NOT IN MY BOOK

NOT IN MY BOOK

A Novel

A Novel

KATIE HOLT

alcove
press

Published in the United States by Alcove Press, an imprint of The Quick Brown Fox & Company LLC.

Alcove Press and its logo are trademarks of The Quick Brown Fox & Company LLC.

Library of Congress Catalog-in-Publication data available upon request.

ISBN (paperback): 978-1-63910-975-3
ISBN (ebook): 978-1-63910-976-0

Cover design by Ink and Laurel

Printed in the United States.

www.alcovepress.com

Alcove Press
34 West 27th St., 10th Floor
New York, NY 10001

First Edition: December 2024

10 9 8 7 6 5 4 3 2 1

For Momo, Grandma, and my dear ol' Granddaddy.
I wrote this with my best foot in my mouth.

For my parents, who showed me every single day
that the type of love in between the pages of
romance novels exist outside of them, too.

FALL

People say there's a thin line between love and hate.

But with Hunter, it was oceans wide.

— Excerpt from *Untitled* by
Rosie Maxwell and Aiden Huntington

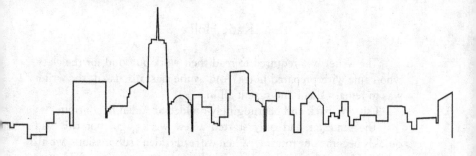

CHAPTER ONE

My mom used to say if I didn't have anything nice to say, then it was best to say nothing at all. It was typical mom advice, but it became my gospel. It was basically one of the commandments of the South. You know, southern hospitality and all that.

I was almost certain Aiden Huntington's mom had told him the opposite. If you don't have anything nice to say, shout it from the rooftops! Repeat it until you instill in their mind just how *worthless* they are!

It would explain why Aiden felt the need to berate me. Every. Single. Class.

"Sensory details need a lot of work." It was the first thing out of his mouth when it became his turn to offer up thoughts on my chapter. Most people started their comments with one or two nice things and ended with some gentle constructive criticism. But Aiden cut right to the chase and through the heart. He flipped through the pages, his mouth turned down in a frown, like my chapter personally offended him.

"And the dialogue. I mean, come on. If Rosalinda—"

"Rosie," I interrupted. He lifted his eyes to mine, peering at me through his lashes, his brow raised slightly. "We've been over this. My name is Rosie."

Our professor, Ida, cleared her throat from the front of the room, giving me a dark look. The first rule of workshop? Do *not* talk during workshop.

The writer was required to read their work out loud for the class, who came with prepared notes. And as the class discussed, the writer was to remain silent and take it all in.

I shrank back and begrudgingly nodded at Aiden to continue.

The semester had only started a few weeks ago, but this had quickly become our routine. When we read Aiden's submissions, we all gave praise and *critiques*. Not insults—mere *suggestions*. We were always very kind and gently told him what was working and what wasn't. The worst part was that most of the time, his pieces worked.

In return, he gave comments that were harsh, yes, but, sadly, helpful. Aiden had an annoying editorial eye that ended up making everyone around him a better writer. Except when it came to me. This was our second semester doing this dance—he'd done this last semester in our master fiction workshop, too. He hadn't cared enough to dig into my work because he didn't think the romance genre was worth his time and didn't care to help me improve.

He continued for a few more minutes, saying what he always said about the pieces I submitted:

I get this is a romance, but does the love story really have to be the center of the plot?

Don't these characters have something better to do than fall in love?

What does it even mean *to darken your gaze?*

I stole a glance at Jess, the only other romance writer in the class, from across the workshop table. She rolled her eyes in solidarity with me. As a full-time student, Jess was taking two more classes than I was, and I couldn't even *imagine* how exhausted she must be. I was only part time, extending my MFA degree for years to be able to even afford NYU.

We'd initially bonded over our love for romance last year, and that bond only strengthened this year with Aiden's blatant distaste for our genre. I'd spent all last semester complaining about him, but now that she'd witnessed his brutality toward me, which funnily enough *she* never experienced, she was extra sympathetic. Now, whenever I complained about Aiden, she would say, "It's all the pent-up sexual frustration. He probably critiques the length of his partner's moans in bed."

"Above all else"—Aiden dropped the stack of papers onto the wooden desk between us, grimacing as if he couldn't bear to look at them for a minute longer—"it falls flat. There's almost no emotion in it.

You'd think a romance would make you feel *something*, at the very least joy. It's actually impressive that you haven't been able to convey this."

I sent a death glare to Aiden, but stuck to our golden rule and kept my mouth shut.

"Rosie, you're free to respond to any of the comments if you'd like," Ida said once Aiden had finished.

I went through the notes my classmates had given me. It was the third first chapter I'd submitted, hoping that something, *anything* would stick. We were in a selective two-semester novel intensive, which meant we had to submit the first half our novel at the end of this semester for our midterm and the full thing at the end of the course. This class was an elective, but it counted toward our course requirements, and it was designed to help those of us who were choosing to submit a novel as their final thesis.

We had until the end of the add/drop period to test out chapters if we weren't certain about our plots, and I was struggling.

I had grown up determined to be a novelist. I'd decided I *had* to publish romance novels and make hopeless romantics around the world swoon—there was nothing else for me out there. Romance had shaped my world view, molding how I lived with optimism and hope. I wanted to give that to someone else. And this was my chance to finally push past the agonizing writer's block and finish a manuscript.

"I'm trying to set up the tension between them. I want their romance to really explode by the end—"

A scoff cut me off. Aiden leaned back in his chair, rolling his eyes. *Ages* ago, I'd thought Aiden was cute. Before I knew him, I would've been excited by the idea of sitting across from him. But after our workshop together last semester, the very sight of Aiden left a bad taste in my mouth. There were nine of us in the class, but the seats we'd sat in on our first day of workshop had seemed to become our permanent seats—otherwise I would've sat at the opposite end of the table far, far away from him.

"I'm sorry, Aiden. Was there something you'd like to say?" I narrowed my eyes at him, challenging him to speak.

His green eyes flashed at me the way they always did before we got into a fight. The sadist loved it when we argued almost as much as he loved torturing his characters with depressing backstories and tragic endings. He was the antithetical romance hero and every time he opened his mouth, he proved it.

Surprisingly, he said, "I've said what I wanted to."

"No, go ahead. I *insist*." I leaned forward across the table toward him. My hair fell in front of my shoulder, a smile creeping up my face. I was no masochist, but I couldn't ever resist confrontation with Aiden. I wasn't scared of him like everyone else was.

"Fine." He straightened in his chair, pushing his sleeves up his forearms. The only thing more infuriating than Aiden's phenomenal writing was the fact that he was the most gorgeous man I'd ever seen. He was historical romance cover hot. He had a strong jawline and perfectly combed hair that looked incredibly soft. His long-sleeved shirt stretched over his arm, tight enough I could see the swell of his bicep. I looked away, trying to convince myself that he was as ugly as his personality. "It's a contemporary romance, right?"

"Right."

"So, how much tension could there really be? We live in the age of instant gratification. The only tension nowadays is whether your thumb will swipe left or right."

"I disagree," Tyler spoke up. He was one of the only other voices of reason in class. Despite Tyler and me being good friends, he refused to take sides. The whole class had fully taken the side of Team Rosie or Team Devil, but Tyler fell squarely in the middle. I smirked at Aiden as Tyler spoke because having Tyler on your side meant you won in our unspoken competition. "I think a lot of people still meet organically, and when they do, there's definitely some tension. My sister met her wife in a coffee shop. No Tinder or Hinge, just a pure meet cute."

Aiden rolled his eyes at "meet cute." The same way he did at "happily ever after" and "puppies" and "sunshine."

"That doesn't mean much to me."

"Well, when I'm writing a book for disgruntled assholes in their late twenties, I'll ask for your opinion," I snapped, growing more irritated by the second.

"Great. And when I'm writing a book for lonely, old cat women, I'll ask for yours."

I jabbed a finger at him, flushed. "I *told* you that was an outdated stereotype for romance readers. A *sexist* one, too."

"And *I* told *you* literary fiction isn't for sad people."

"I don't think literary fiction is for sad people!" The class was watching our exchange like it was a tennis match, heads turning with each word. "I think whatever the hell *you* write is!"

"Okay, okay." Ida stood up from her seat at the head of the table, glowering at us. From appearances, you wouldn't expect her to be intimidating, but the first time Aiden and I fought, she proved how scary she could be. She had curly red hair that expanded around her head, and when she was mad like this, it looked like flames.

Aiden and I slumped back in our seats like five-year-olds, shooting daggers at each other. I crossed my arms over my chest, resisting the urge to stick my tongue out at him. Even though the semester had just started, there was lingering tension from last semester, and I knew the class could feel it, too. No matter what I said, he'd disagree with me, so I followed suit. I was sure there were more than a few stories floating around about us from our workshop last semester.

"Let's remember to keep things civil in this room and make it a safe space to share our work." Ida gave each of us a pointed look. "We all need to respect the content of everyone's work, even if it's not our preferred genre."

She began to give me her thoughts on my chapter, and I tried my best to focus, but Aiden had riled me up. Once she finished and we moved onto someone else's work, I shot a glare at Aiden from across the table willing him to vanish into thin air. He caught my eyes, and his lips curled in distaste before he turned his gaze toward Ida.

I dug my nails into my palm, vowing that one day, I would write a character named Aiden and give him the most excruciatingly painful death. Then again, the real Aiden might enjoy that too much.

"Don't forget to finalize and outline your plot before add/drop because afterward, we're going full steam ahead on drafting," Ida said. "I know it's intimidating, but we're about to begin a marathon sprint to finish your novels. As always, come by my office hours if you're stuck. I'll see you all next time."

"Rosie, you coming to drinks tonight?" Jess asked as I stacked all the pages of critiques I'd received today and placed them carefully into my tote bag.

Tyler, Logan, Jess, and I hung out regularly after class at a nearby bar, the Peculiar Pub. Jess and I had become fast friends during our first semester together, stressing over deadlines and writing frantically in cafés across Greenwich Village. Tyler was Jess's on campus crush. We'd spotted him a few times at the library and in the Writer's House before he walked through the door of our workshop last spring. She barely held it together in that moment, and like a true friend I invited him and Logan out for drinks with us one day. The group kind of fell together after that.

"I can't tonight," I said apologetically. "I picked up another shift at the Hideout. But I'll be there next time?" I glanced at Tyler from across the table and whispered to Jess, "Make your move tonight."

Jess rolled her eyes. "As if. He isn't interested."

"I think he is," I insisted. "But if you don't want to tonight, I promise next time I'll be your wing woman."

"I'm holding you to that," she said before heading out.

I glanced at my phone and winced. I'd have to race to Union Square to catch my train in time for my shift.

"I'll see you at office hours tomorrow, Ida," I called as I left the classroom.

She smiled kindly at me and said, "Bring your chapter and feedback with you."

Our workshop was off Fifth Avenue in the Lillian Vernon Creative Writer's House. You would never know from the outside that it was home to NYU's Creative Writing program. It was a lovely townhouse with tiny classrooms, and I adored spending my time there. After every class, when I rushed across crowded Fifth Avenue to the train, I felt like a real New Yorker. Fall was just beginning in the city, and I took in every crunch of leaves beneath my feet and shade of brown against the concrete buildings.

The great thing about NYU was the city was your campus. But the bad thing about NYU was the city was your campus. I didn't just have to fight the crowds of students, but busy New Yorkers as they went about their day and tourists who stopped every three steps to take a picture.

Throngs of people were pushing their way through the street, and I tried to keep up with them. When I had first moved here, I wasn't used to the fast pace of New Yorkers. In Tennessee, we ambled. We smelled the roses as we took our sweet time. We moseyed and said *hi* to nearly every person we encountered. That was not the case here.

I pushed my legs faster to make it to the 6 train arriving in two minutes, going against all my Southern nature.

"What's the rush, Rosalinda?"

I jumped at the sound of Aiden's voice. He was nearly a foot taller than I was, but still found a way to creep up on me.

"I'm trying to find the nearest bathroom. Your cologne makes me want to puke," I said sweetly. Some guy pushed between us, walking in the opposite direction, shoving my shoulder in the process. He nearly knocked me over, but Aiden placed a firm hand on the small of my back, steadying me.

"Just so you know, it's Italian," he said, raising his chin. He had pulled a black sweater on, and it made him look so fall and cozy. I quickly pushed the thought from my mind.

"Just so you know, that's pretentious."

We finally made it to Union Square and walked together down the stairs that sat at the edge of the park. My brows furrowed as we tapped our phones on the turnstiles. I took this train every Monday and Wednesday after class and not *once* had I seen Aiden here. I glanced at him from the corner of my eye as he walked down the stairs alongside me. Surely if he was going to murder me, he wouldn't do it in public. Right?

He stood next to me on the platform, waiting for the train. I looked between him and the empty train tracks and took a step back behind one of the poles. Just in case.

We stood in silence, the low rumbles of nearby trains surrounding us. When I couldn't take it anymore, I turned to him, suspicious.

"Are you stalking me?" I asked. I placed my hands on my hips, trying my best to look intimidating even though I had to crane my neck to meet his eyes.

He looked down at me briefly, amused. "Who's to say *you're* not stalking *me*?"

"Do you even take the 6?" I asked suspiciously. "I've never seen you here after class."

He spared me another glance. "No."

"See? You're stalking me."

The train rushed past us, the wind from it causing my hair to fall in front of my face. Over the noise of the train, Aiden leaned down until he was eye level with me, smirking.

"This is the L."

"Do you always have to be this annoying?" I drawled. *"Don't you ever get tired of it?"*

She narrowed her eyes at me. If she got any angrier, I'd expect fumes to sprout from her ears.

Her hands curled into fists at her sides. Maybe if she were taller, I'd be intimidated. But it was a little adorable.

"Do you always have to be such an asshole?"

I paused, pretending to consider the question. *"Yes. I do."*

— Excerpt from *Untitled* by
Rosie Maxwell and Aiden Huntington

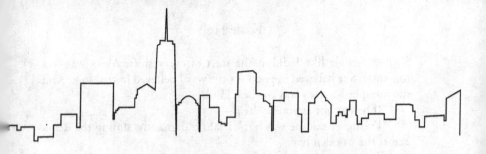

CHAPTER TWO

"I know I'm late, I'm sorry." I stuck my head in the office after I clocked in. "I took the wrong train, and then I got lost, and I still had to change."

"It's okay, Rosie, it's only a few minutes." My boss, Luke, didn't even look up from his desk. He waved his hand dismissively and said, "Bar's empty anyways. Just go start your shift now."

I'd moved to New York City on a whim. My town in Tennessee, Rogersville, had fewer than five thousand people, so New York City was an entirely new *world*. This month marked my first full year in New York, and it was tougher than I'd ever expected. There was no Southern hospitality as my safety net, and I'd learned quickly I had to harden my doe-eyed view of life. I finally felt like I was adjusting and finding my place in the city, as hard it was.

"Running a little late, huh?" Alexa leaned over the other side of the bar. Her dark brown bob swayed around her face as she grinned at me.

"Aiden," I explained as I tied the small white apron around my waist. "He distracted me as we were walking out of class, and I ended up at the L platform instead of the 6."

"¿Cómo te distrajo?" Alexa wagged her eyebrows at me.

"Shut up, you know that's not how it is." I rolled my eyes, turning toward the wall of different bottles of liquor and glasses to make her a

Shirley Temple like I did at the start of every shift. Alexa wasn't a romantic. She believed in good sex the way I believed in true love. And she thought hate-sex was the best kind.

"If he's as hot as you say he is—"

"I've never said he was hot," I said indignantly, sliding the drink across the wooden bar.

She easily caught the glass in her hand, lifting it to her lips. "Yes, you have. You say it every time you blush when you talk about him and whenever you make a point to mention his green eyes."

"They're green like snot."

Alexa tilted her head back and laughed, her dark eyes filled with delight. "One day you'll see I'm right. Thin line between love and hate, Rosie. Thin line."

"Not that thin," I muttered.

The truth was, though, that I'd had a bit of a crush on Aiden Huntington last fall. Jess had dragged me to some student reading that Tyler was reading in, and Aiden stood up to read. It was the first time I saw him, and he was undeniably handsome with broad shoulders and dark hair. It was hard to see him in the dim lighting, but I could make out his square jaw and green eyes. The way his nose narrowed and turned up slightly when I caught a glimpse of his profile. I couldn't stop myself from placing him as a romance hero in my head.

"Good evening. I'm Aiden, and I'm in one of the fiction sections. This is from a short story titled 'Home.'"

Instantly, I was captivated by his words. The low hum of his voice filled the house and sent an electric shock down my spine. His story was about a young boy who'd never had a home, who'd searched for it in other people for so long, but eventually stopped.

Maybe it was because I was homesick, but tears sprung to my eyes and streamed down my face. I was leaning forward, hanging onto his every word. The five minutes he spoke felt like two seconds, and I craved more. I wanted to be envious of how naturally he strung words and sentences together, but I was in awe.

Then, on the first day of spring semester last year, he strolled in from the winter cold wearing a peacoat. Men nowadays didn't wear *peacoats*. They wore North Face jackets with the logos facing out or hoodies with a ketchup stain on the front.

And it only got worse—he took off his coat to reveal a navy sweater that he subsequently rolled up to his elbows. It was almost *appalling* how attractive he was.

He sat directly across from me that day and returned my smile with a tentative one. I convinced myself that when class ended, I was going to ask him out for coffee. I envisioned it all in those few moments: We'd chat over coffee, I'd tell him that I'd thought he was cute at the reading, he'd confess his undying love for me, and I would get my Happily Ever After. The romance novel basically wrote itself.

My dad used to say I didn't have a rose-tinted view, but a Rosie-tinted view. I saw what I wanted to see. I saw Aiden and fell head over heels. But you know what they say about la vie en rose—the red flags look just like all the other ones.

We all went around the table, introducing ourselves and what we liked to write, ranging from horror to comedy. But the minute "romance" left my mouth, Aiden's demeanor shifted. Any warmth from him disappeared and was replaced with his signature scowl. His nose crinkled in distaste as if to say, *"Really?"*

Sitting high and mighty on his horse, Aiden said he wrote "literary fiction." He literally turned his nose up when he said it. And, hey, lit fic wasn't my thing, but I wouldn't ever shit on it the way Aiden shit on romance.

Things spiraled quickly from there. Aiden and I disagreed on nearly everything we could. He condemned romance every time I submitted a piece and would make snarky remarks like, "Oh, how coincidental there was only one bed," or "No, it makes total sense for him to secretly be a prince. *Sure.*" I only wished I could hurl the same insults as he did and let it leave a mark. I tried, but I had to dig deep to find any critique for him, really.

I'd made the worst mistake of telling Alexa about the tiny crush I'd had on Aiden before I got to know him. Now she wasn't convinced that I was over him, even though I *was*.

"How was class today?" Alexa pushed up on the wooden bar, trying to get a glimpse behind it. "Do you have any cherries?"

I pulled the small cup of them out from the fridge under the bar and plopped them into her drink.

My relationship with Alexa was trifold: friend, coworker, and roommate. The Peruvian network of worried moms encompassed the whole globe. When I decided to move to New York, my mom went into panic mode and called all my tías to see if they knew anyone I could live with. Turned out my tía's friend who sent her ají amarillo paste from Peru had a niece who was moving to the city around the same time as I was. Alexa had already secured an apartment in the East Village, and we quickly bonded over our lack of knowledge of city life. Our roommateship morphed into a strange, unlikely friendship. When the year ended, we hadn't even thought twice about renewing our lease.

There was a learning curve in living together, though. Although we got along great, we were total opposites. She loved partying and night clubs and spontaneity whereas I preferred a weighted blanket on Friday nights and detailed to-do lists.

It had been hard to stay in touch with the Peruvian side of myself in Tennessee when the only store that sold Inca Kola was two hours outside of town. But Alexa kept a steady supply of Morochas in the apartment and taught me how to make a few traditional dishes, like lomo saltado or pollo a la brasa.

We rarely got to see each other outside of the apartment and the restaurant. She was studying fashion at The New School full time and was working here part time. Alexa had lucked out with financial aid from The New School, but NYU wasn't as generous with me. I couldn't even afford to *consider* being a full-time student. I spent my weekdays after class as a bartender here and spent the weekends writing and studying.

"Aiden was particularly vicious today. We got into it a little bit in class."

Alexa took a seat as I rested my forearms on the dark bar. "How so?"

"He tore up my piece—and I was really proud of that one, too. I thought it could be a good start to my manuscript, but apparently not. We fought in front of everyone."

"Ooh, foreplay." She smiled, fishing a cherry out of her drink before popping it into her mouth. "Dime más."

Heat crept up my neck. "I'm telling you, it's not like that. He's so horrible. And only to me, just because I like romance." I sighed. "It's Simon all over again."

"Simon was a self-righteous prick."

My neck prickled at the thought of my narcissist ex. I had spent the past year moving on. "I don't see much of a difference between Simon and Aiden then."

"Simon didn't value you or your passions. Simon couldn't have cared less if you spoke the same language."

"I wish Aiden spoke a different language than me," I muttered.

A couple walked in at the other side of the restaurant. Alexa patted the bar and said, "Duty calls. Don't let him get to you."

As she walked off, I started to organize the glasses and liquor bottles.

The Hideout was one of the best restaurants in Flatiron. It was a bit of a hike from our place, but the pay and tips were great. On weekdays there was usually a small crowd of regulars, but the weekends were wild. I refused to work them—even if they guaranteed a week's worth of pay in one night—because the staff shuddered every time they talked about it.

Paying for school and rent was a struggle. I spent my nights eating free meals on a box of dried food in the storage room at the back of the restaurant. I hated that I would have to drag out my MFA for years longer than anyone else. But even though I wasn't the New York socialite I'd dreamed I would be, I was *here*. And that was all I had ever wanted.

My ex-boyfriend Simon and I had met freshman year of high school. Almost immediately, I fell head over heels. Even now, I couldn't really explain why. Maybe because he seemed put together and wasn't a complete jerk like every other guy at fifteen. Maybe it was because he had swoopy hair that he combed every morning.

We didn't end up dating until sophomore year. He was my best friend and one night after I confessed how I felt, everything changed so quickly. Suddenly it wasn't Simon the Best Friend, but Simon the Boyfriend. I was so happy to finally be with him, to be Simonand-Rosie, that I let myself become blind to the red flags.

He encouraged me to go to our local college together and skip out on Barnard College, insisting that you didn't find what we had twice, and we had to hold on it. He hated when I talked about New York or how I dreamed of being a novelist. He thought it was ridiculous and that I should either do something practical like teaching, or just stay home and raise our children. And even then, I still spun it in my mind as romantic that he wanted to have a family with me.

Once we graduated, he became even more controlling. It was frustrating, but I just assumed that every couple fought. Everyone had preferences and differences, and this was where ours lay. But as time went by, Simon still didn't propose, citing he "wasn't sure yet."

Then I read Ida Abarough's article "Why We All Should Read Romance," and my long-lost confidence in writing romance was suddenly regained. She eloquently expressed why women read romance and how it showed women taking control in their lives while still being desired instead of wholly objectified. And how it had expanded to include different gender identities and become a safe space for people of color. No matter how bad life got in the romance novels, there would be a Happily Ever After that proved nothing was unfixable.

That night, I developed a two-step plan: get into NYU, then take as many of Ida's classes as possible. I had been listless the few years after graduating, still working in my town's diner. I knew this would get me on track and by a miracle, luck, or something in between, just after my twenty-fifth birthday, I was admitted into the MFA program.

When I told Simon I was admitted to NYU, he laughed. He thought it was some prank I was playing on him and when I told him it wasn't, he said, "Rosie, you don't have to go to school to sell those kind of books. Slap a hot guy on the cover and the work is done for you." Everyone in my life, Simon included, deemed romance a "guilty pleasure." You didn't go to school to study it, and you certainly didn't uproot your whole life to do it.

But I went anyway. The first class I registered for was a Fiction Craft lecture with Ida.

Simon and I tried long distance for a while. I'd always thought long distance was the true test of love. If you loved someone, you'd stay up late even if you were tired. You'd put in the hours and the work. But every time Simon and I spoke on the phone he said, "Rosie, when are you going to forget this pipe dream and come back?" Every time I texted him and he didn't text back, I told myself he was just busy.

I'd never thought the long distance would break us, but ultimately I'm glad it did. Reality hit me hard my first fall in New York, and I sometimes felt like I was still reckoning with the whiplash.

But Ida's class had opened a new cavern in my heart, pouring out a new love for writing. At the end of lecture one day, she said, "If you have any questions, about this lecture or otherwise, come by my office hours and we can talk about it."

Perhaps this had been an empty gesture. But it was my opening, and I came every week and stayed for hours, all but forcing a mentorship onto her.

I would pore through all my ideas, and at first, she'd shake her head, smile tightly, and say, "Rosie, maybe you should spend this time writing or go talk to your workshop professor."

I had only smiled and said, "I'm only taking the craft class. I've got nowhere else to be."

It took a while, but I slowly peeled back the layers of Ida. I knew she *hated* when we called her Professor Abarough because it made her feel old. She'd just gone through a nasty divorce but she won her dog, Buster, in the settlement. She always kept a Lisa Kleypas book in her desk (*Marrying Winterborne*) to flip through when she got overwhelmed. *And* I knew that she secretly loved having me as a mentee even if she acted like she didn't.

Today, like I always did, I headed toward her office at the NYU English Department on Greene Street. But when I noticed a flyer on the bulletin board near her office, I gasped, snatching it off the board and reading it carefully.

It encouraged students to apply for the Sam Frost Fellowship that would pay *half* of next year's tuition. *The Frost* was a prestigious national literary magazine on par with *The Paris Review*. If I got this, I'd not only be able pay my rent and become a full-time student, but I'd get my name out there. I stuffed the flyer in my bag before entering Ida's office without knocking.

Her office space was tiny, her desk and chair facing a wall of books of different genres and colors. She generally tried to keep it clean, but clutter always took over her desk in the form of stacks of papers and coffee cups. As soon I stepped through the door, I fell into my usual chair.

Without looking up from her laptop, she said, "We need to talk about that chapter." Her red hair was pulled back into a bun, her black glasses sitting at the tip of her nose as she typed away on her computer.

"I know. Not my best work." I pulled out my workshop notes and first chapter, laying them across the edge of her desk.

"Can I ask what you were *attempting* to do here?"

"You know." I waved my hand vaguely in the air. "Angst."

She gave me a flat look. "Try again."

"I'm waiting for something to stick."

"Rosie," she said gently. "There's not much more time to wait. You need to decide on your storyline soon or you'll be stuck with something you have no passion for. By the end of your time here, you *will* have to submit a thesis, and it's better to start now than later. I can't guarantee your thesis advisor will be as kind to romance as I am, so it needs to be as strong as possible."

"You really don't think there's anything workable here?"

She hesitated. "Not necessarily. But it lacks your usual personality and voice and that's what makes your writing so good. Everything you brought me from your other workshop last semester came alive off the page, and this feels . . . forced. Unlike you." When I deflated the tiniest bit, she said, "Why don't we both read through and see what we can keep and where to go from there?"

We sat in silence as she read through the copy I'd emailed her, and I sifted through my classmates' comments, hoping something would spark inspiration. I narrowed my eyes at the impeccable handwriting, gripping the paper tightly in my hands.

Description isn't working here.

Dialogue sounds unnatural.

Every statement ended with a period. What kind of psychopath took notes and included the periods? Anger simmered in me at the sight of his words.

"Oh my God. Look at this." I handed her Aiden's notes. "Have you reconsidered his expulsion from the class?"

She rolled her eyes. "You're just as bad as he is." She read through his comments, her lips quirking a bit before handing it back.

My mouth hung open in shock. "I am a goddamn *delight*. Aiden is a menace upon our class."

"I do recall you threatening to toss his notebook off the Empire State Building last week."

I waved her off. "Oh please, that was a joke."

"Oh really? What about the time you told him his writing was nothing but bathroom graffiti?"

"Oh that?" I scoffed. "That was a *compliment*. Bathroom graffiti can be very poetic," I said sagely.

She laughed and handed me back his paper. "I don't know why you two act like this."

"C'mon, indulge me. You know you want to gossip about Aiden. It's our favorite pastime."

"It's *your* favorite pastime." She gave me a pointed look. "I swear half the time you come in here, it's just to talk about Aiden. Finish looking through your notes for this chapter."

I huffed but did as she said. She wasn't wrong about Aiden. It was hard not to be affected by his words when he was an annoyingly good writer.

And I was secretly hoping every day that he'd wear that peacoat to class, even though the fall weather hadn't gotten cold enough to require it yet.

"Rosie," Ida said softly. She said it in the way she always did when she told me something wasn't working, and she didn't want to hurt my feelings. (The first time she used this voice with me was when I burst into tears after Aiden called my chapter "One big, lousy cliché.")

"I know." I looked up from my notes. "But I don't *know* where to go."

"I still don't understand why you can't continue the last one. I thought it had a lot of promise."

"But you didn't think it was good," I pointed out.

"I didn't think it was there *yet*," she corrected. "But I feel like you quit writing it for more significant reasons than you're letting on."

My gaze flicked away from her intense one. She was right. I hadn't been able to continue that project or start a new one because I felt like a fraud. I was writing about some epic, sweeping romance and all I had to show for that in real life was *Simon*? I hadn't even come close to my own Happily Ever After; how could I write one for my characters?

"I want to write something new," I said, ignoring her unasked question. "I want to write something that'll challenge me."

"Okay." Ida pulled out a notebook from her desk drawer and poised her pen above the paper. "Let's brainstorm."

That was by far my favorite thing about Ida. She never made my writerly goals feel ridiculous. We spent the next hour discussing different rom-com ideas and tropes to play around with and not once did I feel like the idiot Aiden made me out to be.

I left Ida's with a newfound determination. I would write a romance that was funny and sexy and charming, and Aiden could choke on his own dick.

I didn't come all this way to let some pretentious asshole in a peacoat (albeit a very nice peacoat) tell me I'm not good enough. If he could destroy me in just a few words, I was a writer. I could do the same.

"Don't you two ever get tired of fighting with each other?"

Max and I shared a glance as if that was a ridiculous notion. "It's my favorite pastime."

— Excerpt from *Untitled* by
Rosie Maxwell and Aiden Huntington

CHAPTER THREE

I vowed revenge when it was Aiden's turn to be workshopped. And all the stars aligned—this was his worst chapter yet. Like me, he was struggling to figure out what he wanted his book to be about. I felt a lot better knowing I wasn't the only one trying to find their footing. He was trying to imitate some stream of consciousness, Faulkner-style writing, but it made no sense. As we discussed his work, everyone had their brows furrowed, but I was smiling.

I patiently waited as the class went around the room sharing their thoughts until it was my turn. Aiden's dark ember eyes settled on me. I ignored how my stomach flipped, a wave of uneasiness flowing through me. But there was no way I would lose my nerve.

"I don't know." I sighed heavily, gently placing the pages on the table in front of me. I tried to look casual despite my hammering heart and shaking hands. Confrontation wasn't really my thing, but I had to stand my ground. I refused to let Aiden shame me for being a genre writer and walking around with this stupid air of superiority. I looked up at him through my lashes and lifted a single shoulder. "It's a bit . . . *derivative*."

Shock rippled across Aiden's face for a moment before he rearranged his features to appear impassive. I bit back my smile and continued.

"I mean, I get that you're probably a Faulkner fan, right?" I drawled, looking to him for confirmation, but I didn't need it. Once, last semester, he'd gone on for hours about him, explaining the inspiration behind a short story. Aiden gave a terse nod, the muscle in his cheek jumping. "I figured. I mean, it's so obvious and, God, the way it drones on and on, no offense. It seems like it's trying so hard to be meaningful that it's . . . lackluster. This reads more like Faulkner fanfiction than anything else. Fanfiction is great, though! I just didn't know it was your thing." I gave him a sickly sweet smile from across the table.

He looked up at me, setting his pen down. Aiden sat back in his chair, watching me intensely as I tried my best to appear cavalier.

"Above all else, it falls flat." I said, repeating his words to me from workshop a few weeks ago. To hell with dignity and maturity. I wanted *revenge*. "This doesn't seem like a feasible start to a novel, but instead feels like the ramblings of a guy on a blog from 2003. It's nearly useless, I would say." I folded my hands on top of the pages. The silence in the room was deadly as I turned to Ida, beaming. "That's all from me."

Aiden was glaring at me, his eyes hard, hatred seeping between us.

"Okay," Ida said cautiously. "Any thoughts, Aiden?" She looked tentatively between the two of us, waiting for the bomb to go off. Honestly, I was waiting, too. I was longing to see Aiden lose his cool, to watch my words creep into his mind and stain it like his did to me.

Instead, Aiden sat up, cleared his throat. He looked at each of our classmates as he politely addressed their notes. I expected his voice to quiver, I craved *tears*.

But he was so obviously unbothered by what I had said, his eyes looked almost bored. Irritation flared in my chest. He had a way of doing *anything* and just making it seem like he was better than the rest of us. He was succinct, and I wanted to strangle him.

Finally, his eyes flicked over me for just a second before turning to Ida.

"I've responded to all the opinions that are worth acknowledging. Like I've said before, I'm not writing for lonely women who live out their fantasies through mass-produced paperbacks found in a Duane Reade. I'm writing for a deeper meaning."

"Oh, c'mon," I huffed.

Aiden barreled on. "I'm writing for an audience that cares about more than overdone tropes and unrealistic men."

"Well, at least my book won't be a coaster for some deadbeat forty-year-old who thinks Matt Rife is some sort of God," I bit out.

"No, your book will be a coaster for a bored cat lady's vibrator."

I snorted. "Your *wife's* vibrator because you couldn't please a woman to save your life!"

"At least I'll be married!"

"At least—"

"*Enough*," Ida snapped. Half the class's mouths were open in shock, the others were holding back laughter. "I don't want to hear another word from you two for the rest of workshop."

She shot us both a glare, and I shrank back in my seat as shame flashed through me. What was I doing? Trying to get back at a man whose opinion I didn't even care about? I was in this class for *me*, not a petty, childish rivalry. I certainly wasn't trying to disappoint Ida in the process. On our first day, Ida had emphasized the importance of respect during the workshop. Aiden and I had been toeing the line she'd drawn since day one of this class, but now we'd barreled past it.

For the rest of class, I kept my head down, too embarrassed to make eye contact with anyone. And I knew the moment I looked at Aiden, I'd feel nothing but the uncontrollable need to smother him to death.

When class ended, I beelined it toward the door, hoping to avoid any more confrontation with Aiden. I had plans to meet up with my friends at Peculiar Pub for drinks after class today, but the last thing I wanted to do was relive the past few hours.

We met at the edge of the block on the corner of Fifth and 10th. Jess and Logan were giggling as they walked toward me and when they saw me they laughed even harder. Tyler side eyed the two of them, his lips quirking up.

"It's not funny," I complained.

"You're right. It's *hilarious*." Logan grinned. "God, that was so entertaining. Remind me to sign up for workshops with you and Aiden from now on."

"He was being a dick, and I wasn't going to stand for it," I said defensively.

"To be fair, you started it," Logan said.

"Hey!"

"You did! I *love* that you started it because it's usually Aiden that starts these fights, but today it was totally you."

Embarrassment flooded me. I looked to Tyler and Jess. "You don't think Ida is going to hate me for starting it, do you?"

"No," Jess said reassuringly. "Add/drop just ended; there's no class you could move into. She might dock your participation grade or something, but I think you're fine."

"Let's just go to Peculiar." I sighed heavily.

Since I loved romance and I loved Jess, I got Logan to keep talking to me as we walked toward Peculiar Pub, giving Jess some time alone with Tyler. Every so often on the walk over, I heard her giggle.

The more I'd gotten to know Logan and Tyler over the past few months, the more they'd become really great friends. Tyler was always so serious and stoic, every word out of his mouth thoughtful, like in his writing. He wrote contemporary fiction that read like poetry and instantly captivated you. It was easy to see why Jess liked him so much.

Logan, on the other hand, was Tyler's exact opposite. Logan wore every emotion and thought on his sleeve. He had no filter and didn't care. He wrote horror comedies and was able to make our skin crawl on one page and have us bursting into laughter on the next.

The Peculiar Pub was aptly named: At the front there was the bar with plenty of room to stand around and talk, but toward the back was a different vibe, with booth seating and bottlecaps lining the walls. Once we had asked the bartender for the most peculiar drink on the menu, and she brought us a raspberry cheesecake flavored beer.

"I'll grab the first round," Tyler said. "The usual for everyone?"

We nodded as he walked off to the bar, and Jess's eyes lingered on him.

"You know," Logan said thoughtfully. "I think my favorite part of class today was when Aiden said vibrator."

"Oh my God." I hung my head low.

"You know, I've never had a vibrator. Do they usually come with coasters?" He looked between Jess and me, waiting for an explanation.

Jess reached across the table to smack him playfully and said, "Shut up." She paused. "No. They don't."

Tyler returned with our happy hour drinks, placing margaritas in front of Jess and me and beers for him and Logan.

Logan sipped his beer and said, "I wish you two would fuck and get it over with."

I coughed, chocking on my drink. "What?"

"Well, there's an *obvious* amount of sexual tension between you two. You guys would probably be nicer to each other if you would just have sex. Then you wouldn't hate him so much."

I shook my head vehemently, nearly gagging at the thought. "No one would want to hear his complicated metaphors as dirty talk. Besides, I don't hate him because I'm *attracted* to him."

Logan's eyebrows raised. "So you *are*?"

"No." I blushed. "I hate him because he's elitist about romance. Right, Jess?"

Jess nodded in solidarity. "He's harshest whenever we submit our stuff. We're only a few weeks in, and he's found something wrong with all of Rosie's chapters."

"But not yours," Tyler said, frowning. "He's not as harsh to you as he is to Rosie, and you write romance too."

"I don't want to talk about this anymore," I declared. "I want to enjoy tonight with my friends and not have to think about Aiden at all."

"Fine, fine, I'll drop it," Logan said. "Tyler, what happens next in your book? I want spoilers, I have to know."

We chatted for a while about everyone's projects. Now that I couldn't transfer out of Ida's class, I had to stick with my current plot line. No restarting my novel or testing out new chapters. I didn't have time to dwell anymore—I had to *write*. Especially now that Ida wasn't the happiest with me.

When we finished our second round of drinks, Jess yawned and said, "I've got to get home. It's a forty-minute train into Brooklyn for me."

"I should go, too," I said. Alexa was probably still at work, and it'd be nice to work in the silence of my apartment.

I lingered on my walk home, hoping to find inspiration in the eclectic streets of the Lower East Side. But nothing struck me. When I got back, I headed straight to my bedroom, changing into some sweats and a cropped tee and settling into my bed with my laptop propped on my knees. I scrolled through the Notes app in my phone, through the random scene ideas and the strings of sentences, hoping there was something good enough to fully develop and turn in.

There wasn't. I groaned, frustrated, deciding it was better to just succumb to the writer's block. I snatched my bag off my floor, digging through it to find my current read. Instead, I pulled out the crumbled flyer from outside Ida's office door.

Everyone in the literary community knew about *The Frost* magazine, but I'd never heard of this fellowship before. Jess told me Tyler had been published in the litmag, and it had helped him get published in even *more* magazines since his name was out there a little more. But I hadn't really thought much of it at the time.

Some quick googling revealed that this fellowship was a *huge* deal. Only ten MFA students in the country were selected, and a group of professors from different universities would mull over the submissions. The winners would receive a scholarship for an amount that, at NYU, would cover half the *full-time* tuition. That money would change my life.

I widened my eyes as I read the list of the few NYU alumni who'd won the fellowship. Most were now published authors or even editors at *The Frost*. All the archives were available online, too.

I was deep into an edition from a few years ago when my phone buzzed with an email from Ida. The blood drained from my face when I saw it was addressed to Aiden and me. The subject line: *Class Today.*

Rosie and Aiden,

I would like to discuss what happened during today's class. It hasn't been sitting well with me all afternoon, and I believe a conversation is necessary. Since we don't have class tomorrow, please come find me at my office on Greene Street tomorrow at noon. If that time doesn't work for you please let me know right away as I believe this is an urgent matter.

I immediately sent a screenshot of it to the group chat with my friends. The name of the chat changed nearly every week, and this week it was *aiden huntington's worst nightmare.*

Logan: you're fucked
Jess: you'll be fine!! i bet she just wants to tell you two to knock it off

I bit my lip.

Rosie: tyler? what do you think?

Tyler was the voice of reason in the group. He would be truthful with me and tell me if it was as bad as I was imagining.

Tyler: Try not to worry about it.

I groaned. I was definitely screwed.

On the way to Ida's office, I decided I would apologize. I was twenty-six years old; I could be the bigger person. I'd walk in, apologize profusely to her, then maybe mumble an apology to Aiden. Besides, Ida was my mentor. Nothing *too* bad could happen. She'd want me to succeed as her mentee, right?

Aiden and I approached Greene Street at the same time from opposite ends of the street. He rolled his eyes when he saw me and whipped open the door, stepping past me.

"I can't believe I'm getting called to the teacher's office like I'm in elementary school," he muttered as we waited in the small elevator.

"You started it," I said. The elevator dinged and together we walked down the hall to Ida's office.

"What are you talking about? *You* insulted *me* last class." He knocked on the door as we waited for Ida to answer.

"Because you trashed my chapter the other week!"

His jaw dropped in disbelief. "This is all over something I said *two weeks* ago?"

"And because you're a snob about romance!" I narrowed my eyes up at him. Taking in our height difference, I stood on my tiptoes to make myself seem taller and more intimidating, but I still fell at least half a foot shorter than him. "You think you're such a better writer than me."

"Oh, here we go." He rolled his eyes and leaned down to meet my eyes. "Rosalinda, I'm going to be very clear: I don't think I'm a better writer. I know I am."

All plans to apologize went out the window. Anger burst into my chest and my hands curled into fists. "I'm going to make you regret ever writing a *word* down. I'm going to put a curse on your family for *generations*. I'm going to—"

"Enough," Ida snapped as she opened the door. "Come in."

We walked in at the same time, getting stuck between each other and the doorframe. I elbowed him, trying to move forward, but he did the same. I twisted my shoulder to get through, stumbling as I stepped into the room.

I smoothed my top down before elegantly taking my usual seat in front of Ida's desk, lifting my chin. Aiden sat in the seat next to me, and I made a point to scoot my chair away from him. I was comfortable being in Ida's office since I spent so much time here. Aiden was on *my* turf now; I had the home field advantage.

She was sitting forward at the table, her lips in a thin line. She was as short as me, but she found a way to be as intimidating as Aiden. My confidence began to wane as I noted the severity of her expression.

"Ever since our first class you two have been incredibly rude, disruptive, and made us all subject to the Rosie and Aiden show day after day. I'd heard rumors from your professor last semester but assumed it wouldn't be that bad. Then, when it turned out to in fact be *that* bad, I remained hopeful it would get better as the semester continued, but I've had enough." Aiden and I shared a guilty glance, knowing she was right.

"You both are wonderful writers, but I can't keep making excuses for you."

I opened my mouth to object, but she held her hand up. "Rosie, I'm not arguing with you on this. I expected more from you. After all we've talked about wanting respect as a romance writer, this is how you respect other writers?"

She was right. I felt so small, mortified by how I'd acted.

Ida cleared her throat. "I'm sorry to have to do this, but I'm asking the two of you to drop this class and go into a different fiction workshop or elective. I know add/drop has already ended, but I can't allow you two to disrupt my class further. I told the entire class my number one priority was a safe space to share our writing. I suggest you reach out to your advisors to see if there is a class they might be able to place you in."

I sat up, alarmed. "Please, I'm so sorry. *We're* so sorry. Please don't do that." I couldn't face my parents and tell them the reason I'd failed a course was because of some stupid feud with Aiden. If I dropped the class now, there was *no* way I'd be able to get into another one. Since it was a yearlong class, I'd be shit out of luck for next semester, too. And I would lose all the money I'd already paid for the course. I could barely afford NYU as it was, I couldn't throw away this money.

"I can be nice, look." I turned to Aiden. I couldn't tell if he was more startled by the desperate expression on my face or the bomb Ida had dropped. "Aiden, you have great sentence fluency and write beautiful prose, especially with your metaphors." I turned back to Ida, my eyes wide. "See? We can change."

"Rosie, I'm sorry. I know how much this hurts, but I can't let you two set an example for what's acceptable. The way you've been acting is not congruent with the standards of the NYU Creative Writing Program. I'm doing *this* so I don't have to go to the Dean of Student Affairs."

Aiden remained silent, but I knew it had to be getting to him, too. His hands had curled around the edge of the chair's armrest, his knuckles white.

Ida was the best professor I'd ever had. Dropping out of this course meant losing her respect, her mentorship, and a lot of money I didn't have. I couldn't stomach the thought.

"There has to be something we can do," I urged. "We'll behave for the rest of the year, I swear."

Ida gave us each a long, hard look. "I may have a proposition for you."

My heart leapt. "Anything."

"Great negotiating skills," Aiden muttered. I shot him a quick, warning glare.

"You two don't respect each other or each other's writing. If you want to continue in the MFA program, you'll have to learn to respect the people around you. Aiden, I know you're struggling with continuing the plot of your project."

Aiden gave a terse, reluctant nod.

"And Rosie, we've talked about how hard it's been for you to start." I flushed, nodding. "So. I'm willing to reconsider—*if* you two spend the rest of the course writing a novel together."

The room was silent.

"You'll each still submit chapters for workshop, and I'd expect you to make sure you deliver around the same number of words."

The silence grew, spreading to every inch of the room. Heat began to pull at my skin, sweat pooling behind my knees and on my forehead. The only thing I wanted to do less than fail this class was write a novel with *Aiden Huntington*.

Not in My Book

"I'm really appreciative of this opportunity," I said carefully. "But is there literally anything else? I know one thing Aiden and I can *really* agree on is that he doesn't want to write romance and I don't want to write litfic."

In my peripheral, Aiden nodded.

Ida nodded. "Exactly. Rosie, what defines a romance?"

"The Happily Ever After," I said immediately. I didn't look at him, but I could practically feel Aiden roll his eyes.

"So the project you'll write together will be a romantic story—but without the happy ending. That way Aiden gets to write a romance, and you get to write an emotional literary fiction ending. You'll write a *love story*."

Fuck no. I lived and breathed the rules of romance novels and rule number one was the Happily Ever After. Breaking that rule was the last thing on Earth I wanted to do. What was the point of making two characters fall in love for nothing? The best part of a romance, besides the steamy scenes obviously, was the happy ending.

I bit my lip, trying to think of a way to get out of this and stay in Ida's good graces. I looked over at Aiden for help, but I could tell he didn't want to do it either, by the grimace plastered on his face.

As immature as it was, revenge flashed in my mind.

If we *did* write this book together, that meant Aiden would have to write sex scenes and swoony lines. He'd hate that. It would anger him and mortify him. It would make him feel exactly how I felt every time he critiqued my work.

"I'll do it," I said happily. Aiden threw a disbelieving glance my way which only spurred me on. "I mean, how hard can it really be?" I lifted a casual shoulder. "But, Aiden," I turned to him with a sympathetic expression. "I know romance isn't your thing and since the majority of the book would be romance, I get why you wouldn't want to. I mean, I know that *I'm* not too intimidated to . . ."

"Fine," Aiden said sharply. "I'm in. There's not much to a romance. We'll lock them in an elevator, have them fall in love, then let the elevator collapse."

I dug my nails into my palms, wishing they were Aiden's eyes instead.

For the first time since we'd entered the room, Ida smiled. "Then, it's settled. First and second chapter due next week. And no more fights in class," she warned.

She dismissed us and once again we both got caught in the doorway. This time, Aiden pushed through first. I closed the door behind me only to turn around and find an angry Aiden looming over me.

"I can tell you don't want to do this," he accused. The cold look in his eye made me feel victorious.

"Neither do you. I think you hate romance more than you hate *me*."

He let out a breathy laugh as we made our way into the elevator. "You don't know what you're talking about."

"Our romance is going to be the most swoon-worthy, gushy, romantic love story of all time," I threatened punching the ground floor button angrily. "And it'll have a *million* sex scenes."

"Oh yeah? I'm going to kill off one of our main characters," he said simply. The elevator doors opened, and I followed him onto Greene Street and down Waverly.

"You can't do that," I protested. I stood in front of him, stopping him from walking any further, but he wouldn't meet my eye.

"Watch me."

"That's the most horrific, evil thing you can do in a romance!"

"But we're not writing a romance, are we?"

"That doesn't mean you can just kill them off." I wanted to write the type of book that made me believe and hope for love, even when it seemed impossible. Not something out of Aiden's wet dreams that fed his tortured-man aesthetic.

"Guess we'll just have to see." He walked away, and I stuck out my tongue at his retreating figure, my nose snarled in anger.

I could barely focus during my shift at the Hideout. I messed up drinks and couldn't keep my hands steady as I poured them. I was too busy planning all the ways I would make Aiden suffer through this project. He was bad enough with his critiques in class, but now I wouldn't even be able to have a first draft without him berating me.

My phone wouldn't stop buzzing from my back pocket so I snuck a quick look around the restaurant to make sure my boss wasn't around and pulled it out.

Logan: rosie. tell. us. everything.
Tyler: You don't have to.
Jess: uh, yes she does. spill

Tyler: She's at work guys she's not going to answer.
Logan: but i have to know!!!!!
Jess: me too!!!!!
Tyler: She probably just told them to start being more respectful during workshop.

I sighed, sending a quick text.

Rosie: can't talk. at work. but we have to cowrite the final project

I slipped my phone back in my pocket, but almost immediately I was bombarded with texts. I huffed, pulling it out again.

Logan: HAHAHA
Jess: you're joking
Tyler: Wait, really? Is it a romance?
Logan: i can't believe we get to witness this for free
Jess: actually we're paying a lot to witness this
Logan: shut up jess
Jess: rosie are you fucking with us

I rolled my eyes and punched my response into my phone.

Rosie: no. i wish. we have to write a romantic story without the hea (??) so it's pretty much a guarantee that the devil's henchman is going to make us kill off a character
Logan: can we pls only refer to aiden as the devil's henchman

Logan changed the name of the group chat to *aiden = devil's henchman*.

Tyler: Are you okay Rosie?

I paused, letting the anger wash over me. In all honesty, I didn't know if I was okay. I was embarrassed by my childish behavior. I was mad I'd have to interact with Aiden more than two times a week now. And I was beyond worried that this wouldn't work, and I'd ruin any chance of becoming a better writer and finishing a book.

I closed my eyes for a moment and tried my best to picture my parents' faces when they'd found out I was accepted into the program. Dad's face had opened in shock, but my mom had had a knowing grin, like she wasn't surprised. The reminder of their belief in me settled my beating heart.

Rosie: i'll be fine

I put my phone on silent and slipped it once again into my back pocket. I wouldn't disappoint my parents, and I wouldn't disappoint myself. And more importantly, I wouldn't let Aiden Huntington get in my way.

"I never knew you could be nice. Are you sure you didn't pay them to poison this?" She eyed the cup of coffee in front of her suspiciously. She even had the audacity to pull off the lid and lift it to her nose, inhaling.

"If I did, those are poisonous fumes," I replied, sipping my own cup. "But, no, I didn't. Believe it or not, Maxine, I can be nice."

"Sure." She snorted.

"Most people say thank you."

"Fine. Thank you." She paused. "I guess you can be nice. Sometimes."

"I'm actually nice most of the time."

"I wouldn't go that far."

"Just shut up and drink your coffee, Maxine."

"There's that nice guy charm."

— Excerpt from *Untitled* by
Rosie Maxwell and Aiden Huntington

CHAPTER FOUR

Since I was the romance expert, it was on me to write the first chapter. Initially, I'd tried to bully Aiden into writing it, but an evil glint appeared in his eye, and I could practically see the morbidity and angst rolling around in his brain. I couldn't trust him to write a meet cute that didn't turn into a *murder* cute.

I wanted the perfect story with the perfect characters to wash over me. Then, I'd sit elegantly in front of my laptop, gracefully typing out the best first draft of a first chapter ever to be written.

That did not happen.

I was walking around the Village, trying to find any source of inspiration around me. I loved Bleeker Street; when I was a little girl, I'd always dreamed I would live in this area. I'd live in a brownstone and wake up to the sounds of sirens and cars, and I'd go to a bakery on the corner for breakfast each day. I hadn't known what New York was really like, of course, and my apartment in the East Village was nothing like I had imagined. But walking down Bleeker now reminded me of how badly I wanted this life.

After walking nearly to Chelsea and back, I decided it was probably best if I sat down and tried to churn something out. Think Coffee was one of my favorite places to study and write. Hordes of students came after classes and settled in with their laptops and textbooks. I loved to sit in the back of the café when it was cold. The warm lighting and cozy music made it easy to fall into my own words.

I marched in and promised myself I wouldn't leave until I had something to work with.

I knew I wanted to write an enemies-to-lovers story. A hallmark of romance novels were the different tropes employed. A lot of people called them overdone or predictable, but readers (including me) *loved* them.

The enemies-to-lovers trope would also piss Aiden off, which was an added bonus. Not only would he think it's cliché, but we'd have to drag out the romantic part of the novel before we got to whatever horrific ending he wanted to write.

I was the last in line to order, right near the door. Every time someone opened it, the autumn wind hit me. I was used to the cold from back home, but in Tennessee it was momentary. You braced the cold for maybe ten seconds on the jog to your car, where you sighed in relief over the seat warmers. New York made you face the cold head on in order to survive.

I longed to visit home soon. I was picking up every single shift I could at the Hideout in hopes of being able to not only swing the flight home but also the full week off without pay. Not easy, when the tuition for NYU went up every year and so did rent. Still, I was determined. I knew if I worked hard enough, it'd pay off.

The bell above the door chimed as another customer entered, but this time I heard a small "Oh" as the door opened. I turned around and Aiden was standing behind me, wearing a white cable knit sweater. He gave me one of those smiles that was more of a grimace. Like it pained him to be semipleasant toward me.

I narrowed my eyes, before turning around quickly.

"Come to get some work done?" he asked. I ignored him, pretending to scan the menu a couple of feet in front of us, even though I knew exactly what I was going to get. He repeated his question, but I turned my chin up, continuing to give him the silent treatment. Although I had agreed to Ida's stipulations, I wasn't eager to become Aiden's friend. "Ah, what else could I expect other than the utmost maturity from Rosalinda Maxwell," he muttered.

"Just so you know," I said over my shoulder. "I'm more mature than you. I am *maturely* not responding to you."

"Just so you know, you just did."

"What're you even doing here? This is *my* coffee shop. You can have Starbucks." I turned around to face him and had to look up to even make eye contact with him since I was wearing my sneakers. Aiden was as tall as he was broad. He took up nearly all the space in front of the door of the coffee shop; every time the door opened, he was big enough to block me from the wind. His cheeks were still slightly flushed, the tips of his ears pink, and he looked a little adorable as much as I hated to admit it.

He raised his eyebrows. "You own Think Coffee? Congratulations on its success, Rosalinda," he said, sarcasm dripping from this voice.

"Shouldn't you be, I don't know, killing puppies? Or other writers' dreams?"

His green eyes flashed, his eyebrows raising in disbelief. Up close, it was impossible to deny how attractive he was. "Shouldn't you be dreaming about shirtless men alone in your room?" he asked mockingly.

"You're just jealous because you've never been one of those shirtless men."

"Really?" he asked, incredulous. I knew he was just making fun of me, but with his eyes trained on me like this, it was as if he was looking right through me.

"Really." I prayed he would blame my blush on the cold. It was hard to ignore how attractive he was when he was this close. I usually had the barrier of the workshop table between us, but with him leaning down and looking me dead in the eye, I had to force away the thoughts of how infuriatingly soft his hair probably was.

"It's you."

My head jerked back, my heart hammering against my chest. "What?"

"It's your turn." Aiden nodded behind me to where the cashier was waiting for my order. I rushed to the counter, apologizing profusely. Once she took my order, I reached into my bag for my wallet.

"I know it's in here," I muttered. I set my messy tote on the counter, digging through it. "Fuck, fuck, fuck." I looked at her, smiling sweetly. I've learned one thing since moving here: New Yorkers either love the country accent or they don't. I've gotten eyerolls, but hey, I've also gotten discounts. I exaggerated my accent now—a twang on the "a"s and a drawl on the "o"s, hoping it'd save me from another embarrassing moment in front of Aiden. "Do y'all happen to take Venmo? Or can I start a tab here, like a bar?"

She furrowed her brow, confused. "Um . . ."

"I got it." Aiden stepped forward and inserted his card into the machine.

"No, it's okay." I tried to pull his card out, but he grabbed my wrist to stop me. His hand warmed my skin, and I still felt his touch even when he pulled away. "I can pay for it," I said through gritted teeth. The last thing I needed was to owe him a favor.

"Just let me do something nice for you," he hissed.

"You probably paid them to put laxatives in my coffee."

He spluttered out what would've been a laugh if Aiden were capable, his eyes opening in shock. The cashier handed me my receipt, and I walked to the end of the bar, Aiden following suit after placing his own order.

"Thank you," I said begrudgingly to Aiden from the corner of my mouth. "You can be nice. Sometimes."

He nodded. "I'm actually nice most of the time."

"Oh, well, I wouldn't go that far."

"I'm just not nice to *you*."

The barista called my name, and I turned to Aiden.

"Well, I'll see you on Monday. Thanks again for the coffee." I lifted my drink as a goodbye and walked toward the back of the shop where the tables were full of customers. The semester had just started, and it felt like every student had crowded into Think Coffee to study. I was able to snag an empty one in the corner and pulled my laptop out.

I opened an empty doc and willed words to come. The cursor blinked back at me tauntingly, as if it knew I had nothing. Last semester, it had been near impossible for me to write anything romantic. I'd had to force myself to listen to Taylor Swift and reread my favorite books to find inspiration because I realized I didn't have anything to draw from in real life. I'd come to terms with the fact that the man who I'd thought was my first love didn't love me, and I didn't love him. Since then, I'd quickly learned how careless the men of New York were, most of them looking for a casual hookup to forget in the morning.

My fingers hovered over the keyboard, rubbing against one another.

Anything, I told myself. *Just write anything.*

My gaze flicked away from my screen momentarily only to find Aiden standing near the front of the seating area. His neck was strained, surveying the cafe for an empty table, but there were none. I'd been lucky to find a place to sit myself. Guilt started to pool in my stomach as he began to turn around to leave.

My southern nature had a hard time leaving me, even after a year in the city. Before I could think better of it, I stood from my chair.

"Aiden," I called out. He turned around and looked at me with a questioning glance. I beckoned him to the small table and hesitantly he made his way over.

"The least I can do is offer to share my table," I said, sitting back down. "You know, as a thank you for the coffee."

"Are you sure?" His brows were pulled down as he hesitated in front of the table.

"Positive." I moved my bag from the seat across and made room for him.

"Well, thank you. That's very nice," he said appreciatively, clearing his throat.

"I can be nice sometimes." I repeated his words and smiled at him, but he only gave a terse nod.

"I won't disturb you. I'm just trying to get work done." He pulled his laptop from his bag.

Almost immediately, he started typing. No thinking, just writing. I was envious. How come the words came so easily to *him*? What did *he* do to deserve the relief from writer's block?

I'll admit, his melodic typing soothed me more than the cafe music, as much as it pissed me off. There was a calming rhythm to the ebb and flow of the words pouring out of his fingers. It was so soft and gentle, like he cared for each and every word he wrote. The act of writing itself was so vulnerable. It was strange to witness someone in those moments of privacy.

Back when I decided that Aiden was my mortal nemesis, I did some research. I liked to know the people I hated because what if Aiden was donating his time to underprivileged children? Could I *really* hate that?

Jess and I asked around in the program about him last year, and, as it turned out, Aiden was a full-time first-year grad student—a second-year now. This semester he was teaching an Intro to Creative Writing Class at the undergraduate school. Aiden as a workshopper was bad, but as the facilitator? I wouldn't be surprised if the students left that class *sobbing*.

I tried to focus on the blinking cursor on my own screen as it stared back at me, daring me to write even a single word. I looked at Aiden over my laptop. He had pulled his lips between his teeth as he typed, his eyes narrowed in focus. His white sweater complemented his tanned skin so well that I had to force my eyes away.

Despite myself, I couldn't help but wonder what it was like to *be* with Aiden. Would it be like this? Sitting across from each other at cafés, writing? Did he always dress without wrinkles or would he be the kind of boyfriend to wear hoodies and sweatshirts for snuggling on the couch?

Realistically, he was probably as cold in a relationship as he was in class. He'd probably pick every dinner and every movie. And maybe he was like that in bed, too. He'd take exactly what he wanted and—

I closed my eyes. Aiden was *not* a romantic hero, and he never would be. I was just lonely. I missed home, I was frustrated over school, and Aiden was wearing a *sweater*. These factors combined were quite dangerous.

After a few minutes, Aiden was still typing, like he never ran out of words to say. I couldn't stand the clacking of his keyboard any longer.

"What're you writing?" I asked.

He looked up at me briefly, the relentless typing pausing. "I'm working on a short story for my other fiction workshop."

"Oh." I wrapped my hands around my coffee cup, trying to keep warm. I looked down at my own empty doc, deflated. When I glanced back at him, his gaze flickered up from my collarbone to my eyes, his cheeks flushing.

"What are you *not* writing?" he asked, not unkindly, nodding at my laptop.

"Our chapter," I admitted. "I know we said we'd go off the cuff, but I have no idea where to even start."

"Shouldn't it start with a meet-cute or something?" He squinted, waving a hand. "I thought this would be easy for you. You're the romance expert."

I laughed softly. "It's not that easy. I just—" I broke off, taking a deep breath. "I just can't find the words some days. I know they're somewhere within me, but then I look at an empty page and nothing comes up. It's worse than just a word on the tip of my tongue—it's *painful*. It's like when you know you should cry, but the tears won't come."

"Have you ever heard of the shitty first draft?"

I titled my head. "That's what you turn in for workshop, right?"

"Funny," he deadpanned. "The shitty first draft is when you get everything out. You don't care what you're writing or if every word is perfect, you just write."

"So?"

"So." He shrugged. "Writing's in the revisions. Nothing's set in stone, you know. Your backspace works as well as the other keys."

"Har har." I rolled my eyes. But I considered what he said. I'd never admit it to him, but it *was* good advice. "I just wish I knew where I was going. If I knew what we were aiming for, I feel like the words would come easier. I mean, it's all up to me as of now. What if you don't like one of the names? What if I name the girl after your mother, and you can't distance yourself from real life enough and you end up writing a love story about your mother? What if—"

"No more 'what ifs.'" He shut his laptop and took his black notebook from his bag. "Okay. Let's plan it out."

"Really?"

"Really. Come on, tell me what you've got."

With our laptops closed, I noticed how many empty tables there were now. The cafe's rush had ended, and we didn't really *need* to sit with each other anymore. But neither of us got up to move.

"Well, I decided on enemies-to-lovers because it's the best trope to write." He opened his mouth, but I barreled on so he couldn't object. "But there are still plenty of things I need to figure out. Why do they hate each other? What makes them stop hating each other? Also, I'm really hung up on what their names are. What's their backstory? What do they look like—"

"Jesus, Rosalinda, how do you ever get any work done? You're stressing *me* out." He rubbed his eyes with the heels of his palms.

I ignored him. "To me, the most important thing would be their names."

Aiden's nose crinkled. I hadn't noticed the freckles on it before.

"What? You don't think names are important?" I asked.

"No, I do. But I feel like the characters decide those when the time comes. After we decide what to do with them."

"Fine. What's our plot then?"

"Well, we have to know the character's name to even start putting them in situations."

I threw my hands up, exasperated, but the corner of Aiden's mouth twitched. I squinted at him in disbelief. "Did you just make a joke? I didn't know you were capable. Will your hardware start malfunctioning soon?"

The hint of a smile left, only to be replaced with a frown. "I was thinking maybe they work together?"

"Ooh, a workplace romance." I sat up, intrigued. "Tell me more."

"Maybe they're always competing. They're in sales, and there's a big client or something so they have to team up for a presentation. They're always bickering, but they go away at a company retreat and things get romantic from there."

"I hate to say it," I said, closing my eyes, "but this, surprisingly, sounds like a good romance. How will we ever make it literary fiction?"

His eyes twinkled. "This is where it gets good."

He went through a couple of different scenarios, all of which made me want to cry. He gave the characters tortured pasts, he killed them off. He kept going until I couldn't take it anymore and cut him off.

"No way." I shook my head vigorously. "We can't make either of them evil. Then, the reader won't even care if they end up together."

"I didn't say evil." He might not have said it, but I heard it.

I couldn't understand why someone *wouldn't* want a happy ending. Before I could stop myself, I asked, "Why don't you like happy endings?"

He lifted his shoulder. "It's unrealistic."

"Plenty of people get their Happily Ever After."

"Even more don't."

"Maybe not *you*, but people who deserve it usually get it," I said jokingly.

I must've hit a nerve because he tensed, his eyes turning cold. "Are we talking about me, or are we talking about the characters? Let's just make this painless and spend as little time together as possible." Before I could respond, he stood from his chair, nearly knocking it over. "I have to go. I trust you're capable of writing a single chapter."

With that, he slung his bag over his shoulder and stormed out of the coffee shop.

Maybe I'd taken it too far, but it wasn't fair for Aiden to just flip on a dime like that. I fumed to myself as I packed my own bag. He was self-righteous and arrogant. He thought he was so much better than me just because he made people sad instead of happy.

I hadn't known how to start my chapter before, but I sure as hell did now.

My mom used to say if I didn't have anything nice to say, then it was best to say nothing at all.

So, I won't say out loud that I wish Hunter would fall off the edge of a cliff.

— Excerpt from *Untitled* by
Rosie Maxwell and Aiden Huntington

CHAPTER FIVE

I texted Aiden almost an hour ago that I had finished the chapter. After he left Think Coffee, I was so mad I couldn't see straight. We were stuck in this stupid project because neither of us could be nice to each other, but we had to at least *try*. I couldn't mess up my second chance in this class.

We had a shared Google Doc for our project. Instead of sending each other chapters and scenes back and forth, it was easier to just have it all in one place. I'd also be able to see whenever he logged on and what changes he made to my writing . . . and if he got too cruel, I could change his writing, too.

After I texted him, I kept the doc open, waiting for his name to appear on the screen. I nervously bit my thumbnail, rereading the chapter, trying to see it through Aiden's eyes.

I hadn't intended for it to actually be good. I'd set up a feud between the two characters and had written some great banter that I was proud of. Maybe we could use some of it in the *real* first chapter, but for now, I had another goal in mind.

When Aiden's name appeared on the doc, I pushed the bag of plantain chips off me and slid my laptop closer, watching his cursor go through each line. My heart was pounding by the time he finished, his cursor blinking on the last word.

Then my phone buzzed.

Aiden: Rewrite it.

I laughed giddily, stuffing my hand in the bag of plantains and shoving them into my mouth.

Rosie: no
Aiden: Rewrite it, we can't submit this.
Rosie: why ever not

The three bubbles appeared and disappeared for the next minute. I was sitting hunched over my phone, anticipating his words, slowly chewing.

Aiden: Because the point of this assignment was for us to get along. Not to find another way to fight.
Rosie: i don't know what you're talking about

I fell back on my bed giggling. So what if I *did* have to rewrite it? At least I'd had the chance to piss him off.

Aiden: You named the main guy after me.
Rosie: his name's not aiden
Aiden: No, his name is Hunter. Hunter . . . Huntington. I'm not stupid, Rosalinda.

I could picture the wrinkle between his eyebrows that always formed whenever he was pissed. I wondered if I'd made him mad enough to make the vein pop out from the side of his neck. The last time I'd done that was last semester when I said one of his main characters was whiny and had a superiority complex.

Rosie: hunter is a really common name. you need to get over yourself a little bit, i'm saying that as a friend
Aiden: Rewrite it.

I rolled my eyes and pulled my laptop up in front of me. The chapter was due at midnight so everyone had time to read it by tomorrow. I had already played my joke on him. It'd be easier for both of us if

I just started something we could actually work with. My eyes snagged on a few of the lines, and I couldn't help but reread the pages. I hesitated as my finger hovered over the backspace. It *was* pretty good. Honestly, I didn't know if I could write something better. Even if it was just a joke, I'd put a lot of thought into this chapter.

> Rosie: be honest . . . what would you think about it if the character wasn't named hunter?

The three bubbles did their little dance again—up and down, up and down, for the next few minutes. I continued to shovel handfuls of plantain chips in my mouth, anticipating his harsh words.

> Aiden: I'd say it was near perfect.

I straightened, rereading the words. An involuntary smile flitted across my face. His approval was rare and I hated how much I valued his opinion.

> Rosie: then we should keep it!!!! no one's going to know it's you
> Aiden: Everyone will know. Just change the name.

I snorted. If we were keeping it, we were keeping all of it. I heard Alexa open the front door and kick her shoes off, each thumping against the floor.

> Rosie: sorry, can't. i'm too attached. let me know when you finish our next chapter!!!:-)

I put my phone on silent and slid off my small bed. I found Alexa in our tiny kitchen, pulling off the tie from her Hideout uniform.
"Hey, how was work?"
She gave me a murderous glare. "Trabaja los fines de semana."
"My brain hurts, English please," I begged.
She tsked. "Si nuncas practicas tu español, nunca aprenderás."
When she discovered I wasn't fluent in Spanish, Alexa had made it her personal mission to teach me. Coming from a mixed household, I'd mostly spoken English growing up. It wasn't until I moved to

New York and tried to share my heritage with others that I felt any less Peruvian for being mixed. It was like other Peruvians thought I wasn't as in tune with my culture just because I couldn't conjugate in the preterit instinctually or had to really focus when listening in on conversations in Spanish. But I wore red on Peruvian Independence Day and cooked lomo saltado when I missed home (okay, I asked Alexa to, but still).

"I know, I know." I waved her off. "I've been writing for the past few hours, my brain is mush."

She sighed, relenting. "I want you to work weekends."

"No way." I shook my head.

"Benji is so terrible at the bar! They mess up every drink anyone orders, and they spend the whole time flirting with their partner!"

"I can't," I said apologetically.

"But why?" she whined, stomping her foot.

"Because," I dragged out. "The weekends are my only time to write. And y'all make the weekend shifts sound like absolute hell. If I can avoid them, I'm going to."

"But if you start working weekends, you'll have more money to go home in time for Thanksgiving *and* take more classes." Alexa grabbed a mug from the cupboard and shoved the kettle under the faucet. Each of her moves were sharp, as if she were just as mad at the objects in her hand as she was at Benji. She slammed the kettle on the stove, turning up the flame for it to boil. "Tips are way better on weekends."

"You couldn't pay me enough." When the kettle started to whistle, she poured water in her mug, dunking a tea bag in and out.

She pouted, lifting her mug to her lips. "How was your day? Were you able to start that chapter?"

I laughed lightly. "Yeah, eventually. Funny thing—I actually ran into Aiden at a Think near campus today." Alexa's eyes widened, but I stopped her before she could make a crude comment. "Nothing happened. He was fine, then out of nowhere started being a dick."

"Maybe the raw sexual tension was getting to him." Alexa wiggled her eyebrows. "Did you at least end up finishing your chapter?"

I ran my fingers softly along the counter. "I did."

She hopped up onto the counter, still sipping her tea. "What'd he think about it?"

I bit back a smile. "You know, I think he really resonated with the main character."

Alexa gave a soft *ha*. "Maybe this crazy scheme will work after all."

On Monday, I ran into Aiden before the start of class. He was waiting outside the Writer's House, leaning against the gate surrounding the entrance. When he saw me, he pushed off the gate and peered down at me. "Hi, Rosie."

"You're weirdly chipper." I frowned, automatically suspicious that he'd called me Rosie.

I narrowed my eyes at him, hoping I could read on his face what game he was playing at. My jaw nearly dropped in shock when he stepped forward to hold the door open for me.

I hesitated. Had he been possessed? The Aiden I knew would never do this. In fact, he'd pretend to open the door for me, then shove past me to walk through it first. Something was up.

"Are you sick?" I asked, stepping past him. I got a whiff of his cologne, somehow warm and *sharp*. I pretended I didn't love it.

"No."

"You're being nice. It's weird."

"I literally just said hi to you."

"Exactly."

"I'm guessing you didn't read chapter two," he said as we walked down the hall toward our classroom. He bent his head just a fraction as he spoke to me, his ear titled toward his shoulder.

"*Shit*," I said, stopping in place. I looked up at him and grabbed his hand. "I'm sorry, I completely forgot! Don't tell Ida." He looked between my hands and his, raising his eyebrows. I dropped his hand like it was fire, wiping my own off on my coat. "I don't want her to think we aren't getting along."

"No worries," he said coolly. Obviously, worry seeped through me at his tone. Since when was Aiden *calm*? "I won't say anything if you won't. After you." He nodded me into the classroom.

We'd each have to read our respective chapters out loud. Ida had already explained to the class what she described as "our special project" in her weekly email to the class.

"Rosie, why don't we start with you and Aiden today? I'm excited to see what you two have put together."

My leg bounced rapidly against the table. My skin prickled, my fingers clenching into fists. Aiden caught my eye and glared at me.

"Stop it," he mouthed, nodding at the table shaking slightly.

"Bite me," I mouthed back.

He glanced at Ida before mouthing, "Stop worrying. It'll be fine."

"Rosie, you can begin whenever you're ready."

My eyes flickered across the table to Aiden's, and he nodded once in encouragement. My chest warmed, for just a second. Maybe the other day at the café was a fluke. Maybe he'd been nervous and *that's* why he left. Maybe the hatred had shifted to playfulness, and we were on our way to becoming friends. And maybe I wasn't too opposed to that idea.

I began reading my chapter. Along the way, my shaky voice became stronger and, as I reread my words, I *knew* they were good. I glanced at Ida, hoping to gauge her reaction, but she was unreadable.

When I earned a few chuckles, I straightened, pride blooming. It was times like these, when my writing seemed indestructible, that I was so certain I'd made the right choice to move to New York. *Of course* this was what I was meant to do with my life.

Just as the dialogue began, I frowned. Something was off. Aiden had changed my character's name to Max.

I had originally named her Meg, after Meg Ryan. I planned to find a way to pay homage to her later in the novel, too. I kept reading, annoyed that Aiden would do something so petty without asking.

Once I finished, Ida spoke up. "I think it's best if we go straight into Aiden's chapter, then discuss the two together."

I glared at Aiden from across the table. I wasn't stupid, either—he was getting back at me for naming the male lead after him. Clearly Max had been named after my last name, Maxwell. I had no doubt this next chapter would be as slanderous to me as mine was to him.

He cleared his throat, shifting in his seat. "*Max's delusions of grandeur would always hold her back. Her naivety holds her back from witnessing reality.*"

I cringed.

"*She trusts freely, laughs easily, even when it's obvious she shouldn't.*"

He must've felt my eyes burning holes into his head because he glanced up between paragraphs. The side of his mouth quirked up and he barreled on.

"But she's not fooling anyone with her act. I see right through it—and her."

I closed my eyes, trying to control my breathing. He was just trying to get a rise out of me. Hadn't I written, *His stoic exterior is the perfect complement to his even colder heart?*

There was a difference in the way we read our chapters. I was on shaky ground, nervous with each word, building up confidence. But Aiden's steady voice carried his every word.

Once he finished, Ida said to the class, "Well, who wants to start?"

Every hand shot up.

"I loved it." Logan leaned forward in his seat, smiling. "It was by far my favorite submission this week, no offense everyone. If Aiden and Rosie don't keep writing together, I think I'll *die*."

Jess kicked his chair and muttered, "Tone it down."

"I liked the dynamic," Tyler said on a more serious note as Logan quietly snickered. "I think the dual point of view is an interesting aspect, and it'll be fun to see the romance play out with that."

Each of our peers offered up comments, but when it was Aiden's turn Ida held her hand up.

"I'm sure Aiden and Rosie have spoken at length about the chapters. I won't make them repeat it for the class." She smiled at the both of us, as if she hadn't given us the dressing down of the century a week ago. "As for my comments, I'll say this for now—I'm impressed with you two. I'm looking forward to the next chapters."

For the first time since The Incident ™, I relaxed. Although I was relieved, I narrowed my eyes at Aiden trying to say, *This conversation isn't over.*

When class ended, I filed out of the classroom silently. I could feel Aiden's brooding, stalker presence behind me. I usually liked to view the world in a rose-colored light, but I was seeing red. I didn't so much as look at him until we were outside on Fifth, in the New York autumn chill and outside of Ida's sight.

I turned around and stabbed Aiden right in the chest with my finger.

"Whoa." He held his hands up, taking a step back with each step I took forward until his back was against the traffic. New Yorkers paid no attention to us, used to ignoring every character on the street. Aiden was a thorn in my side that just wouldn't go away.

My jaw was tight. "How could you change my character's name to *Max*?"

Amusement danced in his eyes. "I got attached to the name, what can I say?"

"What you wrote about me was way worse than what I wrote about you!" I exploded.

He stepped forward, looming over me. I looked up at him through my lashes, my chest rising and falling quickly in anger.

"Who said I was writing about you?" His face was so close to mine I could feel his breath fanning against my skin. I couldn't stop my eyes from briefly flickering down to his lips. "I'm writing about Maxine. An optimist—"

"A romantic, you mean," I said flatly.

"An optimist," he corrected. "Who sees the best in everyone when they don't deserve it. Who lives in a fantasy world. Who finds a way to make every inch of my fucking skin itch." His voice quiet, but sharp. My mind betrayed me as, the closer he got, the more I wondered how his lips would feel on mine. I hated how he made my mind stray from anger to lust so quickly. I prayed he didn't notice as a shiver ran up my spine at his soft, low voice. "Doesn't sound like you, does it?"

No. It didn't. I was an optimist, and I saw the best in everyone because they *did* deserve it. I didn't live in a fantasy world, I just tried to make mine better. And I didn't make every inch of his skin itch, I made it *burn*.

"Just like I wasn't writing about you. I was writing about Hunter, who's desperate to make everyone sad so he can feel just a little bit better about himself. Who goes home to an empty apartment and jerks himself off to fantasies from years ago to make himself fall asleep because it's been too long since he's had the real thing and it shows. Who'd rather see the worst in people than admit there's some goodness left in the world."

His gaze was intense. We dared the other to back down, but neither one of us would. His jaw ticked. "Perfect. So, we're not writing about each other."

"I guess not."

"No reason to read in between the lines then, huh?"

"None at all," I answered sweetly.

"Then I guess I'll see you in the next chapter."

He brushed past me and walked off, lost in the crowd. I stayed where I was, trying to calm my racing heart. As much as I hated him, I couldn't turn off the part of my brain that turned everything into a scene from a romance novel. I hated how I wished he would've leaned forward just a *bit* more to plant his lips on my jaw. The intense look in his eyes was enough to make any girl need to close her eyes and collect herself. Next chapter, he was *really* going to know what I thought about him.

I couldn't take the incessant ringing anymore. I promised myself I'd stay away from him today because I had to focus on my portion of our presentation. But it was impossible when he ignored every call that came through.

"Can you pick up your goddamn phone?" I snapped, turning in my chair. Hunter and I were cursed with desks in the same cubicle, our backs facing each other every day, only a gray half wall surrounding us.

He didn't even look up. "No."

I watched as he continued to write slowly and carefully in his black notebook, paying no mind to the blond hair falling into his face.

The phone was still ringing.

"Fine." I pushed my rolling chair back and reached across him to pick up his phone. "You've reached Hunter Adrian's office. He's way too busy to take your call because he doesn't find you as important as Max Daisy does. You can call her at extension 9412."

I slammed the phone back into the receiver before rolling my chair back.

"Well done," Hunter said. His blue button down was rolled up to his forearms. Whenever he had his shirt like that, I had to force my eyes not to stray. He carefully crossed them over his chest. "Sounds like you just stole one of my clients."

"Well, if you're not going to take their calls." I turned toward my desk, trying to calm my beating heart.

"Aren't you at least a little bit curious about who your new client is?" he pressed. I envisioned the purse of his lips, the dip in his brow—the face he always made when he was upset with me.

"I'm sure I'll find out soon enough," I said over my shoulder. I straightened my keyboard in front of me and pretended to type, my fingers bouncing lightly off the keys.

"Alright," he said. I heard his chair roll and the scratch of his pencil. "When my mom calls, tell her I said hello."

I paused. "Your mom?"

"Great job, Maxine. You've secured Durgis Agency's newest client."

I whipped around, my chair spinning a little too out of control. I had to use my foot to stop myself from going all the way around.

"Why aren't you answering your mom's calls?"

"Why aren't you focusing on your own work?"

Not in My Book

"When your mom calls me, I'm going to tell her how horrible you are, and she'll make you move back home. You'll be destined to live forever in her basement."

"Tell her I'll be late to dinner on Tuesday." He didn't even turn around.

— Excerpt from *Untitled* by
Rosie Maxwell and Aiden Huntington

CHAPTER SIX

"Just so you know," Aiden said as soon as I answered the phone, "I'd take my mother's calls."

"Sure, sure." I balanced my phone between my shoulder and ear as I bent over my knee, carefully dragging the brush across my toenails, making them bright red. We'd graduated from texting to phone calls over the past couple of months of working on the book together. It had started when he tried to get Maxine fired from her job and enter a period of depression, and I couldn't help but call him on the phone and yell at him. "Just like you look up from that notebook when I say something to you."

It annoyed me all last semester how he refused to make eye contact with me whenever I spoke. I'd say anything, and he'd start writing in his stupid notebook; when I gave critiques, he'd do the same.

Aiden cursed under his breath. There was a low, steady stream of noise behind him. "Where are you?" I asked, sitting up. Then I heard the music and could practically feel the bass through the phone. After a few more curses from Aiden, the sound started to fade. "Are you at a party? Were you reading my chapter at a party?"

"No, of course not," he said sharply. He must've been able to tell from my silence that I didn't believe him. He sighed, relenting. "It's my cousin's middle school dance."

I spluttered a laugh. "Please tell me everything."

I could basically see him dragging his hand down the side of his face as he groaned. It was strange how well I knew Aiden, even though I hated him. I'd spent so long sitting across from him I could picture him so clearly now. "They were short one chaperone, and she said if they didn't get another they'd have to cancel."

"Aww. And you volunteered? That's so—"

"Please don't say romantic."

"Romantic," I sighed. I fell back onto my bed, the springs creaking. "Who knew Aiden Huntington was such a romantic?"

"Don't say that." I bet he was scowling. "My hands were tied."

"So, like a valiant romance hero, you stepped forward and defended your cousin's honor and saved her middle school dance."

"Or I sacrificed a few hours of my life to stand with a bunch of sweaty preteens in a gym listening to Taylor Swift."

"Hey, take out the preteens and gym, and that's my kind of night."

A laugh, that shouldn't really count as a laugh but instead was a harsh exhale, surprised me. Since when did Aiden Huntington laugh? It made him seem so *human*, and I couldn't stop myself from wanting to know more about him. I sat up to inspect the polish on my toes, testing to see if they were dry. "Do you really take your mom's calls?" I asked casually.

"I did," he said softly. He cleared his throat and said, "Why are you working on our pages on Thanksgiving weekend?"

My throat tightened as unexpected tears sprung in my eyes. Thanksgiving had been this past Thursday, and I hadn't been able to swing a flight. I was still holding out hope for Christmas, though.

"Do you have siblings?" I blurted out, ignoring his question. Despite working together on our manuscript for nearly two months, I felt like I didn't know anything about him.

"Rosalinda," he warned. I knew what he was thinking. He didn't want to give me ammo for my next chapter.

"I'm not trying to use it against you. I just don't know anything about you," I confessed. I picked at a stray string in my white comforter. "Isn't that weird? I hate you, but I don't know anything about your life."

"Hate, huh?"

"Dislike," I conceded. "I didn't know you saved middle school dances. You've been promoted from hate to dislike, congratulations."

He laughed fully this time and warmth blossomed in my chest. The last thing I ever expected was for Aiden's laugh to make me feel like the drive home after a long day. I hated the part of me that wanted to see the smile paired with this laugh. Did he tip his head back? Shake his head?

"No siblings," he said softly. "Just me. What about you?"

"I've got a sister," I said. "A year and a half younger than me." I was tempted to tell him how homesick I was. How she was my best friend in the entire world, and I had felt so lost these past two years without her.

"What made—" He was cut off by sounds of children's laughter. "Hey! Is that a vape? Get over here." His authoritative tone was enough to scare *me* over the phone. "I've got to go, Rosalinda. I'll write the next chapter soon."

He hung up without another word, and I ignored the small part of me that wanted to call him again just to hear his laugh.

I'd been avoiding Ida's office hours ever since The Incident ™, worried I had forever ruined my relationship with her.

I stood in front of her office door, trying to gain the courage to go in. Usually, I entered without preamble and got right to it, but I was so nervous now that I did something I hadn't ever done before: I knocked on her door.

After her soft "Come in," I opened the door and stepped into her office. She looked up from her papers, eyebrows raised.

"Rosie, I'm surprised to see you. You haven't stopped by in a long time."

I hesitantly took a seat in the chair opposite her desk, running my hands against my skirt to wipe the sweat off.

"I know. I just . . . I want to say I'm sorry for what happened. With Aiden. I swear we're being nice to each other now."

"Rosie," she said softly. "I'm not mad at you. I just have to set boundaries within the workshop so you two don't set a precedent for what's acceptable. But you and I are fine, okay?"

I nodded. "Thank you. Because I *did* have a lot of questions for you."

She smiled. "I'd expect nothing less. Do you have the chapter you're going to workshop for next class? Let me see what we're working with."

I handed over the folded papers and she skimmed through them quickly.

"I know it's not my best work," I said in a rush. Writing had been so much easier when I was just a little girl sitting on my bedroom floor, without the pressure of Ida and Aiden as my primary audiences, and I wanted to find that feeling again. "I feel like I don't know Aiden well enough. I'll set a scene up for what I want it to be, but then Aiden will take it in a different direction."

She hummed. "You two lack chemistry."

"That's not true," I said quickly.

She raised a brow. "So, you two *do* have chemistry?"

A blush spread across my cheeks. I don't know why I felt weirdly protective over the dynamic Aiden and I had. It wasn't a typical one, but now that we'd spent some time working on the project, I surprisingly felt like we worked well together. Even if it was in opposite ways. Half the time when he insulted me, I wanted to write it down because it was such a good insult.

"I don't know." I shrugged. "I don't think it's that bad."

"What you two need is to communicate better. Think about how successful Christina Lauren is. Their voices blend so well because they're so in sync with each other."

"They write the same genre."

Ida shrugged. "I didn't say it would be easy."

I sighed, knowing she was right. If Aiden and I were able to miraculously communicate with no problem, we'd have to be semivulnerable in front of each other. I wasn't ready for that.

"Let's see what the workshop thinks tomorrow. I'm really impressed with what I've seen so far from you two. I think it's been your best writing yet."

"I don't know about *that.*" I laughed. "Sometimes when I read it back, it doesn't even feel like my voice."

"Sure." She bowed her head, conceding. "But it might just be a new side of your voice you hadn't discovered yet. And, honestly, I really like it. But let's see what we can do with this chapter."

We continued revising my latest chapter and going over her recent notes for me. There were some writers who had no ability to teach, instead opting to preach from their pedestal. But Ida wasn't like that. She took the time to sit with me and go through line-by-line edits and guided our plot as much as she could. I always left her office with a renewed sense of purpose in the program.

As I packed up, I said, "I meant to ask you about this earlier. Have you heard of the Frost Fellowship? I was thinking of applying for it."

I'd done the math, and if I won, I'd be able to do a full-time schedule to finish my MFA sooner *and* afford to go home more than once in a blue moon. Besides, being published in *The Frost* would be an incredible honor that'd help me build up my writer credits.

Ida's eyes brightened. "You *absolutely* should! It's a really great opportunity."

"Obviously I want to, but . . ." I hesitated.

"But you're afraid of what'll happen if you submit a romance," she finished.

"The only thing I know how to write is romance. But I know what other people think of that. I don't want it to hurt my chances."

She sat forward at her desk, leveling her gaze with mine. "I'm going to be honest—I don't know if they'll be kind to a romance piece. I don't know if that'll be a deciding factor or not. But you'll regret not having taken this chance. You know I think you're a great writer," she said softly. "I say submit romance and fuck 'em if they can't appreciate it."

It was so easy to say *fuck the man! I won't submit any sad, serious literature. I'll submit my witty romance chapter!* But rejection was disheartening. It was immortalized in words echoing in my head and doubt in my hands over a keyboard.

"Would you be able to look over my piece before I submit it?" I asked finally.

Ida smiled. "I'd love nothing more."

"That's it for today. Keep up the good work, everyone." Ivy stacked her papers against the conference room table and stood.

I remained in my seat across from Maxine. Despite sitting next to each other at our desks daily, we always picked the seats across from each other in the conference room. Perhaps because it was another way to hurl glares or get under the other's skin.

She didn't leave either. She pinned me down with her light blue eyes as the room emptied out. I had become addicted to that look. It was my biggest vice—figuring out what words I could say to make her mad, to make her focus only on me, to get the look.

She bounced her leg rapidly, causing the table to shake. "Would you quit that?" I snapped.

She narrowed her eyes, her leg speeding up.

"You're going to bruise."

"So, I'll bruise," she said. Her velvet voice surrounded me in the conference room; it was nearly suffocating. She commanded attention from everyone she met, even if she didn't know it. She was often larger than life, fearless.

It was annoying. And admirable.

"How's your portion of the presentation coming?" I asked casually.

She lifted a shoulder, acting like my words were of no consequence to her. "Just as you would expect. I heard yours was all cold hard facts." She frowned, as if the idea brought a bad taste to her mouth.

"Oh really? Where'd you hear that?"

"You know how much the break room likes to gossip." A grin spread across her face. Hope flickered in my chest at the thought that she'd asked about me. "I'm sure everyone will like my portion better. Mine appeals to the emotions a bit more. It's happier."

"Unrealistic," I corrected.

"To you, there's no difference."

I resisted the urge to smile. I was always doing that around her, terrified of what would happen if I let someone in again. I tapped my fingers on the glass conference table, leaving smudges, deciding it was better to push her away.

"It's time to wake up, Maxine. You're in the real world now with real stakes, one of them being your career. Don't come crying to me when you're knocked on your ass by reality. I won't help you up."

— Excerpt from *Untitled* by
Rosie Maxwell and Aiden Huntington

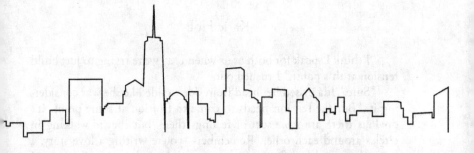

CHAPTER SEVEN

Safe to say, I was shaking my leg under the table during the next class. I hadn't even known it annoyed Aiden before or that I did it that often, but I wasn't about to stop now.

He glared at me from across the table.

"Knock it off," he mouthed.

"Pay attention," I mouthed back.

Our classmates were still giving out their comments on our latest chapters. It felt like everyone was edging around the truth until finally someone spoke up.

"I like what you guys have done, but this isn't an enemies to lovers. This is just enemies so far," Tyler said. Out of the corner of my eye, Ida nodded in agreement. I frowned. That was intentional. I mean, if the enemies became lovers too soon, then no one cared.

"It's obvious Max and Hunter hate each other, and you're doing a good job of *hinting* toward some feeling, but there's no progress. There's nemesis chemistry, but it's not translating into any sort of romantic plotline, and without that, all the yearning feels a little stalkerish."

From the front of the room, Ida gave me a pointed look as if to say, *See?* I snuck a glance at Aiden, but he was unfazed. I rolled my eyes. He probably wasn't even listening. I bet he was doing his taxes in his head.

"I agree," Ida said.

Katie Holt

"I think I speak for both of us when I say we're trying to just build tension at this point," I rushed out.

"Sure." Ida tossed her head from side to side like she was considering it. "But the tension needs to come to fruition at some point. It's obvious there are *some* sort of feelings there, but they're walking in circles around each other. Remember—you're writing a love story. I need there to be *definitive* romantic moments between the two of them, not just thoughts in their heads." She paused. "I have a proposal for you two."

"Another?" Aiden muttered. He held his pen carefully above the lines of his black notebook, preparing for whatever she was about to say.

"You two need to get to know each other better so these characters can really experience the romance they'll eventually have. Try a little roleplay."

I started coughing in surprise, and Aiden finally looked up from his notebook.

"Go on a date—as Max and Hunter—this weekend," Ida said. "Then go home and write about it. Pretend you're the characters, and let the romance build in your book."

Aiden frowned. "Is this a suggestion, or are you telling us?"

"If anyone else asks, I'm suggesting. But since you're asking, I'm telling."

Aiden and I shared a quick, panicked glance.

Ida laughed softly. "You two will be fine," she soothed. "Just focus on not killing each other so we can hear all about it next class."

When my friends and I left the Writer's House, they were silent for a minute, sharing glances with each other.

"Go ahead." I rolled my eyes.

At once, they all burst into laughter.

"It's not *that* funny," I scolded. "I'm glad you find the inhumanity of forcing me to hang out with Aiden hilarious."

"Oh God," Logan said, wiping a tear from his eye. "Don't make us laugh any harder."

"That really does suck," Tyler said sympathetically. "But hopefully it'll go by fast."

"It's going to be a slow painful death," I muttered.

"It *is* a lot like a romance novel," Jess said thoughtfully between laughs. "Enemies to lovers, forced proximity—"

66

"Don't even say that around me," I said grouchily. "It's *nothing* like that. We aren't enemies to lovers. We're enemies to near murderers. I swear every time we talk we come this close to strangling each other." The door to the Writer's House opened and as Aiden began walking down the stairs, I said, "I'll text y'all later." I chased after him until I fell into step with him outside.

Now that the weather was turning frigid, his peacoat had *finally* come out of the closet. I hadn't seen it since last winter, and I hated how much I liked it on him. I'd tried not to stare at him too hard at the beginning of class when he walked in with it on.

"We need to plan out tomorrow."

He jumped at my words and looked down at me, bewildered. "Jesus Christ, you scared the shit out of me."

"We need to plan our 'date,'" I deadpanned.

He scowled, crossing the street toward University Place and Union Square. "Can we not call it a date?"

"Why? Too romantic?" I teased.

"Yes," he said, matter-of-factly.

"You'll need to get used to romance." I had trouble keeping pace with him as we walked through the streets. The holiday season had begun, which meant there were more tourists around than normal. Not only did I have to dodge groups of people standing side by side, crowding the sidewalks, but his long legs made easy, long strides. I was nearly jogging trying to keep up with him. "Or at least the word 'date.' That's some free life advice for you. Most women won't date a guy who calls what they're doing 'hanging out.'"

"I can say the word." He noticed my struggle, and I swear he sped up. "I just don't want to call it a date with *you*."

"Oh, you should be so lucky. I'll have you know, I'm an excellent dater."

"That's right, what's your boyfriend's name again?"

"The same as your girlfriend's," I spluttered. He stopped at a busy intersection and turned to face me. I had to crane my neck to look up and meet his gaze. "Be real—what do you want to do for our date?"

Aiden studied my face for a moment silently, before shaking his head. "Let's not, and say we did." He continued walking, his hands shoved into his coat pockets and his shoulders pulled up against his ears as the wind picked up.

"No!" I protested. "I think they're right, we need to do this for the book. A few weeks ago, I didn't even know if you had siblings, let alone a cousin who's in middle school. Or a mom!" He rolled his eyes at that. "If we want our characters to connect, we need to learn things about each other."

He squinted. "I thought we weren't writing about each other."

I let out a frustrated sigh. "Is the idea of a couple of hours with me so unbearable? I can at least *tolerate* you."

"Fine, fine. I'll pick you up from your place tomorrow, alright?"

His pace increased once again, and I nearly sprinted after him. "You can't just phone it in."

He jumped again. "Jesus, I'll be sure to bring a bell, too."

"It needs to be romantic. You can't just take me to McDonald's and expect everything to fall into place."

When we reached a crosswalk, I tried to walk despite the red light. But Aiden held his arm out as a bike whirled by, stopping me from stepping in its path and giving me an annoyed glance. "I can't plan something romantic." He grimaced. "I'm not good at that."

"I don't care." He gave me a flat look. "I don't! Okay, if it's not romantic, then whatever. We just spruce it up in the chapter. Anything is romantic if you look at it in the right light. You just have to *try*, Aiden. I will, too."

He rubbed his hand at the side of his jaw where stubble was just appearing. The muscle in his jaw ticked back and forth, making me lose all coherent thought. "Text me your address. I'll pick you up at seven tomorrow."

The next morning, I whipped Ida's door open and, once again, she didn't even look up from her laptop.

"I'm glad we're back to normal," she murmured. "I was afraid that you'd start knocking and coming in here like a quiet mouse like you did at the beginning of the semester."

I fell into my usual seat as I pulled off my coat. "You've *betrayed* me. You're a traitor. You've crossed enemy lines."

She rolled her eyes and shut her computer. "Oh please, don't be so dramatic."

"That man is my worst nightmare. And now I have to sit across from him *by myself* and make polite conversation."

Ida looked like she was trying to suppress a smile. "You'll be fine."

I narrowed my eyes at her. "Why are you so invested in our book? You don't ever push anyone else like you do us."

She frowned. "That's not true. I made Logan go to a comedy show last week after his chapter about the stand-up comic made no sense. I suggested three young adult novels to Amelia when hers kept including scenes set at house parties with weed *and* I made her call her fifteen-year-old niece to see how real kids talk these days."

I huffed. "That's convenient."

Ida laughed. "Listen, I believe in you and Aiden as writers. But you're both stubborn and too comfortable in what you're writing. I'm just trying to push that comfort."

"You rarely write anything other than romance," I pointed out.

"But I had to learn to write other things before I could feel comfortable in the genre. I had to learn how to give my female characters agency and control over their lives and sexuality by making them believable. I wrote so many character studies and character-driven novels before I ever attempted my first romance novel."

She leaned forward. "I know romance is a big passion of yours. And it's a big passion of mine, too. But what makes romance novels so good is the fact that they're a complex dive into human emotion. There's so much more to a romance than just love. That's important too, don't get me wrong, but your characters need a bigger range than that. A tragic ending may not be what you want, but I think writing a scene like that and making that pain visceral will help you in the long run."

I knew she was right. My characters had only ever felt flat, never dynamic. I was too afraid to hurt them or make them suffer. Working with Aiden was going to force me to *go there.*

"Fine." I reached into my bag, pulling out my laptop. "Besides complaining about how you stabbed me in the back, I was hoping we could look at some pieces I was thinking about submitting for the fellowship?"

She smiled. "Of course. I'm really glad you decided to submit."

"Me too. I mean, I might not get it, but I think it's important that I try."

"As a writer, Rosie, you're going to face a lot more rejection than praise. We all do. I personally think you have a good shot, but it's important to get out there and pick yourself up when you're told no." She reached out for my laptop. "Let me see what you've got."

"I was thinking of submitting a piece I worked on last semester. It's an epistolary story about a couple trying long distance."

We went over the story for a while, discussing plot and some line edits. But it was the way her eyes lit up when she read my story that made me really believe I had a good shot at this thing.

Of course I wanted to grab dinner with Max. This felt like my one shot to prove to her that I wasn't as bad as she thought. I felt like the best version of myself around her and I wanted to chase that feeling.

I wanted to prove to her that this mattered to me. This opportunity wouldn't come twice, and I couldn't risk squandering it. When it proved difficult to get a reservation on such late notice, I did the one thing I hated: I called my father.

— Excerpt from *Untitled* by
Rosie Maxwell and Aiden Huntington

CHAPTER EIGHT

That night, I pulled out a bunch of different outfits and laid them out on my bed. Usually on a date, I'd wear my jeans or a miniskirt and a nice shirt. But what do you wear on a date with a man you don't actually like?

Alexa was lying on top of my bed, her head hanging off the side, watching me hold up different shirts in front of my chest.

"So, tell me again how this isn't really a date, because I'm not buying it."

No one was. My group chat was blowing up with texts, mainly from Logan and Jess. Logan was convinced this was a date, but Jess was convinced Aiden was going to murder me by the end of the night.

Logan: this is the funniest possible outcome of the cowriting, i can't believe we get to witness this for free
Jess: again, not for free
Tyler: Rosie, text us if you need us.
Jess: ^^ who knows what weird shit aiden might be up to
Logan: oh pls we all know theyre going to fuck tonight
Jess: don't be so crude
Logan: i'm not!!! but . . . rosie you have to let us know if he's a freak in bed i bet he has a red room
Jess: he definitely has a sex swing at the very least

Tyler: What's a sex swing?
Logan: i'll send you some links
Tyler: Please don't.
Jess: rosie at least send your location so we know where the body is in case he murders you
Logan: yeah that way we can all see when you get to his place
Jess: not going to happen logan
Logan: wow who knew none of you believed in the power of winter nights. it's cold outside and its cuffing season and that makes people CRAZY HORNY
Jess: pls shut up
Tyler: ^^

I let my phone buzz on my bed, not replying to the texts.

"It's not a date, it's homework," I insisted to Alexa. That's what I kept telling myself at least. If I didn't repeat this in my head over and over, my mind would drift. I'd start to romanticize everything and read into details that weren't even there, and then I'd fall in love with a version of Aiden I created in my head. It'd happened to me with Simon when I was fifteen and I didn't snap out of it for almost a decade.

It had been a while since I'd been on a date. After Simon and I broke up, I said yes to every guy who asked me to get drinks. I was so eager to step into this pool of dating and get over Simon, but I quickly learned love could be a ruthless game. The guys would frown when I ordered something with a carb or refused to kiss them or go back to their place. One guy left in outrage after I said I wouldn't Venmo him two hundred dollars because he was low on cash.

"Are you nervous?" Alexa sat up, resting against my headboard.

"A little," I admitted.

"He's not Simon, you know."

Honestly, that's what I was afraid of anytime I went out on a date. That I wouldn't be able to read the signs and would fall for someone like Simon all over again.

I wanted the kind of love you treated gently, like it could break. The kind that was intense and real. The kind you fought *for*, not against. And maybe I was wrong and love like that didn't exist. But I wanted to get as close as I could to that feeling.

"I know that." I decided to wear a long sleeve maroon top with a sweetheart neckline and my black jeans. I put them on and turned around to show Alexa. "How do I look?"

She smiled. "You two are definitely going to fuck by the end of the night."

I groaned and threw a nearby pillow at her. "It's not like that."

"Suuuure," she dragged out. "Your tits are basically hanging out of that shirt. The minute Aiden sees you his tongue is going to roll out of his mouth like a cartoon dog."

Maybe the *tiniest* part of me hoped Aiden thought I looked nice. It was probably just the delusional romantic in me, but I hid my smile at the idea.

At seven exactly, as I was finishing my makeup, there was a knock on our door. I jumped, nearly smearing my lipstick, and turned to Alexa still sitting on my bed.

"Did you buzz him up?"

"No. Ronny Jr. must've let him in."

I sighed, trying to ignore the nerves as I opened the door to Aiden Huntington—looking mad as ever. His peacoat was buttoned up, a black scarf tied around his neck. His hair was usually perfectly tousled, but tonight he had combed it back neatly. The smell of his oaky cologne overpowered me from the second I opened the door. What did it say about me that he looked extra hot when he was mad?

"There's a brick holding open the door to your building," he said hotly. His words were harsh. His jaw was clenched, the muscle in his cheek jumping.

"Nice to see you, too, Aiden," I said.

"Rosalinda," he cut in. "Anyone can just walk in your building."

"I'll have you know that brick is named Ronny Jr. He helps Ronny Sr. get in the building when he forgets his keys," I said lightly, hoping he would move on.

His eyes narrowed dangerously, a grim expression overtaking his face. "You know about this brick? And you haven't done anything to stop it?"

"It's not a big deal, I have a lock." I pulled at the chain on my door frame to prove it to him. "Are you going to keep critiquing the safety of my building or are we going to dinner?"

"Rosalinda, this is ridiculous. Even for you."

Aiden had a Rolex. He wore expensive, Italian cologne and probably only took the subway instead of an Uber because he got inspiration for his writing from it. It was obvious he didn't have to worry about money, but I did. I'd learned to love the poorly built building that I called home, and I didn't appreciate Aiden talking shit about it.

"Great, I'll move out tomorrow now that I have your approval. Can we go?"

"That's not what I—"

"Leaving," I called out to Alexa. "I'll be back later."

"Hopefully not," she sang back from her bedroom.

I rolled my eyes and all but pushed Aiden out the door. "Where to?"

He led me to an Italian restaurant a few blocks away called il Buco. I'd passed this place plenty of times, lingering in front of the building just to get a whiff of food that wasn't coming from a ramen noodle package. It was a small restaurant, but there were plenty of people standing on the sidewalk, waiting for their tables. Once we entered, I immediately fell in love with the place. Nearly every inch of the interior was decorated. Pots and pans hung from the ceiling, glowing in the candlelight of the room. The bookcases along the walls held old cookbooks, vases, and bottles of wine. The restaurant felt more like a grandmother's home than an upscale eatery in the Bowery. Soft Italian music blended with the conversation of all the customers. The smell of fresh basil and rosemary filled the air and my stomach growled in anticipation.

I frowned as I watched the hostess sympathetically shake her head at everyone in line before us. I had worked at the Hideout long enough to recognize that look. With how busy it was, there was no way Aiden and I would get a table in a timely manner.

"Are we going to be able to eat here?" I asked Aiden. "It looks busy."

"I've made a reservation," he said.

"How'd you do that so last minute?"

"I pulled a few strings."

"But how—"

He sighed, resigned. "Are you going to keep asking questions or are we going to eat?" Nearly every table was full, couples huddled close together over the tables. I eyed him skeptically as he stepped up to the hostess stand. "I have a reservation for Huntington." She nodded and grabbed two menus.

"Right this way." She led us through the restaurant to a small table in front of a brick wall. Aiden motioned for me to sit on the booth side of the table and took the wooden seat.

Aiden and I sat uncomfortably across from each other. I crossed my ankles, forcing them as far away as much as possible because my knees were already grazing his. The last thing I needed was to be caught in a game of footsie with Aiden Huntington.

"Seriously Aiden, how'd you get a reservation so quickly?"

His lips were set in a tight line. "I called my father."

"You called your father?"

He flipped through his menu and hummed noncommittally. I wondered what it was like to have a father that could get you anything you wanted within just a few hours. A nice reservation at a fancy restaurant, a car, maybe a palace or two. If I called my dad for something, he'd laugh loudly and say, "I can send over some fresh basil from the garden, but that's about it."

I frowned and opened my menu, balking at the prices for each entree. Christ, even a side salad cost fifteen bucks, no way would I be able to afford any of this.

"Good evening." A waitress stopped at our table. "Are we celebrating anything tonight?"

Just as Aiden was about to shake his head, I had an idea. My foot drove into his shin under the table and said, "It's our anniversary!"

Aiden's hand shot down to rub his shin, shooting me a bewildered look.

"Oh, how special! How long?" The waitress beamed at us.

"Happily together for three years! Isn't that right, honey?"

Aiden narrowed his eyes. I widened my eyes, telling him to play along. "Three years of pure bliss," he strained.

"Thank you for celebrating with us at il Buco. Anything to drink?"

Aiden nodded for me to go first. I didn't have to open the menu to know a cocktail would be at least eighteen dollars. "Just water for me."

Aiden ordered the same and our waitress smiled down at us, "I'll come back in a little while to take your orders!"

I smiled sweetly at her as she walked away.

"What was that about?" Aiden asked, his brows drawing a V between his eyes.

"We're supposed to be pretending to be a happy couple. I thought maybe she'd offer us champagne or whatever. It's what they'd do in Tennessee."

Aiden scoffed. "Welcome to New York. Nothing is free here."

"I just thought it'd be a good idea," I snapped. "We're supposed to be Max and Hunter while we're here."

"Max and Hunter don't like each other," he countered. "They haven't been together for three years."

"Fine. Then I guess we can just sit here in silence and tell Ida it went fine."

"Fine."

"Fine." I snatched up my menu and skimmed it for the cheapest item. A light Caesar side salad should hold me over until tomorrow, and it wouldn't be too costly on my bank account. I'd gulp it down, then get out of here as soon as possible.

I took in the tables around us. We must've looked like we were on a first date. A first *blind* date. The restaurant was bustling, the staff running around. I winced, knowing that this was what was probably happening at the Hideout tonight, too. I felt bad for all the workers, hurrying to bring food to tables and fill water glasses.

The minutes felt like agonizing hours as we waited for our waitress to return. I couldn't take it anymore and had to break the silence.

"You know, this place is really romantic. I mean look at all the couples here." I nodded toward another table where a couple was sitting on the same side of the booth. "It was a good choice."

He gave me a tight smile. He was watching the crackling fire of the candle between us like it was the most interesting thing he had ever seen. I blew out a breath, annoyed that Aiden wouldn't contribute to the conversation, but pushed forward, nonetheless.

"This won't work if we don't talk." Aiden's eyes flashed at me again, then he carefully unfolded his napkin and placed it in his lap. "I just meant that maybe everyone in workshop has a point. As much as I love hurling insults at you in our chapters, we do need to make Hunter and Max fall in love. I know they aren't there yet, but it's up to us to get them there."

"I'm having a hard time *not* hurling insults. It's the norm with you."

"Well then. Maybe we should say mean things." I straightened.

"What?"

"It's the only way you and I know how to talk to each other. So I say we act normal and be mean." The corners of Aiden's mouth quirked up, but he didn't say anything. "Fine. I'll go first. You were rude at my apartment."

He frowned. "No I wasn't."

"Yes, you were. About Ronny Jr.?"

"It's a stupid way to keep the door open. Especially in your neighborhood—"

"Blah, blah, all I hear are insults about the place I pay a very high rent for." I waved my hand. "But I'm over it now that I've said you're a jackass to your face."

"You didn't say I was a jackass."

"*Anyway.* Your turn."

"Fine. You're not very good at walking in heels," he said, hesitating, as if he wasn't sure if it was okay.

I gasped dramatically. "Not true!"

I had tripped nearly every step of the way, but I'd hoped he hadn't noticed it. In my defense, we'd walked down Bond Street—which was *cobblestone.* It was practically impossible to walk on cobblestones even in sneakers.

"So I just imagined when you nearly face planted a few minutes ago?" He smirked, leaning back in his chair.

"You know, I think I meant it when I called you a jackass earlier."

Aiden ignored that comment. "I just pretended not to notice because I'm a gentleman."

I scoffed. "Yeah, right. If you were a gentleman, you wouldn't have mentioned it at all."

"If you were a lady, you'd be able to walk in heels," he pointed out, his voice light.

"Hey, I never claimed I was."

The waitress finally came back to take our orders. Aiden's frown deepened when I only got the salad, but he didn't say anything. She left us with a small basket of bread and butter. I knew that salad wouldn't fill me up so I snatched a piece up immediately.

"How'd the middle school dance end up going?" I asked, stuffing a piece of bread in my mouth.

He grimaced. "Most of those kids haven't figured out deodorant yet. And I can't tell you the amount of grind lines I had to break up."

I wrinkled my nose. "Gross. I always stayed by the snacks when those started. By far, the best part of the middle school dances were the moms who brought in cupcakes."

"You went to those dances?" He must've caught me eyeing the bread-basket because he scooched it closer to me. I flashed him an appreciative smile, taking two more pieces. Then the final one for good measure.

"You didn't?"

He shook his head. "It was always just an excuse to show off for girls and dance awkwardly in front of parents and teachers. I didn't ever see a reason to go."

"I went because of Trent Walsh," I said dreamily. "He was the hottest guy in middle school. He had swoopy hair, his jeans sagged, and he had a chain."

"So what? You went in hopes he'd dance with you?" His tone wasn't judgmental, but curious. As if he hadn't experienced the normalcy of having a crush as a middle schooler.

"I went because I *knew* he'd dance with me," I corrected. "He told everyone that Friday that he liked my hair and thought I was the smartest girl in the grade. We danced to Coldplay. The gym lights were dim, we were in a corner, and he didn't even try to grab my ass. It was so romantic. He was my first kiss."

Aiden cleared his throat, suppressing a smile. Why was he always so reluctant to smile? Why did he force them away instead of inviting them to cover his face?

When our food finally arrived, I stared at Aiden's plate of pasta with envy. It was piled onto his plate and garnished with fresh basil. He expertly twirled the noodles around his fork as I angrily stabbed at the lettuce of my pathetic salad. I couldn't even afford the grilled chicken add-on.

I must've been staring at Aiden's plate for too long because he stopped eating. He raised an eyebrow and offered his fork forward to me.

"Do you want some?"

I shook my head, shaking myself out of my pasta daydreams. "No, that's okay."

"You know," he said carefully. "Dinner's on me tonight."

I stilled, narrowing my eyes at him. "What makes you say that?"

"I'm just saying, order what you want from the menu. I'm paying."

"I can pay for my own food."

"It's a date, Rosalinda."

"I'm a feminist—"

"So am I," he cut me off. He cleared his throat and carefully placed his fork next to his plate. "I took you out, I'll pay for your meal. Get something more filling."

"I'm plenty full." I was lying, but I was also too proud to tell him I was starving. Maybe this was all a ploy. He knew to offer to pay for my food because he told the staff to—

"Stop overthinking," he interrupted my thoughts.

I sighed. "This place is already expensive as it is. I'm not letting you pay for *two* of my entrees."

He rolled his eyes, like *I* was the one being annoying. He flagged down our waitress and asked for an extra plate.

"What're you doing?"

He gave me an impatient look before he carefully moved half of his pasta onto the extra plate and set it in front of me. "There. Now I don't have to pay extra *or* watch you stare glumly at your little salad."

"Did you just say glumly?" I raised my eyebrows, smiling slightly.

"Eat your food." He sighed, as if he was tired of me. But he didn't start eating until I hesitantly picked up my fork.

Aiden turned his attention back to his own meal as I stuffed as much pasta as I could in my mouth. He looked up when I moaned, shifting uncomfortably.

"Oh Lord," I said through a mouthful of food. "This is so good. This may be the best meal I've ever had." The corners of Aiden's mouth twitched as I continued to shovel food into my mouth. "Aiden, I owe you big time. We can kill a character. We can do whatever, this is the best pasta I've ever had. Thank you so much."

"You've got marinara sauce all over your mouth."

"That may be the sexiest thing I've ever heard."

I didn't know why I said it. Maybe it was my food starved brain. Maybe it was the pasta. Or maybe it was the slightly authoritative tone

Aiden seemed to always take around me. But he was a man wearing a nice sweater, sitting across from me, and had offered me half of his pasta. How did a girl *not* find that romantic?

"Aren't we supposed to be pretending to be Max and Hunter?" he asked, sipping his water.

I shrugged. "I don't know, don't we do that anyway?"

"Fair enough, but it might be worth a shot."

I sat up, straightening the napkin on my lap. "Well, Hunter, how are you?"

"I'm doing fine, Maxine. How about you?" he said flatly, but still playing along.

"What's with the Maxine? You know everyone else calls me Max."

He shrugged. "I don't know."

"Yes, you do." I tipped my water glass up, swallowing it down. "You do it for some reason. You've always called me Rosalinda."

"Maxine," he corrected.

I waved a dismissive hand. "Same thing and you know it."

"Next question," he said.

"That's not how you move through life, you know. You can't just avoid questions in conversations because you're uncomfortable—"

"I'm not uncomfortable."

"Oh puh-lease, you're basically squirming in your chair."

"You're deluded."

"A little bit," I said with a laugh. The waitress interrupted us with a dessert menu.

"Are you lovebirds thinking about dessert?"

"Oh, no." I pushed it away from me. "I think we'll just take the check. If you could split—"

"Rosalinda, order dessert," Aiden said, sounding utterly exhausted.

"No," I said, pushing the menu toward the waitress.

"I know you have a sweet tooth. I know you want dessert. Just order some." He was pushing his own menu toward me. The waitress looked between us, hesitantly stepping away.

"Why don't I give you two a few minutes to decide?"

"That's not necessary," I said.

"Thank you," Aiden said at the same time.

I glared at him from across the table. He held out the menu again. I folded my arms across my chest, lifting my chin defiantly.

"Just order some damn dessert, Rosie. I'm paying."

"No way. I'm not letting you buy me a salad that I didn't even eat, give me half of your food, *and* pay for dessert. It's too much."

"It's not too much," he said. His brow was furrowed, that same stern tone in his voice that made my insides melt. "You come into class nearly every day with a different form of chocolate. Just order."

I tried not to let my shock show because that was true. I couldn't go a few hours without some sort of sweet. I usually kept M&Ms in my bag but sometimes if I got a nice tip, I bought cookies or a chocolate croissant from the bakery a few blocks down. And sometimes I stole Morochas, Peruvian cookies, from Alexa.

Then again, maybe it was obvious that I did this. Maybe it meant absolutely nothing that Aiden paid attention to what I did in class and remembered it. Stored it away in a file in his brain of random facts about Rosalinda. It was probably ammo for later.

But I really did want dessert.

"Fine." I took the menu from him. "But you have to eat some, too."

"Oh no, am I being forced to eat chocolate cake? Whatever shall I do?" he deadpanned.

I raised a brow. "How do you know I'm getting the chocolate cake?"

"Because there's no way you're getting the tiramisu," he said as if it were obvious. He sat forward and gently took the menu from me. His green eyes were shining in the candlelight and I wished, just for a second, that this was real. That we were on a real date. I quickly dismissed the thought because in no universe would Aiden Huntington and I ever be together.

"Am I right?" he asked, pulling me from my thoughts.

"Yes," I muttered.

He lifted his chin. "Knew it."

The waitress brought out the dessert soon enough. When Aiden dove in for a piece of cake, my spoon clanked against his, stealing it. He paused at this, but when I did it a second time his gaze flew up to mine.

I popped the spoon in my mouth, giving him a cheeky smile. Something flashed in his eyes and then he stole the next bite from me.

We continued to battle it out and when Aiden shoved my napkin off my lap to distract me while he snatched the next bite, I gasped.

"Cheater."

He stuck the spoon in his mouth and said, as close to playful as Aiden got, "I don't know what you're talking about."

When the waitress came with our check, I put up a valiant fight to pay. "Let me," I said, reaching for the black book.

Aiden was unamused, not even looking up from the check. "We've already discussed this."

"I've changed my mind."

"No."

"Please, I want to—"

"Fine." Aiden snapped the black book closed and slid it over to me. "Go for it."

I slowly flipped it open, my eyes widening at the number at the bottom of the receipt. "You know, I was thinking about it and maybe it's best—"

He rolled his eyes once again and snatched it back from me.

Later, as we walked home, the same silence that had haunted us for most of the night reappeared. It wove around us, between skyscrapers and city lights, to wrap us fully in discomfort.

"Tonight was . . ." I paused, trying to find the right word. I looked up into the night sky, trying to find the politest way to say disaster.

"We'll make it better in the chapter," he said as we stopped in front of my apartment building. "Writing's in the revisions, yeah?"

To fully meet his gaze, I had to crane my neck. I tried not to let the atmosphere get to me, but God he was handsome in this surprisingly rugged way. In the way his eyebrows stayed furrowed and complemented the darkness of his hair but contrasted the lightness of his eyes. His nose was slightly crooked but it only made him look even more *perfect*. Sometimes when I looked at him I was sure somebody just like him had been the inspiration for Clark Kent.

We stood there, our breaths visible in the cold, the white puffs as prominent as the silence we were entrenched in. I believed anything could be romantic if you looked at it in the right light. But *this* was not romantic. We waited for the other to say something that gave us an escape. He shifted his weight, looking toward my building, and

Katie Holt

I pulled my coat around me, looking at the ground. Eventually, I couldn't take it anymore and shoved my hands in my coat pockets.

"Well, I'll see you next week." I awkwardly turned around and rushed into the building.

"¿Por qué estás aquí?" Alexa demanded when I entered the apartment. "You should be at his place. Naked."

"We already did that," I said sarcastically, walking to the kitchen. I pulled a glass out from the cabinet and ran it under the tap.

"Ha ha, very funny. How was it?"

"Exactly what I expected." I gulped down the water. "Horrible, awkward, painful." Sure, there were a *few* moments that didn't make me want to die. But how was I supposed to write those moments knowing Aiden would read it? "I can't imagine it helping to inspire anything for our chapter."

She smiled. "I'm sure something will come through."

After I took off my makeup and threw on some sweats, I checked my phone and scrolled through the millions of texts from the group chat.

> Logan: i'm telling you guys she's at his place
> Jess: or dead
> Logan: don't say that!!!!
> Jess: it's a real possibility. we don't really know aiden
> Tyler: To be fair, none of us really try to talk to him.
> Logan: oh pls, that's bc he scares us
> Jess: we need to save rosie
> Tyler: They're probably still on the date. Let's not panic yet.

I rolled onto my side, pulling my blanket around my shoulders.

> Rosie: date is over. so bad. i want to die
> Logan: tell us everything.
> Rosie: we went to a nice restaurant, didn't rly speak, and then he awkwardly walked me home
> Tyler: He walked you home? That was nice of him.
> Jess: or the BARE MINIMUM. can we pls stop praising men for doing the bare minimum??
> Logan: sooo true bestie

84

Not in My Book

Jess: shut up logan
Tyler: I can't wait to read about it in workshop.
Logan: this is more of a horror than a romance
Rosie: y'all are ridiculous

I muted the conversation and spent the next hour scrolling through Twitter. Just as I was drifting into sleep, I got another text.

Aiden: Chapter done.

Eagerly, I reached for my laptop on my nightstand and opened our shared doc. The icon with his picture was still on the doc, his cursor at his last words, which meant he was still online and viewing the document. I scrolled to the top of his chapter and started reading.

It was unexpected when Maxine invited me out for dinner. It was even more unexpected when I couldn't shake my nerves.

I tried to remind myself it wasn't a real date. Rather a dinner between two colleagues. Who despised each other. Who'd never really seen each other outside of work. Who I desperately tried to make conversation with every day only to ruin everything a moment later.

I willed the anxiousness away, but there was something more hanging in the air. That's the way it always was with Maxine. We hurled insults back and forth, but how much of them did we really mean?

It's not a date. It's a dinner between colleagues. That's it. I repeated it like a mantra in my head. I hadn't been on a real date since my last relationship, and even then I wasn't in the right mind to focus on my date because of everything that had happened with my mom. I wasn't in any position to put myself out there when it felt like my world had crumbled. The truth was Maxine was so deep under my skin, it was like she had become my veins, not leaving a single part of me untouched. Dating had never been my priority, but I couldn't say no to her.

— Excerpt from *Untitled* by
Rosie Maxwell and Aiden Huntington

CHAPTER NINE

A million questions bloomed in my mind. His chapter was so brutally honest, I really couldn't tell if he was writing as Aiden or as Hunter. I kept reading.

When I arrived at her apartment, I stopped short at the door to her building. Anger and fear for her bubbled up in me. Her first initial and last name were clearly displayed on the buzzer for apartment 9C, but I didn't need to buzz myself up. There was a brick holding her door open. One of her neighbors, or an intruder, walked past me into her building without batting an eye. I followed, trying to unclench my fists, my nails pressing crescents into the palm of my hand. The elevator groaned with each movement, and I swear I thought the cables would snap.

I would never admit it to her, but Maxine was the smartest woman I'd ever met. During her first staff meeting, she'd been unafraid. Even new to the team and in a room of strangers, she'd had no problem clearly stating her opinions. She even made the entire room laugh once or twice.

I hesitated as I continued to scroll down. I didn't want to believe he was referring to our first class together last semester. I'd been so nervous during our first workshop that I kept babbling and raising my hand and . . . I *did* make a few people laugh. Surely it was a coincidence. I was just reading into it; there was no way he was actually talking about *me*.

But I was starting to seriously doubt her intelligence if she lived here.

Okay, maybe he was.

It was reckless, putting her safety in such blatant danger. I knocked on the door in three quick knocks. I could hear her quiet murmurs through the door and although her voice usually soothed me, I couldn't shake my anger.

She unlocked at least three different locks and answered the door with a smile that was like a constellation in a clear night sky. I didn't want to look away, I wanted to study it and her. To know who she was outside of the one building we were seemingly confined to. This was the chance I had been waiting for and her smile reminded me why. I wished I could tell her I wasn't mad at her, but for *her.*

Instead, I said, "There's a brick door holding open the door to your building."

She blinked, her lashes long, fanning against her cheek, and said, "Oh, that? My neighbor, Andy, forgets his keys, so he just leaves it there."

Rage unfurled in my chest until I was suffocated by it.

"You know about this brick?"

"I have a lock. It's no big deal."

I narrowed my eyes at her as my mind worked through a million solutions to solve her problems. I couldn't buy her an apartment, I couldn't report the building, but I could convince her to move out.

Eloquently as ever, I said, "Maxine, this is ridiculous. Even for you."

Immediately, her face flushed in anger. I'd meant to come across as kind or caring, like the type of man she deserved. But as always, I got in my own way.

My eyebrows flew up in surprise. Until now, writing as Max and Hunter had always meant throwing insults we wished we could say in person. It had never crossed the boundary into anything more. But . . . did Aiden really like my smile that much?

I had figured his comments on the brick were because he was entitled. That he looked down on me for being poor. Not because he was genuinely worried for my safety. He was probably just turning it up for the chapter. Maybe he was better at romance that I had anticipated.

"Let's just go." She brushed past me into the tiny hallway, and I had no choice but to follow. After she sent me her address, I did some research on nice restaurants in her area. I wanted to go to a place she would actually like. Or somewhere she'd never treat herself to.

Once we neared the restaurant after an intensely awkward walk over, she asked, "How'd you manage to get us a reservation here?"

I shrugged. "I pulled a few strings."

Meaning, I'd called my father and promised to have dinner with him soon if he could get us a reservation here. He liked to catch up with me precisely once a year, and he liked to spend that hour and a half berating my life choices. He ensured that I knew he was disappointed and wasting my life. But I'd trade the most excruciating dinners with him for just a few hours with her. If I could keep my foot out of my own damn mouth.

My heart was pounding. He had copied this evening almost verbatim, but the romantic in me couldn't tell the difference between the lines of reality and fiction.

He was still on the doc when I reached the end of the chapter, and he was still on the doc when I started to write:

Hunter brought me to a blissful Italian restaurant. I had passed this place a million times before. During spring, when it was barely warm enough for people to sit outside, I'd linger on the sidewalks as whiffs of fresh basil and pasta filled the street. When we walked in, the music immediately captured me just as much as the mouthwatering aromas. I was annoyed with Hunter for what he'd said at my apartment, but even though I would never admit it to him, I was looking forward to tonight.

I paused, considering my next words.

Besides, I'm sure I'd misinterpreted his words. He was probably being nice and I was being the asshole by getting mad on a whim.

Almost immediately after I typed that last line, the chat box appeared on the side with a notification.

Aiden: Rosalinda.
Rosie: what?? it's the truth!

I couldn't take my eye off Aiden's icon in the corner as I wrote. I closed my eyes, and I could see the same intense look he gave me every session of workshop. Doubt blossomed.

Rosie: you're making me nervous
Aiden: How so?
Rosie: you're just watching me write. i feel shy
Aiden: Pretend I'm not here.

An idea popped in my head, and before I could stop myself, I quickly typed to him.

Rosie: or you could write it with me

I sucked in a breath, gnawing on my bottom lip as I watched the bubbles of the chat appear and disappear.

Aiden: Okay.
Rosie: just jump in whenever!!
Aiden: Okay.

I smiled triumphantly and continued to type.

"The reason I asked you to dinner was because I wanted to call a truce," I said, tilting my chin up, feigning confidence. Underneath the table, I wiped my palms on my skirt.

His brow furrowed, lines appearing across his forehead. *"A truce?"*

"I want this presentation to be as painless as possible. There's no way out of working together." He nodded, conceding. *"And frankly, I'm exhausted by hating you and working so hard at the same time. So, I thought I'd eliminate one of the factors."*

I waited for Aiden to jump in, but he didn't.

"A truce," he said as if he was tasting the word on his tongue.

Aiden finally jumped in.

"What would this truce entail?

I straightened, beaming at him. "I've decided I don't hate you anymore. Once we're done, however, feel free to hate me."

I paused, unsure if I was writing solely as Maxine now, and he was writing as Hunter. He started to type.

"All it took to get you to stop hating me was taking you out? I should've done this years ago."

I ignored him. "Truce?" I held my hand out across the table.

He shook it once. "Does this truce mean we have to be friends now, or is it more of a ceasefire?"

I pondered this for a moment, my nose scrunching. "Well, if we were friends, you'd have to give up valuable information about yourself."

He rolled his eyes, sipping his water. "Oh really, like what?"

"I don't know. I sit five feet away from you every day, but I hardly know anything about you. I don't even know where you're from."

He frowned. "I'm from here. I thought you knew that."

I waved him off. "I know you're from New York, but where? I bet you went to some prep school on the Upper East Side."

"Upper West Side," he corrected. "From kindergarten to high school."

I placed my elbows on the table in an unladylike manner and held my chin in my hands. "What was it like growing up in New York?"

"What was it like growing up in Tennessee?" he countered.

I watched the shield in his eyes go up to protect himself. I didn't want to push him too far, but I was so desperate for even the smallest tidbit about him to satiate my curiosity.

"It was okay," I said thoughtfully. "It wasn't always easy being a Hispanic kid in school in the south."

"You're Peruvian, right?"

My chin jerked back, surprised. "Yeah. I am. How'd you know that?"

"You came in one day with a bag that had a pin with a red flag," he said, sheepishly. "I looked it up after class."

Aiden's cursor quickly backed up, deleting *class* and replacing it with *work*. My heart leaped a little in my chest.

It was true. I had a tote bag decorated with pins, and, pinned right next to the Tennessee flag, was a small Peruvian flag. I hadn't known Aiden had even noticed it.

"Half-Peruvian," I said. "My dad's from good ol' Rocky Top and my mom's from Peru. It's made for some weird family reunions."

He laughed softly. "I'll bet."

"What about you?" I snatched a roll from the breadbasket between us. "Were family gatherings also unbearable for you?"

Hunter paused, not meeting my eyes. He cleared his throat and said, "I didn't really have a lot of those."

"What about for the holidays? Thanksgiving was always confusing—we'd have sweet potato pie on one end of the table and ceviche on the other."

He paused again. "I didn't really have holidays either." Just as I was about to press for details, he said, "I'm sure your family has some Christmas traditions."

It was obvious that Aiden was staying away from the topic of his own family. Not everyone was as lucky as I was to have such a loving support system. But this was the kind of conversation I'd been hoping to have at dinner, and he knew me well enough to know I *did* want to press for details. I wanted to know more about his lonely Thanksgivings and why it had been so hard to call his father for a reservation today. And why he was avoiding a dinner with him. But how could I be certain this was all true? Aiden crafted his words so carefully that there was no reason to believe this was all real, but I still knew it was.

"We have a few Christmas Eve traditions," I said. "My mom usually makes a big feast and everyone from my mom's side comes. We open presents right when midnight hits, and we dance until everyone gets tired and goes home. Afterward, my dad makes us watch It's a Wonderful Life. *On New Year's, though, we have a big party." I couldn't stop the joy from radiating from me as I remembered those cold December nights. "There's a small Peruvian community in my hometown, and for New Year's they always came to our house, and we do all the traditions we can."*

"Like what?"

"Well, the color you wear represents what you want for the New Year. Yellow for luck, green for money, red for love . . ." I trailed off.

"Ah." He leaned back, his head nodding in understanding. "And you always wear red?"

"Not at our last party," I confessed. "I wore yellow. I just . . . really needed some luck. I figured I'd start with that then move onto red when I felt like I was ready."

The conversation fell so easily between us throughout the meal that I forgot that only a few hours earlier, I'd hated him.

In these few pages, I was learning more about Aiden than I had in the past year of workshop. He was funny and sometimes even flirty. I had to keep my head on straight and remember that he was creating a romance hero, not charming me.

"Tell me what it was like growing up in New York," I begged. "Just one thing."

Hunter sighed, as if he didn't really want to answer.

"Wow, okay, message received," I murmured. I waited anxiously for the words to appear before me on the doc. I'd given up memories, real ones, to Aiden. All I wanted was one of his own.

When he saw the hope in my eyes, he relented.

"There," I said triumphantly, and waited.

Finally, after what felt like an endless moment, Aiden typed, *"I did go to a prep school on the Upper West Side, but I lived with my mom in Alphabet City after she and my dad split. So, as a nine-year-old, I took a forty-minute subway ride by myself to school and back every day."*

My jaw dropped slightly. "I'm not too proud to admit that at twenty-six I get a little nervous taking my ten-minute train ride."

He shrugged and picked his fork back up, moving his food around. "You get used to it. You know which train cars will be safe and which ones won't be. I always got on one with a mom and her kids so I knew she'd look out for me."

My heart broke a little for Aiden. I had always dreamed of growing up in New York, but the image of Aiden in his little prep uniform and backpack, sitting alone, nearly brought tears to my eyes.

He gulped down his water, avoiding my eyes. "It's no big deal. By the time high school started, my mom and I had moved to the West Village, and I transferred to a school around there."

"So you didn't see your dad at all?"

"Not really, no."

"Your mom must be the best."

Suddenly, our words started to erase from the doc. I sat up, panicked there was some glitch, before I realized it was *Aiden* removing our last few lines of dialogue.

I quickly moved to the chat box to the side:

Rosie: what're you doing??? this is so good, don't erase!!
Aiden: It's not. It's your chapter anyway. Write it yourself, Rosalinda.

Just as I was about to beg him to stay, his icon left the doc.

"Fuck," I groaned, rubbing my eyes with the palms of my hands. Part of me knew I was pushing Aiden too far. He had walls built so tightly around him, it was near impossible to break through. I'd gone too hard too fast, and now I'd ruined the little progress we'd made.

"Whatever," I muttered, angrily closing out of our shared doc. If Aiden didn't even want to *try* to be friendly, I wouldn't force him. I had my own stuff to do.

Ida and I had been emailing back and forth about my piece for the fellowship. I was over the word count for the submission guidelines by four hundred words. I'd thought it wouldn't be a big deal, but Ida emphasized how strict they were on it. Apparently, they would disqualify me if I submitted even a word more than the five-thousand-word limit.

I'd come to New York for me. I wasn't going to let Aiden derail my dreams just because he was throwing a little hissy fit.

So instead of letting my mind wander to Aiden and our conversation, I spent the night cutting words and rephrasing sentences in my fellowship submission.

"Why do you always call me Maxine?" she asked as we split dessert. Our spoons clinked together as we battled for the last bit of brownie.

I won, scooping the last bite into my mouth. "I know everyone else calls you Max, but when Ivy introduced you the first day, she called you Maxine before you corrected her."

She stabbed her spoon at me, her dark eyes narrowed in suspicion. "That doesn't explain why you call me Maxine."

I shrugged, like it was inconsequential, but my gaze locked with hers hoping she could see what I felt. "I don't want to be everyone else to you."

— Excerpt from *Untitled* by
Rosie Maxwell and Aiden Huntington

CHAPTER TEN

"Well the date obviously worked." Ida shot me a smug look. "But before I continue with my thoughts on Rosie and Aiden's submission this week, I want to hear everyone else's."

Logan raised his hand immediately. I shot him a warning look, but he was very purposely not looking my way. "You two did a great job of creating a romantic atmosphere. The way we got Hunter's chapter before the date, where he showed his vulnerability, really evoked the feeling of falling for someone."

Ida hummed from the front of the room.

"It's falling before you even know it," Tyler said quietly.

"Exactly," Jess said. "And the *date*." She shot me an apologetic glance before she said, "I think whatever happened on your mock date really worked. Max and Hunter finally opened up to each other. I'm rooting for them now."

We got plenty of other comments like that, too, and I tried my best to scribble them all down. Since the asshole commanded it, I had finished the chapter without him. And now he wouldn't meet my gaze, which pissed me off just the tiniest bit.

He was taking notes, but his pencil moved back and forth slowly. I leaned forward, trying to catch a glimpse of his paper. Part of me thought he wasn't even taking notes, and I wanted to catch him in the act.

Growing more and more frustrated, I started to bounce my leg. At first, I did it subtly, only hitting the table every other time. I watched him as I did it, but his guarded expression didn't loosen.

So I sped up.

His jaw tightened and finally, *finally*, he looked up at me. He *glowered* at me. His pencil was making sharper movements on his paper, but he was still looking at me.

I smiled sweetly at him and went faster.

"Just like Max and Hunter," Logan muttered under his breath.

Aiden's neck snapped toward him. He gave him a death glare that made Logan shrink back and send a panicked glance to Jess. Even though Logan wrote some of the scariest horror I'd ever read, he was still petrified of Aiden.

Aiden's gaze snapped back toward me, but I wouldn't back down.

"Knock it off," he mouthed.

"Never," I mouthed back.

"This is what we need out of a romance to start with," Ida said, dragging our attention away from each other. "But I need *more*. More stolen touches and physicality—the *good* parts of a romance. You're *close,* but it's not there."

I shot Aiden a look as an idea popped in my head. What if we went out on another fake date? We'd been so closed off to each other and that night was the closest we'd gotten to opening up.

He must've known what I was thinking because he immediately shook his head.

"You're right," I spoke up quickly, before Aiden could stop me. "We'll go on another fake date."

"But more romance this time," Ida said, hesitantly. "Are you sure you two are okay with this?"

"Don't worry about it," I said before Aiden could answer her. "I'll plan it this time so it'll definitely be more romantic."

"I picked a literal candlelit restaurant," Aiden protested.

"And it was a good start, but we need a little more."

"What's more romantic than a *candlelit Italian dinner?*"

"Look, if you're in *Lady and the Tramp*," I countered, "it's plenty romantic—"

Aiden rolled his eyes. "*Lady and the Tramp?* Did I miss the part where we shared the same piece of spaghetti?"

"Oh, you *wish* we—"

Ida cleared her throat, cutting us off. "Everything okay over there?"

"Of course," I said quickly.

She tsked. "Regardless of what you two do in your free time, I expect the romance to progress in the next chapters."

Once we were outside the building, Aiden cornered me the way I'd done to him the other day. Except he used his height to his advantage. My back was against the wall of the building, his hand pressed to it near my ear.

"Ooh so scary," I teased. My heart was pounding against my chest, which was moving up and down heavily with every breath. He was hovering over me, his eyes boring into mine. I pressed my thighs together as the image of him like this wandered in my mind way farther than I wanted it to. If he hadn't pissed me off so much, this would've been hot.

"What the hell is your problem?" he snapped.

"What's *my* problem? What's yours?" I demanded.

"Why are you proposing fake dates? Wasn't the first one painful enough?"

"Yes! Which is why we need another one." I pushed him away from me and glared up at him. "You're the one who shut down when we were writing the chapter. If you hadn't, maybe Ida would've thought it was romantic enough."

"I didn't shut down," he said tersely. "I had to go, that's all."

"Oh please, you deleted half of it."

"You're the one who wouldn't stop shaking the fucking table. You're the one who said our date wasn't romantic enough."

"Well, it wasn't!" I moved past him and started to make my way toward Union Square. It was rush hour, and I was hoping I'd get lost in the crowd. I walked quickly, my height finally an advantage as I blended into the crowd.

Suddenly a hand wrapped around my wrist. Aiden pulled me out of the throngs of people.

"Don't walk away," he growled.

"I'm over it," I said. "I'm over *you*. If we can't have a friendly conversation—"

"A friendly conversation? It felt more like an interrogation—"

"How can I get it through your head? That was *Max and Hunter*, not Aiden and Rosie."

"Great!" He threw his hands up in the air. "Then romance me, Rosalinda! You're the romance expert. Since I did such a shit job at it, plan the perfect second date for Maxine and Hunter."

He stalked off. I curled my fists at my side and shouted after him, "It's Max!"

By the time the weekend hit, my plan for our date was falling perfectly into place. Winter in New York was nearly in full force, gusts of wind and rare hints of sunlight made walking outside unbearable. And on a cloudy day like today it was near frigid.

A nice, long walk with Aiden sounded *perfect*.

I was willing to suffer for the greater good. I had thick tights on under my jeans, an extra sweater on under my coat, and gloves and a hat safely secured in my tote bag. That peacoat alone wouldn't keep Aiden warm.

I texted him to meet me at one of my favorite parks, Jefferson Market Garden. I had stumbled upon this park in the Village when I first got to New York. It was small, but they always had two food trucks hanging around there at lunch time. It had walkways with hedges surrounding the trees and a fountain. In the summer, there were colorful flowers everywhere, but in the thick of winter, they had hung fairy lights between the trees and fence.

We were supposed to meet around two. The park was just a fifteen minute train ride for me, so I left at five after two to make him suffer just a bit longer in the cold.

Twenty minutes later, because I knew I could rely on the MTA being unreliable, I found Aiden at the entrance of the park, his shoulders pulled to his ears and his chin tucked against his chest. I smiled in victory at the sight of his peacoat. He was blowing air into his bare hands, trying to keep warm in the cold.

"I got here early, just so you know," he said as I approached him. His breath puffed in a cloud in front of him. "You shouldn't be late for dates."

I tsked at him. "Fashionably late."

"Can we just go to the restaurant? It's freezing out here."

"Sure." I shrugged. I moved to stand between the two trucks sitting outside the park. "Take your pick." I shoved my hands in my pockets and smiled up at him. He had slicked his hair back again, and I hated how handsome it made him look.

He gave me an incredulous look as he looked between the two trucks. "You can't be serious."

"Is something wrong?" I asked innocently.

"It's freezing, Rosalinda," he clipped. "I'm not eating outside."

"Well, I'm hungry. Feel free to leave, but you'll have to explain that to Ida." I stepped toward one of the trucks, pushing myself up on my tiptoes to see over the makeshift counter.

"Hey, Rosie." Mateo smiled down at me from the truck. "Do me a favor and go to hers today?" He nodded toward the second truck. "Business has been sparse."

"Aw, c'mon, I want tacos, not a burrito," I whined.

"It'll be on the house next time. Please."

"Fine." I stalked over to Juanita's truck.

"Rosie!" she said, delighted, standing from the small chair she had in her truck. "In the mood for a burrito?"

"Always." I smiled. "Any progress with Mateo?"

"None." She pouted as she dumped food into the tortilla. Aiden stepped forward next to me, observing the menu.

"I told you," I said to Juanita, "He likes you. Just go talk to him!"

"No way." She shook her head. "If he likes me so much, he can come over here."

"Has it ever occurred to you that he's shy?" I raised an eyebrow, but she only huffed.

"Well, I'm shy, too." She eyed Aiden. "And for you?"

He shrugged. "Whatever she's having."

Juanita's hands started moving quickly, collecting ingredients.

"It's nearly a year now that we've been working out here together. If he wanted to make a move, he would've. Besides, he told me this morning when we were setting up he was thinking of moving his truck to Washington Square."

"But only for finals at NYU!"

Not in My Book

"We all know when he moves his truck and rakes in the money with those college kids, he's never coming back," she said sadly. She handed Aiden the burrito wrapped in tinfoil.

I pulled my wallet from my bag, but Aiden held out his hand to stop me.

"I got it."

I shook my head. "I asked you, I'll pay."

"Rosie, it's okay."

"Juanita, don't take his money."

"Whatever you say, hija." She smiled affectionately at me as I slid over a twenty and slipped the change in her tip jar.

"Talk to him tonight," I called out as we walked away.

"Shh." She widened her eyes in the direction of Mateo's truck.

I turned to Aiden. "You ready?"

I led him to the semisecluded path and stopped in front of the benches. "You get to make one choice on this very romantic date. Do we sit or do we walk?"

Aiden studied the small walking loop and the benches. Then he peered down at me, watching me carefully.

"What?" I asked, shifting under his gaze. His stare could be really intimidating when he wanted it to be.

"I'm trying to figure out which one you want to do less."

"Okay, that's it, we're walking. Let's go."

We unwrapped our burritos, letting the dead, fallen leaves crunch beneath our feet.

"What was that all about?" Aiden asked between bites.

"What do you mean?"

"With the two food trucks? And what you were saying to her."

I blushed slightly, pulling my lip between my teeth. "My first couple of weeks here, I took a lot of walks. I stumbled upon this park and the two of them are always here. Turns out, they're both really into each other but won't say anything. Mateo often sells more than Juanita and when he does, he asks me to go to her truck in exchange for free tacos next time."

"Why haven't they said anything?" he asked softly. I could feel the heat of his gaze on the side of my face as we walked.

I sighed. "It's complicated. They're both too shy and too scared of rejection so neither of them wants to ask the other out. But Juanita tells me that Mateo always helps her pack up at the end of the night if he finishes first, and he makes sure she leaves safely."

"Hmm," Aiden said, eyebrows furrowed.

"I'll admit, the burritos aren't that great, but I'm too invested in their relationship to go somewhere else. I'm hoping I'll be asked to be a bridesmaid or something at their eventual wedding."

"You really do love romance, huh?" He eyed me, and I could tell he was genuinely curious, not just trying to make fun of me.

I nodded, taking another bite. "In movies, books, food trucks, you name it."

He hummed and silence fell between us. We walked the loop a few times, eating away. There were a few benches and tables scattered around the park, but they were covered by frost and snow from a few days ago. The flowers that were usually in bloom were hidden beneath the ground. The stretches of green lawn, even covered in snow, were comforting to me. To have a small space with nothing but nature surrounding me felt, even for just a moment, like I was home again.

I wanted to fall into conversation with him like we had in our chapter. It was so easy on paper; why was it so hard in person?

By the time we walked the loop a fourth time, I couldn't take it anymore.

"I can't take this."

Aiden slowed, lifting his brows. "Is the burrito too spicy?"

I squinted at him, trying to figure out if he was serious. "What? No. I can't take *this* anymore." I motioned between the two of us. "I'd literally rather do calculus than walk around this circle again without saying anything." I moved to stand in front of him so he'd stop walking. "I can't act like we have nothing to say to each other, then vomit it out on our doc."

Aiden turned away sharply. The tips of his ears were pink, but I didn't know if it was from the cold or something else. He pulled his lips into a thin line and for a brief moment, I thought he was going to walk away.

He tossed his tin foil wrapper in the nearby trash can. "Tell me more about Tennessee."

I smiled and said, "You're not getting out of talking, but okay."

I told him about my summer days as a kid. When my dad would set the sprinkler up in the front yard, and my mom would bring out a tray of homemade lemonade. How my dad tried so hard to learn Spanish for my mom and made Peruvian Independence Day special for her. He would spend hours stringing up lights in our backyard and curating the perfect playlist for the party.

"What made you decide to move to New York?" Aiden was walking with his hands tucked into the pockets of his peacoat, his head titled just a fraction to hear me.

I tossed my head back and forth, not wanting to dump Simon and my lifelong dreams of New York on him. Simon wanted me to stay, and I thought I loved Simon, so I stayed.

"Enough about me," I said. "Tell me more about what it was like growing up here."

"Boring," he said dismissively. "You've asked me this a million times, and I always tell you the same thing. Tell me more about that diner you worked at."

"Oh no you don't. You're not getting out of talking about yourself." I tugged on his arm.

His eyes roamed my face for a moment before he gave me a small smile, conceding. He tentatively told me stories, and it occurred to me that maybe Aiden was *shy*. Sure, he was still a raging asshole, but it seemed like he also didn't really feel comfortable talking about himself. It was only when I would nod or respond to what he said that he would keep going.

When he let it slip that he hadn't ever visited most of New York's most famous tourist attractions, I paused and faced him. "You're telling me that you, Aiden Huntington, native New Yorker since *birth* have never been to the top of the Empire State Building."

He shrugged. "Plenty of New Yorkers haven't."

"That's *ridiculous*. It's not only a historic New York landmark, but a historic romance one."

He side eyed me. "What sense does that make?"

"Tom Hanks. Meg Ryan. *Sleepless in Seattle*. Cary Grant. *An Affair to Remember*. Top of the Empire State building. *Supremely* romantic."

"I haven't seen either."

"Aiden, I might puke. That's so horrible." He wasn't smiling, but it was as close as Aiden probably got. It hit me, out of nowhere, that I would do anything to keep that shy smile on his face. There was a light blush on his cheeks from the cold, but he wasn't complaining about the weather like I'd thought he would.

I hesitated. "Can I ask you something?"

He spared me a glance. "As if I could stop you."

I puffed out a quick breath of air, the white showing in front of me. "Why do you hate romance?"

He stiffened. "Rosalinda," he warned.

"Anytime someone in workshop introduces a romantic plot line, you turn . . . vicious. How can something so happy make you so mad?"

Suddenly, he wouldn't meet my gaze. "It breeds unrealistic expectations."

"Tell me you didn't just say 'breed' in a conversation about romance."

He ignored me. "It's unrealistic."

"So? Isn't fiction supposed to be an escape?"

"Sometimes, you just need something to relate to." He paused and finally met my gaze. He took a long, deep breath, swallowing slowly. "My dad cheated on my mom. He was out with his mistress while she was giving birth to me." Before I could respond, he continued. "My mom had a hard life. She grew up poor and ran away to New York with him. Even after she discovered his affair, she stayed with him. She thought they were destined for a happy ending." He glanced at me from the corner of his eyes.

Slowly, he started walking again, and I trailed behind. I couldn't keep my eyes off him. I was trying to worm my way into the small opening he gave me, but he said all of this like it was just a story. As if he was speaking about a character he'd created instead of himself.

"She stayed with him for far too long. At first she thought she won the lottery with him, but"—he shrugged—"turns out my dad's a piece of shit. Those first years where it was just the two of us were rough. Along the way, I think once she accepted not everyone gets their happy ending, everything changed. She fell in love with herself instead."

"Aiden, I'm—"

"Tell me why you like romance," he interrupted. I knew he was desperate to get out of this conversation. He finally looked down at me, and his eyebrows creased down the middle.

I gnawed on my lip. "I don't know. I just do."

"Oh please, as if you don't have some elaborate answer already worked out." He knocked his elbow against mine.

It was my turn to be vulnerable with him, but I found that I didn't really mind. I kind of *wanted* to share my life with him.

"My mom was the one who taught me how to read. She was always so patient with me. She'd point out words on billboards or cereal boxes, anything really to help me. Then she started taking me to the library every day, and we'd sit and read forever in the kids' nook."

My heart warmed at the memory of my mom's soft voice in my ear as we read in our town's small library.

"She reads a lot of romance novels. She moved here, to the US, for college, so she spent a lot of time in airports, going back and forth for the holidays. She loved the Harlequins and had a collection of them back home. She eventually caught me reading her stack when I was *way* too young to be reading them."

Aiden hummed, his cheekbones rising just slightly in amusement.

"She took a Sharpie and blacked out . . . *those* scenes, but soon enough I was buying my own at the bookstore."

A wave of homesickness washed over me. I loved being here and having what felt like the whole world in front of me in just a few blocks, but some days I would give just about anything to be back home on the front porch with my family.

"Even though I was probably too young, she still let me read them because she didn't want me to miss out on one of her favorite things."

"And so you love romance because . . ." His voice was like honey, enveloping me despite the cold. It was low and smooth in comparison to his sharpness in class.

"I guess it's because no two love stories are alike. I mean, sure, most of them get their happy ending. But no one meets the same way and falls in love the same way. Sometimes you know just after an hour with a person. Or it can span decades. The only thing every love story really has in common is that it's worth it. Love is *always* worth fighting for. I mean, that's why there's all the songs and poems and movies about it. It has to be something spectacular if everyone's chasing it."

"You really believe that, don't you?" There wasn't any malice in his voice, just pure curiosity.

I nodded. "I don't think Happily Ever After is an 'if' thing. I think it's 'when.'"

"If I was as bad as you thought, I'd be killing puppies behind dumpsters." I paused. *"You're not as bad as I thought either."*

— Excerpt from *Untitled* by
Rosie Maxwell and Aiden Huntington

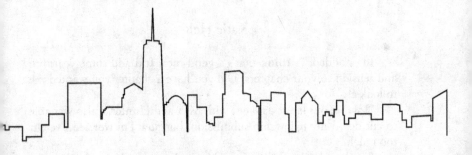

CHAPTER ELEVEN

Ida smiled as I walked into her office. "I'm eager to hear all about these dates," she said.

It was snowing outside, the snowflakes covering my hair and dampening my jacket. I pulled off my gloves one by one and shrugged. "There's not much to tell."

She shot me a disbelieving look, but didn't push. "Do you have a lot to work with for the chapter at least?"

"Can we talk about literally anything else?" I groaned. "I feel like all I do nowadays is talk about Aiden. If I keep this up, I'll come into class next time with a peacoat, black coffee, and a Murakami novel tucked under my arm."

She laughed. "I thought you two were getting along better?"

"We *are*. But . . . I don't know." It was getting confusing. I was more attracted to Aiden now than when I'd had my brief crush after the reading because now I *knew* him. I found myself *wanting* to spend time with him; I was still mad at him for how he had acted all semester, but not mad enough to want to destroy him like before. "It's complicated."

"Okay," she said slowly. "How are you two on the deadline for midterms at the end of the month? Are you on track?"

"I think so. We have a little way to go now that the romance is picking up. I want Max and Hunter to at least *kiss* before the halfway point."

Ida nodded. "I think that's a good idea. It'd add some yearning and tension to your chapters. Did you have a chapter you wanted me to look at?"

"I wrote our latest date out with Max and Hunter. I also was able to cut down my fellowship submission, but now I'm worried I've cut too much."

She waved me off. "That's fixable. Let's start with the chapter, and we'll finish off with the other."

I shared my docs with her, and we went over them for the next hour. I loved having Ida all to myself like this, being able to pick her brain on anything. She was just as eager to talk about romance as I was. I'd spent so much time secretly loving romance and reading as many books as I could with no one to talk to, but now I had someone who loved it just as much as I did. Who understood it even *more* than I did and was helping me develop my work. In moments like this, it felt like everything was coming up Rosie.

Saturday, I had the apartment all to myself since Alexa worked the weekend shift at the Hideout. Her shift didn't end until around ten, but with closing duties I didn't expect her home any sooner than midnight.

I had *very* exciting plans for my Saturday night in New York City. I had my favorite soft, white blanket and a new romance novel. I was settled on my bed with Taylor Swift playing quietly on my phone.

My phone started to buzz, but I ignored it, turning the page. I tried to focus on the words in front of me, but it buzzed again. And again.

I reached for it on the nightstand; Alexa's face was flashing on the screen.

I frowned. "Everything okay?" The sound of chatter and music overwhelmed even me from the other side. "Alexa?"

"Is there any way you can come down tonight?" Alexa's voice was wobbling. "Marianne called in sick, but she has the rush shift, so it's only four hours but we're short staff—"

"Marianne doesn't work at the bar though, why do you need me?"

"Can you come . . . wait tables?" she pleaded. "Luke asked me to beg you. We're overbooked, and everyone and their mother decided to visit New York for the holidays."

I stared longingly at my book, hesitant to leave it.

"You're guaranteed to make at least double your usual tips tonight. People tip better this time of year."

"Fine," I ground out. I was close to reaching my goal in savings so I could buy my ticket home, but not quite there yet. And I needed the money sooner than later because the price of the tickets went up every minute. "I'll be there in half an hour."

"I fucking love you," she said. "You're a lifesaver."

"Yeah, yeah, see you in a few." I tossed the phone on my bed and pulled open my closet. I quickly changed into my uniform before heading out into the cold.

There was a line out the door of people just waiting to *speak* to our hostess. Plenty of people were also littered across the sidewalk, buzzers in their hands. There were Christmas trees on either side of the entrance and garland hanging low overhead.

I had to push through the crowd to get to our hostess stand. When the hostess, Janie, spotted me, she sighed out of relief. "Thank God you're here, I don't know what to do." Wrinkles were lining her forehead, her voice crumbling.

I gave her a sympathetic smile. "Just keep seating people but let them know how long the wait is. Take it one guest at a time, okay?" I said gently. She nodded her head, her bottom lip wobbling. "Have you seen Alexa?"

"Last I saw she was entering tickets by the kitchen."

I hadn't been to the restaurant on weekends yet. It was a madhouse. Every table was full and every seat at the bar was occupied. On weekdays, there was usually a dull hum of conversation in the restaurant, but it sounded like music now. The clinking glances harmonized with the laughter from across the room and it was *suffocating*.

After I ducked in the back to clock in, I found Alexa placing plates on her tray. Her black hair was in disarray and her tie was crooked. Her eyes widened when she saw me.

"I love you," she said immediately.

"What table is this for?" I asked. "I can bring it, go take a minute."

"Wow, I really love you. Table six."

She handed off the tray and rushed toward the dry storage room. When I was first hired here, I was adamant about only being a bartender, even though Luke had tried to convince me to wait tables. Back home, I worked at our local diner, where I'd quickly learned how to find peace amongst the chaos. I knew how to handle the angriest customers and fall into a rhythm with the chefs.

One time here at the Hideout, *one time,* I filled in for a waitress and after that Luke begged me to switch to waitressing. He said, almost in awe, "Rosie, I think you were born to work in the restaurant industry." I *did* love it while I was in the flow of it all, but no amount of tips could convince me to deal with jerk customers every weekend.

I'd only been at the restaurant for five minutes, and I already reeked of garlic and cheese. I stared longingly at my bar, wishing to be behind it. But I continued to wait on Alexa's tables until she came back and explained the situation to me.

"Marianne is scheduled for that corner of the restaurant. I've got most of their orders so far, but they don't have food yet."

"What about drinks?"

"Fuck." Her face paled. "I knew I forgot something."

"Don't worry about it, I'll fix it. It'll be fine."

I spent the next three and a half hours running around the restaurant, delivering food, and spilling plenty of drinks on myself. Every time I asked the bar for a drink, I thought about begging one of the tenders to switch with me, but I wouldn't inflict the hell that is food service on anyone.

Even though the holiday season had officially started, the customers weren't acting like it. They'd send food back, complaining it wasn't to their standards, and more than one server complained about tables giving shitty tips.

Finally, *finally,* the closing waitress came in to switch off our shifts. I began to pull my tie off, but something caught my eye. A peacoat.

Aiden was here. He and an older man were being seated in my section. This must have been his father. They had the same square jaw and angular nose, and they were around the same height. But where Aiden had gorgeous, full dark hair, the man's was graying. Lighter strands peppered around the nape of his neck and into his beard. Both of them were dressed in finely pressed suits, Aiden's peacoat hanging off the back of his chair.

"You ready to get out of here?" Lisa asked. She was straightening her tie and reaching for the notebook in the pocket of her apron.

I nodded but continued to watch Aiden. His back was turned toward me, but I could see his dad clear as day. Like Aiden, he didn't smile. He seemed to have permanent frown wrinkles by his mouth, quickly spitting out angry words. Aiden still had his perfect posture, but it looked like every muscle in his body was tensed in defense.

"Actually, I can take this last table," I told Lisa, my eyes not leaving Aiden. I knew I shouldn't have interfered, but when Aiden's knuckles turned white as he gripped his glass, I couldn't help it. "Why don't you grab some food from the kitchen before your shift?"

Before she could answer, I stalked off toward Aiden.

"You've proved your point and had your fun," Mr. Huntington scolded. "It's time you quit and—"

"Hi," I interrupted. I smiled down at them, my ponytail swaying slightly behind me.

Aiden's head jerked up from the menu to meet my gaze. "Rosie?"

He blinked up at me, dumbstruck, as if he couldn't believe he was seeing me. I knew now was not the time to gloat about how *I* was the taller one for once, but man, I really wanted to.

"Hey," I said softly. I turned to Aiden's dad. "Hi, Mr. Huntington, I'm Rosie. I have a class with Aiden, but I'll be your server tonight." He only hummed and picked up his menu. I glanced at Aiden, and he was watching me with a look I couldn't discern. "What can I get started for you guys?"

Aiden spoke quickly, his words in clipped sentences like always. But I could hear the distress and the strain in every syllable, and my mind flashed to the little boy alone in the subway car.

"I'll take the steak, cupcake," Mr. Huntington said, his eyes never straying from my chest. "Medium rare."

"For your sides?" I asked, scribbling it down.

"What, you gotta write all that down to remember? That's what you go to that big, fancy school for?" Mr. Huntington looked to Aiden to share a laugh, but Aiden's jaw was clenched. He turned away from his father and to me with an apology in his eyes.

"Your sides," I prompted flatly.

I thought Aiden was bad, but I'd take him every time over his father. Back home, men often called me "sweetheart" or "sweet cheeks," which was horrible, but preferable over the demeaning way Mr. Huntington had reduced me to nothing but a servant.

"I'll be back in a little while with the food." I snapped my black notebook shut and slipped it into my apron. "In the meantime, let me know if y'all need anything." I gave Aiden a kind smile for the first time in my life and went to enter their tickets.

As I waited for the kitchen to finish up the food, I kept my eyes on Aiden and his father. Aiden took quick sips of his water, just like he had on our first date when silence fell between us. He looked nervous now—had he been nervous then?

Finally, their food was ready. Neither of them spoke as I set the plates in front of them, adjusting their utensils and drinks accordingly. Just as I was about to leave, Aiden's father stopped me.

"Cupcake, what class do you take with Aiden?"

My gaze slid over to Aiden. He looked straight ahead, his jaw clenched.

I smiled, hoping to lighten the mood. "Is this a trick question?"

His father's glare sent shivers down my back. "No."

My smile dropped quickly, my heartbeat pounding in my ears. "We're in a fiction workshop that preps us for our thesis."

Surprisingly, he asked, "Is it fun?"

I blinked at him. I looked to Aiden for help, but his face remained stoic. "I mean, sure. It's still class, but I think whenever you do something you love, it's fun."

"Ah." His father leaned back in his chair. "So, it's not about forming a career?" He looked eerily similar to Aiden as he did this. That coldness Aiden presented was obviously inherited from this man. Every word seemed to be calculated to drive home some point.

"Writing is a career," I said tersely.

"Please." His father's laugh was humorless. It was more like a cough than anything. "Even if you get published—and that's a big if—do you really think you'll make enough money and be successful enough to write day in and day out?"

This thought had always lingered in the back of my mind. Of course I *wanted* to be able to write full time, but it was rarer these days. But there was no way I would admit that to *him*. "Yes. I do."

"You write novels, you said. What kind?"

"Dad—"

"I write romance." I lifted my chin. Maybe a few months ago I would've mumbled it or just said fiction. But I'd had enough tonight.

I was tired of every needy customer and the Huntington men's judgment.

"Oh." His father sat back in his chair, waving his hand at me dismissively. "Well, then, never mind. That's different."

"Dad," Aiden warned.

"I don't want Aiden to be a writer, but at least there's a bit of a challenge to what he writes. You'll have no trouble getting published. I'll buy your book next time I'm at CVS." He sniffed.

"Don't talk to her like that," Aiden snapped. He narrowed his eyes dangerously at his father, but Mr. Huntington ignored him. I had seen Aiden mad plenty of times over the past year, but never quite like this.

My lips parted in shock, fire igniting in me. "Listen, just because—"

"Oh, c'mon," Mr. Huntington said. "Write those bodice rippers, make your quick buck, and slip your change into my kid's cup when he's living out of a box."

Aiden's been rude but he's never quite dismissed me like *this*. If Mr. Huntington was rude to a total stranger, what was he saying to his own son?

"Aiden is extremely talented," I started, placing my hands on my hips.

"Rosie, you don't have to," Aiden said pleadingly, looking down at the table and shaking his head.

"No, Aiden. He doesn't know—"

"Really." Aiden finally looked at me, and I saw what he was hiding in those eyes. Annoyance. Anger. Fatigue. "It's okay."

Taking the hint, I nodded and turned on my foot away from them. I curled my hands into fists, digging the nails into my palm. I'd known what Aiden's father was doing, and I played right into his hand. Now I'd probably made things worse for Aiden.

"Woah, who pissed you off?" Alexa came up behind me. She followed my gaze to Aiden and his father. "Who's that?"

"Aiden."

"Your Aiden? *Peacoat* Aiden?" she asked, craning her head to get a better look at him.

"Yes."

"A su madre, Rosie. He's *hot*. Tell me again why you haven't hit that?"

"Shut up." I shook my head. "His dad's being a dick."

She arched an eyebrow. "To you or to Aiden?"

"Me. Him. Both." I stretched out my fingers, watching Aiden and his father. His dad was cutting his steak in sharp movements, angrily piercing it with his fork. But Aiden only sat in front of his untouched chicken and pasta. It didn't matter that Aiden was my worst enemy; no one got to talk to him like that.

Except me, obviously.

They were arguing now. Aiden spoke in quick, quiet words, but his father spoke in sharp angles, spit flying out with every word. It was so sad to watch someone you viewed as larger than life shrink into themselves under someone else's thumb. "It doesn't matter."

"Sure," Alexa sang. "You know, you're free to go."

I looked at her nervously from the corner of my eye. "Oh. Yeah, for sure. I think I'll just finish this last table—"

"Aiden's table?"

"I'm just worried," I said defensively. "He's casually mentioned his relationship with his father a few times and it doesn't seem great." I nodded over at their table. "*Obviously.*"

Alexa nodded thoughtfully. "That's really nice, Rosie, but what can you do? Luke's been singing your praises all night, but you know if we get a bad review because you're mean to Aiden's dad, he'll blow his top off."

I bit my lip. "I'm just going to keep an eye on them."

I spent the next half hour dawdling by their table, refilling bread baskets and waters. Lisa eventually took over the other tables because she needed the hours, but I insisted on finishing off Aiden's table.

I was standing by our ticket system as Alexa was telling me a story from earlier tonight about some hot girl she waited on. I was biting the nail on my thumb when Aiden's shoulders tensed. They went straight back, and his hands found their way to the table, folded.

"Do you have Aiden's ticket?" I interrupted her.

"Are they done?"

"Can you print it?" I looked back at them, and his father was leaning across the table now, slowly getting redder in the face. I couldn't help but think about the way Aiden had said his mom needed saving from his dad. Maybe Aiden needed saving, too. "Quickly."

I snatched the ticket from the printer, almost ripping it in half in the process. I rushed over to their table and plastered a smile on my face. Almost instantly, Aiden's father stopped speaking.

"Hi, I just thought I'd bring your check over."

Mr. Huntington frowned. "We didn't ask for it."

"Oh," I said, gripping the black book tightly in my hand. "We have a reservation for this table in thirty minutes, and we need to get it prepared."

Mr. Huntington made a point to look at the empty tables surrounding him as the night died down. "Just leave it there, we'll get to it soon."

I gave an apologetic smile. "I was actually hoping to go ahead and get your payment now, so we can begin the process of setting up for our reservation. We have a time limit for each table because of this."

His face hardened, like he wanted me to back down. I held his gaze, not letting up. For a second, I thought he'd say no—or worse, ask for Luke. Instead, he shook his head and placed his card in the book. He spared Aiden a glance. "You're welcome for the meal."

I snatched the book up and hurried through his payment process. While I was away from the table, Mr. Huntington looked like he was picking up where he left off.

"Come on," I urged our machine.

"You know"—Alexa peered over my shoulder—"you're doing a lot for someone you claim to hate."

I rolled my eyes. "It's not like that."

"Uh huh." She smiled and walked away, balancing her tray on her arms.

I snatched the receipt and rushed off. When I returned with the black book, I handed it to Mr. Huntington.

"Thank you guys again for coming in."

As Mr. Huntington hastily signed the receipt, probably ignoring the tip line, he said, "Well, son, we can continue this conversation over a cup of coffee."

My gaze flew to Aiden's. He didn't react, just gave a terse nod. And I couldn't help it, I wanted to save him. I hated the hurt look he was trying so desperately to hide but that showed in the wrinkle in between his eyebrows and the way his hands curled into fists. It broke my heart into tiny pieces, knowing that this man was making the terror of my Wednesdays feel so small.

"Actually." I laughed softly, cocking out my hip, trying to seem as casual as I didn't feel. "I absolutely *hate* to interrupt this little father-son date, but I was wondering if I could borrow Aiden for an hour or two? I need help with something for class—midterms are coming up and all that."

His father narrowed his eyes at me. "Isn't it just writing? What could you possibly need Aiden for?"

"I'm her critique partner." Aiden cleared his throat. "I need to look over her work before she turns in her midterm."

"Fine." He stood up and began to tug on his jacket. "This conversation isn't over, son."

"Thanks for coming to the Hideout," I called after him as he stalked off. I turned to Aiden, whose head was cradled in his hands on the table. His eyes were clasped shut, tension residing over him like a disease. Carefully, I set a hand on his shoulder, feeling the hard lines of his body beneath his suit, hoping I was being comforting at the very least. "Are you okay?"

At the sound of my voice, he sat up straight, like he'd just remembered I was standing there. He shook his head, wiping any signs of distress away as he faced me and said, "Thank you. For all of that. You didn't have to do that."

I shrugged. "I don't know what you're talking about."

Aiden exhaled, short and quick. "I'll let you finish your shift."

I rubbed the edges of my apron between my fingers. "Oh, uh, I actually finished my shift a while ago. I was just . . ." I trailed off, heat rising to my cheeks.

Aiden blinked slowly. "You stayed for me?"

"It's not a big deal." The words fumbled out of my mouth, tripping over each other. "Bless his heart, but your dad's kind of a dick. No offense."

Aiden Huntington had the audacity to smile at that. A *real* smile, the smile that I'd spent months secretly craving was here now, in full force. Crooked nose, crooked smile. Aiden Huntington was every romance reader's favorite daydream.

"None taken." He stood from the table, and I followed his gaze until he did so. He was looming over me and a pressure formed in my stomach at the intensity of his eyes. My mouth turned dry, but I couldn't force myself to look away. He hesitated only slightly before saying, "Let me buy you dinner."

My eyes widened. I started to shake my head, but he held his hand up.

"I owe you that. I promise, no candlelit Italian places."

A shy smile spread across my face and I shook my head. "I won't make you do that. It's okay. Besides, you just ate, and I'd feel weird sitting there the whole time while you ate nothing."

He squinted at me and it was almost . . . *playful*. "You look like the kind of girl who can't refuse ice cream."

I groaned. "Am I that easy to read?"

"My treat," he insisted. "I owe you."

I hesitated but caught Alexa's eye over his shoulder. She was nodding aggressively and basically shooing me out of the store. "Okay," I said finally. "Meet you out front?"

It was a known fact that New York in the winter was intolerable. The piercing wind caught between the skyscrapers, and the people, just as cold and calculated, didn't care. I'd developed a thick skin and braced myself against the city, knowing that when it came down to it, I was truly by myself.

But walking around with Maxine, the city felt different. The sidewalks and concrete buildings grew warmer with every step, like someone had lit the fireplace in my heart and she was tending to it. Carefully adding logs every so often to stoke the flame. Walking side by side with her, ignoring every blaring car and streetlight, I knew I was far gone.

— Excerpt from *Untitled* by
Rosie Maxwell and Aiden Huntington

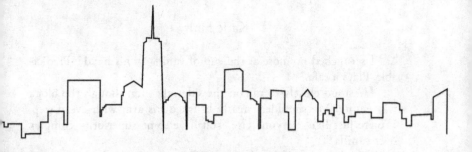

CHAPTER TWELVE

Van Leeuwen, a popular ice cream shop, was around the corner from the Hideout. I told Aiden he didn't have to walk me home after he paid for our ice cream because the walk from Flatiron to the East Village was always long, but longer in the winter.

But Aiden only said, "You'd probably find some way to hurt yourself, and then I'd spend the rest of my life feeling guilty."

It wasn't necessarily the words of a romantic hero, but it made me smile.

December was just beginning, and although New Yorkers tended to hibernate in the winter, the city came to life during the holidays. We couldn't walk a block without seeing some sort of holiday window display with poinsettias and red ribbon.

We hadn't realized what a mistake we'd made until we ambled under streetlights, holding our ice cream. Aiden had been sensible enough to get a cup, but I got a waffle cone and the ice cream slid down my fingers, numbing them even more, especially since I forgot my gloves in my mad dash to the restaurant.

"I think you can tell a lot about a person by the ice cream flavor that they choose," I said between licks.

"Oh really? What's mine say about me?" He stuck his spoon in his mouth.

I scrunched my nose at the cup of vanilla in his hand. "Predictable. Plays it safe."

He stood closely to me on the sidewalk even though the block was empty. My shoulders nearly brushed his arm with every step. "You're just like everyone else. You have some superiority complex over vanilla."

"That's not true!" I paused, considering it. "It may be a little true, but what I said still stands."

"Ask my father—I do anything but play it safe," he muttered. He jutted his chin toward my cone. "What's yours say about you?"

"You tell me."

"Hmm." He slipped his spoon in his mouth again, speaking against it. "Birthday cake flavor is a pretty bold choice."

"Yeah, if your usual is vanilla." I snorted.

Aiden studied me a moment. "I think it means you probably had a childhood with fun birthdays."

"What's in a cone? That which we call birthday cake ice cream would taste as sweet?"

"Not Shakespeare," he groaned.

"What do you have against Shakespeare?" I gasped. "He was like the ultimate sad boy; shouldn't he be, like, your God?"

He gave me a flat look. "Maybe yours, you romantic. I prefer other writers."

"Okay, like who?"

"I love Hemingway—"

"Ugh."

"I also like Austen." He nudged my shoulder.

"You were able to stomach a romance? Where did you find the bravery to do it?"

"Shut up, *Pride and Prejudice* is a classic." He smiled warmly down at me, though. I was becoming addicted to his smiles, and I was willing to do whatever I needed to do to earn another one. "And who could resist Mr. Darcy?"

I laughed in delight. When we started walking down the residential blocks toward my apartment, the streets emptied out until we were practically alone. The sirens echoed off the buildings around us. Once or twice, a loud group stumbled past, but for the most part it was just us, and neither of us seemed to want to change that. Sometimes we stopped at the crosswalks even if there were no cars, making our walk unnecessarily longer. But whenever we crossed the street, Aiden would silently move to stand on the side of the oncoming traffic so I wouldn't be in harm's way. And when we walked down the street, he'd maneuver us so I stood closer to the buildings. It was truly the first time we'd enjoyed each other's company as just Rosie and Aiden, without hiding anything in our written words.

"Hey," he said, knocking my shoulder with his. "Thanks for tonight. Really."

I bumped his shoulder right back. "What're coauthors for?"

"I rarely ever see my dad even though he lives in the city. But when I do, it usually goes a lot worse than that." He rubbed his jaw, turning away from me.

"Why is he so hard on you? If you don't mind me asking."

Aiden hesitated, choosing his words carefully. "He was the founder of a tech startup that got pretty popular in the financial world. He decided when I was younger that I would follow in his footsteps and is upset that I'm refusing to do so."

He tossed his cup in a nearby trashcan while I lifted the bottom tip of my cone to my mouth.

"How'd he react when you told him you wanted to be a writer?"

"Poorly." He gave me a deadpan look, as if that were obvious. "How did your parents react?"

"I think they knew from the start." I took another bite of the tip of my cone. "I always loved to read. I wouldn't even go to parties in high school without a book in my bag. I studied English during undergrad, too. I think it was inevitable."

"Do you miss them?" His hands were tucked in the pockets of his peacoat, his head once again tilted toward me. From the corner of my eye, I admired his profile. How had I been able to resist him for so long? How could he have been sitting across from me all of this time, and all I noticed was his peacoat?

It was so unfair that someone so annoying got to be *this* attractive. I was trying with all my might not to be turned on by him, but I knew the more time I spent with him the harder it would become. I couldn't force myself to stop, though.

"Every day," I said. "Leaving was one of the hardest things I've ever done, but I had to do it. I haven't seen them since I left." I shrugged, feeling another wave of homesickness. "Sometimes *all* I do is miss them."

"But you're going home for winter break, right?"

I felt my cheeks tint slightly. "Money's a little tight . . . It's the only reason I took a shift tonight. I have to save up to pay rent and buy groceries, and once I have enough for rent, I have to save to pay off school. By then, there's nothing left for a plane ticket. And even if I could swing the cost, I can't afford to miss out on a week of pay."

Aiden nodded in understanding.

"I've been doing everything I can to make it possible to be home for Christmas . . . but I think in the back of my mind, I know it's a lost cause." A lump suddenly formed in my throat. I hadn't admitted that out loud yet and doing so made it feel all the more real. I loved being home, but I loved being home for Christmas even more. My mom spent hours decorating our house, carefully placing our homemade ornaments on the tree. Christmas by myself last year had felt so pitiful in comparison. Tennessee and New York were nearly complete opposites, but somehow I longed for both. A tear fell, and I quickly swiped it away.

"Hey," Aiden said softly. He grabbed my elbow and took the mostly eaten ice cream cone from my hand. "It's okay. You'll go home soon."

"God, I'm sorry." I sniffled, swiping away a rogue tear. "I shouldn't be crying in front of you."

He made a face at that. "What's that supposed to mean?"

I sniffled and wiped the tears that were quickly falling. "I don't know. We get close, but not close enough to get burned, right?"

He looked away, a tight grip still on my elbow, clearly lost in his thoughts. A part of me that I hadn't known existed was dying to be in there with him, even for just a brief moment. Finally, he turned back to me. "I think if Max and Hunter can call a truce, so can we," he said softly. "So long as you promise to stop bouncing the workshop table with your leg."

I laughed through my tears. "I don't know, that's a pretty big ask. I like messing with you too much." He didn't respond, but I had a hunch he felt the same way. The best part of my day was fighting with him. "I think we can call a truce, too."

"I'm sorry about not being able to go home, Rosie. I know that's tough." His hand slipped down to mine, his thumb rubbing slowly over my wrist.

"I'll be okay," I said. "I'm sorry, I don't even know what came over me. I prided myself on not crying over this . . ."

"Hey," he stopped me, just as soft. I looked up—this wasn't the man who sat across from me every day in class. He was the man consoling me under a streetlight on an empty block, shielding me from the world with his broad shoulders like he could protect me from it. Like he wanted to. "You're allowed to be sad. You're allowed to miss the people you've spent your whole life with. You're allowed to miss the people who were good to you, Rosie."

"Thank you," I said, holding his gaze. Neither of us spoke. I was pinned beneath those green eyes until I couldn't bear it and looked away. He unwrapped the napkin from my cone and handed it to me to wipe my nose.

"C'mon." He nodded toward the street. "Let's get you home."

Each of her fingers tapped across her cheek as her chin rested in her hand. I tried not to let my eyes linger too long on her face. On the beauty mark beneath her eye or the way her lashes swept across her cheek when she blinked. I looked away reluctantly when she caught me studying her.

"You know," she said. "We should've done this friends thing a long time ago. It's not as bad I thought it would be."

"Even when you're complimenting me, you're insulting me."

"Oh please, you like it better that way."

The truth was I liked her no matter what she did, no matter what she said.

I grinned. "I really do."

— Excerpt from *Untitled* by
Rosie Maxwell and Aiden Huntington

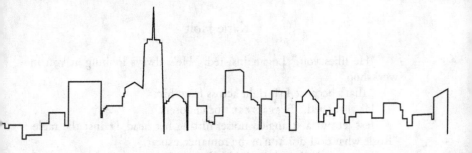

CHAPTER THIRTEEN

"Wait so you two are *friends* now?" Logan's brow was furrowed. "I thought you two would be more likely to duel at dawn or something."

"We came close last semester," I admitted, then looked at Tyler. "Remember the em dash debate?"

We were sitting in the corner booth at Peculiar Pub. When I'd told them what happened over the weekend, Jess declared an emergency meeting after class on Monday.

"That was horrible," Tyler groaned. "I swear sometimes you two just fight to hear yourselves talk."

"Hey!" I said defensively. "It's not my fault Aiden prefers commas."

"I can't listen to this again," Tyler muttered. "Anyone want another round?"

Tyler slid out of the booth when we nodded and made his way toward the bar.

"How's it going with you two?" I turned to Jess. I felt bad I hadn't been much of a friend to Jess lately. I've been so caught up in my own drama with Aiden, I've been neglecting my best friend duties of helping her get together with Tyler. Then again, she refused to do anything the last time I mentioned it. I've encouraged her to at least *text* him outside of our group thread, but she barely even talks to him when he's sitting right there.

"Literally nothing is happening." She placed her forehead on the table in despair. "He's so hard to read."

"He likes you," Logan insisted. "He's always looking at you in workshop."

"That's because I sit right across from him."

He shrugged. "Beggars can't be choosers."

Jess let out a strangled noise, hitting her head against the table. "Rosie what do I do? You're the romance expert."

I grimaced. "I wish I could help, but Tyler *is* really hard to read. Half the time I wonder if he even enjoys hanging out with us."

"We should confront him," Logan said, slapping his hand down on the table.

"You're just tipsy." Jess sat up. "Actually . . . maybe I should get super drunk and confess my feelings to him."

I shook my head. "Tyler is too good of a guy for anything to come from that. If that happened, he'd probably apologize to *you* then never bring it up again. I say ask him out for coffee after class. Maybe next time he gives you a comment in workshop ask him to 'elaborate further,'" I said slowly, widening my eyes.

Jess brightened, tucking her dark hair behind her ears. "And this is why you are our resident romantic."

Tyler came back then, setting down the beers in the center of the table. "Can we circle back to you and Aiden being friends?" he asked, sipping one of the beers. "I feel like we moved on from this too quickly."

I hesitated. Being friends with Aiden was nothing like I had expected it to be. I'd thought maybe we'd just start being nicer to each other, but lately I'd found myself always reaching for my phone to text him. It started when I asked for advice on one of our chapters, but soon I wanted to know his opinion on everything. I kept reminding myself the feelings weren't real, just a result of spending so much time with him. But I couldn't stop my heart from beating harder every time he nodded at me on the way into class or told me he liked my chapter after I sent it. I craved more and more, and I wasn't sure when this newfound desire for his attention would be satiated.

"It's not a big deal," I said finally. "He's not that bad."

"I think it's a great thing," Logan said. "The chapters have been getting better."

Our characters were no longer enemies and were slowly but surely making their way toward lovers. Our truce really allowed us to put more of ourselves in the characters, and we couldn't stop writing. I had written more words in the past few weeks than I had in the past *year*. Suddenly, everything looked different.

"And you two have been way nicer to each other in class." Logan waggled his eyebrows at me suggestively. I rolled my eyes and sipped my beer, hoping they couldn't see my blush.

Today in class, we'd been mid-discussion about our chapters when Aiden spoke up.

"I haven't been able to give Rosie feedback on this chapter, actually."

I'd held my breath, a little nervous that our new friendship meant absolutely nothing to him, and we were on our way back to insults.

Ida had reluctantly nodded before saying, "Go ahead."

"I think one of the strengths of this chapter, and really the work as a whole, is your ability to make dialogue seem so realistic. It's never stilted or awkward." He was reading off his notes from the chapter, flipping through the pages. "And, obviously, something I'm not as good at is the romance of it all, but you're able to fill in the blanks with surprisingly tender moments."

"You may not be as good at the romance," I had blurted in response, "but I think you do a really good job of keeping us grounded. I tend to want to romanticize everything, but you make it feel real."

"Well, to be fair, the reason the characters have become so dynamic is because you set them—"

"Sure." I'd waved him off. "But when you rein me in it adds more tension—"

"While I'm loving this friendly exchange for once," Ida interrupted, "I think it's time to move onto other pieces."

"Right." I had sat back in my seat, a blush forming on my cheeks.

"That was nothing," I insisted to the group now. "Everyone's nice to each other in workshop."

"I guarantee you, Aiden has never been that nice to anyone in his *life*," Logan said. "Maybe he has a little crush." He reached over the small booth of the table to pinch my cheek, but I shoved him away.

"Shut up."

"I wouldn't be surprised," Tyler said, smiling softly. "He has a soft spot for you."

My heartbeat sped up again. Maybe I had the smallest, tiniest, most insignificant crush in the world on Aiden. But it was a pipe dream—I never would imagine him to feel the same toward me.

"Now that I think about it," Jess said, "lately, if someone else in workshop gives you a harsh critique, he glares at them."

I deflated a bit. "I bet he just wants to be the only one to insult me."

"In a *sexy* way," Logan piped up. "It might be a kink. It's always the quiet ones."

"Shut up." Jess kicked Logan, shaking the table. She must've been able to tell I was uncomfortable because she said, "Let's talk about something else."

"I agree, enough about Aiden and me." I sipped my beer, letting the bitter taste wash down my throat. "Did I tell y'all I'm applying for the Frost Fellowship?"

"You're kidding!" Jess said in surprise, a smile taking over her face. "That's great! Tyler, didn't you apply last year?"

He nodded. "You definitely should, Rosie. I'm a finalist at *The Paris Review* right now for a short story, and I think my fellowship helped a lot."

"I've been working on revising a short story from last semester with Ida. I'm hoping they'll be kind to a romance."

"You should have Aiden look over it," Logan said.

I scoffed. "No way."

"I mean, he *knows* your voice. It couldn't hurt."

I fiddled with the label on my beer, peeling it off. The submission deadline wasn't until the end of January, but I wanted to get it done now. I was so nervous for all of it, eager to just submit everything and be done.

"Maybe," I conceded.

"And since Aiden's got a fat crush on you, I'm sure he'd be more than happy to help."

"That's it," Jess declared. "Next round on Logan."

During the next class, I found myself staring at Aiden more than I ever had. He caught me once, and I felt myself turn so red that I thought about faking a stomach bug to leave.

After class, Aiden caught up with me to discuss the path for our next chapters. We walked down Fifth Avenue toward the Arch at

Washington Square Park, our chins tucked against the cold as we walked quickly and stiffly together. Like a natural New Yorker, Aiden walked at an alarmingly fast pace. But he seemed to be making an effort to slow down so I wouldn't basically be jogging next to him.

"They need to break up," he said.

"No," I whined. "They're not even together yet! We have to at least let them kiss."

He gave me a bewildered look. "In my head, I thought they would just fall in love, not *be* in love."

"Not much of a difference, buddy."

We walked around the park, between the trees and grass that reminded me so much of home. Even though it was freezing out, there were plenty of people ambling about—street performers and people walking their dogs. *This* was what I loved about New York.

As we neared the fountain, Aiden stopped and turned toward me. "I don't think they should kiss at all," he said.

"Yeah, that's not happening," I scoffed. "They need to kiss. They should have sex, too."

He pressed his lips together. "I'm not writing a sex scene, Rosalinda."

"Uh oh, we're back to Rosalinda, you must be serious."

"I thought you said not every romance has sex scenes."

I scowled up at him. "We don't have to write erotica, but you know . . ." I looked away from him, suddenly embarrassed. "They should do stuff."

"Is that what they call it in romance novels? Doing stuff?" He laughed, and despite the rowdy park, it cut through all the noise and landed so beautifully in my mind that I wished it was a physical item that I could hold forever.

"Shut up, you know what I mean. It'll be a display of intense love for our characters. All the tension between them will finally pay off." Aiden's dark brows furrowed, skepticism flitting across his face. "Don't worry, I think we're a little while away from writing their sex scene. But even though we're writing a slow burn, I still think they should kiss before we turn in what we have."

He raised a brow. "A slow burn?"

I smiled. "A slow burn is when it takes a really long time for the couple to get together. When you build up so much tension and yearning between them, that it makes the reader burn and die for them to finally kiss."

He thought about that for a moment, then nodded once. "Well then, where do we go from here?"

"I'm not sure." I bit my lip. "Do you want to grab some coffee? I'm freaking out just a little about getting everything done in time. Maybe we can sketch out the next bit together?"

He stiffened. "Okay."

"We don't have to if you're busy." I frowned.

"No! I'm definitely not busy. Not busy at all." He shifted back and forth on his feet, his cheeks reddening. He closed his eyes and breathed in deeply like he was collecting his thoughts. "Yes, I want to go get coffee with you."

I eyed him. "Okay, weirdo. Think Coffee?"

"Lead the way."

After we had ordered our coffee, we sat at a small table in the back corner. As I unpacked my laptop and notebook, Aiden rolled up his sleeves, revealing his forearms. He was wearing a black shirt, which made his green eyes look brighter and his hair look even darker. In romance novels, there was always such a focus on body parts that had rarely seemed attractive to me in real life. I'd never cared much for jawlines or clavicles or forearms. But around Aiden, I couldn't help but always notice how his shirt would tighten around his biceps and make his forearms look so *strong*. I loved making him mad for plenty of reasons, but my new favorite one was the way his jaw would tick when he was particularly irked.

"Let's outline," I said before I went into cardiac arrest at the sight of Aiden running a hand through his hair.

For the next few hours, we entertained a few different story ideas. Mine romantic, his morbid.

"But! If we kill one of them off now, it gives the realistic ending that we need," he reasoned. His shoulders were squared as he laid his hands on the table to speak.

"We can't call it a romance if they don't even kiss before one of them dies! They're just friends right now, they're not even lovers."

"It'll surprise the reader."

"They'll throw the book away!"

I pulled my hair away from my shoulders into a low ponytail. I had learned to dress in layers during the winter. Today I was wearing my puffer, a sweater, and a white V-neck with my jeans.

Aiden was looking up toward the ceiling as I arranged my hair, his jaw tense.

"I think there's enough tension," he said. "Let's just cut it off—"

"And have them kiss! Perfect!" I clasped my hands in front of my chest joyfully. He suppressed a smile, his cheekbones lifting but the lines of his lips pressed together.

The sight of his unwanted smile made my chest warm because I knew I'd put it there. I was finally getting to know the real Aiden. Not the version of himself he hid behind his iron mask, but the one who relished in sad moments and awarded people with smiles, even if he didn't want to. "Opposites attract" wasn't just a romanticized idea in my head, it was a scientific fact, right?

Aiden cleared his throat, pulling at the collar of his shirt just a little. "Hey, would you ever want to grab—"

"Piel Canela" by Los Panchos, a song my mom and I always danced to in the kitchen, started blaring from my phone, my mom's face flashing on the screen. Blood rushed to my cheeks as I snatched it from the table.

"Sorry, I should take this." I turned away from Aiden and said in a low whisper, "Mami? Is everything okay?"

We usually had our weekly calls on Sunday nights. When she called during the week it was usually an emergency. Albeit they were always stupid emergencies like "Where did you get the blackberry jam from again?" or "Do you know where your father keeps the weed eater?"

"Mi vida, estoy pleaneando la cena de Navidad y necesito saber si vienes o no."

"I don't know right now, Mami," I said through clenched teeth. I glanced over at Aiden who was staring intently down at his notebook, very obviously listening but trying not to.

"Hijita, your tía and I want to start cooking before the grocery stores turn crazy. We need to figure out how many potatoes, eggs—"

"I shouldn't throw off your count by *that* much."

"You eat a *lot* of Papa a La Huancaína."

I switched to Spanish. "Te llamaré más tarde. Estoy con un amigo."

"Un amigo?" She gasped. "¿Es guapo? Es su—"

"Te llamaré más tarde, Mami. Te quiero mucho." I hung up before she could say anything else and turned back toward Aiden with an apologetic smile. "Sorry, my mom's just . . ."

"No worries." He waved me off. "Family's complicated. You've met my dad." He cleared his throat and looked down at his leather watch. "Actually, I keep meaning to thank you again for saving me. Do you want to grab dinner? My treat."

"Um . . ." I stuttered, thrilled at the prospect. I sat forward, leaning over the table—and knocking the rest of my iced coffee over in the process. "*Shit*."

"Here, let me grab some napkins." Aiden stood from the table to grab napkins while I sat helplessly at the table. This was why I didn't have a boyfriend and this was why I didn't like going on dates. I freaked out the minute I got asked out and ruined it. Romance was always better in my head and in books.

I helped Aiden clean up the ice and spilled coffee in silence, trying to find a way to say YES. *I DO WANT TO GET DINNER WITH YOU.*

"If you're busy tonight," Aiden said, rubbing his hand across the back of his neck, "then we don't have—"

"*No*," I said a little too forcefully. I squeezed my eyes shut, taking deep breaths. "Sorry, I'm just flustered."

His eyebrows raised and my face got so hot, I was surprised it didn't melt off.

"I'd love to go to dinner with you. Let's leave this God-forsaken coffee shop as soon as we can." I slipped my jacket on quickly, and he stuffed his black notebook in his bag.

"I know of a pretty good burger place a few blocks down, if that sounds good?"

"Sure," I said, trying to calm my heart rate down. "I'm hungry for anything."

He followed me closely out of the store, placing his hand carefully on the small of my back.

As we walked toward the burger joint, I tried to conjure ways for him to press his hand on my back again.

She was so obviously sad about the prospect of being alone; gone was the brightness in her eyes, and I was so afraid they would fill with tears that I was willing to do whatever it took to soothe the wrinkle between her eyebrows. The offer to spend time with her spilled out of my mouth, the color of hope, tinged with regret.

"You don't have to do that." But even as she said this her voice wavered. "I don't want charity. I'll be okay."

"It's not charity if I genuinely want to be around you, Max."

— Excerpt from *Untitled* by
Rosie Maxwell and Aiden Huntington

CHAPTER FOURTEEN

"No onions, no mustard, not too much mayo, and not too much ketchup," I said to our waitress. "But could you mix the ketchup and mayo up? Oh! And do you have barbeque sauce?" She had a dead look in her eye that turned vicious as I started to order. "And a side of fries, unless they're crinkle fries, then I'll just do without them. But if you have waffle fries, I'll have two servings." She angrily punched my order into her tablet, glaring at me.

Aiden had cleared his throat and leaned forward. "I'll just have the number three."

"You know," he said once our food arrived. "I'd wondered why the burrito at Juanita's food truck had such a unique selection of toppings in it. Now I get it."

"Listen," I said between bites. "It's not bad to be picky."

He nodded at my plate. "Are you going to eat the pickle?"

"Ick, no it's all yours." I stabbed it with the toothpick from my burger and placed it on his plate.

"You don't like pickles?" He frowned.

"It's the juice." I shuddered. "Kids at my middle school used to drink it, and it grossed me out."

He laughed, biting off half the pickle.

"What about you?" I asked. "Any food you despise?"

He titled his head, his eyes turned to the ceiling in thought. "I don't like beans. Of any sort."

"Me either!" I beamed at him and reached across the linoleum black and white table and raised my hand for a high five. Aiden rolled his eyes before slapping my hand back, the corners of his mouth turned up in a small smile. "It's the texture."

"I watched this movie as a kid," he began. "*Dennis the Menace*? He was kidnapped and he had dinner with the guys who kidnapped him, but all they had to eat were beans. They stuffed their faces with it, and that scene always made me sick."

I nodded in understanding. "My dad knew I didn't like beans, so when he would get mad at me, he'd make beans for dinner." The restaurant was nearly empty, our voices echoing in the small building. "I used to hide them under my rice, and he always let me get away with it."

Aiden finished off the rest of his pickle and grinned. It was so *rare* for Aiden to grin. Sure, he smiled and would laugh sometimes, but to watch his whole face morph because of a grin that I'd caused made me glow. "Rosie's dark side finally comes out."

"For that, I'm stealing a fry."

And that started us eating off of each other's plates. Sometimes when we reached across the table, our hands brushed, and I'd ignore the shock it sent through me. A while later, I hadn't touched my own fries, but I had eaten most of Aiden's, and he'd eaten mine.

"Have you ever been in love?" I asked.

Aiden paused with his arm halfway across the table. "Why do you ask?"

I shrugged. "Because you hate romance."

He popped my fry in his mouth. "I don't hate romance. I hate romance *novels*."

I rolled my eyes. "I feel like you can't say that when you haven't read one."

"I told you I've read *Pride and Prejudice*," he said defensively.

"That's not what we both mean, and you know it."

"I've been in love before," he said carefully. "Sort of. I don't know."

"You don't know?"

"I'm sure *you* have," he said, ignoring the question. "Tell me about your first love. I bet you had some sweeping romance with fate and sparks and all the things you read about."

"Honestly? I don't think I've been in love." I swirled the straw in my water around, avoiding his gaze. "I thought I was in love, but in retrospect I wasn't. Because I read romance novels and the love in those stories is just so different from what I've experienced. With my ex-boyfriend it was . . . routine and habitual, a cycle we couldn't break. When I *am* in love, I don't want to have to wonder if it's love, you know? I want to know with certainty that there is nothing else I would rather feel."

He opened his mouth, but I cut him off before he could say anything. "And I know romance novels can be unrealistic, but there *are* Happy Ever Afters. And, I don't know . . . sure, love can be messy, and it can hurt, but I think it's supposed to heal, too."

"I know what you mean," he said quietly. "Every time I've been in love, or at least thought I was, I thought I had to give up a part of myself. I couldn't be completely me."

I snatched one of his fries and gestured for him to take one of mine. I held it up. "To easy, true love."

"To easy, true love," he agreed, and we clinked.

Aiden and I had way more in common than I ever thought. We both watched *Big Brother*, and dipped our French fries in our milkshakes. Aiden was apparently super into making playlists, too.

"I used to spend hours debating the transition from one song to the next, burning CDs in my bedroom," he admitted.

"Did you ever make one for a girl?" I asked, cheekily.

He rolled his eyes. "No. I would make them based on a book I'd just read. I'd try to emulate the plot or the vibes of it. I would—"

My phone started buzzing. I cursed and silenced it. But it buzzed again. "Jesus Christ," I muttered. I shut it off again and shoved it under my leg.

"Do you need to get that?"

"No," I shook my head. "My family's just—" My phone buzzed again, the chair amplifying the sound.

"Take it," he urged. "I don't mind, really."

I hastily swiped the green. "What?" I asked sharply.

"Is that any way to greet your baby sister?"

I rolled my eyes. "Hi, Maria. How are you?"

"I'm good," she said brightly. I paused, waiting for her to continue.

"Is that it? You're not calling about some urgent matter?"

"I can't call to say hi to my big sister?"

"You can call, and when I don't answer, you can send a text."

"Look at you. Goes to New York for one year and becomes too busy to care about us southern folk," she tsked. "So are you coming home for Christmas or not?"

"I already told Mom I don't know," I whispered, angling my body away from Aiden so he couldn't hear. Maria and I both spoke broken Spanish, and we couldn't really speak it to each other. We needed someone like my mom or our tías to guide us in conversation or else we'd be completely lost. I wished we were fluent as I sat here trying to have this conversation in front of Aiden. "I'm just trying to figure out the plane ticket and work stuff," I lied.

I knew it wasn't happening. I'd had an alert for flights set up since Halloween and nothing had been in my price range. Even if I took on more shifts at the Hideout, I still wouldn't have enough for a roundtrip flight and rent next month. I knew I needed to tell them soon, but I hadn't found the courage yet.

"I really need you here, Rosie." I could hear the panic in her voice and frowned. Maria was the calm one. The one who did yoga in the morning and had an elaborate skin care routine she claimed was "meditative."

"Is everything okay?" I asked softly.

"I just miss you. A lot."

"I miss you, too. I'm sorry I don't know yet. I'm going to try to pick up a few shifts—"

"Peter and I can help pay for your ticket." Peter was Maria's husband. They were high school sweethearts and got married just before I left for New York.

"No way. I know you two are saving up to get the house on Lott Street. Don't worry about me. I'll let y'all know soon, okay?"

"Fine. Fine. Love you," she said as I hung up.

"I'm so sorry," I said to Aiden.

"Don't worry about it. Is everything okay?" I hesitated, reaching for another of the last of his fries. "You don't have to tell me," he said kindly. "But we're past using personal information against each other, okay?"

Loose strands fell out from my ponytail at the side of my face, and I pushed them behind my ear.

"I still haven't told my family I can't come home for the holidays," I said, my voice small. "I've been trying so hard for the past few weeks. Balancing school and my social life and working myself dead, and I really thought I would make it. But the plane tickets are crazy expensive now that Christmas is two weeks out, and I won't have anyone to cover my shifts." My voice was wobbling. I shrugged and said, "It just sucks."

"I'm sorry, Rosie," he said affectionately. He reached over to grab my hand, his fingers curling around the back of mine.

"It's not world ending." I wiped away a stray tear with the hand Aiden wasn't holding. "I'll survive it. I just spent last Christmas by myself, and I hoped this year would be different. New York during this time is so fun, but only if you have someone to spend it with, you know?"

"Yeah," he said sympathetically, his thumb sweeping over the back of my hand. Such a small touch that sent shivers down my spine.

"It's okay, though. I'm applying for the Sam Frost Fellowship, have you heard of it?"

He paused. "Yeah," he said carefully. "I have."

"I'm hoping that if I get it, it'll solve some of my money problems since tuition wouldn't be as big of a problem. Then I'll be able to go home more often. That kind of money is life changing."

He hummed, nodding. "I get what you mean."

"It's alright, though. I'm just being dramatic."

He tilted his head. "I could do Christmas with you."

I took in a sharp breath. Aiden's eyes didn't leave mine.

"Oh, Aiden," I said carefully. "You don't have to do that."

"I want to," he insisted.

"No, really, it's okay."

"Do you not want me to?" he asked tentatively, and my heart broke into a million little pieces. I didn't know much about Aiden. I had pieced together his father's feelings for him quite easily, and it was obvious to see that he had spent his life neglected and unwanted by his dad. But he wouldn't feel that way from me.

"No!" I rushed. "I'd love it if you did, but really, I couldn't make you—"

"I want to," he said forcefully. "Seriously. A dinner isn't enough to repay you for what you did. My dad—" He shook his head. "You saved me." He blew out a breath. "I spend Christmas by myself anyway. You'd really be doing *me* a favor."

"I like to do touristy things," I warned. Part of me was trying to deter him, to push him away just so I could see if he really wanted to step closer.

He nodded, his smile reaching his eyes. "I figured."

"I want to go to Central Park and probably Macy's—"

"Rosie." He squeezed my hand, wrapping his fingers around mine. "You're not going to talk me out of it. I want to."

I bit my lip, smiling. "Okay. I'll buy you a hot chocolate as a thank you. Obviously."

"Really, don't worry about it. I'm excited."

My smile kept growing wider. "Me too. I really can't thank you enough. At least when I tell my family I'm not going to be alone, they won't be as worried. And they won't think I'm sulking about Simon—"

"Simon?" he asked. "Is that the boyfriend?"

Something about the way Aiden was looking at me, his face so open, made me want to spill my guts. My gaze slid away from his. "Ex-boyfriend. We dated back home for . . . well, *years*. We broke up last fall." He raised his eyebrow, encouraging me to continue. I sighed and ran my hand down my face. "I was a little doe-eyed as a kid."

"You? No way." His voice was dripping with sarcasm.

I tossed my napkin at him. "Shut up. Before we started dating our sophomore year of high school, I had this *huge* crush on him. But I think I liked a person I created in my head, not Simon himself. And then when we started dating, I convinced myself that he *was* that person, and I wasn't seeing it."

"So what happened?"

I shook my head. "It took me way too long for me to realize how much of a jerk he was. I just . . . wanted to be loved so badly that I thought being hurt was part of the deal. He convinced me to stay in town for college, told me romance novels made my standards too high . . . It wasn't until I moved here that I woke up from this decade long nap." I hesitated. I hadn't talked about this in so long. I had to blink back the tears because even though I was over Simon, I wasn't over what he'd done to me and how he made me feel. "He told me I was destined to become an old lonely woman, surrounded by books."

"*What?*" Aiden said sharply, pulling his shoulders back. His voice dropped to a deadly level.

I shrugged as if it meant nothing. As if I hadn't wasted a near decade of my life hoping Simon would be who I wanted him to be.

"Everything sort of fell into place after we broke up. Why I couldn't write anything romantic, why I was so unhappy, why I felt like there was something missing in my life."

"Jesus Christ." His eyes were narrowed, and his jaw was clenched. He was breathing slowly and barely moving his jaw.

"I think maybe he was right," I said quietly. "I probably *do* need to lower my expectations."

Aiden immediately shook his head. "No, Rosie. You don't have to lower your expectations. You deserve more than your highest one. Any guy you're with should be falling over himself to make you happy."

I tried not read into his words, but I could feel my mind shifting. I'd once thought that Aiden was the antithetical romance hero. But maybe I was the antithetical heroine. I was argumentative and stubborn, but Aiden didn't seem to mind anymore.

"Weak guys like that are just intimidated by strong women," Aiden continued, each word a sharp cut into the air. "You shouldn't have to beg someone for the bare minimum. He got too comfortable being with someone as wonderful as you and took you for granted." He hung his head. "Rosie, I'm sorry. I never would've said that stuff about romance novels—"

"You didn't know," I said quietly. "I mean, it sucks that you *did* say it. But you haven't since we started being friends. And besides, I make fun of literary fiction all the time."

His face screwed up. "That's different."

"It's not."

"I didn't know *other* people were making fun of you for romance. God, you must've thought I was exactly like that asshole this whole time."

I frowned. "We were mean to each other. But we're done with that now. I like hanging out with you too much."

Aiden smiled, and my breath caught in my chest. "I like hanging out with you, too."

I was the *worst* version of myself when I had a crush on someone. I couldn't control my words or actions, both of which ended up coming off too strong and too cringey. It was like my mind became its own person with one goal in mind.

So, really, I couldn't be blamed when I couldn't stop talking about him.

"Aiden really liked that line, though," I said to Ida as I sat in her office. I had rewritten a recent chapter and wanted to get Ida's opinion on it.

"Okay, keep it then if you both like it," she murmured, continuing to read on her screen. "You know, maybe Hunter's best friend could also be into Maxine? Create some tension there."

I frowned. "There's no way Aiden would be open to introducing a love triangle. He's already hesitant about the main romance as it is."

Ida pushed her laptop screen down and glared at me. "Stop talking about Aiden. This is your book, too."

"I know that," I said defensively, crossing my arms across my chest.

"You've used his name in every single sentence since you walked in here."

"Not true." Ida gave me a deadpan, until I relented and said, "It's *your* fault! You wanted the two of us to be friends!"

"Because I thought it would bring peace to my daily life but turns out you're just as bad as friends." She paused, studying me. "Is there something going on between you two?"

"No!" I nearly shouted. I cleared my throat and regrouped. "No. Nothing. We're just . . . friends. We've been getting to know each other and spending a little bit more time together."

"Uh-huh." Ida bit back a smile, pushing her screen up.

"It's true," I insisted.

"I'm sure."

I rolled my eyes, settling back in my seat. "Are you done antagonizing me or can we go over the chapter?"

"I think it's looking good. Are you two ready to submit your pages for the midterm?"

"Nearly. The last chapter Aiden wrote kinda of screwed up my plan, so I need to fix that, but we're close to done with our first half."

"Perfect. And the fellowship piece? It's due early January," she reminded me.

"It's going well," I said excitedly. "I keep rereading it, and I think I'm almost ready to submit it, but something still feels a little off about it to me."

"Well, you already know I think it's great. But maybe a different set of eyes would serve you well?"

There was one obvious person to be that second set of eyes. Aiden knew my voice better than anyone by now, and I was sure his feedback would help me take the piece to the next level. I just had to work up the courage to ask.

"I missed you," Maxine said, walking further into the room. My heart was pounding, a loud rush in my ears, but I hung onto her every word like she hung the moon.

"You missed me?"

"Don't act so surprised. We're friends now. Honestly, you might be my best friend."

A Maxine-shaped space had been undeniably carved into my soul. Around her, I couldn't ever stop the smiles that spread across my face—and given the way her eyes lit up every time my lips quirked, I didn't want to.

I hadn't really thought about Maxine as my best friend before, but for the first time in a long time, I felt like I could be myself around someone else. She might've been the best friend I've ever had.

"You might just be mine, too, Max." I shot her a look. "Don't let it go to your head."

— Excerpt from *Untitled* by
Rosie Maxwell and Aiden Huntington

CHAPTER FIFTEEN

"I can't *believe* you didn't make them kiss," I whined as soon as Aiden answered the phone.

"It's not the right time," he said. "They're not ready."

"Uh, yes they are. They're basically screaming at me to let them kiss."

"Then make them kiss in your chapter," he whispered harshly.

I stopped in the middle of the street, basically asking to get run over. The streets surrounding Union Square were extra crowded now that the Holiday Village had opened up. A smile took over my face. "You're scared of writing a kiss scene."

He scoffed. "Please."

"You are!" I let out a giddy laugh. "Oh my God, Aiden Huntington is scared of a little kissing."

"Shut up," he hissed.

"Why do you keep whispering? Should I be whispering, too?" I whispered.

"That's typically what you do when in public spaces to be polite," he said.

"That's typically what you do when in public spaces to be polite," I repeated mockingly in a low voice.

"Very mature."

"Just write the kiss scene so I can write the next chapter," I said. "We can't be wasting time like this."

"Or you can write the kiss scene in *your* chapter," he said again.

I shook my head. "It throws off my plan for my chapter if they haven't kissed by now."

"I thought we couldn't be wasting any time?"

"Ah, sorry, connection is breaking . . . have . . . go . . . can't . . . hear." I hung up on him and slipped my phone into my pocket.

The truth was, I didn't want to write the kissing scene either. I'd written kissing scenes before, some damn good ones, too. But something about exposing to Aiden the way I imagined other people kissing and inadvertently showing how *I* liked to be kissed was embarrassing. Naturally, the only thing to do was bully Aiden into it.

Now that all the extra money I was going to spend on my plane ticket was just going to be sitting in my savings account, I thought it'd be responsible to buy myself a few books. I heaved open the heavy door of the Strand, immediately relaxing as I stepped in. Despite how many times I visited the bookstore, I always had to pause in awe over the sheer number of books. On weekends when I had nothing to do, I spent time wandering the stacks and flipping through pages. I'd go up into the Rare Book Room and sit on the comfy chairs, reading until they yelled at me to leave. It was like a second home.

The Strand was full of people today, nearly wall to wall. Customers stood around the tables, lingering as they read the backs of books. They had decorated the store for Christmas: garlands hung between the lights and Santa hats sat on the cards that named each table. Christmas music played softly in the background, barely audible over the chatter of the store. I walked through the crowd of people toward my favorite section.

The romance section of the store was small, near the back of the store. If I was lucky, I'd be the only one in there, scanning through the titles—but someone was already in the stacks when I got there. I gasped. I'd know that peacoat anywhere.

"Aiden?"

Aiden, wearing a hoodie beneath his peacoat and a beanie, turned around. His mouth parted in surprise when our gazes met. He appeared so *boyish* standing there. I hadn't thought Aiden even *owned* hoodies. But he looked so warm and cozy that I couldn't help but take a step closer to him.

"Hey," he said, raising a single hand. He held the other behind his back, and I narrowed in on it suspiciously.

"Whatcha got there?" I gave him a cheeky grin. When I stepped forward, he stepped back. When I tried to peer around him, he angled his body away from me. The horror section was right next to romance. He was probably a secret horror fan, which would explain why he'd found such glee in torturing me for the past few months.

"Nothing."

"So prove it."

He scowled. "I don't have to prove anything to you."

I rushed him then, and his eyes widened in surprise. He tried to sidestep, but he ended up bumping into an endcap bookshelf. With his back pressed against it, I pulled his arm in front of him.

Aiden Huntington was holding a romance novel.

"Oh my God."

"Shut up."

"*Oh my God.*"

"I said shut up." He snatched his hand away from my grip and held the book to his chest. "It's for my cousin."

"Your cousin in middle school?"

"Yes," he said defensively.

I unfolded his arms from his chest. "Wow, your preteen cousin must be very mature to be reading what *The New York Times* called 'Extremely sexy.'"

"I'm leaving." He brushed past me, out of the aisle.

"No!" I rushed after him and moved to block his path. "I was just teasing. I think guys *should* read more romance novels, and I don't think they should be made fun of it for it because it really isn't a gendered genre like people make it seem and—"

"How'd you know I was here?" he cut me off.

I blinked. "I didn't. But now that I'm here, I can help you pick out a book you'll actually like."

"What's wrong with this one?"

"Nothing. I really love that one, but you'd hate it, honestly."

His eyes narrowed at me. "Aren't you supposed to be writing?"

I glanced at him over my shoulder as I scanned the romance section. This area of the store really was *tiny*, barely taking up a fourth of the wall. I had spoken to a bookseller about expanding it because they apparently didn't see how lucrative of a market the romance genre was, but they'd just nodded absently and walked away. "Look, you'll need to write the kiss scene in your chapter first, so I can continue with the story."

"We have to submit it for class *tomorrow*, Rosalinda."

"Details, details," I tsked. "Their selection is lacking, but we can work with this." I grabbed one of the nearby ladders and climbed to the top. I pulled books from the shelves, handing them down to Aiden, explaining the plot of each as I did so.

"You know"—Aiden looked up at me from the side of the ladder facing me—"I was planning on maybe getting one book."

I crinkled my nose. "That's pure nonsense. You're going to need these and *obviously* a Christina Lauren."

"What the hell is a Christina Lauren?"

I moved down the ladder and handed him a copy of one of their books. "They're a lot like us, you know. They're a best-friend writing duo. One is Christina and the other is Lauren."

His eyes softened, and he smiled down at me. "Okay. I'll read one by them. But I don't think I need all of these."

He gestured to the stack I had placed in his arms, reaching from his waist to his chest. I couldn't help zeroing in on his biceps. My gaze traveled up his arms and for some reason my eyes snagged on his *neck* of all things. Sure, shoulders and backs were attractive, but Jesus fucking Christ, I couldn't stop staring at the slope of his neck.

I cleared my throat. "You're right. Let's refine this stack to only the best."

We ended up staying in the romance aisle for almost an hour. I kept picking up books and explaining their tropes and basic plots. He flipped through each one, then he'd either shake his head and push it back on the shelf or add it to the pile.

Eventually, I started picking out my own books and handing them down to him from the ladder. "Keep the stacks separate!" I said anxiously whenever he put one of mine in the wrong pile.

"Why?" He leaned against the bookshelf behind him. Handsome men like Aiden should be *banned* from leaning. I didn't understand the science behind it, but it made him a million times hotter. "You know which ones you've read. This is just creating more work for me."

"Just do it."

He rolled his eyes and separated our books into two stacks.

When we were finished in the romance aisle, Aiden grabbed a basket and places our books in it. "My turn," he said.

He grabbed my hand and dragged me to the fiction section around the corner in the E-F-G aisle. It was different from all the other straight, narrow aisles. This aisle had a small alcove that Aiden and I could barely fit into. His hand had slipped so easily into mine, our fingers were now intertwined. I tried my best not to read into it and convinced myself this was just him being friendly. *Platonic.*

But Aiden didn't seem like the type of guy to hold a girl's hand through a bookstore if he didn't feel anything toward her.

Still, if this was all I ever got from Aiden, I'd be okay with that. Just sweaty palms pressed against each other and taking up too much space in the tight aisles of a bookstore. The line between reality and fiction was almost as big as the one between love and hate, but I was desperate to convince myself it was thinner. That this wasn't all in my head.

He was still holding my hand as he searched through the shelves. The aisle was so small that we had to stand chest to chest with our faces craned toward the shelves. I studied him as he scanned through the Fs, his brow furrowed.

"I'm not reading Faulkner, no matter how big your crush is on him," I said as his finger ran along the spines. He ignored me, deep in concentration.

"Aha." He pulled a thick book out of the shelf and turned to me with it. *As Best I Can* by Maggie Frantel. "This book is sad, but it's a little romantic too." He held the book out to me, and I regretted having to let go of his hand to take it.

"Are you kidding? I love Maggie Frantel," I said, flipping through the book. Everyone and their mother had heard of her. She had started off doing literary fiction tinted with romance, but over time she'd morphed into a Nora Roberts kind of writer. Under a pseudonym, she had churned out a mystery every year up until her death a few years before. The television adaptation of her Detective Pierre St. Clair books was currently the longest running series on ABC.

"*Down Your Block* is one of my favorite movies *ever*." I peered up at him. "I didn't think you'd like anything that has so much romance in it."

He shrugged, "These are my exception. Always."

"You know, I've never read this one. It was her debut, right? Didn't it win the National Book Award?"

He nodded. "About fifteen years ago. It's one of my favorites. You really get submerged in the main character's head." He continued on, talking about how the prose was beautiful without even trying and how, by the end of it, the book would be all I could think about. You could tell how much Aiden admired this writer. Even in class when he talked about his favorites, his eyes never quite lit up like this.

"Did you cry when you read it?" I asked.

"Yes," he said, unashamed.

"If I read this and I can't stop crying . . ."

"You can call me. Any time. And we'll talk about every detail," he promised.

"The same with your books." I nodded at the basket. "You'll cry tears of happiness at the Happily Ever Afters."

He smiled at that. "Oh, definitely."

We stood in the aisle, chest to chest, with no space for either of us to move. I was so *happy* to be in my favorite bookstore with someone who was slowly becoming my favorite person. I couldn't help my eyes flickering down briefly to his lips. And when I did, his eyes fell to mine, too. His head moved, just a centimeter closer to mine. No one would be able to see us if we did kiss, with my back pressed against the shelves, the alcove hiding me from the rest of the store.

But just as quickly as he'd moved toward me, he moved away and said, "C'mon, let's keep looking around."

"Sure," I said, trying to hide my disappointment. My heart was beating rapidly even *thinking* about what kissing Aiden would be like. I wanted to stay in this small aisle and learn exactly what it felt like when Aiden took what he wanted.

We spent nearly all day together at the Strand. We went to every floor and pointed out books we loved or ones we'd want to read. I could barely focus with Aiden's touch always finding me. His hand would linger on the small of my back when someone wanted to scoot past us, or it would fall on my shoulder when he wanted to point something out to me.

By the time we were ready to check out, the sun had begun to set.

"We need to go in there with a clear head," I said as we neared the line. "Oh shoot, I should probably move my money now."

"What're you talking about?"

"I swear the Strand line is the scariest one in all of Manhattan. Those booksellers will yell at you if you delay. They're *notoriously* grouchy. We've got to be focused while we're in line."

"No," he said. "I meant the part about moving money."

"Oh, I just need to figure out the tax for my books so I can make sure I have enough in my checking." I pulled out my phone and began crunching the numbers on my calculator. It wasn't like there was a *ton* of money in my savings. I never seemed to have enough money, but I always found the spare change I needed for books.

"Don't worry about it." He pushed my phone away. "I've got it."

He walked stepped in line and I followed quickly after him. "No way. You paid for my coffee—"

"That was just to piss you off."

"My ice cream, my dinner. I can't let you pay for all these books too." The line was moving rapidly and as soon as the bookseller called for the next person in line, Aiden moved toward the counter.

"Fine. Stop me."

"Fucker," I muttered. I started furiously typing on my phone as the cashier scanned our books. He had already stuck his card in the machine and as soon as I moved to pull it out, he plucked my own card from my hand. "Hey!"

He held the card above his head and even on my tiptoes, I couldn't reach him.

"This is ridiculous. We're *adults*, not in middle school. Give me my card back."

"Sure," he said calmly. "In a few minutes."

I glared up at him, even though I was secretly touched because book buying was basically one of my love languages. Aiden must've known how much this meant to me, especially in the midst of my money troubles.

Once Aiden had finished paying, he handed me back my card.

"You didn't have to do that."

"Funny. That doesn't sound like 'thank you,'" he said teasingly. He grabbed the bags from the cashier and carried them out of the store with me trailing behind.

We started walking, side by side down Broadway. "The Strand was the first place I came on my first day in New York, after I settled into my apartment," I said. I kicked the pebble in front of me with each step, my hands shoved in my pockets to protect them from the cold. "I would spend days there if I could."

"I used to go there as a kid. My mom took me nearly every day after school." He cleared his throat, shaking his head. "She'd let me wander up and down the stacks on every floor and let me pick three books. Always three."

"What was your go-to book as a kid? I know you had a comfort book." I nudged his shoulder.

"*Dear Mr. Henshaw* by Beverly Cleary."

I smiled at him. "Mine was *Stargirl* by Jerry Spinelli."

"Of course." He rolled his eyes but was smiling. "Small town girl who's different and finds love?"

"Boy who falls in love with reading and can't help but obsess over it."

"Boy without a dad who writes to his favorite author," he added quietly. "That's why I liked it so much. I could always relate to that kid."

"Soon enough you'll be Mr. Henshaw to some other kid," I said.

He smiled at that. "Hopefully."

"Speaking of," I said, checking the time on my phone. "I should probably head home to write the kiss scene *someone* slacked off on. I'm freaking out that we won't get these chapters done in time."

"You know," Aiden said sheepishly. It was the first time I had seen him be anything but positively confident. "I live close by—we could write it together." My eyes widened, excited and dumbstruck. When I didn't answer immediately, he said, "Obviously you don't have to if you're uncomfortable or don't want to—"

"No, I do!" I said quickly. "Lead the way."

He lived in the West Village on Perry Street and Bleecker, a small walk away from the Strand. As we neared his street, I was almost tempted to ask him to keep walking around. Tennessee sunsets were special, but a New York City one hit different. The light would bounce off a skyscraper and land between buildings in a beautiful way. But today I had a new appreciation for them, now that I'd seen the evening light dancing in Aiden's hair. His eyes. His smile.

I kept waiting for him to lead me into to some fancy apartment building, but when he stopped in front of a brownstone and jogged up the front steps, my jaw dropped. I glanced at the doorbell—there was just one, rather than a series of buzzers like most apartments had.

"What the shit? Is this *yours*?"

I was too stunned to move. I'd had a suspicion Aiden had money. I mean, he had paid for so many of my meals that I figured he was at least comfortable. But *this*? This was an anomaly. This was the holy grail of apartments—*houses*—in New York.

He walked down the few steps and grabbed my hand, interlacing our fingers. "C'mon, let's go in."

He dropped the bags instead of my hand to reach in his pocket for his keys, then he pushed the door open for me.

"Holy fuck, Aiden."

I'd been raised in the South, where we learned certain rules of hospitality. That meant waiting for your host to guide you into the living room and asking politely if you should take your shoes off. But all of that flew out the door when I walked into Aiden's apartment.

Past his foyer, the room split to a kitchen straight ahead and a living room to my left. I walked in, and if it was possible, my jaw dropped even further. There were floor to ceiling windows facing the streets, only covered by thin white curtains. Aiden had placed a small table and reclining chair near it; a stack of books rested on the table. At the center of the room, facing the wall with a TV mounted, was a large couch.

"I'll grab my laptop and we can start working. Make yourself at home," Aiden said, walking down a hallway.

Remembering myself, I toed my sneakers off and placed them near the door. I peeked into the kitchen to find it was just as spacious. An island sat between the stove and the dining room table, white granite covering it. But it wasn't one of those places where you were afraid to touch anything. There were splashes of color in the backdrops and plants and dish towels that made it feel homey.

I went back into the living room as I waited for Aiden, the rug under my feet incredibly soft. At the edge of the room near his reading nook were tall bookshelves, each one filled with books facing upright and pulled to the edge of the shelf. I ran my finger against the spines, reading all the different titles, and then I peered at his table—*Pride and Prejudice* was sitting at the top of the stack of books, a pen stuck in the middle as a bookmark.

The sun through the windows was fading fast. It cast a golden glow over the room, shadows emerging at nearly every corner.

Aiden came back with his laptop in hand, turning on a lamp. "I thought we could work on the couch? But if you want to work at the table—"

I shook my head. "The couch is perfect."

I sank into the cushions, and he sat carefully next to me, balancing his laptop on his thighs. Our knees were *this* close to touching. I'd never thought about hands or knees or collarbones this much in my life.

"So, are we going to talk about it?" I asked expectantly.

"About what?"

"About the fact that you're clearly a secret billionaire."

He smiled, opening the laptop. I don't think I would ever get used to the lines that formed on the sides of his face when he smiled.

"Secret billionaire is a *great* trope," I muttered to myself.

"What?" He side eyed me.

"Nothing," I waved him off. "So we're not going to address it?"

"We're not."

"C'mon." I knocked my shoulder with his. "Indulge me."

He hesitated. "Fine. But I don't want to talk about it afterward."

I saluted him. "Scout's honor."

He gestured to the Strand bag sitting in his foyer. "That book I gave you, the one by Maggie Frantel? That's my mom."

My chin jerked back, my mouth parting. "But your last name is Huntington."

"She wrote under her maiden name. She didn't want my dad's name to be associated with her work."

"Hold up hold up." I waved my hands to indicate I needed some more time to process this. "Maggie Frantel is your *mom*? Like *the* Maggie Frantel."

"Yes."

"Like the Maggie Frantel who basically had her own shelf in the Strand?"

His eyebrows flew up smiling. "I didn't know you were such a fan."

I shot him a look. "Everyone's read at least *one* of her books in their life . . . So *that's* where you got all this money?"

He sighed heavily, running a hand down his face. "It's complicated. She left me *everything* when she passed instead of her sisters because the only way I could inherit the trust fund from my dad was if I followed in his footsteps as the 'heir' to his company. I've been surviving off her money for years."

I was quiet for a moment. "I didn't know your mom passed."

"Almost seven years ago. My freshman year of college."

"I'm so sorry."

"I've learned to live with it. It's why I enrolled in the MFA program. She was depressed for a really long time after she left my dad, but writing saved her. She filled my childhood with literature and words flying around the house. All I've ever wanted was to follow in her footsteps so I took some classes in college, but then my dad started breathing down my neck about taking some finance position at his company. This program felt like the only way I could say 'I'm doing this, whether you like it or not.'"

"You're a great writer. I'm sure she'd be so proud of you, Aiden," I whispered.

He smiled slightly and said, "Thank you, Rosie." We held each other's gaze for a second. I wanted to climb into his mind and dig out everything he was hiding. I wanted to assure him that we were okay—that he could tell me these things without judgment and I'd be a friend, not the adversary I was in August.

His eyes didn't leave mine as he whispered, "We should probably . . ."

"Right! Right. Yes. The chapter." I snatched the laptop from him and skimmed through the ending of the last chapter. "You left them at a good place. They're at the company retreat, right?"

"In separate hotel rooms," he reminded me.

"If there's anything you can learn from being friends with me," I said, turning to him seriously, "it's that any moment can become a romantic moment."

"Bullshit."

I lifted my chin. "Try me."

He rubbed his hands together. "Alright, walking your dog."

I scoffed. "Oh, c'mon, give me a hard one at least. Picture this, you're walking your dog in the park—it runs off and what happens? You find it sniffing another dog's butt, but that dog's owner is the love of your life."

"Dinner with your mom." He held my gaze, raising his brows in a challenge.

"She sets you up with the server," I said with an easy shrug.

"Jury duty."

"He may be a murderer, but he has a really nice smile."

At that, Aiden burst out in laughter, his head tipping back. "I stand corrected."

"Let me get them together then I'll give the laptop back. I'll work my magic." I tried to crack my fingers, but nothing happened.

"Intimidating," Aiden muttered. "Do you want something to drink?"

"Ooh, do you have hot chocolate?"

He shook his head as he stood. "How does tea sound?"

"Not as good, but doable."

For the next few minutes, as Aiden clattered around in the kitchen and I typed, things felt . . . normal. I straightened at the idea. Could this ever be normal for us? A life where he's making tea and I'm sitting in the living room writing?

Snap out of it.

I needed to focus and write this kiss scene before I lost my mind. I couldn't keep doing this—setting myself up for disappointment and letting my naivety get the best of me.

"How're we doing?" he asked, setting a white mug on the coffee table in front of me—with, of course, a coaster underneath it. Steam was rising out of my mug, but Aiden had ice cold water in his glass.

"I made up a pretty good excuse for Max to go to Hunter's room," I informed him.

"What's that?"

I shrugged. "She missed him."

"What?"

"They've been spending a lot of time together, it's natural. She was going to eat dinner by herself, then she realized she missed him, so she went to his room."

"So, they're going to kiss at dinner?"

"Noooo," I dragged out. "They're not going to *make* it to dinner. They're gonna start talking and end up kissing."

"But—"

"Shh, you'll see." I tilted the screen of the laptop toward him so he could read as I continued to write.

"You missed me?" Hunter asked, incredulous.

"Don't act like you didn't miss me, too." I peered into his hotel room. *"You were going to eat dinner alone, weren't you?"*

He sighed. "Yes."

"Well, do you want to get dinner or not?"

"What if we ordered in?" I hesitated, but Hunter jumped back in. "You know everyone else here with us will be waiting for one of us to snap."

I shrugged and shoved past him into the room, plopping onto his bed and settling in. "Your bed is way comfier than mine."

His eyes darkened as I lay in his bed, but he quickly looked away. "I'll get something off UberEats."

Aiden eventually got into it and we started passing the laptop back and forth. We fell into a rhythm that was so natural, like we had been doing it for years. Sometimes he'd peer over my shoulder and suggest something, or I'd call out an idea as he typed. I knew exactly when he ran out of words, and he knew when I would take the characters too far too fast.

"Here we go," I muttered. I turned to him and pouted out a bottom lip. "Aw, your kiss scene virginity." I reached up to pinch his cheek, and he smacked my hand away.

"Just write." He pushed the laptop closer to me.

We faced each other on the bed, picking fries out of each other's boxes. Knee to knee, face to face.

"Can I ask you something?" I asked, popping a fry into my mouth.

He reached over, his hand brushing mine. "Shoot."

"Why do you hate me?"

"I don't hate you anymore." He frowned.

"Well, why did *you hate me?"*

Aiden took the laptop.

He hesitated, searching for the right words. "Do you remember your first day here?"

"Vaguely. There was a tour and lots of paperwork."

"Ivy introduced you to the team. After you left the room she said, 'That woman is optimistic to a fault.' I'm not like that. I'm brash and rude. And . . . even though I thought you were beautiful, I knew I wasn't what you needed. Or deserved, really. I figured I might as well keep my distance, but that became impossible. I lose sense of myself whenever I'm around you."

His hands were still on the keyboard when I took it from him.

"Ask me why I hated you when I first met you," I said.

"Why did you hate me when you first met me?"

"Because I thought you were the most handsome man I'd ever met, and you seemed to want nothing to do with me. And I wanted everything to do with you."

How had our faces gotten closer? How were our knees almost overlapping?

"Sounds like a lot of wasted time," he whispered. His breath fanned my face.

I looked over my shoulder to Aiden, who wasn't even watching the screen, he was watching me.

Our legs were pressed against each other as a result of me basically crawling over him to grab the laptop. When had our faces fallen so close together that our breath mingled? When did we start looking like Max and Hunter, yes, but Rosie and Aiden at the same time?

I cleared my throat, pulling my gaze away from his mouth. "We need to decide what kind of kiss scene we want."

"What're our options?" he whispered, his voice husky. I tried to ignore the shivers racing down my spine, but Aiden's voice was so low and his eyes were so intense. I was drunk on this moment, desperate to sip on it forever.

"Well," I started slowly. "There are the passionate kisses—you know, the ones you can't control. Where the characters just can't get enough of each other."

"Mhm." I could've drowned in the deep lull of his voice. My eyes fluttered without control, and I instinctively leaned closer to him.

"Or the slow ones. They're still passionate . . . uncontrolled. Unrestrained. But tentative."

"I see."

"It has to be well-written, too. Kisses are always better in books so we have to make the right choice about what kind of—"

"What did you say?" he interrupted me.

Our heads were tilted to each other, close but not close enough. I could see the curve of his mouth as it deepened into a frown.

"We have to pick the right—"

"No, about kisses being better in fiction."

"Oh." I blinked. "I mean, kisses *are* just better in books."

He gave me a bewildered look. "What're you talking about?"

"Kisses in romance novels are *world altering*. The characters see everything differently after, and they have this *spark*. In real life, kisses are just . . . wet."

His lips quirked before he swallowed and said slowly, "No. They're not."

"Yes. They are."

"If you think that, Rosie, then you haven't been kissed the way you should be. You haven't been kissed by someone who really *wants* you."

My eyes flickered from his eyes to his lips for a second, my chest rising up and down. When his nose nudged softly against mine, I fought to catch a single breath.

"Then show me," I whispered.

In an instant, his mouth covered mine. He decided what kiss we would have, but it wasn't any of the options I had listed. It was questioning and exploring, hungry and slow. His hand slipped underneath my jaw, tilting my mouth toward his. I arched up, pressing myself closer to him. His hand slid from my jaw, anchoring itself in my hair, a fist curling around my curls.

He nudged my mouth open and at the first slip of his tongue, I turned greedy. My hands curled into his T-shirt, wanting more of him. Obligingly, his other hand slid around my waist, his grip tight on my hip.

Aiden was right. He was *so* right. Kissing Aiden was nothing like any other kiss I'd experienced. I could feel my heart beating with every time his tongue swept over mine, and I didn't have to fake the moan that came when his teeth tugged on my bottom lip.

This was what it was like with someone who wanted me. This was better than any kiss I'd read.

A gasp here, a lick here. A smile there, a moan there. If I could die like this, my body turned uncomfortably on the couch, but Aiden's hands and lips on me, I wouldn't mind it one bit.

As if he could sense my slight discomfort, his hands moved down the curve of my body, landing on my waist. He lifted me onto his lap, my knees straddling him.

My hair fanned down, covering us, and I finally got my hands on him. Underneath me, I felt the proof that he wanted me as badly as I wanted him. His hands spanned across my hips, slowly moving me across his lap. I had spent too much time being distracted by the breadth of

Aiden's shoulders and the strain of his biceps against his shirt; I couldn't stop my hands from running over the rigid lines of his muscles.

Like always, this was a competition between us. He was experimenting, trying to figure out what would make me moan, sigh, or gasp. I was doing the same—occasionally, I got a sharp intake of breath or a sigh into my mouth. And now that I was on his lap, I had the upper hand. I ran my fingers up his neck to his hair, my fingers threading through the dark strands. When I tugged ever so lightly, I won with his low moan.

I took control and rolled my hips against his. His fingers tightened on my waist, and he tipped his head back, groaning. Still moving, I took advantage and ran kisses along the side of his jaw.

"God, Rosie, you feel so good," he murmured into my hair. "So good."

He opened his eyes and met my gaze. He smiled and something inside of me froze.

What was I doing? What was I risking? What would happen after we woke up tomorrow? We'd continue to write a romance novel where the characters don't end up together, then we'd do the same? Of course we would—Aiden had made it very clear he didn't like romance.

I couldn't do heartbreak again. I knew what would happen if I let us get carried away on this couch; I've seen this film before. It would end in a whole lot of nothing, I would let my unresolved feelings for Aiden fester in my head until they consumed me, and Aiden would never give me a second thought after we went our separate ways. Aiden wasn't the boyfriend type; he didn't value romance the way I did. If anything happened tonight, it'd be no skin off his back but it'd leave an open wound for me.

"I'm sorry," I stuttered. I moved off him, falling on my ass in the process. I scrambled up and Aiden followed suit.

"Rosie—"

"I've got to get home, I'm sorry." I stumbled into the foyer, slipping my shoes on. I whipped the door open and Aiden followed me out onto the stoop.

I turned around once I was on the street. Aiden stood in his doorway with swollen lips and mussed up hair, confused. I wished I could explain all the thoughts racing through my head, but nothing came out except "I'm sorry."

It may have lasted only a few minutes, but I'd remember every sigh and gasp she gave me for years to come.

In those few minutes, with her thighs parted and me in between them, I envisioned it all. I envisioned waking up and smiling down at her in my bed. I envisioned the moment I could finally tell her that I loved her and although I wasn't good enough to deserve it, I'd do all I could to get there. I'd wake up every day and figure out how to ensure she knew I valued her.

But perhaps I was too late.

— Excerpt from *Untitled* by
Rosie Maxwell and Aiden Huntington

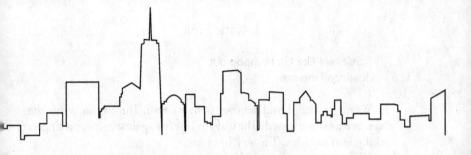

CHAPTER SIXTEEN

I woke up and stared at the ceiling for what felt like hours but what was probably twenty minutes. I pulled the blankets up to my chin and squeezed my eyes shut, replaying last night in my head a million times. I told him to kiss me, he gave me the best kiss of my life, and then I ran away. But I was right to stop it all. I mean who knows what would've happened if we kept going? Maybe a shirt would've come off and we would've made our way to his bed, and he would've—

I sat up, stopping the thoughts. Aiden and I were friends. *Finally.* There was too much to lose in the uncertainty of us.

I sent a quick text to Jess.

Rosie: sos.

She replied almost instantly.

Jess: what's up?
Rosie: you cant tell anyone
Jess: i won't is everything ok?
Rosie: aiden and i kissed last night.
Jess: YOU'RE JOKING. YOU'RE ACTUALLY JOKING.
Rosie: im not

Rosie: we like kinda made out
Jess: call me now

When I called, I told her every single detail. The way we wrote the kiss scene until we kissed. The way his lips felt against mine, his fingers sinking into my hips. The way I ran out.

"Wait, so was this a *good* kiss?"

I sat back against my headboard, groaning. "That's the worst part. It was hands down the best kiss of my life."

"No *way*. So why'd you run out? I don't get it."

"Because it's *Aiden*."

"Right."

"Like, it's *Aiden*."

Jess laughed softly. "It's Aiden who you haven't been able to stop talking about all year. Aiden who you allowed to become your friend without so much as an apology for how he treated you."

"I was mean to him, too," I said defensively.

"Aiden who you protect without a second thought."

"It's too complicated. Right?"

Jess sighed heavily. "I don't know, honestly. If he was just in the workshop, you know I'd say go for it the way you would tell me to with Tyler."

"But?" I prompted.

"But you two are writing a book together. It could get messy and complicated and put you in bad graces with Ida if this doesn't work out. You're already walking a thin line. What happens if you hook up, break up, and go back to fighting? She'll dismiss you both from class if you cross the line again."

I groaned again, smacking my head lightly against the headboard. "You're right. He's just so hot. I couldn't help it."

"It'll be okay. Just spend as little time with him as possible going forward."

"I can't do that," I moaned. "We're writing the romantic parts of our novel now. We have to write these mushy romantic scenes together—" I cut off when I realized the other end of the line had gone silent. "Jess?"

"I'm trying not to laugh." Her voice was wobbly. "You're fucked Rosie, good luck."

Later that afternoon as I approached the Writer's House, Aiden was leaning against the gate, holding two coffees. One iced, the other hot. His head was bent, chin pressed to his chest, and he was wearing his eternal scowl.

"Hey," I said once I got near him. His head snapped up and his face transformed from one of deep thought to deep concern.

"Hey." He straightened, looking down at me. He looked like he was afraid to say anything. Instead, he shoved the iced coffee toward me. "Vanilla latte with almond milk."

I nearly melted at the fact that he'd gotten my coffee order right, but I had to set the record straight with him. I took the cup from him, giving him a small grateful smile. "Thank you."

We went quiet again, looking anywhere but at each other.

Before we were friends, the hatred looming between us was a dark cloud that made every word we said venomous. But now there was something else. It wasn't dark, but it wasn't clear either. It hung in the air, daring one of us to speak and blow it away.

"Rosie, look, I'm really sorry about last night. I know it was late and you were tired, and I didn't mean to take advantage—"

"You didn't take *advantage* of me." I blanched, semimortified.

"Then I didn't mean to take it too far too fast, if you're not—"

"Let's just forget about it." The words left my mouth before I could think better of them.

His eyebrows drew together, confusion the clearest emotion on his face. "Forget?"

"It was for the book, right? I mean we just got caught up in the moment."

Aiden's green eyes searched my face, and I tried to remain impassive. I tried not to let it show how much I wanted to return to his apartment—the place that had quickly become a safe haven for us to want each other.

"Are you serious?" he asked quietly.

"Let's just forget about it," I repeated. We were still at a point of return, but if we had gone further? I would've confessed I'd started to have feelings for him, and he'd tell me he "wasn't looking for anything serious." It was better to salvage what little of our friendship I could before we got to that point.

Disappointment flashed over his face before he quickly rearranged his expression into a neutral one. He straightened and gave me a curt nod. "Fine. Forgotten." Then he turned on his heel and walked into the building without me.

"Oh, I'm sure this'll be fun," I muttered, following him in.

As the class settled in, I tried to catch his eye, but he wouldn't meet my gaze. He laid his notebook out on the table very carefully. He folded his hands over it, and it looked like he was zoning out, staring at the wall.

Jess caught my eye and tilted her head. She widened her eyes at Aiden and mouthed, *What's up?*

I made sure Aiden wasn't looking before I mouthed back, *I'm an idiot.*

I still wanted the truce. I wanted to be friends with him. But I also wanted . . . *him.* I was petrified of the way my heart hadn't calmed down until I finally fell asleep last night. I hadn't felt this way with anyone before, and I figured if I didn't allow myself to claim it, I wouldn't have to have it snatched it away from me.

And Jess was right. There was so much riding on our successful coauthorship. I was too scared to throw it all away.

It was our last workshop before the end of the week, when our midterm was due. After that, we had a month break. Hopefully by the time we returned in January, I could sit across Aiden without hearing *"You feel so good, Rosie"* on repeat in my head.

"Let's start with my favorite writing duo," Ida said from the front of the class. "Aiden and Rosie, who's first today?"

"I am," Aiden spoke up. He read his chapter aloud. In the lead up to the kiss, the tension between Max and Hunter was impenetrable. They were longing for each other but didn't know how to move forward.

When he finished, Ida turned to me. I read our kiss scene out loud. I'd finished it when I got home from Aiden's. It was the easiest kiss scene I'd ever written because Aiden was a *really* good kisser. I didn't have to think about the mechanics of hand placements or try to conjure words to describe how good the kiss felt. It was sweeter than any fiction I had read.

As it started to heat up, I couldn't stop the blush that rose to my cheeks. I had to remind myself that only Jess knew the truth even though it felt like the entire workshop had read my diary.

If only I had put in my chapter that Max was desperate to hold onto little pieces of Hunter, but she was scared that they'd be sharp and leave an unmendable wound.

When I finished, Ida was smiling. "Let's start with what's working."

Logan's hand went up first. I shot Jess a nervous glance because Logan loved to tease me about Aiden and no doubt he would take this opportunity.

"That kiss scene was hot," he started. Jess jabbed him with her elbow. "Ow. It *was*. Rosie, I think you did a great job of really conveying the urgency both of them felt in that moment, and I think that's due to how Aiden sets you up for it. It felt so realistic, like it really happened and—Jess, knock it off."

"Oops my bad," she muttered.

We went around the workshop table; the consensus was that these were our best chapters yet.

"It breaks my heart knowing they won't get the Happily Ever After," Ida said. "But I'm excited to see what you do with it. Let's move on to what's not working."

We had a few comments about sensory details and amplifying the setting, but mostly our classmates didn't have much to say. Aiden's expression remained impenetrable—he didn't smile once at the nice comments and apparently couldn't care less about the bad ones, like this was all beneath him. Anger rose in my chest and, just like it had throughout the rest of the year, it spread through my body.

"Alright, great work you two. I think we're ready to move on to Tyler's piece?"

Aiden raised his hand. "I actually didn't have a chance to share my critiques with Rosie."

"Oh." Ida was pleased, obviously thinking he was going to say nice things like he had earlier. But, I was too familiar with that look in his eye and what it meant for me. "Sure, by all means."

He picked up my chapter and started flipping through it. "This kiss scene was okay in my opinion. I thought Max and Hunter were lacking a chemistry that we've been building up to this whole time—"

"Is that so?" I muttered.

"Sorry, what was that?" I looked up and he was staring me dead in the eye for the first time.

"Just keep going," I snapped.

"It's frankly unrealistic that the two of them would be so okay with all of this after years of hating each other. They're willing to put that all away?"

Ida hummed, her gaze shifting between the two of us.

"It seems more likely that one of them would shy away from all of this. Or even run away."

"I agree," I said, looking him in the eye. "I think Max wouldn't want to ruin what she has with Hunter. You know, the newfound friendship."

He tilted his head. "She may even want to 'forget it,' right? I wouldn't be surprised if she was playing with his emotions."

I scoffed. "As if she could do that. For that to happen, Hunter would have to *have* emotions."

"Really?"

"And you know, I bet his ego may be a little bruised after this, so maybe *he's* the one that runs away. Save him some humiliation."

"Perfect." Aiden threw the papers down. "So we're agreed, in the next few chapters Hunter and Maxine will no longer be friends."

"Or anything that resembles lovers. You can have your sad ending."

"I'm not sure I'm the only one who wants it."

The class was watching us go back and forth. Plenty of people were whispering between each other, their brows furrowed in confusion. But Aiden and I glowered at each other from across the table.

He always had to do this. He had to win, and he had to do it by embarrassing me in the process.

"Alright," Ida said carefully. "Why don't we move on? Aiden and Rosie, you can discuss this outside of class."

I glared at Aiden, but he looked away from me. For as much as I wanted him, I couldn't *stand* him. He was so determined to not let anyone in, he didn't understand that some people *wanted* to go past his walls. For the first time in his life, he hadn't gotten what he wanted and now he was throwing a temper tantrum.

I tried to pay attention to the rest of class and give critiques to my classmates, but every so often my eyes would flicker back to him.

Once, I caught his gaze before he quickly looked away. My chest grew tighter at the thought of all I'd ruined.

Once we were dismissed for winter break, Aiden quickly left our classroom, but I followed him onto the street. The harsh chill hit me extra hard since I hadn't taken my time wrapping myself in my scarf and gloves like usual.

"Aiden," I called after him once we were on the street, but he kept walking. I repeated his name louder, but the jerk pretended not to hear me. "You are such a *jackass*!" I shouted. People turned to look at me, especially our classmates who were lingering outside of the building. With his back still turned to me, he paused. Then he carefully and slowly turned around.

"I know you weren't speaking to me." His words were impatient, like he didn't even want to waste a breath on me.

"What the hell was that in there?" I demanded. "You did that to embarrass me."

"No, I didn't." His face was hard, his eyes stormy. He clenched his jaw, ticking it back and forth.

"Yes, you did!"

"Rosalinda, I'm not going to do this with you. Stop."

"Or what? You're gonna write about it in the next chapter? Then critique my response in class?" I taunted.

His eyes narrowed a fraction. "This is about Max and Hunter. What they do has nothing to do with us—"

"*Bullshit*. You're just mad about last night."

His head tilted to the side. "Now what happened last night?"

My chest was rising up and down, anger boiling inside of me threatening to spill over. He wanted a reaction, like always. I wanted to call him a child and scream at him until his ears bled. But he just stood there, perfectly still, unbothered. The cold look in his eye worse than any wind of the city. This person was so different from my Aiden from last night. I didn't know what to do to bring him back to me.

"Aiden, I like being your friend so much more than this," I said angrily. I wanted to avoid getting hurt, but it seemed as if that was my only option with Aiden. "I don't want to fight with you again. That wasn't what I meant."

His head turned away from me toward the traffic. It was rush hour, and we were being the type of assholes that stood in the middle of the sidewalk. New Yorkers shoved past us, uncaring about our drama.

He spoke in a low voice, his eyes deadly. "I'm not looking for friendship from someone who'd rather live in a world inside her head. You can't write me into one of your heroes like you tried to with Simon. Grow up and stop thinking life is a romance novel. It *isn't*."

I wasn't sure if it was the sound of the traffic or the heartbeat pulsing in my ears that brought on the headache, making tears spring at the back of my eyes. But I wouldn't ever give Aiden the satisfaction of seeing them fall.

"That was a low fucking blow," I said, my voice wobbling. "I guess I was right about you in the first place."

When the tears began to pool, something washed over Aiden's face. He stepped toward me, but I had already turned around for the train station, glad I wouldn't have to see him for a month.

WINTER

"I'm sorry," I said, meaning every word. If I had an ounce of courage, I would look Maxine in the eye and tell her how wonderful I thought she was. How I wanted to pick her brain and find a way to weave myself into her thoughts.

But I wasn't brave. I was a coward, unsure how to apologize to someone who meant more to me than even I'd realized. If only I could tell her how it tore me up, knowing I was the reason she had shed tears. I was drenched in regret, stuck replaying the way her lips felt against mine for the rest of my life. I knew I'd compare the feel of every woman to the small sliver of skin I felt on her waist.

Words were the deadliest weapons Max and I had. We learned how to sharpen them and wield them with extreme efficiency. And when it was time to strike, we did it to kill. But I don't think either of us realized how deep the wounds were until the knife had already been dug in.

"Forgive me." I apologized because I'd been the one to dig the knife in too deep. I apologized because I couldn't stand the idea of causing her pain. I apologized because I missed her, more than anything.

— Excerpt from Untitled by
Rosie Maxwell and Aiden Huntington

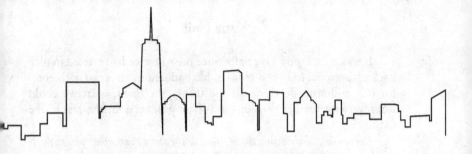

CHAPTER SEVENTEEN

Aiden and I had barely spoken in almost two weeks. Okay, *technically* we had, through Max and Hunter. He apologized and I accepted it for the sake of the story:

"I can't hate you anymore," I said quietly. "We're too far gone for that. I don't want to go back to where we were."

"We won't," Hunter replied immediately. "I promise, I won't let you down again."

But I'd be lying if I said his words didn't echo in my head. If it didn't change the way I thought about him as he carved out all my insecurities and laid them out between us. Still, I knew I'd miss him too much to stay mad for long.

It had no consequence on our real lives. I hadn't seen him since our last class. I'd thought it would be easier this way, but the radio silence between us was so much worse than us being outwardly angry with each other. I missed his assholery.

It was quiet in my apartment; the only sound was the Christmas music playing softly on my phone. Christmas Eve was in a few days, and Alexa had gone home for break, so I had the place to myself.

I had nothing better to do than spend the holiday working ahead in our book. Aiden must've had the same thought because every so often, he'd text me: *Chapter's done.*

It was pure agony, especially since the romance had started to pick back up between Max and Hunter. Ida had sent us an email with notes for our midterm, detailing all the things she liked, what we could improve with further revision, and some guidance for the rest of the manuscript:

I'm sensing there's something more to the story than what you're writing here, which is fine so long as it doesn't interfere with the class environment. However, you two are meant to be writing a love story and although there is often conflict in a love story, Max and Hunter have to be together for at least a brief period of time before you take it away from the reader. It'll make the lack of HEA all the more painful.

So, reluctantly, we'd made them get back together.

Even though I had technically forgiven Aiden through Maxine, I was still upset over what he had said. I don't know if my heart could survive another break, but part of me wanted to risk it with Aiden.

And given our recent falling out, I still hadn't asked Aiden to read my litmag piece. Once he did—*if* he did—and he gave me notes, I would submit it. It wasn't due until the end of January anyway. But I knew Aiden would tell it to me straight. He would tell me if it was horrible, and I shouldn't even bother submitting. Or he would tell me what to fix so I had a better chance of getting accepted.

As I reread through my short story for the millionth time, my phone pinged with a message from Aiden telling me the next chapter was done. I switched tabs on my laptop and began scrolling through the chapter before straightening.

As my lips pressed against hers, I felt her shudder against me. I clutched her waist, pulling her closer to me, even though close would never be close enough. I savored the taste of her, sweet and perfect. I wanted more.

One hand slid up to her jaw, pressing at the side until she opened her mouth for me. Her tongue slid against mine, and I couldn't hold back my low groan.

The chapter had taken Aiden's kiss scene virginity. And it was *hot*. He must've been reading those romances he bought at the Strand. He had Max on top of Hunter, running her fingers through his hair. I had to walk away from it once Hunter started whispering dirty things in Max's ear because all I could hear was Aiden saying, "God, Rosie, you feel so good" over and over.

I expected the kiss to progress into a steamy scene, but Aiden had cut the chapter off, leaving it to me.

"No way," I muttered, slamming my laptop closed. "He can't do this."

He'd put me in a position where if we wanted to include a sex scene, then *I'd* have to be the one to write it. There's nothing wrong with a closed-door romance, but I preferred it when the door was taken off the hinges. He knew as much. There was no way that I was going to be forced to write a full sex scene while he got away with just a measly kiss.

I snatched my phone from my nightstand, settling against my headboard. Before I could think better of it, I called Aiden.

"Rosie?" he answered.

"You can't end the chapter like that."

"Why not?"

"Because I thought we agreed there would be a sex scene—"

"*You* agreed."

"—and I'm not going to write it."

I could barely look him in the eye now. My face would be on fire every time I spoke to him knowing he'd read words I'd written like "slick" and "hardness." The reasons sex scenes were so good in romance novels was because the characters were vulnerable, but safe with their love interest. No fucking way was I being vulnerable by myself over here.

He scoffed. "Why should I be the one to write it? You're the one who reads them religiously."

"I know you're trying to insult me, but I'm not ashamed of that," I snapped.

"Just write it, Rosalinda," he snapped back.

"No way." I couldn't help the flush that took over my whole body at the idea of writing a sex scene for Aiden to read. "You were setting them up for it. You write it."

"Wouldn't the reader rather hear it from Max's perspective?"

"Uh, no. Hunter's point of view can be equally hot."

He sighed dramatically. I could see it now. Aiden was probably sitting in a swiveling desk chair in his big office in his big expensive apartment. He was probably rubbing his temples, grimacing. He'd done that a lot during our first semester together.

"You're not going to make me write this by myself," I said.

There was silence on the other end for a moment.

"So, what then?" he said, his voice softening into curiosity. "You want to write it together?"

"Please. As if you'd ever agree to that," I huffed.

A beat passed. "You're on."

I looked down at my phone, shocked. We'd written online together before, but a *sex* scene? I'd just been provoking him—I hadn't thought he'd *agree*. I was mostly hoping he'd write it on his own, but I couldn't back out now.

"Fine." I put my phone on speaker then reopened my laptop to our document. Aiden's icon was now in the corner. "You first."

"No way. I wrote the last chapter. You start us off, Rosalinda."

I curled my fingers in my hands, hesitating over the keyboard. I gathered all the courage Aiden didn't have, closed my eyes, and began to type.

I'd wanted this longer than I ever really knew. Maybe from the moment I met him. And here he was, hands on my hips, mouth on mine. I couldn't believe I finally had him.

"Go," I said. It took a minute for him to start typing. As I waited, I heard the creaking of a chair, and the soft clicking of his keyboard.

"I want you on the bed," he said, his breath ragged. His hands drifted up to the zipper at the side of my dress and tugged it down, the sound filling the room. "Now."

His hands were shaking slightly, like he couldn't control himself but was trying to. He slipped my dress over my head and pushed me gently on my back, his gaze darkening as it roamed over my body. As I watched, he stripped off his shirt and dress pants before settling between my thighs.

He cleared his throat. "Your turn."

Of course I'd thought about what Hunter looked like under his button up shirts. But nothing I'd dreamt about compared to the reality. My hands flew to his back, desperate to feel his muscles work under my palms. He planted kisses up the side of my neck, until he reached behind my ear. He kissed the same spot over and over until I couldn't take it. With a gasp, I tried to push his briefs off, but he brushed my hands aside, chuckling. "Eager?"

"Shut up," I said, breathless, finding his mouth.

Nothing was as sweet as kissing Hunter. No one had ever kissed me with such urgency and tenderness, like they were bordering on the line of self-control. His tongue slipped against mine, his hands sliding up the side of my body. He reached behind me to unhook my bra and tossed it off.

To my surprise, Aiden interrupted. "My turn." I'd expected him to drag his feet and to have to force him to write a few words. Not for him to be so eager to jump in. I shifted my legs underneath my laptop, feeling a little breathless with anticipation.

"I knew you'd be this perfect in real life," he said. His eyes drifted back up to mine, studying me as they went, as if they were trying to memorize every detail about this moment. His mouth covered mine again as his hand moved down to slide his thumb across my nipple. I hissed out a breath, slightly arching my back at the sensation.

"Real life?" I asked.

"Don't act like you haven't been the star of every one of my fantasies," he said with a wry smile.

"Really?" I asked, a tinge hopeful.

"Really. I've wanted you exactly like this for so long. Longer than you know," he murmured against my mouth, his voice rumbling.

"I'll go," I said quickly, before he could start typing. I vaguely wondered if he could hear my breaths coming faster as my chest rose up and down. My eyes were glued to my screen, hanging onto Aiden's every word, and I could only hope he felt a fraction of what I was feeling right now.

His eyes stared down at me, intense. "Do you ever think about me?" he asked.

"All the time," I whispered. "When I'm in the shower. When I'm lying in my bed all alone."

"Fuck," he bit out, pressing his mouth back to mine. He cradled my jaw in his hand, pulling me up toward him. He pulled back for a second, licking his thumb and index finger before coming back to me.

His wet fingers found my nipple, pinching, pulling, sending heat right down to my core.

"Oh fuck, Hunter, if you keep doing that—"

"My turn," he rasped. I pressed my thighs together, trying to relieve the pressure. I wasn't sure if I was more turned on by his words or the image of him sitting and writing, slowly losing control like I was.

"What? You'll come for me just like I want you to?" His gaze had shifted down to my breasts, watching me writhe against his fingers. Then his mouth moved down my chest until his mouth covered my nipple, taking it between his teeth.

"My turn." I tried to control my breathing. Part of me registered that maybe I should be embarrassed, but my mind was clouded with images of Aiden. My thighs pressed together under the laptop, wishing I could hang up the phone and close my laptop so I could be alone and get rid of this ache.

I nodded, already so close to the edge that I could taste it. I closed my eyes, letting the pleasure wash over me—

—when he yanked his hands and mouth away. He took my hand that was curled in the sheets and guided it down my stomach to the top of my panties. "Show me what you do when you think of me."

I slid just the tips of my fingers into my panties, teasing myself, looking up at Hunter through my lashes. "Do you want to hear what I think about, too?"

He was sitting back on his heels now, rubbing his length through his briefs. His jaw clicked, then he nodded.

"My go-to fantasy," I whispered, slipping my hand fully into my panties, feeling the slick between my legs. "Is in our office. I say something rude, and you say something just as rude back. Finally you've had enough of me and grab my arm."

I gasped when my fingers reached my sensitive bud. I teased the area around it, not yet ready to give myself that pleasure.

"I want these off," he said through gritted teeth, tugging at the fabric at my hips. I lifted my hips in time and in one quick move, I was fully bare in front of him. His eyes narrowed on my hand and he gritted, "Spread your legs."

I eased my thighs apart as I teased myself. "You pull me out of my chair, your jaw tense and eyes blazing like they are now." I gave in and circled my clit just once. "Fuck," I sighed.

His hand slipped into his briefs, and he shuddered at the first stroke.

"You say, 'I'm tired of that mouth of yours.' I pout, and you aren't able to take your gaze away from my mouth. Then I lick my lips and you inhale

sharply. I lean in closely and say, 'This mouth can do other things besides talk.' Your eyes don't widen—you aren't even surprised. They just darken, completely focusing on my lips. Then you say, 'Well, get to work.'"

I slipped one finger in and closed my eyes, crying out. It felt so different with someone watching you, wanting you. I rocked slowly against my hand, keeping a taunting pace, the heel of my palm firmly pressed against my clit. All of the pent-up aggression and lust for Hunter only made me want him more. I battled between opening my eyes to confirm he was still there and keeping them screwed shut from pleasure.

"You're so fucking hot, Maxine. Some days I can't take it."

"Always with the Maxine, even now." My eyes flashed open this time, watching his hand massage his length. I curled my finger, and closed my eyes, whimpering.

"I know your little fantasy's not done," he urged.

"I sink to my knees. Your eyes don't leave mine as I slowly undo your belt and pull down your zipper. I pull you out and run my mouth over you—" I gasped, not being able to bite the last words out. I slipped another finger in, speeding up. "I'm close."

He pulled my hands from me. "When you come, it's going to be all over my cock, not on your fingers."

Hunter took the fingers I just had inside me and lifted them to see them in the dim lamp light. He watched as they glistened, rotating my wrist. Slowly, he took them in his mouth and swirled his tongue around them, tasting me. His eyes never left mine. "Exactly how I imagined, baby."

"Fuck me," I breathed. I was desperate to come now that I had gotten close twice. I reached forward and pulled his briefs down. His hard cock laid against his stomach, and I couldn't help it.

I leaned forward, swirling my tongue around the tip. He hissed. When I took more of him in my mouth, his fingers curled in my hair.

"You feel so good, Max. So good."

My fingers froze over the board. Those words had been on a loop in my mind ever since I left Aiden's place.

That had to be on purpose, right? I would be lying if I said I wasn't imagining Aiden as Hunter. But was he imagining me as Max? His end of the call was as silent as mine. I only heard occasional typing, so he must've heard my hesitation. Quickly, I began again.

I looked up at him through my lashes, reaching the base of him.

"Yeah, just like that," he said. Carefully, he moved my head up and down. When I nodded and he felt no resistance, he moved faster, harder, harsher.

He groaned and hissed as if I was hurting him, but I knew from the look in his eyes he was in total bliss. Aiden's eyes were burning with—

Oh fuck. FUCK. I immediately erased his name and replaced it with Hunter's. Fuck fuck fuck. My cheeks flamed as I thought of a million ways to move out of the country with no notice.

"Sorry," I rushed. I smacked my palm against my head, mortified, my eyes squeezed shut. "I didn't—"

"It's okay," he said, his voice thick. "Keep going."

I took a deep breath, wishing I could just disappear off the face of the Earth. But I wasn't done with this scene, and I craved more of his words.

His eyes were burning as he watched me. I couldn't tear my eyes away from him as I moved my tongue around his head. When I moaned just a little, his hips thrust forward. But suddenly, he grabbed my shoulders, pulling me up.

"I don't want to come in your mouth," he said. "I want to come in that pretty little pussy of yours."

He pushed me back onto the bed, his mouth seeking out mine, urgent. He settled between my legs, his hands gripping my hips, rubbing himself against me.

Eventually, he leaned back on his knees, admiring the heat between my legs. My thighs were slick with arousal.

"I have an IUD. I got tested a few months ago and haven't been with anyone since . . ." I whispered.

"Me, too. Whatever you want, Max, I can grab a condom—"

"No," I said immediately. "I want to feel you."

Once, twice, three times he slapped his cock against my clit. "Are you sure you're okay with this?" he asked.

I pulled him back down toward me, answering with a kiss. His lips moved slowly against mine, changing the pace completely. "I've wanted you for so long."

"I've wanted you the whole time," he said against my lips.

I leaned back to look him directly in the eye. "Really?"

"The minute you walked in with your sweet southern smile. I was a goner when that smile was aimed at me."

"Do you really mean that?"

I was asking as Rosie now. Surely he was caught up in the scene, and I was just reading into it. But Maxine wasn't from the south. Both of them had been born and raised in California; it was a strategic plot point for us.

"The whole time," he promised, leaning down for a kiss.

I gasped when he finally, finally entered me. I stretched slowly around him, feeling just a hint of pain at his size. Desperate whimpers escaped me the more he moved.

"Hunter," I gasped, my head falling back onto his pillow.

He paused for a moment, letting me adjust. "Can you take more?"

I nodded, desperate for him to keep moving. Slowly, he pushed further inside me and when his hips settled against mine, I cried out in relief, biting my lip. I reached for his shoulders, my hands running up the landscape of his body until they settled around his neck.

He smiled down at me. His hand caressed my cheek, holding my head so gently.

I turned my face into his palm, kissing it.

"Hi."

"Hi." I smiled. Slowly, he began to move his hips. I gasped, clutching at his shoulders. He started slowly, but eventually we built to something so much greater. "More," I begged.

"You're doing so good, baby," he said, still holding my cheek with one hand, his other falling down to rub my clit in circles.

"Please."

Both Aiden and I were breathing heavily now. Our fingers were moving rapidly across our keyboards. Heat was rising to my cheeks. It was a mix of sexy and pure mortification writing this with Aiden.

"I'll give you anything you want," he said, groaning. "Anything you want. You want me to smile? I'll never stop. You want me to go harder, faster? I'll exhaust myself. Just for you." His hips moved faster, and I writhed underneath him, gripping him hard. My hips bucked up to meet his, seeking more and more from him.

I pulled him closer to me. I needed all of him, every part of him touching me. His face fell into my neck, kissing behind my ear.

I felt his breath hot on my skin. "Are you close?"

"Uh-huh." I nodded, my eyes squeezing shut.

"*Look at you, writhing on my cock. Fuck,*" *he bit out, moving* *faster.* "*You're so fucking tight.*"

My head fell back onto the pillow, my hips twisting. "*Oh God, Hunter. I can't take it.*"

"*You're taking it right now. Every inch of my cock, baby,*" *he* *repeated. I squeezed down on him, and he drove his hips forward, groaning.* "*You're so fucking sexy, Max. I'm losing my mind over here trying not to come.*"

"*Fuck,*" *I whimpered.* "*Hunter, I'm gonna—*"

"*Come for me.*" *He rose up and watched me as we moved* *together.* "*Come on baby, come. Come for me.*"

Pleasure wracked my body, my legs shaking. Hunter's movements quickened, the strength of them nearly pushing me further up the bed. With a jerk of his hips, he groaned as he spilled into me.

He collapsed on top of me, pushing my sweaty hair away from my forehead. I could tell it was on the tip of his tongue. Everything we meant to each other, ready to burst from him.

He wasn't ready to say it, though, and I wasn't ready to hear it. **But I knew I wanted this—and so much more—with him.**

I wanted Sunday brunches.

Lazy Saturdays.

Writing together in a living room.

Shopping at bookstores and kissing in between the stacks.

But I didn't know how to say it. So, I reached up and pressed a soft kiss against his mouth, wishing he could tell all that I meant by it.

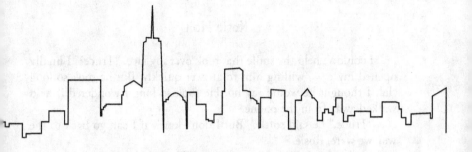

CHAPTER EIGHTEEN

"Are you still there?" I asked quietly.

"I'm here." He sounded breathless, his voice rough.

"That was . . ." I paused searching for the right word. "Good. That was good. We did a good job."

He laughed softly. "We did."

A silence blanketed over us. I was desperate to break the awkwardness of the call, but I was too scared. We had just crossed a million lines in less than an hour. I tried to calm my still beating heart, but the scene we had written was playing in technicolor in my mind. I shivered, wishing Aiden were here, next to me.

I picked my phone up from my bed carefully, lying back and placing it on my chest.

"Aiden?"

"Yeah?"

"I don't want to fight with you anymore." My eyes were squeezed shut, ready to block out the world in case this didn't go as planned. "We don't have to be friends if you don't want, but I'm tired of fighting with you."

"Me too," he confessed. "Fighting with you isn't as fun as it used to be." He hesitated. "I miss you."

"You miss me?" My heart leapt, hope blossoming.

"Don't let it go to your head."

I couldn't help the smile that took over my face. "Truce?" I finally opened my eyes, willing him to answer quickly. But he took so long that I thought he would say no. He took so long I wondered if he'd walked away from the phone.

"Truce," he said softly. "But I don't know if I can go back to the way we were, Rosie."

My head jerked back in surprise. "Why not?"

"It's complicated. I think we're better for each other at a distance."

"Oh. Okay." I tried not to let him hear the disappointment in my voice. I wanted more—I wanted everything we'd written, and I wanted it to be us. "I'll work on the next chapter and send it to you."

I tossed the phone on my bed and flopped back onto my pillow. Blindly, I reached for my other pillow and stuffed it over my head, screaming into it. All of this would've been avoided if I kept my hands to myself. If I'd let my romantic fantasies stay fantasies.

Aiden was right, though—I did live in a world inside my head. But it was because I liked it so much better. In my made-up world, I was everything my soulmate wanted, and my soulmate was real. He existed and he was waiting for me and he loved me—flaws and all.

I sat up and reached for my laptop, torturing myself by reading my short story another time.

"What if we don't feel the same tomorrow?" I whispered. Hunter and I were lying face to face, the sheets bunched around our waists.

"I will." He brushed a lock of hair behind my ear. His finger continued to trace my jaw, then my chin, then back up to my lips. His thumb brushed over my bottom one, pulling it apart from the top.

"How can you be so sure?"

"Because." He shifted onto his elbow smiling down at me. *"I've always felt this way, Max. There hasn't been a second where I wasn't wondering what you were thinking and if it was of me. I'll feel this way tomorrow, the day after, and all the days after that."*

— Excerpt from *Untitled* by
Rosie Maxwell and Aiden Huntington

CHAPTER NINETEEN

It was Christmas Eve and I was alone. I tried to not let it get to me. I put on a Christmas movie as I brushed my teeth and made breakfast, trying to get into the spirt, but it just made me feel more pitiful.

Back home, my mom would wake us up early with "Ay, Ay, Ay, It's Christmas" by Ricky Martin and make us peel potatoes and shell hard-boiled eggs. My sister and I would be covered in food by noon and if we'd complain, then my mom would just point at the Christmas tree with all our presents lovingly wrapped underneath it. Then my tíos and tías would come over with their families for dinner—which would last for hours, everyone filling our house with chatter and laughter. My Tío Alejandro would get too drunk, and my dad would try not to roll his eyes and when he inevitably did, my mom would elbow him. Then when midnight would hit, we'd open all of our gifts and dance and talk until three in the morning.

It was so quiet now, though. I moved gingerly as if, if I made even the smallest noise, I'd disturb the roaches lurking in the corners of my apartment.

It was nearly noon. I'd spent the morning writing chapters and going over my fellowship application yet again. It was *Christmas*. In *New York*. It felt anti-Christmas to stay indoors all day.

I knew Jess was going home, but I couldn't remember when. And maybe Tyler and Logan were still here? I pulled out my phone and texted our group chat (which had been renamed to *ho ho hoes*)

> **Rosie:** anyone still in the city? i was thinking of hitting up rocke-feller to see the tree?? maybe hot cocoa at central park
> **Jess:** my flight leaves today i'm on my way to JFK:(
> **Tyler:** I've been home since last week. Sorry.
> **Logan:** on a train to Westchester but i'll get hot cocoa w u when i get back tho!!!

I groaned, tossing my phone on the couch next to me and picking up my laptop again. I was working chapters ahead of Aiden at this point. We were supposed to alternate chapters but I went ahead and wrote three consecutive ones. It's not like I had anything better to do, and I figured it was best to churn it out while the words flowed freely. When I finally reached a good stopping point, I texted Aiden absent-mindedly that I had finished, like I always did.

I was queuing up *Frosty the Snowman* when my phone rang. It was *Aiden's* name flashing across the screen. I tossed my phone away from me, unsure what to do. But it kept ringing and ringing. Finally the ringing stopped—only to start up again when he called right back. I snatched it up quickly, contemplating for a moment before clicking the green button. "Aiden?"

"Why are you doing homework on Christmas Eve?" he asked, worry tinting his voice.

"Hi, hello. How are you?" I said pointedly. "Merry Christmas."

"Answer my question."

"I already told you. I'm doing nothing for Christmas. *These* are my Christmas plans."

The other line was quiet for so long that I pulled my phone away from my ear just to check if he'd hung up. He hadn't. Well, in for a penny, in for a dime. I already had Aiden on the phone, so I mustered up some courage and said, "Aiden, you know I've been meaning to ask you something." I sucked in a breath. "Remember how I told you I was applying for the Frost Fellowship?"

He was quiet for a moment. "Yes, I remember."

"Would you look over my submission?"

"*What?*"

"Will you look over my submission?" I pulled the doc up on my computer. "It's due in a couple weeks, and I really want to be selected this year. I've been working like crazy on my piece. And I know you'll tell me if what I've written is shitty or not, and I trust your judgment since we're quasi-friends now and—"

"Rosie, it's Christmas Eve," he interrupted.

"Well you don't have to read it *tonight.*"

He exhaled sharply and said, "No, that's not what I meant. Of course I'll look at it . . . but you shouldn't be working on Christmas Eve." He paused for a second and said, "Meet me in Union Square."

My head jerked back. "What? Now?"

"Yes."

My heart was beating with so much hope that I didn't allow myself to believe it. "Aiden, I'm not going to force you to—"

"You're not forcing me. I'm asking you."

"But you said you wanted us to keep some distance . . ." I was pushing him, I knew that. Aiden giveth and Aiden taketh away. But I was confused. I'd rather spend Christmas Eve by myself than with someone who didn't really want to be with me.

"I know, I know. I was wrong, Rosie, I shouldn't have said that." He sighed, and it sounded a lot like he was letting go of something that had been weighing him down. "Rosie. Will you go to Union Square with me?"

I smiled, pressing my ear closer to my phone as if that would somehow get me closer to Aiden. "I can be there in an hour."

"I'll see you then."

The minute he hung up, I raced around my apartment. After I showered and dried my hair, I shucked on a Christmas sweater and slathered on makeup. So much adrenaline kicked through my veins, I had to redo my eyeliner three times.

The Holiday Village at Union Square was always a mad house. On Christmas Eve, it was unbearable. I stood at the southeast entrance, where all the crafts people held their booths, and was immediately overwhelmed. Aiden had texted me to meet him at the Wafels and Dinges booth (most likely because he knew I would drag him there anyway), but there was an impenetrable crowd of people surrounding the booth.

I was so short that it was impossible for me to peek my head up over the crowd, but I tried as hard as I could on my toes.

"Rosie!" a voice barked out.

I whipped around and Aiden Huntington was pushing past people in a black knitted Christmas sweater. His peacoat was open, a beanie snug on his head.

I warmed looking at him despite the cold and smiled, trying my best to get to him.

When I finally made it, people were swarming all around and I was pushed forward into his chest—but he caught me, his arms grasping my waist steadily. He sent a death glare to whoever had shoved me before looking down and meeting my gaze. The smell of his cologne and the feel of his hands on me had been the star of my dreams since we kissed, since we wrote that scene together. I was thrilled to finally be standing here with him after wishing I could fix everything between us. Aiden Huntington was better in reality than any sort of fiction.

"Hi," I said softly, reluctantly stepping away from his touch.

"Hi." His lips quirked up. "Merry Christmas. I like your getup."

I pulled back, pulling my coat open even wider. "What? This old thing?" A couple of Christmases ago my dad bought the entire family llama Christmas sweaters. He was so eager for us to be in touch with our Peruvian culture that whenever he saw anything with a llama he bought it immediately. This particular sweater had a llama with a scarf around its neck and a Santa hat on its head. Real bells hung off the sweater, and I'd paired it with my jingle bell earrings. "And look at you—I'm shocked you own a Christmas sweater."

He looked down at his sweater, pulling his peacoat open so I got a better look. It was more wintery than Christmassy, but it was probably as festive as Aiden got. It was a thick black sweater with a red pattern across the chest. A thin black scarf was hanging loosely around his neck.

"It's my only one. My mom got it for me in high school; I'm surprised it still fits."

"I like it." I smiled up at him. His green eyes met mine briefly before looking away, toward one of the booths. I rubbed my fingers together, suddenly nervous. I had been so excited to see Aiden and to have something to do on Christmas, I'd forgotten that the last time I saw Aiden I was close to crying and yelling. "Aiden," I said tentatively. "Are we—"

"I'm sorry," he blurted out, then grimaced. "You should know how sorry I am. I know . . . what I said wasn't right or fair, and I keep turning it over in my head. I didn't mean it. I'm sorry."

I took a breath. "I think if Max can forgive Hunter, then I can forgive you," I said softly. "I'm sorry, too."

"You've got nothing to be sorry about." He smiled softly. "How about for the rest of break, you be Rosie and I'll be Aiden?" His gaze met mine, unwavering, determined. "No secret messages, no unspoken words. Just us."

I nodded once, smiling. "I'd like that."

"Good. Because as Aiden, I'd like to tell you, Rosie, that you're delusional if you think I'm waiting in this line for a Belgian waffle. I had no idea it'd be *this* long."

I tsked, observing the line. It had wrapped around the small booth, infringing on the space of another. The waffle makers were moving at lightning speed, adding Nutella and powdered sugar.

"It's not just *any* Belgium waffle. It's Wafels and Dinges. It's a New York staple."

Aiden rolled his eyes and said, "As a New Yorker, I can certify it's not a *staple*. C'mon, let's keep walking. When I walked in, I saw a booth you're going to love."

Aiden led me toward the other side of the park. I tried my best to follow him but people kept walking between us, bumping into me and pulling us further apart. Aiden looked over his shoulder for me, frowning when I wasn't there. I raised my hand and when he spotted me, he stopped in the middle of traffic. Plenty of people gave him glares, but he ignored them and just held his hand out to me. A silent question that I hesitated to answer. I told myself that the kiss was still forgotten, and he was only doing this so we wouldn't get lost.

When my glove-clad hand slid into his palm, I could feel the warmth of his skin. He squeezed once before he continued walking, and I clung to him.

He nodded at a booth as we approached and I immediately gasped. "Oh my God."

He grinned. "I thought you'd like this."

"Aiden, I *have* to get one. I don't care the cost. I will go bankrupt for these."

I stepped into the booth and started flipping through the small prints. They were dogs in the place of iconic movie scenes. It had the *Titanic* Jack and Rose pose but with a corgi and a pug. A poodle was holding their skirt down a la Marilyn Monroe. A beagle was dancing to "Greased Lightning."

And then I found it—the perfect print to hang in my room. "Aiden!" I said, waving him over. "This one. This is the perfect one."

He stepped forward, his head tilted. "What's this from?"

I snapped my head toward him. "*When Harry Met Sally.* The greatest film ever made."

A German Shepard and a golden retriever were facing each other in Central Park like on the movie poster, fall leaves decorating the background. The golden retriever, Meg, was standing dignified, her hands clasped in front of her. The artist had even captured Meg Ryan's unruly hair.

"How much for this one?" I asked the man in the booth.

"Twenty."

I turned to Aiden. "Chump change for a masterpiece like this. Twenty bucks? I would've paid *fifty.*"

"Maybe don't say that so loud, Rosie," Aiden muttered.

I happily paid the man, who wrapped my print carefully and placed it in a bag. He held it out for me, but Aiden grabbed it before I could.

"I'll hold it. C'mon, let's keep looking around."

We walked around the Holiday Village twice. I kept getting distracted by the holiday foods and unique booths. They had nearly everything I would never need but desperately wanted.

We stopped at a booth that sold antique jewelry and when my eyes snagged on a delicate silver locket I couldn't help but gasp. I carefully held up the necklace, turning the piece over in my hand.

"That's pretty," Aiden said, peering over my shoulder.

"My lita gave me one *just* like this when I was little. I would wear it all the time. But one day the chain broke, and I didn't notice until it was too late."

My lita, or abuelita, had worn it the first time I visited Peru when I was seven. I was sitting in her lap at dinner one night and I couldn't stop playing with it. I gushed over how beautiful it was, my mom translating for me. She slipped it over her head and over mine. The cold metal pressed against my skin. I clutched onto the locket all night, afraid to lose it. I wore it everywhere after that.

In high school, my friends and I had a tradition that after any winning football game we'd go to Waffle House. One night, sitting in our usual booth, I realized the locket was gone and the chain must have broken. Simon drove me back to the stadium, and I spent hours looking through the field and stands, only to come up empty handed.

"How much?" Aiden asked the vendor.

"Three hundred," the man replied. "It's an antique, pure silver."

"Oh," I said softly, setting it back down. I couldn't justify spending that much on a necklace. "That's okay, thanks anyway."

We finished our walk through the park and after I detoured to the nearby Whole Foods to use the bathroom, we stood at the edge of the square, away from the crowds.

"Where to now?" I looked up at Aiden.

"Wherever you want. You mentioned Macy's earlier."

My mouth parted in surprise. "You would suffer through Midtown for me?"

Aiden smiled and nodded. "Yeah, Rosie. I would."

I hoped it didn't show on my face how much I *liked* Aiden in that moment. He'd never smiled at me like this before we were friends. When we truly despised each other, I got frowns all day, etched into his face. I used to take satisfaction in the fact that he'd probably develop wrinkles from the frown lines. But now, the wrinkles had floated up his face toward his eyes, crinkling in the sunlight. This smile was especially designed and produced for *me*.

"Train or walk?" he asked.

"Walk," I said immediately. "I want to check out the window displays on our way there."

He grabbed my hand, like it was the most natural thing in the world, and said, "Lead the way."

"I can't."

"I'm begging."

"I *won't*."

"Aiden, it won't be that bad. I promise."

He shot me a dirty look. "You *know* it'll be that bad. That's why you're begging."

"No one even *cares* about Rockefeller Center. All the tourists care about Times Square and Broadway. Who cares about some dumb tree?"

"Exactly. It's a dumb tree so we don't have to go."

I gasped, slapping his arm. "It's not *dumb*. It's the Christmas tree of New York. Take some pride in your city."

We had spent *way* too much time at Macy's, but it was nearly impossible to walk in the store of wall-to-wall people. I settled for just looking at the window display outside. Every year it featured Tiptoe the Reindeer and a cute little inspirational story. I couldn't get enough of it. Aiden walked through the display *twice* with me.

But now I really wanted to go to Rockefeller Center to see the tree. I figured once we were there I could convince Aiden to go ice skating, but he was flat out refusing to go to that part of the city, claiming it would be "too busy."

He leveled his gaze with me and said, "I take pride in New York. I just don't think the epitome of Christmas in New York is *Rockefeller Center*. It'll be at least ten times the people here."

I pouted. "I warned you I wanted to do touristy stuff."

We were standing in the middle of Herald Square. Busy, last minute shoppers were rushing around us as the sun began to set. I shivered slightly, and Aiden didn't say anything as he unwrapped his scarf from his neck and pulled it snug around mine.

"You're shaking so hard your earrings are ringing." He smiled down at me.

"I don't need your scarf."

"Me either." His nose and cheeks were adorably red from the cold. "We need to decide what we're going to do."

"Okay. Rockefeller Center. Times Square. Central Park—"

He covered my mouth with his hand laughing. "I'm not doing any of that. It won't even be fun. With your luck, you'll probably get mugged. I have an idea. It's going to get dark soon. We head somewhere on the Upper East Side, if you're up for it."

I furrowed my brow. "What's uptown?"

"It's a surprise."

I *did* want to go to Rockefeller Center, but Aiden was right. It was an overwhelming crowd here, I couldn't imagine what kind of hell there would be around the plaza. And if Aiden had a surprise for me, there was no way I was saying no.

"Fine, fine let's go," I agreed.

We took the train uptown, heading toward Aiden's surprise.

"I think you'll really like this place, but it's okay if you don't. We can leave if you don't want to," Aiden insisted as we walked down the block.

"I'm sure I'll like it," I assured him.

We stopped at a restaurant I'd never been to before, Serendipity Three. There were people waiting in the cold, sitting on a bench outside.

"C'mon, we've got a reservation," Aiden said.

Before he could pull the door open, I placed a hand on his arm stopping him. "Aiden, not if you had to call your father. Not if you traded this for a dinner with him, it's not worth it."

"It would've been worth it, Rosie, just so we're clear," he said, firmly, his gaze locking with mine. "But no, I didn't call him. I made this reservation that night we got burgers on the off chance you'd want to spend today together."

How was I expected to *not* fall for this man? All day he'd been nothing but thoughtful and to know he'd made a reservation so far in advance on the off chance I'd like this place? I was feeling more certain that wherever he went, I'd go, too.

When I stepped inside, I gasped, wide eyed. The restaurant was a lot bigger on the inside than I had expected. It was pure camp—pink everywhere, with unique art lining the walls. A stained glass chandelier hung from above. There were giant bells and garland covering every inch of the store. I turned in a slow circle, trying to take in every detail and stow it away for later. It was *glamorous*.

The waitress seated us at a small table upstairs and placed two giant menus before us. It was impossible to take everything in at once. My eyes would snag on a different decoration every second. The table was small, and my knees kept brushing with Aiden's, but I didn't mind.

"How'd you find this place?" I asked.

Aiden opened the menu and said, "My mom liked to celebrate here. Whenever something big in our lives would happen—she'd sell a book or I'd make a good grade—she'd tow us all the way up here and order a big sundae to split."

My heart burst in my chest. I pushed his menu down so he'd meet me gaze. "Aiden, this made my Christmas."

His cheeks tinted and said, "I'm glad you like it. If you trust me, I'll order for us?" I opened my mouth, but he held a hand up to stop me. "And my Christmas gift to you is that it's on me. Don't worry about the money, okay?"

I sighed. "Normally I would protest, but after learning you're a secret billionaire—"

"I'm not even a *millionaire*," he said with a laugh.

"—I suppose I can allow it."

A little while after he ordered, the waitress came back with a giant plate of fries and two bowls of decadent hot chocolate with straws sticking out of them.

"This," Aiden said, scooting one of the bowls closer to me, "is the iconic Frrrozen Hot Chocolate."

My eyes lit up. "Explains the straw."

"Since you live essentially off sugar and nothing else, I thought you might like it."

I took a sip and moaned. The texture was a bit unusual, but the chocolate was so sweet that I eagerly sipped more. "How have I never known about this?"

Aiden took a sip from his own and said, "The first time I asked a girl out on a date, I took her here. She *hated* it. She thought there was something morally abject about having something frozen and hot simultaneously."

I raised a brow. "Did you two go on a second date?"

"No. Not liking frozen hot chocolate is a deal breaker."

I smiled. "Did you bring all your dates here to test it out?"

"A few," he admitted. "The worst was a girl who was lactose intolerant but was too embarrassed to tell me. She had the frozen hot chocolate and spent the rest of the date in the bathroom downstairs."

I winced. "Poor girl."

He shrugged. "It could've gone worse."

"The worst date I went on was when I was in middle school." I leaned forward.

His eyes sparkled in excitement as he sipped on his drink.

"Back then, I *really* liked this guy. He had Justin Bieber hair and said 'swag' after everything. Somehow he got my number, and we texted back and forth. We never really talked at school though so I thought it was more of a love letter type of romance, which made it even better for me."

"Of course," Aiden said.

"Eventually, he asked me out on a date and *obviously* I said yes because it was my first date *ever*. I gave him my address for his mom to pick me up and everything. We were going to see *The Hunger Games* together because I had read the books and loved them, which I also thought was really romantic.

"When I opened my front door, his smile vanished and he started looking around. He said, 'Oh, hey Rosie. Is Lizzie here?' Turns out, he thought he was texting Lizzie, my best friend, the entire time and was going on the date with *her*."

"Oh no." Aiden's eyes widened.

"He'd never said my name, and I thought it was so romantic that he only ever called me 'babe.' His mom saw the whole thing from the car and forced him to go out with me anyway."

Aiden's elbow was bent on the table, his hand covering his mouth. "I'm sorry, it's not funny."

I rolled my eyes, sipping my hot chocolate. "It's a little funny."

He shook his head, but his eyes still had that glint. "Rosie, that's kind of traumatic."

"Thank you!" I said, tossing my hands in the air. "That's what I said! My parents were like, 'Oh, you'll get over it. It's character building.'"

"What happened when you explained the situation?"

"Let's just say it was the worst two hours of my life."

Aiden burst out laughing, his eyes squeezing shut. It was the infectious type of laugh that bubbled at the bottom of your throat. Soon enough, I joined in.

"I needed that," Aiden said, wiping his eyes. As we sipped our drinks, we exchanged more embarrassing stories from our childhood. I was sworn to complete secrecy about the time he laughed so hard milk came out of his nose and it landed on his crush in third grade.

Later, as we slurped up the last bit of Frrrozen Hot Chocolate, Aiden said hesitantly, "I didn't know you were so serious about the fellowship."

"I'm a little embarrassed that I had no idea it existed even though it's such a big deal. But when I mentioned it to Ida she really encouraged me." I shrugged, pushing the mug away from me. Even though my diet consisted of mainly sugar, I had a hard time drinking all of the hot chocolate in one sitting like Aiden. "Obviously it would provide so many important opportunities for me, and it'd help with my writing career in the future . . . but getting that tuition money would be life changing. I'm already drowning in student loans; if I got this I wouldn't have to drag out my MFA for years. Maybe I could go home more, too."

Aiden stiffened, his gaze not quite meeting mine. I knew money talk could throw people off, especially for people like Aiden who had so much of it.

"I guess I also want to prove that I *can*," I said. "That the romance I write is good enough for people to forget their bias with genre lines, you know?"

Aiden nodded. "I get that. I can't wait to read it—but I can't promise that just because we're friends, I'll be nice."

"That's kind of why I want you to look over it." I said honestly, smiling sheepishly. "Don't get me wrong, you *suck* in workshop. You're mean. Like *really* mean."

"I get it," Aiden said flatly.

"But you're *honest*. It's rare when you compliment someone and when you do it feels good." I blushed. "With your feedback, I'll know if I'm in over my head with the submission."

"I'm sure it's great," Aiden said confidently. "You're an amazing writer, Rosie."

My heart glowed in my chest. I never wanted this day to end, but the restaurant was closing up soon. Aiden so graciously paid the check and we ambled out into the street.

"I can barely walk, I'm so full," I groaned.

"Just wait till you get their Blackout Sundae. They put a full piece of cake on top of a giant ice cream sundae."

I turned around to study the restaurant. "You think they have one they could give us to go?"

Aiden laughed and grabbed my hand, tugging me toward the subway. "C'mon. Let's get you home."

We made our way to the station together, but I dreaded the moment we passed through those turnstiles. Then the most perfect

Christmas of my entire life would come to an end, and I'd go home to my lonely apartment.

We were shoulder to shoulder as we went down the stairs to the station. It wasn't as crowded as usual. Everyone was most likely back home with their families, preparing their turkeys and presents.

The way the station was divided, the N, R, and W trains—which I assumed Aiden would be taking—were on the platform immediately following the turnstiles, but I had to go down another set of stairs to get to the 6.

I stopped and turned to him. "Thank you for today. I had the most fun I've had in a really long time."

He smiled softly. "Me too, Rosie."

An N train came whirring into the station and my gut clenched. "Well, I don't want you to miss your train so . . ."

He tilted his head in confusion. "I figured we'd take the 6? The Astor Place stop isn't too far from you, right?"

"Right," I said slowly. "But I don't want to make you go all the way to East Village when you're on the other side of town."

He rolled his eyes and gently grabbed my elbow, leading me toward the platform. "You're ridiculous. Of course I'm going to get you home. C'mon, I think I hear a train approaching."

I wasn't used to this Aiden that I had spent the day with. The one who considered my feelings and safety before his convenience. I'd *hoped* he would take the train with me just so we could prolong our time together, but I thought I was just living in my own world again. That I was making Aiden into someone he wasn't.

When the train arrived, we got on a semicrowded car. Aiden and I stood, facing each other, holding onto one of the bars toward the center of the car. It jostled us slightly, him stepping forward so he wouldn't lose his balance. His chest was nearly pressed to mine. I couldn't tear my gaze away from his green eyes. I wished with all my might for this to be real. For Aiden's hand to slide around my waist, his hand moving the few inches on the bar to grasp mine.

At every stop, either of us could've stepped away, but as if by silent agreement, as if we craved this closeness with each other, we didn't.

Soon enough, the jostling stopped, feeling more like swaying. If I really wanted to be delusional I could pretend that Aiden and I were dancing on this subway together.

"Rosie," Aiden whispered at one of the stops, his voice thick. "I—"

"Helloooo, New York!"

Aiden was interrupted by a group of performers coming onto our train. One of them held a speaker on their shoulder. "We hate to interrupt your Christmas Eve, but we have a little show for you!"

"This is hell," I whispered to Aiden. "This is my nightmare scenario."

One side of his mouth hooked up in a grin. "You obviously haven't had a mariachi band on your train yet."

The performers were rapping and dancing on one side of the car while another guy passed around a hat that was barely getting any tips.

"Just don't look at them," Aiden murmured. "New York rule number one is to not make eye contact." I nodded, wanting to follow his instructions, but I couldn't help but glancing at them from my peripheral. "Rosie," he warned.

"I'm sorry!" I whispered. "They're kinda good."

The train came to a stop and Aiden tugged me out of there before I had a chance to compliment the performers.

"It's Christmas," I insisted as we walked up the stairs. "We should've given them something."

"You're gullible," Aiden said gently. "If you gave them a dollar, they would've asked if you had Venmo to give more. That's how it goes."

"Whatever," I huffed.

The Astor Place station was only a few blocks away from my place, and the walk went by too quickly. I wanted to find an excuse to take another loop around the block with Aiden.

We stopped in front of my apartment building, facing each other. Aiden glanced over at my door, his eyes rolling.

"What?" I asked.

"It's Christmas so I won't even *mention* the brick."

"Ronny Jr.," I corrected, grinning up at him.

He nodded. "I'm really glad we're okay. I was . . . worried. I didn't know what to do."

"Me either," I admitted. "I think maybe you and I are just destined to fight with each other. We both need to develop a thicker skin so this doesn't happen again."

"You're right," he said. Then quickly added, "Don't let that go to your head. You're *rarely* right."

"Not true, but I'll let it slide. It's Christmas after all." I nudged his shoulder with mine, playfully.

We fell silent for a moment before a surge of determination went through me. I had spent so much time sitting in the passenger seat, waiting for other people to make the sweeping gestures. It was time that I did it. I liked Aiden. I had been lying to myself about it for so long, but I couldn't anymore. Not when my smile was fading quickly at the thought that I might not see him again until classes started back up.

He shifted his feet. "Well, I should—"

"Do you want to come up?" I forced the words out of my mouth, my cheeks blazing. Aiden's face remained impassive, making my cheeks heat even further. "My family just always stays up late for Christmas. And we usually do dinner, then gifts, then dance, and when everything winds down my dad will convince us to watch *It's a Wonderful Life* and we'll all be half asleep but you know, I still cry when George Bailey—"

Aiden's hand settled heavily on my shoulders and said, "Shut up before you run out of breath. C'mon, let's go up."

My lungs were filled so tightly with hope, my mind and heart had no room for anything other than Hunter. Fissures from every past heartbreak were repaired with every smile he gave me from across the room.

I wanted to walk to him and grab his hand. To feel his skin against mine and hopefully, one day, his heartbeat against mine. I wanted to run my fingers through his hair and tell him I was his . . . if only he could be mine.

— Excerpt from *Untitled* by
Rosie Maxwell and Aiden Huntington

CHAPTER TWENTY

Aiden had never made homemade cookies before. He said he'd only ever done it from the Nestle rolls, and I immediately had to rectify that situation. I'd thought it would be a cute thing for us to do before we watched a movie, but I'd forgotten how competitive we were.

"Rosie, it says you have to put the batter in the fridge for a few hours," he said insistently. He was reading the recipe off his phone, shaking his head.

I waved him off. "It's just a suggestion. The cookies won't be better or worse if we don't."

"That can't be true. It's going to taste like shit if we bake them straight away."

"No it won't," I snapped.

"Yes, it will," he snapped back.

"Well, then it won't be different from your regular diet. You talk so much shit you should be used to the taste. Now, tell me what I need to add after the vanilla extract."

It was a *miracle* that I had all the ingredients, mostly thanks to Alexa. But I didn't have one of those electric mixers, so I was having to do it all by hand. My wrists were about to give out any minute. The batter should've been thick and light brown by now, but there were still clumps of flour at the edges.

"Aiden, I think my arm is going to break."

He didn't even look up from his phone. "You're fine."

"I really do think it's going to fall off," I urged.

He rolled his eyes, nudging me away from the bowl with his hip. "I told you we couldn't do this without a mixer. I knew you'd rope me into mixing."

"If it's the price of cookies, then we just have to pay it."

"I don't know why I thought I could satiate your sugar addiction at Serendipity."

Aiden started mixing so quickly that a gust of flour puffed up into his face. I cackled, but quickly stopped when he threatened to dump the contents of the bowl on me.

Eventually, we were able to get the batter looking kind of like cookie dough. We gave up on the mixing, deeming it was good enough, plopped scoops onto one of my baking trays, and stuck it into my tiny oven.

"You've got flour on your cheek," I said, laughing. I stepped forward, the pad of my thumb swiping against his cheekbone, wiping the spot away. His eyes didn't leave mine and my breath caught.

"Thanks," he whispered.

"S-sure." I stepped back, suddenly feeling nervous. I had *straddled* Aiden before, but it somehow felt different now. More intense. "Let me pull the movie up on my laptop while the cookies bake."

He nodded once before I turned around.

On my way into my bedroom to grab my laptop, my eyes snagged on my window, and I gasped. Flurries were falling from the sky, beginning to blanket New York. Snow in New York always seemed so magical in the movies—whimsical and magical. In reality, New York snowstorms were pretty for about a minute, and then turned gross—piles of gray and brown slush on every corner.

But from the inside of my apartment, along the empty streets, the magic of New York snow was renewed.

Aiden was sitting on my couch when I returned to my small living space. He was studying my apartment, his eyes flying to something new every second, lingering on the sad Christmas decorations Alexa and I had put up after we found them for cheap at a thrift store. There was a wreath on the door, fairy lights up around the apartment, and mistletoe hanging from the arched ceiling between our kitchen and living room. Garland with red berries lined the coffee table in front of the couch.

"It's snowing," I said softly to Aiden as I set my laptop on the coffee table, starting the movie.

Aiden glanced at me. "Oh yeah? First snow of the season, right?"

"It's good luck on Christmas, you know."

"Must be," he murmured. "I like your place. I didn't really get to look around the last time I was here."

"It's no brownstone," I teased.

He nodded, conceding. "Sure, but it's homey. It's the kind of place you could walk around without worrying about breaking anything. Most of the stuff at my place is still my mom's. I still feel like a little kid, nervous to touch her vases and décor."

"You could make it your own." I sat on the couch next to him, folding my legs underneath me. "Add some of the dog art we bought today."

He snorted. "Oh yeah, that screams Aiden."

"You don't have any Christmas decorations up." My elbow rested on the back of the couch, my head resting against my hand as I faced him. I paused and hesitantly asked, "What was Christmas like for you as a kid?"

He took a deep breath and moved his elbow so his position mirrored mine. "When my parents were still together, my dad would drag my mom to some corporate holiday party on Christmas Eve so I'd be in the apartment by myself. I'd go to bed early and maybe read a book."

My heart split open. "Well, what about after they divorced? Did your mom do anything special?"

"They traded off holidays. When I was with my dad, it was the same thing. When I was with my mom," he smiled at the memory, "we had a really quiet Christmas. She'd make homemade hot chocolate and would have gotten some cookies from Levain Bakery earlier in the day. We never sat around and waited until midnight, but we'd watch the classics. *Rudolph, Frosty* . . . Even when I was in high school. She was sick and I . . . I couldn't say no to her."

"She seems like she was a great mom."

"God, the best. She would've liked you a lot."

"Yeah?"

His smile widened. "Big time. She would've told me to be nicer to you."

"Well, at least you *know* you weren't the nicest to me."

"I should've been," he said softly. His hand reached out to touch one of my curls, rubbing it between his two fingers. He focused on my hair, but I studied him in the low light with a pounding heart. Adrenaline rushed through me as I imagined him tugging me closer, onto him, like we'd been at his place.

The timer for the cookies brought us out of our silence and I reluctantly stood. "I—I better go check on them," I stuttered out. Being this close to Aiden had such an immense effect on me, I lost any sense of self.

The cookies turned out to be a *disaster*. We had forgotten to put parchment paper down so the bottoms were burnt, and I might've preset the oven a *little* too high thinking they would cook faster. But instead they turned hard as rocks the minute they cooled down.

I still placed them on a plate and poured two glasses of milk for Aiden and me. I set them on the table next to my laptop and said, "Voilà."

Aiden sat forward to grab one. He eyed it before knocking it against my coffee table. "Huh. Wonder what would've happened if we put them in the fridge for an hour."

"Oh, fuck off. They can't be that bad." I snatched one from the plate and dunked it in the milk. I hesitated before I bit into it. "Delicious," I managed.

I suffered through a few more bites before Aiden pointed at my kitchen and said, "Spit it out."

I rushed to the kitchen and called out, "I'll get the Oreos."

I also grabbed some blankets on my way back. Aiden and I cozied up, side by side on my couch, our thighs pressed against each other, watching the movie. I tried my best to stay focused on George Bailey, but all I could feel was the heat of Aiden's muscular thigh against mine. His touch sent a chill through my whole body and I craved more. But we still had nearly forty minutes left in the movie and an hour to go until Christmas.

"What do you want for Christmas?" I whispered, turning to face Aiden. The only light in the room was from my laptop screen and the twinkle lights. I could barely make out the sharp angles of his face or his full lips.

"I haven't thought about it," he said.

"No letters to Santa?"

"No." His lips quirked. His green eyes flickered down to my mouth before searching my eyes. "Right now I feel like I have everything I need."

His face inched closer, our noses nudging against each other. I inhaled sharply, as his breath fanned against my face, his lips suddenly so close to mine. I could already feel the heat and softness of him. His eyelashes fanned across his cheek, and I marveled for just a second how beautiful he was. I'd been so stupid to run out on him that first time. I was terrified of another heartbreak, but if today had proved anything it's that Aiden would be careful with me. He'd suffer tourist crowds and make reservations just in case. He could be a romance hero if he really wanted to.

Our lips had just barely touched each other when someone started banging at my door.

I jumped back, startled. My heart was still racing as I looked around in confusion.

"They probably have the wrong door," I said. "I didn't buzz anyone up."

"No, but you have that stupid brick." He stood from the couch and said, "Stay here. I'll check."

I nodded, touching my fingers to my lips. When Aiden got rid of whoever was at the door, I'd tell him. I'd tell him I wanted to kiss him, and I wanted to be with him. I couldn't wait a second longer.

I jumped again at a screech that definitely wasn't Aiden's.

"Quién eres? Dónde está mi hija?"

Is that . . . ?

I raced to my front door. Aiden looked back at me panicked as my eyes widened.

My parents and sister stood in my doorway with luggage, wearing matching llama Christmas sweaters.

I was terrified, painfully aware of every move I made. You only get one shot with a girl like Maxine. This was my chance to prove to her that I craved her. That I wanted to spend forever where she was, no matter what. How could I not do everything I could to show her that this, these moments of careless laughter and accidental brushes, were all I had been wanting for months?

— Excerpt from *Untitled* by
Rosie Maxwell and Aiden Huntington

CHAPTER TWENTY-ONE

"What're you doing here?" I asked, managing a little laugh.

"Is that any way to greet you mother? *What're you doing here?* How about Feliz Navidad? Te quiero mucho?" My mom was tiny but fierce. Her dark hair was graying at the edges and pulled into a bun. She was just as short as me, but she could've passed for my older sister. She took care of her skin religiously and even after a flight it looked dewy and youthful.

I stepped forward and wrapped her in a hug, planting a kiss on her cheek. "No, I really mean *what're you doing here?*"

I looked to my dad who smiled and said, "Your mother got us on a flight last minute."

"Are you surprised?" My sister, Maria, stepped forward and pulled me into a hug.

I tried not to let my slight disappointment show. Of *course* I was excited they were here. I'd probably be jumping up and down if Aiden weren't standing right there holding onto a kiss I wanted.

"*Duh* I'm surprised! I can't believe you're here! Come in, come in."

"¿Dónde está Alexa?" My mom looked around my apartment. "Are you burning something in here? Is the gas on?" In true Peruvian mother fashion, she began inspecting every inch of the place.

I glanced at Aiden who was standing to the side, looking mildly amused and nervous. I shot him an apologetic look as I wheeled my family's luggage into the living room.

"Give her a minute to relax, honey," my dad chided gently. He was a big man, the opposite of my mom. His face was consistently rosy and his beard was full and white. As a kid, I'd interrogate him to try to find out if he was secretly Santa. He pulled me away from my mom and into a hug. "Hey, Rosie Posie," he whispered. He glanced at my laptop screen and lit up. "You're keeping the tradition alive! What part are you on?"

He sat on the couch before I could answer and turned the volume up to watch it himself.

Maria gently grabbed my elbow and said, "Sorry. I know they're a lot. It was all my idea. I thought maybe you'd be lonely on Christmas Eve, so I convinced them to fly out for just a few days to see you." She lowered her voice, glancing at Aiden, "I didn't know you'd have company."

I looked to Aiden who was still standing apart from us, his hands clasped behind his back. I was dazed already with the three of them fluttering around my apartment, the sound of my mom's heavy footsteps going from room to room and the movie playing loudly through the laptop speakers. I couldn't imagine what Aiden was feeling.

"I didn't either," I admitted. "Aiden," I called him over. "This is my sister, Maria. Maria, this is Aiden."

Maria's eyes brightened. "So *this* is Aiden. I swear, Rosie doesn't shut up about you. She keeps saying how mean you are, but I actually thought it was pretty funny when you told her—"

"Okay, okay," I interjected. "It's Christmas. No reliving bad blood."

"Nice to meet you," Aiden said to Maria. Then to me, he said, "Can I talk to you?" He pulled me aside, his head bent as he whispered, "Look, I should probably head home. I don't want to intrude on your family . . ."

"¿Quién es él?" My mom's voice rang through the apartment. She stood in the doorway between the kitchen and living room, watching us. "Rosie?"

"This is Aiden," I said. "Aiden, this is my mom, Claudia."

"Are you celebrating with us?" my mom asked, looking at Aiden hopefully. "We didn't know Rosie was seeing anyone, but if we had known, we would've brought you a sweater too."

I blanched, shooting a nervous look to Aiden. It made sense. My mom was pretty old-fashioned despite all the romance novels she'd introduced me to and I guess the low lighting, the cookies, and the fact that it was so late on Christmas Eve had led her to think Aiden and I were together. It'd be too complicated to try to explain what we *really* were to my parents because I didn't understand it myself.

"Right. Yes," I said, panicky. "Aiden and I are *seeing* each other. We are *together*. Obviously. That's why he's here so late. But he doesn't really like Christmas sweaters." I gestured awkwardly at his sweater. "That's as festive as my guy gets." I cringed at my words.

Aiden shot me a look, and I tried to plead with him using my eyes to just go along with it.

"I would've worn the llamas," he said kindly. He stepped forward to shake my mom's hand. "It's very nice to meet you. I was actually just leaving. I don't want to intrude on your family time. I know how much Rosie's missed you all."

"Stay!" I grasped his arm, panicked. Aiden began to shake his head, stepping back. "No, I'm serious. Stay. We'll be partying until Christmas hits, and I don't want you to spend Christmas Eve alone."

"I didn't spend Christmas Eve alone," he said. "I spent it with you."

I held his gaze and lowered my voice to a whisper. "It's not over."

"You've been waiting all year to see your family," he murmured back. "I don't want to ruin it."

"You'd only make it better." I reached for his hand, squeezing his hand three quick times, and said, "Please."

He held my gaze for a minute, before squeezing back and whispering, "Okay. I'll stay."

"Perfect!" My mom clapped. "Rosie, you have nothing in your fridge. What're we going to eat?"

I rolled my eyes. "Okay drama queen, let's go look. Aiden and I just made cookies, so clearly I have *some* stuff."

"That's what these are?" Maria called from across the room. "I thought it was coal to put in stockings or something."

My dad burst into laughter. "You two made these? Yeah, I think your mom and I will take care of the cooking tonight."

"You guys don't need to cook anything," I insisted. "Aiden and I went out to eat earlier. I have some snacks—"

"She has none—" Aiden started.

"I do!" I said defensively. "We have some Oreos left in the package, and I'm pretty sure I have some chips in the cabinet."

My mom tsked. "Amor, can you run to the store and get some actual stuff to eat? It's Christmas Eve for God's sake! We can't sit around all pitiful, we need to have a feast."

"Nowhere is gonna be open, honey. It's nearly midnight on Christmas Eve."

"I can go," Aiden offered. "I think there's a bodega around the corner from here."

"No," I protested. "Mami, we don't have to have a feast." I turned to Aiden. "You don't have to go. I have plenty of food here, we'll survive for the night."

"I want to make a good impression. It's not a big deal."

"Thank you!" my mom piped up, her eyes shining at Aiden.

My dad stood from the couch and said, "Maria and I will go. I've been on a plane and in a car for the past few hours. I want to stretch my legs. Besides, I know we interrupted you two. Your mom will be busy in the kitchen trying to pull together some sort of meal, and you two can have some alone time." I nearly puked when my dad winked at us. What did he expect? For us to run in my room and have sex while Mom was rummaging through my drawers? I didn't dare look at Aiden.

My father and Maria slipped past us out the door, Maria wiggling her eyebrows at me. I wanted to die from mortification.

We tried to convince my mom to let us help her in the kitchen as she tried to whip something up, but she refused. So, Aiden and I sat awkwardly on the couch, waiting for everyone to return. Not even a half hour ago, we'd sat here together, about to kiss.

I looked to the ceiling, praying to any god to somehow dig us out of this hole and make all of this less awkward.

"Hey," I whispered to Aiden eventually, angling my body toward him. "I'm sorry I didn't correct my mom about us being a couple. She'd have bombarded me with a million questions if I had, and it would've made the situation much worse. I hope I didn't make you uncomfortable."

"It's okay." His voice was low and soft. "Family's complicated. You know I get it. You've got a great family, Rosie Posie."

I ducked my head. "They're a lot, but they're really amazing. I can't believe they came all this way . . ." I bit my lip, smiling. I obviously wanted to see my family for Christmas, but I had let go of that dream a long time ago. "They also don't know how to act in front of strangers, so I apologize in advance."

Aiden laughed softly. "It's obvious how much they love you," he said. "Trust me, I'd trade overbearing for what I got any day."

I wished I had the right words to tell him that being with him wasn't as hard as his dad made it seem. That it was one of the easiest and best things in my life. I opened my mouth to try to say as much, but he shook his head, his hand landing heavy on my knee.

"I'm really happy I'm here with you."

A little while later, Maria and my father knocked on the door and I rushed to answer to escape the thick silence between Aiden and me. They had a million bags in tow, snowflakes resting on their eyelashes.

"Did you know there's a brick holding the front door of your building open?" My dad asked, his brow furrowed.

"That's Ronny Jr.," I explained.

"That's stupid, Rosie Posie. You've got to get rid of it and tell whoever's doing that to stop."

"That's what I said," Aiden piped up.

My father nodded approvingly. "Good man."

I rolled my eyes and helped them set the bags onto the coffee table, digging through the array of chips and cookies. I brightened at all the bodega snacks they had bought.

"Mom's cooking something in the kitchen," I told my dad. "I think it's pasta."

"I'll go help. Can you make this look nice and fancy? It'd make your mom happy. We'll watch the movie until midnight hits then do presents."

I turned to Maria, panicked. "I didn't buy anyone anything! I didn't think I was going to see you guys."

She smirked, glancing at Aiden. "I think the best gift you could've given them would be getting over Simon. Dad wouldn't shut up about you on our grocery run," she said to Aiden.

He shot me a panicked glance. "In a good way or bad way?"

"Really good."

He looked pleased but confused. "I didn't do anything, though."

"*Exactly.* He thinks it's really good for Rosie that you're so quiet because Rosie talks a *lot.*"

"Hey!" I said defensively.

Maria only shrugged and said, "It's true. Do you have plates and bowls?"

"I'll grab them," Aiden volunteered, leaving Maria and me alone.

"He's handsome," she whispered. "Clark Kent vibes."

I tried to hide my smile. "I guess so."

She huffed. "Oh please. You don't have to pretend around me." She glanced back at the kitchen. "I know you two aren't together, but I *am* curious as to what you were doing watching a movie together so late at night."

"We're kinda friends now. Maybe more. I don't know." I ignored the burst of butterflies in my chest at the thought of this all being real. "Peter didn't join y'all?"

"No, he's spending the holiday with his family this year. He really wanted to come, though." She hesitated. "Look, there's something I need—"

She clamped her mouth shut the minute Aiden returned with my parents. My mom was holding a small pot of spaghetti with cheap pasta sauce smeared all over it.

"This was all Rosie had." She set it on my coffee table, Aiden trailing behind. "Aiden was kind enough to help us bring out the bowls and forks," Mom said eagerly.

Aiden smiled sheepishly and set them all on the table. "Rosie's been teaching me about southern hospitality."

My sister let out a surprised laugh, snatching a bowl. "Rosie didn't tell us you were funny."

"Rosie Posie didn't tell us *anything.*" My mom pouted. "I can't believe you're seeing someone and never told us, hijita. Is this why you didn't want to come home for Christmas?"

"No," I rushed. "I wanted to come home, but I couldn't swing it. You know that."

My mom sighed dramatically, sitting at the edge of my small couch. "I don't know *anything* about my daughter's life. You're all the way up here in New York, and I'm out of the loop. Tell me how you two met."

Aiden and I shared a look.

"Well, we're in class together."

"So you must know that boy who's bullying my daughter?" Dad demanded, sitting next to Mom on the couch.

I guffawed. "I wouldn't say *bullying*."

"You told us the boy who was picking on you last year is in your class this year, too, right?" Mom asked.

Maria smothered a laugh and looked toward us expectantly.

"He is in our class," Aiden spoke up. "Real jerk."

"Aiden! ¿Por qué no haces algo? You know, Rosie and I read a lot of the same romance novels and she really likes the heroes who are a little overprotective—"

"Okay, thanks, Mom," I cut her off, blushing.

"Rosie doesn't need me to fight her battles," Aiden said seriously. "She does a good job of taking care of him herself."

"That's my Rosie Posie," my dad said.

"C'mon, give us more!" my mom said eagerly. "When did you two start dating? You were in class together, then what happened?"

Aiden looked at me and said, "You know, I should let Rosie tell it. She's the romance expert."

I laughed hollowly and said, "But, Aiden, you've been trying to start writing more romance. This is a good way to stretch your legs!"

My parents were watching us eagerly. I hated having to lie to them, but I'd rather face these awkward questions than have Aiden spend Christmas alone.

"Why don't you both tell us?" Maria suggested, oh so helpfully.

I sent her a quick death glare before stuttering out, "Sure. I guess it all started in . . . class one day."

I cringed and looked to Aiden for help; his lips turned up in a smirk.

"You know, I'll just say it. *I'm* the guy who was giving Rosie a hard time." Maria mock gasped, but Aiden continued. "The truth is, I really liked Rosie, from the moment I saw her. And I'm . . . defensive I guess. I wanted to talk to her, and I didn't know how because she . . . I mean, she's *Rosie*. Larger than life and so kind and confident. I was too scared to go right up and talk to her." He shrugged. "And the only time I ever really was given the opportunity to talk to her was during workshop.

"I was hard on her, probably too hard, but I was trying to push her because—as I'm sure you know—she's a great writer." He turned to me and said, "But I really had to search. I had to look in between the lines because your stories made me wish I could give her that type of love—the kind she wanted and deserved."

My mom was practically swooning at every word and I was, too. We had spent so much time in the liminal space of pretend—first as Maxine and Hunter and now, with my family. I wanted so badly to believe that this was all true, too.

So I took a chance and told the truth. "It was similar for me, too," I said quietly, my eyes never leaving Aiden's. "It was before we even had class together—Aiden was doing a reading at the Writer's House. He read the most *devastating* piece, and it spoke to me so deeply that I couldn't be bothered to pay attention to anyone but him. He read with such conviction and vulnerability that . . . I had this huge crush on him for so long." Aiden's head jerked back just a tad at this. "And then you know, he was mean to me, blah blah blah, but . . . somewhere along the way I guess we got to know each other and didn't want to stop."

I had thought maybe my feelings were too complicated for Aiden. I'd struggled between wanting him so much and being so scared when my heart sped up at the sight of him or at the low timbre of his voice. But now, as we sat in the living room of my apartment, the tangled web unraveled, and I *knew* that I wanted to risk being burned and broken for him.

"How *romantic*," my mom said. "I'm so glad we can all be together. Why don't we start the movie?"

Maria and my parents got comfy on the couch, and Aiden and I sat on the floor in front of them, our arms folded over our knees. The five of us watched the movie in the dim light, eating cheap pasta. I caught Aiden's gaze out of the corner of my eye and smiled softly at him. When he returned it, I knew this was better than any Christmas I'd ever had.

I never thought I'd want to be in a mess like this. One where I couldn't sleep because I was imagining telling her how much I loved the freckle at the top of her ear, and how much I wanted to kiss it. But I'd give just about anything to stay here.

— Excerpt from *Untitled* by
Rosie Maxwell and Aiden Huntington

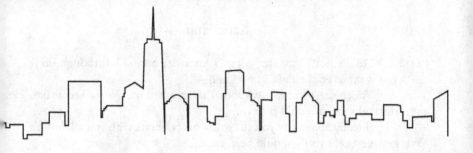

CHAPTER TWENTY-TWO

"I can't believe we missed midnight," my mom said, agonized, when the movie ended. From the sound of her voice, you'd think we just told her Peru lost the World Cup. "We're supposed to open the gifts at midnight."

"It's just thirty minutes after," Aiden whispered to me. "What's the big deal?"

"My mom really loves tradition. When she was a kid in Peru, they'd all count down until midnight and then tear open their gifts. We did that too sometimes, and I think that's what she envisioned."

"Ah." Aiden's tongue clicked in understanding.

"We can just do it now," Maria said soothingly. "Rosie, do you mind if I set our suitcases in your room? I'll grab all of them from there."

"Sure, sure," I said.

Aiden and I were still sitting on the floor, our legs crossed. We faced each other, our knees touching. I could see how tired Aiden was from the way his eyes were drooping. His normally perfect hair was now mussed up. He must've been so uncomfortable in his sweater and jeans. But he didn't complain and had stayed awake through the movie despite how long it was.

"Maybe I should head back," he said, tilting his head closer to mine. His voice was low. "I don't want to overstay my welcome."

"You're not," I assured him. "I know it's been a lot, though, so if you want to go, I would understand—"

"Aiden can't leave," my mother interrupted us. We looked at her, startled that she could hear us.

"I really appreciate you all letting me celebrate with you all, but it's getting late. I really should head back."

My mom crossed one leg over another and simply shook her head. "I can't allow it. As a mother, I cannot."

"Mom, if he wants to leave—"

"It's snowing out there! I can't in good conscience send you out in the cold when you can easily stay here."

I froze, turning toward her wide-eyed. "Mom, you know he wasn't going to *sleep* here right?"

She shared an exasperated look with my father. "While we'd rather not hear about it, we know what it's like to date in your twenties. You don't have to pretend for our sake that Aiden's never spent the night here."

I wanted to sink into the floor. I imagined melting into a puddle just so I wouldn't have to have *this* conversation with my parents.

"*Mom*. No. That's . . . no—"

Aiden's hand rested on my knee, his thumb rubbing soothing circles. "I think what Rosie is saying is we want to be respectful. Besides, I'm not sure if there's enough room for—"

"Nonsense," my mom declared. "If you go out into the snow and slip on ice, I will never live with myself. Maria can sleep on the couch, we'll sleep in Rosie's room, and you two can sleep in Alexa's room? Rosie, do you think she'll mind?"

"I mean, no, I can text her, but—"

"Perfect! Then it's settled!"

I couldn't bear to look at Aiden. I felt bad enough that I'd made him lie to my family, but now he'd have to keep up the ruse overnight and sleep in the same bed as me? It was too much.

"Aiden," I said, "do you mind helping me take the dishes to the kitchen?"

He nodded, jumping up and helping me collect empty bowls and plates.

As soon as we were out of ear shot, I burst out, "I'm so sorry."

He moved past me to set the dishes in the sink. "Don't be."

"No, it's too much. I'll go out there and tell them the truth. You already did every touristy thing in New York with me today, and I know that killed your soul, and now you're having to pretend that we're in a relationship. You don't have—"

"Rosie," Aiden said, his voice low but stern. "I never *have* to do anything. But when it comes to you, I find myself wanting to." His eyes were soft as he stepped toward me. We held each other gazes for a moment before his eyes snagged on my mouth for a brief moment. He cleared his throat and said, "Let's go back in before your mom yells at us. She's kinda scary, you know?"

I laughed softly. "Imagine what it was like when I stayed out just five minutes past curfew. She was halfway to killing me and calling the cops."

I grabbed my phone and quickly texted Alexa.

Rosie: long story but my parents and sister surprised me and came to visit. they're sleeping in my room and my sister's on the couch. is it cool if aiden and i sleep in your room? i'll change the sheets

Alexa: you and AIDEN??? you'll CHANGE THE SHEETS???

Rosie: not like that!! i just meant that i'll change them not that we'll get them dirty

Alexa: proud of u. do whatever u need to do

Maria emerged from my bedroom with a bunch of wrapped boxes and gifts, and something else in a paper bag. Aiden and I apologized again that we hadn't gotten them anything, but they all waved us off. We watched as my parents exchanged gifts with each other and gave Maria her gifts, too. They gave me a few romance novels I'd been wanting and a couple of sweaters. Aiden sat back and watched the whole thing with a light smile on his face. I couldn't stand the fact that he was watching us all give each other gifts without receiving anything.

"I'll be right back," I muttered, running off to get his gift out of my room. I'd made it before we got in our fight and hadn't wrapped it because I didn't know if we'd make up.

I held it behind my back and looked at Aiden. "I haven't had time to wrap this so close your eyes while I place it in your hands." He gave me a flat look, but when I widened my eyes, he relented, holding his hands out. I gently placed the gift in his palms and whispered, "Okay, open."

When he opened his eyes, they widened. "Did you . . . *make* this?"

I hadn't been able to get the picture of Aiden burning CDs based on books out of my head after we got burgers. I loved giving Christmas gifts and when he'd told me, the idea flew into my mind.

"It's based on our book—or at least what we have so far." I nodded at the CD in his hands. "I tried to put one on for every chapter we've written so far. I know people don't really listen to CDs anymore, but I thought for the nostalgia of it all . . . and there's probably *way* too much Taylor Swift, but—"

"I love it." He smiled softly, reading each title I had written carefully on the front of the CD. "I can't believe you made me this." He shook his head. "Hang on a second. I got you something too."

I bit down on a pleasantly surprised smile. I hadn't expected him to get me a gift at all.

He dug around in his peacoat for a second before instructing me to close my eyes. I held my hands out and felt a cool metal touch my hands. My eyes flew open and I gasped in surprise. It was the locket from the Holiday Village. I ran my thumb over the smooth, oval locket before opening it.

There were two empty slots for pictures, one on each side. My lita had had a portrait of her children on one side and her husband on the other. It had felt wrong to take them out, so I'd never really imagined what pictures I would put in a locket of my own.

"Aiden, how did you—"

He shrugged. "When you went to the bathroom, I ran back to get it."

"Rosie, that looks like the one Lita gave you," my dad said quietly.

My throat thickened with tears. It was terribly expensive and even though Aiden *had* the money, he didn't have to spend it on me. So many memories of my lita and that trip to Peru rushed back to me. Now this locket held memories of Aiden *and* Lita in it. I knew I'd never take it off.

I looked up at Aiden, trying to blink back the tears. "Help me put it on?"

He nodded and stood behind me as I lifted my hair, carefully chaining it behind my neck. His fingers brushed against the base of my neck. My breath hitched, resisting a shudder. Once he finished, he brushed his thumb on a spot on the back of my neck slowly, his hand sliding down my shoulder. I held the locket close to my chest and turned around smiling.

"Aiden, you don't know how much this means to me. Thank you."

"Give him a kiss," Maria said encouragingly. I shot her a look, and she shrugged innocently. "What? Y'all are *dating*. You gave each other sentimental gifts. When Peter gives me a gift, I give him a kiss."

Aiden's gaze was like steel on me. I wished I could read his mind because obviously I wanted to kiss him, but I couldn't keep making him do things he didn't want to do.

"Yeah, you're right," Aiden said, determined. "I oughta give you a kiss." He stepped toward me, his hands cradling my face. He leaned in close to me and whispered, "This okay?"

I responded by pushing up to press my lips against his. His lips were warm and soft, and he tasted like peppermint bark. I stepped back from him, suddenly sheepish that I had done that in front of everyone. It was just a peck, but I felt a rush through my body because this was *Aiden*. I'd never run out on him after a kiss again.

"Aiden, we actually got you something, too," my dad said.

Aiden's soft smile morphed into shock as he turned toward my dad. He shook his head, his eyebrows creased. "Oh, you didn't need to—"

"It's not much," Maria said. "But we didn't want you to be empty handed on Christmas."

The paper bag was still sitting there amongst the torn wrapping paper. My mom handed it to Aiden, who took it skeptically. He peeked inside the bag slowly and closed it, laughing.

"What is it?" I asked.

He pulled out an orange and white hat, a T for Tennessee sitting on the bill.

"We knew Rosie was homesick so we brought it for her, but you're with Rosie now, so you must know how much Tennessee means to her. We thought you might like this."

Aiden smiled, flipping the cap around in his hands before pulling it on his head. I had never seen Aiden wear anything other than a beanie and he suddenly looked like every guy from my hometown with the bill sitting low on his eyes.

"How do I look?" he asked.

"You look born and raised in Johnson City," I teased.

"That's a good thing?"

"That's a great thing," my dad said. "I was born in Memphis, raised in Johnson City."

"Where do you two live now? Rosie mentioned it once I think."

"Rogersville," my mom supplied. "You should visit with Rosie sometime."

His gaze slid to mine. "I'd love to. Now that I've got the cap to go with it."

My parents laughed, delighted. My whole body eased at the sight of them talking back and forth, like this could be real. He kept asking them questions about Tennessee, and they asked him a few about New York.

It was nearly three when we all decided to go to bed. It wasn't as rowdy as our Christmases back home, but it felt just as perfect. As the night wore down, we all began to yawn. Nerves ran through me at the thought of having to share a bed with Aiden.

Alexa's room was the same size as mine with a full bed. It wasn't as small as a dorm, but it'd be a tight fit.

My dad lent Aiden an extra pair of sweatpants he'd brought and I gave him an oversized t-shirt. I changed into flannel bottoms and a sweatshirt. After we both were ready, we stood on opposite sides of the small bed, staring down at it.

"You know, I'll be fine on the floor with just a blanket and a pillow. We don't have to . . ." He gestured toward the bed.

"No, no, you're the guest. I'll take the floor."

"There's no way I'm letting you sleep on the floor, Rosie." He puffed out a breath, setting his hands on his hips. "We can share the bed, can't we? We're adults."

"Graduate students."

"Taxpayers."

"A bed is nothing," he said, seemingly convincing himself more than me.

"Nothing."

Still, neither of us made a move toward the bed. I rubbed my arm anxiously. God, this whole situation was stupid. I was acting like a fifteen-year-old girl again, refusing to look Aiden in the eye.

"Well, good night." Aiden bit the bullet, pulling Alexa's comforter and sheets back, settling in.

"Right. Good night." I flipped the light off and slid in next to him.

The last time I'd slept in a bed with someone was Simon over a year ago. I could feel Aiden's body heat radiating next to mine. If I moved even the slightest bit, my leg would be pressed against his.

"Aiden," I whispered after a little while. He didn't respond, his hands folded over his stomach as he slept. I poked him in the shoulder, hoping to wake him, but he still didn't move. "Aiden."

Still no response. Even though this had been one of the longest days of my life, I couldn't sleep. I was too aware of Aiden next to me. I shifted, the sheets rustling, but still nothing woke him.

I moved to my side to face his shoulder and said, "Are you asleep?" With no response, I pushed his shoulder slightly. Okay, maybe a little harder than I should've, but his eyes snapped open.

"I *was* asleep, Rosalinda."

"Uh-oh." I smiled into the dark. "I must be in trouble if you're not calling me Rosie."

"Would you prefer Rosie Posie?" The corner of his mouth quirked up and I groaned.

"I knew you'd use that against me."

"I love it," he said honestly. "I wish I came up with it." He turned to his side to face me, too, his arm curled under his head.

I could barely see him. Alexa had thin curtains covering her windows, but they weren't closed all the way and the light from a nearby apartment building seeped through. Some of the light landed above his face, but the room was still clouded in darkness.

He clicked his tongue, grinning. "You know, ever since your family arrived, you've developed a southern accent."

"No, I haven't."

"No, I haven't," he repeated in an exaggerated southern accent. "You've said 'y'all' at least a million times."

"It's a common term."

"It's cute." He hesitantly reached forward and brushed my hair away from my face, then pushed it behind my shoulder. His hand trailed down the length of my arm softly, goosebumps rising in its wake. "I can see why you like romance so much," he whispered. "If I had parents that in love, I probably would too."

I smiled. "They've always been my proof that true love exists. They're not perfect, trust me, but they really do love each other. They found each other despite growing up in completely different cultures and countries."

"I like them."

"They like you, too. I can tell." I was quiet for a moment. "This has been the best Christmas of my life," I said honestly.

"Me too, Rosie," he said into the darkness. "The absolute best."

The next morning, my pillow was stiff. I frowned and, with my eyes still closed, started to slap it to fluff it up.

"Ow."

I froze. Slowly, I pried my eyes open to discover my pillow was not a pillow, but Aiden's chest. His arm was slung around my body, with his hand dangerously close to my ass. My arm wrapped around his waist, snuggling into him.

"Oh my God," I said when I saw the drool that had gotten on Aiden's shirt.

"What?" he murmured. His eyes opened to meet mine, then widened. "Oh."

I disentangled our legs and pushed myself out of the bed. "Jesus," I said. "Oh my God. I'm sorry. I'm *so* sorry, I don't know—"

"It's okay, Rosie."

"I *drooled* on you," I said, wincing. "I'm so sorry. I'll wash your shirt." My face flamed with mortification. Typical me to drool on someone I had a crush on. Even worse, it was *me* who'd been snuggling with Aiden, not the other way around. He was on his side of the bed, but I was all over him.

"It's not a big deal, Rosie, I promise." He rolled onto his back, his forearm resting on his forehead. His lips were pressed together, trying to suppress a laugh. A new wave of embarrassment washed over me.

Panic began to set in my chest, so I moved toward the bedroom door, falling over myself.

"I'm going to take a shower," I said abruptly, grabbing my clothes.

"Rosie, c'mon, it's okay," he called after me, but I was already halfway out the door.

Not in My Book

Once I had taken the world's longest and coldest shower, I pressed my ear against my bathroom door to hear if anyone was up. I reached for the doorknob but paused at the sound of Aiden's laughter.

I opened the door just a crack and heard my mom and Aiden chattering away. I couldn't see them, but I could clearly make out each word.

"This was Rosie's first ballet recital," my mom said.

"I didn't know she danced."

"She doesn't." My mom laughed. "When she was a little, I tried to teach her the marinera, but she couldn't ever do it. And you know Rosie, she's stubborn, so now she flat out refuses to dance."

I could hear the smile in Aiden's voice. "I'll keep that in mind."

She must've been showing him old pictures of me on her phone. I leaned next to the door, my head resting on the wall. It was calming to hear Aiden talking like this, like he wasn't on guard.

"Can I ask you something?" he said.

"Por supuesto."

"Why'd you name her Rosalinda? I've always loved her name."

I smiled to myself. I must've heard this story a million times growing up.

"Oh, she loves this story." I could hear the smile in my mom's voice. "She used to make me tell it to her every night before bed," she said wistfully. "It's because of her father. I used to work at the flower shop downtown during college. Eric came in one day looking to buy roses for his mother. He bought a bouquet, then pulled a single rose out and handed it to me. He came in nearly every day after that. He always bought one rose, handed it to me after he paid, then walked out.

"Soon after we started dating, roses became our thing. When we got married, he had a rose in his lapel. When I found out I was pregnant, I called him at work and left a worried voicemail. I came home to dozens of roses scattered across our kitchen and living room." She laughed softly at the memory. "There seemed to be no option but to name our first child Rose if she was a girl.

"I pushed for Rosalinda, though," she whispered. "I don't know if you picked up on it, but our Rosie is a little bit of a romantic."

"Really? She's never brought it up," Aiden said.

Mom laughed. I could picture her leaning forward, the light shining in her eye. "She's named after my mother, her lita. My dad *loved*

223

her name, he always called her Rosalindita. She *adored* telenovelas. She and my dad used to sit on the couch watching them so intensely. When Rosie discovered my romance novels, I thought it was destiny—that a love of romance was in all our DNA. I had learned English from a lot of those romance novels going back and forth between Peru and Tennessee during the holidays. I must've read all the ones at the airport. I used to find copies of the books in Spanish and compare the pages until I understood the ones in English just as well. My mother passed away when Rosie was a kid, but they had a cosmic connection. Like they were an extension of each other. Even from the first time my mom laid eyes on her."

"Why Rosie and not Rose?"

The pure curiosity in Aiden's voice formed a knot in the back of my throat. I was so touched that he was taking an interest in me like this, that he was being so kind to my mom.

"Rosie was born with a faint blush on her cheeks and a smile. One look at her and it was obvious she was a Rosie." A comfortable silence fell between them, but it didn't last long. "I've been worried about her ever since she left. But you're good for her. I can see she's okay now that she's got you."

"She was great before she had me. She has everything under control all the time, it seems. I'm always in awe of her."

My heart warmed hearing that. For as much as Aiden had insulted me throughout the year, it was nice to know he thought so highly of me. That he thought I was way more put together than I felt.

I opened the bathroom door. "Good morning," I said shyly. Aiden and my mom were sitting on the couch, still in their pajamas. "Merry Christmas. Where are Maria and Dad?"

"They're getting bagels for everyone," my mom said. "Do you mind if I slip in there to shower?"

"It's all yours."

Once Aiden and I were alone, silence fell between us. He had an extreme case of bed head that made him look so young and *casual*. I took my mom's place on the couch next to Aiden, tucking one leg under me.

"Aiden, look, I want to apologize—"

"Rosie." He shook his head. "You don't need to apologize. Best sleep I've had in years."

"You're just saying that." I covered my face with my hands, mortified.

He gently took my hands into his own, pulling them away from my face. "I'm not. Except for when you started talking in your sleep."

"Liar." I narrowed my eyes.

"Every so often you'd say, 'That's so romantic,' then start snoring."

I pushed his shoulder, laughing. I didn't want to have my heart ripped out of my chest again. I couldn't give my everything to someone who didn't want it and would throw away the spare parts. I just wouldn't survive it. But I wanted *whatever* I could get with Aiden. I was willing to let him stomp over my fragile little heart if that meant I got just a glimpse of his.

"I'm gonna head home, I think."

"You don't have to. I'm not sure what we're going to do today, but you're welcome to join us."

He shook his head. "You're on borrowed time with your family. I'll see you next semester, okay?"

I sighed, knowing he was right. I'd regret it if I didn't spend some quality time with my family before they left.

"Okay," I relented. "I'll walk you out."

We were silent in the elevator ride down. It had snowed all night, the streets blanketed in white.

"You don't even have snow boots on," I said. "Your feet are going to freeze."

He laughed. "I'll be okay." He had his new Tennessee cap on instead of his beanie. "Thank you for letting me stay and for letting me spend Christmas with you."

"I wouldn't have it any other way," I said honestly. I hesitated before reaching up to kiss him on the cheek. "Get home safe, okay?"

He nodded. "Merry Christmas, Rosie."

"Merry Christmas, Aiden."

My family and I spent Christmas Day lounging around, catching up on everything. We watched a few movies on my laptop, talking over all of them. It was how Christmas typically went at home, too. We'd sleep late and spend the day in our cozy clothes, messing around with our gifts.

Their flight wasn't until late at night the day after Christmas, so I thought it'd be nice if I showed them a popular Peruvian restaurant in midtown, Pio Pio, the next afternoon.

Whenever we went out to eat at a Peruvian restaurant, we let my mom order food for the table and shared it family style. Inca Kola and a pitcher of Chicha Morada sat in the middle of the table, and the best food I've had in a year was piled on my plate—and I couldn't get enough of it.

"Aiden is very handsome," my mom said casually, picking at her Lomo Saltado. "Why didn't you tell us you were together?"

I could feel Maria's gaze on me as I shrugged. "I didn't know when to bring it up. It's still new."

"It doesn't look new," my dad said. "He likes you."

"I should hope. He's her *boyfriend*," my mom replied

"How long have you two been together?" Dad pressed. "The way he looks at you, Rosie, it's like—"

"Rosie!" Maria interrupted them. "Tell Mom and Dad about that fellowship thing you mentioned on the phone."

I was grateful for Maria changing the subject, but I was also afraid to tell my parents how important the fellowship opportunity was for me. I didn't want to get their hopes up in case it didn't work out.

"It's a really cool opportunity," I said, downplaying it. The fellowship submission deadline was soon, and I was growing increasingly nervous. The more I worked on my piece, the more I wanted to win. Of course the money was important, but more than that, I wanted to prove that a romance writer could be as good as the other litfic writers. If I won, they'd publish my piece in the literary magazine. I wanted to be able to proudly send a copy of the magazine to everyone I knew and say, *Look! I* am *a good writer. Someone else thinks so!* "I'm submitting a short story I wrote last year and hopefully I get selected."

"How wonderful." My mom smiled at me. "Look at you, making a name for yourself in New York."

"Oh, I don't know about I that," I said, bashful. "I hope so. I think this will help. And Ida and Aiden are looking over it—"

"Aiden's looking over your piece?" My mom lit up.

"I like Aiden," my dad declared.

Maria and I shared a panicked glance. My dad *rarely* liked the guys we brought home. He really hadn't loved Simon—he'd claimed Simon was egotistical and self-centered, but I didn't really care. The only guy I dated that my dad had ever liked was Josh when I was in *eighth grade*. Maria and Peter dated their senior year of high school and all through college, and that was fine, but Dad *hated* all of Maria's boyfriends before him. He had this intuition about people and now that he'd declared fondness for Aiden, it meant he'd probably be asking about Aiden frequently.

"He's not that great," I said casually, shoveling food into my mouth.

"He bought you that necklace." My dad gestured toward the locket. "And you haven't taken it off since he gave it to you."

Instinctively, my hand reached up to clasp the necklace closer to me.

"We've just started dating," I explained. "I don't even know him that well—"

My mom gasped. "You don't *know* him? Ay, Ros—"

"I have to pee," Maria announced. She turned toward me. "Come with me to the bathroom?"

"Of course," I said, jumping up from my seat. The minute the door closed behind us I told her, "I love you."

She laughed. "They're being a lot. They're happy you found someone after, you know, everything with Simon."

"I'll tell them when they go back to Tennessee that Aiden and I broke up or something. Otherwise, Mom'll hound me with questions every time I answer the phone."

Maria pulled her lipstick out of her purse, reapplying slowly in the mirror. Her gaze flickered to me. "They are a little right about Aiden."

I knew that. But they didn't know that Aiden didn't do romance. Even if Aiden *did* have feelings for me, it didn't mean he was looking for a relationship.

"How so?"

"Aiden looks at you like he wishes you're really together . . . he was hanging on your every word. When we opened gifts, I felt so horrible that we only had one thing to give him, and it wasn't even a good gift. But he looked genuinely happy to see you happy."

"Aiden and I are friends," I said more to myself. That's what we had decided, even if I wanted more.

"Peter and I were friends," she sang. She set her lipstick down and turned to face me. When we were little, people used to think we were twins. We had the same dark eyes and hair, though hers had soft waves and mine was a mess of curls, and Maria was slightly taller. But otherwise we looked nearly identical. "I have to tell you something."

"Is everything okay with you and Peter?" I straightened, concerned.

She glanced away from me, nervously. Guilt washed over me. I wasn't being a good big sister, calling her and checking up on her. I'd been so focused on my life, I didn't know much about hers.

"Of course." She waved me off. "But you can't tell Mom and Dad."

My brows furrowed. "I won't."

A beat passed before she said, "I'm pregnant."

My gasp echoed in the bathroom, and I clutched her hands. "Maria, oh my God!"

Her eyes were wide as she squeezed my hand tightly. Her voice was strained as she said, "I've only known a month. I can't stop freaking out. It's why I wanted you to come home so badly for the holidays and when you couldn't, I practically begged Mom and Dad to take a trip to New York to see you."

"Why are you freaking out?" I asked softly. "This is great news. The *best* news. What is Peter thinking?"

Tears were brimming her eyes. "Peter sobbed for like an hour when I told him. He ordered a bunch of parenting books online and has already decided that they're twins, for some reason."

I laughed. "That sounds like Peter."

"But Rosie . . . I'm too *young.*" Her voice cracked and she blinked rapidly. "I'm only twenty-five! I can't be a *mother.*"

"Yes, you can," I said softly. "You'll be great."

"No, *Peter* will be great. He's Mr. Domesticity. Whenever I grocery shop, we're eating like shit for a week. And I somehow always mess up the laundry—"

"That's not what makes a good mother," I interrupted her. "Your baby is going to grow up so loved and with an amazing support system. They'll have us and all the tías and all of Peter's family, too."

She wiped the tears under her eyes. "I'm just scared."

"Everyone's scared of growing up and moving on." I handed her a paper towel and rubbed her arms soothingly as she wiped tears away.

"You aren't."

I snorted. "I'm *terrified*. I walk out on the street, and I'm scared half to death that I'll fall in a pothole or something. And all this stuff with Aiden . . ."

She nodded for a moment, quiet. "You shouldn't be scared about Aiden, though."

"Maria . . ."

"No, I'm serious. I know Simon hurt you and left you bruised and bent, but he didn't break you."

"I don't know if I can survive getting hurt that bad again."

I used to think that, anyway. That I wouldn't ever be able to fall in love, and I'd be stuck in a pit, always trying to climb out of it. But with Aiden . . . it didn't feel so scary. I wasn't there yet, but maybe, with him, I could open myself up again.

She pulled me into a tight hug and whispered, "Love wouldn't seem worth it without the risk of losing it."

I'd lived in this city for my whole life. Every milestone and moment of my history was written into the streets here.

But all of them had been easily replaced with memories of her. I'd turn a corner and swear I smelled her perfume. I'd sit in the car of a subway and my head would snap up, certain I heard the peal of her laughter. I couldn't walk a block with being reminded of her. I loved hearing her name in everything around me and seeing her on every street.

Even if it amounted to nothing, and she left me only with memories, I'd take them all. I'd hoard them to turn over in my head and examine from every angle, just to relive the magic of her.

— Excerpt from *Untitled* by
Rosie Maxwell and Aiden Huntington

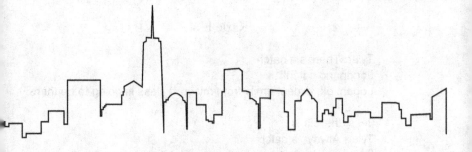

CHAPTER TWENTY-THREE

Logan: we're going out tonight

Logan changed the group chat name to *new years eve or bust*

Tyler: I'm not.
Logan: yes you are. we all are. it's new years eve
Tyler: It's going to be too hectic out—I'd rather just stay in.
Logan: here lies tyler richardson, he was too afraid to do
    anything
Logan: that's what your tombstone will read
Jess: little harsh logan
Logan: someone needs to speak the truth around here
Logan: we have options!! peculiar pub is showing the ball drop
    but it doesn't really seem like they're going to party like we
    are
Rosie: we're partying?
Jess: i guess so
Logan: there's a new club called the new romantics in the west
    village and i propose we go there
Logan: no cover charge, two drink minimum, and they're show-
    ing the ball drop too it'll be more lively there than at peculiar
    pub it's perfect

Tyler: There's a catch.
Logan: no catch!!
Logan: ok, except emily from my craft class is going to be there
    so . . .
Jess: there it is
Tyler: Always a catch
Logan: rosie, u should be on my side! it's romance
Rosie: i agree w logan. we should go out tonight, new year's eve
    is magical!!
Jess: im down so long as logan buys our drinks
Logan: im poor
Jess: we're all poor
Rosie: tyler, are you in?
Tyler: I think I'll stay in tonight, but you guys have fun.

Jess texted me separately.

Jess: you have to get tyler to come
Rosie: what makes you think i can do it?? you're better friends w
    him!
Jess: i can't seem too obvious
Rosie: we're not in middle school
Jess: im begging

I groaned, switching back to the group chat.

Rosie: tyler, you should come out! it'll be a lot of fun
Tyler: I'm not really in the mood

I sighed, knowing what'd get him.

Rosie: fine. the real reason i want everyone to come out tonight
    is because aiden and i kissed and i need to talk about it,
    ok??

Jess texted me privately.

Jess: you're my best friend in the entire world

Logan: YOU'RE KIDDING WHAT WHEN WHERE???

Jess: on her mouth probably. unless aiden is as kinky as we
thought

Rosie: shut up. the point is I need help from my friends process-
ing this

Rosie: tyler, are you in???

Tyler: Fine. Drinks on Logan, though.

Logan: fine. fuck you guys, if this is the price of love then i'll pay it

The New Romantics was probably the *worst* place in New York to have
a conversation on New Year's Eve. The bar sat in the center of the room
with a dance floor on one side and tables on the other. There were
sweaty, glittery bodies all pressed up against each other, jumping to
some techno song. The Countdown to Midnight ball drop was playing
on every screen in the place, muted.

The four of us were sitting at a small booth draped in velvet, silver
glitter adorning the table. Strobe lights illuminated the room every so
often. I could barely hear myself talk as I relayed what happened the
day at Aiden's apartment and then last week at Christmas. I had
already told Jess everything, but Logan's jaw was slack in shock and
Tyler's eyes widened.

"I knew it," Logan shouted over the music. "I *told* all of you when
they were forced to cowrite they would end up fucking."

"But we didn't," I corrected him.

"You're obviously *going* to."

Tyler leaned forward. "Rosie, how are you feeling? That's a lot."

I messed with the straw in my cocktail. "I guess I'm . . . cautiously
optimistic that part of him feels the same way as I do?"

Replaying everything that had happened between Aiden and me
in the last few months for them, it seemed so obvious. It wasn't until
I'd said it out loud that I realized how ridiculous I was being, doubting
how Aiden felt. The last time I'd started a relationship with someone,
I was *fifteen*. I wasn't so great at picking up all the signs, it seemed, but
they were *there*. Adrenaline rushed through me at the realization, and
I became a little breathless.

"So you like him?" Tyler asked.

I nodded, smiling as I touched my locket. I didn't need to think twice about it. Everywhere I went nowadays, he popped in my mind, lingering there. And I wanted him to stay.

"You could invite him here," Jess said.

I shook my head immediately. "No way."

"You could!" Tyler insisted. "We'll be nice. You like him, Rosie, and we like you. If you say he's changed, and he isn't mean to you like he was at the beginning of the semester, we'll be nice, too."

"Aiden *hasn't* changed, though," I said. "And I don't want him to change. I like how . . . surly he is. I just understand him better now than I did before."

"*Invite him,*" Jess said excitedly.

Logan nodded. "New Year's is all about ringing in the new year with people you want to be in your life in the coming year. You *want* to be with Aiden. Take a chance on yourself."

All three of them looked back at me encouragingly. And I knew they were right. The person I wanted to be with most right now was Aiden. Even if he'd frown at the music and crinkle his nose at the drunken dancers.

I nodded once, decided. "I'll be back."

I made my way outside into the last of the December cold. I stood in the smoking area as people continued to stream into the club, girls shivering in their shiny dresses and heels. With one last breath of courage, I called Aiden.

The phone rang twice, before I heard his deep, sleepy voice, "Rosie?"

"Hi," I said. "I didn't wake you, did I?"

"No." I heard some rustling. "I was just reading in bed."

I deflated. "Oh."

"Are you okay? Isn't it almost midnight?"

I pulled my phone back from my face, checking the time. "Twenty minutes."

"What's up?"

I kicked at a pebble in front of me, feeling foolish. Aiden wasn't the type of guy to go out and party on New Year's Eve. Of *course* he was in bed with a book at eleven thirty, not even caring.

"It's nothing. I'm sorry, I woke you. Happy New Year."

"Tell me," he demanded softly. "Are you okay?"

"I'm fine," I assured him. "I'm out with Tyler, Jess, and Logan, and well, we were talking about how you should ring in the New Year with people you wanted to be in your life next year. And I love them, but I kept wishing you were here. With me. Because I want to see more of you in the New Year and well . . ." Gathering my courage, I touched my locket again, reminding myself what that meant. I just had to make this leap. "Because I like you, Aiden. Not in the *oh, I saw this and thought of you* way. But in the *oh you told me this and now I can't stop thinking about it because* you *think about it* way. And in the *I want to end this year with you and start the new one with you too* way."

He was silent a moment. In the five seconds it took him to respond, I regretted every word I said. I wished I could shove them back in my mouth and pretended it never happened.

"Where are you?" he asked.

My heart thumped as I told him the name of the club we were at.

"I'll see you soon."

I looked down at my phone, a little dazed. When I walked back into the club, I found Jess and Tyler by themselves in the booth, sitting close to each other.

"So?" Jess asked the minute I sat down.

"Where'd Logan go?"

Tyler nodded toward the dance floor. "Emily came. How'd it go with Aiden?"

"He said he's coming." I tried to keep my voice steady. "He lives close by so maybe he'll be here before midnight."

"I knew it," Jess said, beaming at me.

"Everyone in the workshop knew it," Tyler said. "It was only a matter of time, Rosie."

The three of us continued to chat, but I quickly got the vibe that they wanted to be alone. Tyler smiled easily at everything Jess said and would occasionally push her hair away from her shoulder.

I sent a look to Jess and said, "I'm going to grab some water. Anyone want anything?"

"We're good," Jess said with an excited smile.

The bar area was crowded, and it was hard to make my way through since I was so short, but I was in no rush. There were only two minutes until midnight and everyone was trying to get their last drink

of the year. My eyes wandered to the door, hoping Aiden would miraculously walk in before midnight, but the clock was ticking.

Soon, the DJ called out, "One minute to go!"

Everyone dissipated from the bar and started searching for their
significant others. Jess and Tyler stood from the booth and made their
way to the dance floor as the countdown started on all the TVs.

When the countdown from ten started, I lost hope. It had been
too short notice, he probably wouldn't make it.

Five.

"Hi."

I whipped around and Aiden was standing behind me—in a red
sweater and dark jeans. My mind told me to play it cool, but my body
wasn't listening. I could hardly believe he was standing there, looking
at me with soft adoration in his eyes. My heart thumped against my
chest. I bit down a smile as I instinctively moved toward him.

Four.

"Hi! You came."

Three.

He smiled. "I did."

Two.

"You wore red."

One.

"Someone told me it's what you wear when you hope for love."

I sucked in a breath. "And you're hoping for love?"

He nodded, stepping toward me. Everyone around us was cheer-
ing and kissing as "Auld Lang Syne" played. "I am. I'm not good at it.
And I've had bad role models, but I want to try."

I nodded, my chest so full of hope. "Me too."

He rubbed the material of my dress between his fingers, his hand
lingering on my wrist. "What does black mean?"

"It means you're taking control over your life," I said. My stomach
dipped when his mouth hooked up on one side, smiling down at me.
"Do you want to dance?"

He held out his hand silently, and together we stood amongst the
swaying couples, our eyes locked on each other's. He pressed his hand
to the small of my back, pulling me closer. I was too short for us to
dance cheek to cheek, but Aiden bent his head so we could.

"I was afraid you were drunk," he whispered, his mouth pressed right against my ear. "And that was the only reason you invited me."

"I was a little tipsy," I admitted. "Liquid courage and all that."

"You don't need liquid courage. You've got me." His hands tightened on my waist and I gripped his shoulder.

"I know we said we wouldn't talk about the book anymore. But . . . if this were a romance novel, and if I were Maxine, which I am, and if you were Hunter, which you are, then this would be the part of the romance novel where we kiss," I whispered. "It'd be the part where I'd tell you that I want you. And that I think about you all the time."

Aiden pulled back from me, his green eyes pining me down. His hand came up to cradle my jaw, his thumb brushing across my cheek, softly and slowly.

"It'd be the part where I told you not a single day has passed since we met that I haven't thought about you. And not a single hour passes where I don't miss you," he whispered. "But we're not writing a romance novel."

"No," I conceded. "But maybe I can change your mind."

His mouth covered mine. He was warm and tasted like mint. I sighed into his mouth, pressing myself closer to him as his hand moved from my jaw to my hair, angling my head up so he could deepen the kiss.

His tongue found mine, tasting, seeking, wanting. I tugged on his bottom lip with my teeth. He groaned and pulled back.

"Rosie, I can't do this if we're going to forget about it tomorrow," he rasped, backing away from my lips the tiniest bit. "I've gotten good at pretending I hate you, but I can't pretend I don't know how you taste anymore."

"Then let's not pretend," I said against his mouth. "Let's go do all the things we wrote about."

"I knew it." A slight smile played across on his lips, his eyes dark and hooded with desire. "I knew you were thinking of me when we wrote that scene."

"As if you weren't thinking of me, too."

"I only think of you, Rosie," he whispered against my mouth before sliding his hand in my hair to pull me into a kiss.

I was shameless in my wanting. I tried to commit every little thing, the way her eyes fell closed, the way she tasted, to memory. There was no metaphor I could write, picture I could paint that would even come close to comparing to the magic of her.

— Excerpt from *Untitled* by
Rosie Maxwell and Aiden Huntington

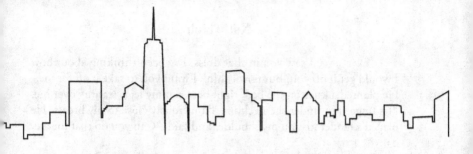

CHAPTER TWENTY-FOUR

We rushed toward Aiden's apartment, stopping every so often to kiss at crosswalks. He fumbled, trying to get his key in the door, then whipped it open, guided us through, and pushed me back against it, lifting me so my legs would wrap around his waist.

"I just can't wait," Aiden muttered, planting open mouthed kisses under my jaw. "I should just take you right here in the entryway."

"I don't care." I grabbed his face, guiding his lips back to mine. His tongue slid against mine as I moaned.

"I've thought of you so much like this," he whispered in my ear. His voice was so low and intoxicating, I lost myself in the hoarseness of it. "Wrapped around me, moving against me. Whimpering like you just can't get enough."

"I *can't*," I gasped. He tugged on my earlobe with his teeth. I barely recognized the sounds coming out of my mouth as my hips moved against his hardness, craving more friction. With my legs still wrapped around him, Aiden carried me up to the second floor of his apartment. He nudged his bedroom door open, then dropped me onto the center of the bed, standing at the foot. His eyes were dark with desire, and I could make out the length of him through his jeans. I looked up at Aiden, who was becoming *my* Aiden with every second. He unbuckled his belt with one hand, tossing it to the side.

"Ever since I saw you in that dress, I've been thinking about how I would get it off you. But now I think I want you to take it off for me." He planted a knee on the bed, right between my legs, leaning over me. His finger ran under the neckline, dangerously close to my breast. He placed a tender kiss on my shoulder and said, "Can you do that for me, baby?"

I nodded. With nervous, shaky fingers, I pulled the dress over my head in a quick motion, leaving me only in a red thong and black bra.

"I wore red, too," I whispered.

He smiled, his hands running up my sides, and although they were rough, he touched my skin so reverently and gently, leaving goosebumps in his wake.

"You're more perfect than I ever could've imagined, Rosie," he murmured against my lips. "And I've thought about you a *lot*. I can't take it some days. You wore a tight pink sundress last year during workshop, and I was hard all class."

I clutched at his back as he ground his hips against me, his mouth taking mine again. Pleasure sparked behind my eyes, and I had to bite my lip to keep all my embarrassing moans in.

Aiden noticed and narrowed his eyes at me, stopping his movements. He pulled my bottom lip away from my teeth with his thumb and said, "None of that. I want to hear you, Rosie. I want to hear the moans I'm earning."

My breath caught, my eyes screwed shut in pleasure from his words. My hands traveled down his back, but I was frustrated with the fabric. "Aiden." I sighed. "I want to feel you, too."

I pushed him off me slightly, creating enough space between us for me to start pulling off his shirt, though my trembling fingers were making me clumsy. "I'm sorry, I'm trying—"

He pulled back and held my hands in his, steadying them. He tried to catch my eye, but I wouldn't look up from his shirt. "Rosie, you're shaking."

He sat up fully. I moved with him, my fingers still gripping his shirt. "It's fine, just help me with your—"

"Rosie, it's not okay. Hey." He grabbed my chin with his thumb and forefinger. "We don't have to do anything you don't want to tonight. I want you only if you want me, and I'm not going to be disappointed if you decide you want to stop." I looked away from him, my cheeks flushing. "If you want to stop here, that's fine. We can go downstairs and put on some Nora Ephron movie and make popcorn or do whatever you want. *Whatever* you want, Rosie."

"No, I want to," I said honestly.

"Let me in there." He tapped on my head delicately. "What's going on?"

"I'm just nervous. I've—" I broke off, not able to meet his eyes. "I've got no moves. None. I've always been so self-conscious during sex that I forget to enjoy it, and then I make the guy feel bad when I can't come and so it becomes this whole thing and—"

"Hold up," he said, disbelief stretching across his face. "Has a guy not made you come before?"

"No." I paused. "But it's fine! I've just accepted that I'm one of those women who can't—"

He cut me off. "Rosie, if we do this, and we still don't have to, we don't stop until you come." Aiden's voice was at an intoxicatingly low level, his gaze intent on mine. "It's no good unless it's good for both of us."

Nerves and excitement spread throughout my body. "But what if I can't?"

Aiden gently took my face between both of his hands and said, "Then I don't stop. I've got nowhere to be. I'm here and you can trust that I'm going to do this for you. But, Rosie, I'm serious if you don't want to—"

I cut him off with a kiss, trying to prove to him that I was exactly where I wanted to be. "I want to, Aiden."

With steadier hands, I grabbed his shirt again and tugged it over his head. I had never seen Aiden without a shirt before. He was toned and muscular, hair dusting his chest. I couldn't stop running my hands over his shoulders, feeling the hardness beneath my fingertips.

He nodded toward the bed and said, "Lay down for me?"

Once I did, he pulled me to the edge of the bed, kneeling between my legs. He ran his hands up and down my thighs, warming me in the process. He met my eyes and said, "If you say stop tonight, Rosie, at any point, we stop. Doesn't matter what we're doing or how close one of us is to finishing, we stop."

"Okay," I whispered.

His lips quirked to the side as he ran a finger along the seam of my laced panties. "I have a feeling you won't want to, though."

Then his mouth was on me. He was kissing me through the fabric, but I was sensitive enough that my hips jerked up. He continued to scatter kisses along me, running his tongue through my center and along the seams until I was heaving.

"You're so wet for me, baby," he rasped against me. "I have to taste you. I can't wait any longer."

Baby. It roared in my ears. Aiden was pulling my panties off, distractedly stuffing them in his back pocket, but all I could think was that he'd called me *baby*. A new wave of desire flooded through me as I released a moan as the feel of his tongue. I grabbed at the bed sheets, curling them in my fists as his mouth moved against my bare skin.

He ran a careful, slow finger through me before teasing my entrance.

"Aiden," I moaned. My mind was in a battle between keeping my eyes on his brown hair between my legs and being screwed shut. But with every swirl of his tongue against my clit and his finger finally, *finally* entering me I couldn't keep my eyes open any longer.

"Tell me how it feels." I hummed in response, but he tsked. "Use your words, baby, you're a writer, aren't you?"

I was barely coherent, needy for more of him. I reached for words to tell him that sex had never been like this for me, not ever, but his finger was teasing me, and he was kissing my thighs. Just as I opened my mouth to respond, he added another finger, sucking my clit into his mouth. At every filthy sound and the sight of him between my legs, I grew wetter. My hands flew to his hair, keeping him against me.

"Faster, *please*, Aiden," I whimpered, finally finding my words. His fingers moved faster, rougher and I couldn't stop from clenching around him, pulling him deeper. But no matter how close I got, I couldn't finish.

I was too self-conscious. I wasn't as skinny as most of the girls who passed me in the street in New York. I had stretch marks all around the tops of my thighs, little white lines of imperfection that made me loathe every bathing suit.

Aiden had been at it for a while now but no matter how incredible it felt or how close I got, something held me back.

"Aiden, it's no use. Let me do something for—"

His laid his arm across my waist, holding me down. His other hand pushed against my thigh, opening me wider.

"I'm not stopping until you come, Rosalinda."

"I *can't*." I was on the verge of tears, frustrated. I didn't feel sexy anymore, but like a nuisance. I had thought of Aiden like this so many times and now that I had him here I was ruining the moment. Even though he said he wouldn't, I knew he would get bored.

"Rosie," he said softly. "Do you *want* me to stop?"

I covered my eyes with my forearm, mortified. "*No*. It's just not going to happen."

He ran his hands up my stomach, cupping my breasts through my bra. "Why don't you let me decide that? Focus on what you feel, nothing else."

"I'm sorry, I'm boring you—"

"I'm hard as a fucking rock, Rosalinda. I'm absolutely *not* bored."

With that, he sucked my clit back into his mouth and slipped two fingers into me. I did as he said and closed my eyes and focused on how he alternated between roughly fucking me with his fingers, then immediately soothing the pain with sensual strokes of his tongue.

"Play with your tits," he said, his voice ragged. I opened my eyes and found his eyes focused on me completely.

I nodded, trusting him and unhooked my bra, taking my breasts in my hands. I pulled at my nipples and as I did, Aiden sucked on my clit harder. I gasped, my back arching.

Soon, the pleasure built up and I couldn't stop my hips from moving against him. I squirmed, trying to satiate the pleasure. Aiden moved faster, his fingers rougher.

"Aiden," I gasped. "I'm going to—"

He curled his fingers, and my hips shot off the bed. He moved with me, his mouth hooked to me as I came. I cried out, my muscles tensing with pleasure.

Once I finished, Aiden shed his pants, grabbing himself through his boxer briefs. He gave himself a few rough strokes, hissing as he watched me.

"God, Rosie, I could come from your taste alone. I'm already so fucking close," he bit out.

He moved up the bed, leaning down to kiss me. Desire pulsed through me, his tongue making silky strokes again mine. I could taste myself on his mouth, but I didn't care.

In between kisses, he began to pull his briefs off, and I moved to help him. We fumbled, laughing against each other's mouths. Finally, I got to see all of him.

"Of course you have the perfect body," I groaned, marveling at his strong arms and broad chest. At a glance down, I blurted out, "Fuck, you're big."

He pressed his mouth to mine laughing softly, "And you're fucking tight. And perfect, Rosie. You're absolutely beautiful."

I always took for granted in romance novels when the hero would call the heroine beautiful. It was typical and expected, but with Simon it was never a guarantee. Sometimes he'd mumble a "you're hot" in bed, but nothing else. But the way Aiden said my name and the way he was looking at me made me believe he truly meant it. Reading it in your favorite book was so different from hearing it from the mouth of your new favorite person. This was so much better.

The urgency returned as our kisses turned longer and more desperate. We grasped at each other, our hands roaming freely on each other's bodies.

"I have an IUD. I got tested after Simon, and I haven't been with anyone since . . ." I trailed off.

"I haven't been with anyone since my last test either. Are you sure?"

"I want to feel you," I said, nodding and pressing a kiss on the underside of his jaw.

I couldn't help but reach forward and take him in my hand, my fist barely closing around him. He tilted his head back, releasing a strangled groan. Just as I was about to lean forward to take him in my mouth, he pulled me away from him.

He let out a shuddering exhale and said, "A man can only take so much, have some mercy."

His chest rose up and down as he watched me. "On your back, baby."

No matter how many times he said it, my heart warmed at the term of endearment. Almost immediately, he settled in between my legs. He gently tapped his cock against my clit, causing me to hiss.

Gently, he entered me. I gasped, my eyes squeezing shut. He slowly stretched me. I gasped as he kept going. He slowed, letting me adjust.

"You look so good taking me like that." With another push, his hips rested against mine. "*Fuck*. Fuck you're so tight."

I squeezed around him, his hips flinching in response.

"Rosie," he warned. The authoritative tone he held in class showing up now made me clamp down on him again. "You're gonna make me come before I have the chance to fuck you the way I want."

His hips began to move. Slowly at first, almost tenderly. Gradually, he picked up speed, his cock driving into me. I moved my hips, trying to create friction, but I was so deep in desire I could barely do anything but moan.

"I know, I know. I've got you," he whispered in my ear. "Go on, take my cock. Look at you, acting like you just can't get enough."

"Oh fuck, Aiden," I gasped, clutching his shoulders. His fingers reached down between us, finding my clit with his thumb. He stroked it in time with his thrusts. My back arched, unable to take all the pleasure.

"You look so good wrapped around me."

My moans filled the room. Aiden kept his pace, sweat dripping from his forehead.

"Such a good girl, Rosie, even now. Taking me like this," he bit out. "Always a good girl for me, isn't that right?"

"Yes," I gasped, fisting the bed sheets. "Keep talking."

He moved down to his elbows, caging my face between them. "You look so pretty like this," he groaned in my ear. "I can't get enough of you."

He picked up the pace as I began to tighten around him. He took my leg and placed my foot on his shoulder, driving even deeper into me. His pelvis was flush against mine now, rubbing my clit with every roll of his hips. I couldn't take it anymore—my eyes screwed shut, trying to accept the pleasure.

"Open your eyes," he commanded. "Are you going to come?" My eyes flashed open and I nodded, helpless to the pleasure coursing through my body. "Look at me when you come around my cock like you're mine. Show me exactly what I do to you."

I cried out, going over the edge. Pleasure from every inch of my body wrecked me. Aiden gave a single thrust, muttering "Fuck," and spilled inside me.

He rolled off me, both of us lying there, panting. He laughed softly and pulled me toward his chest, and I wrapped my arm around his waist.

"I'm all messy," I warned, slurring, still a little delirious from the pleasure.

He softly padded into his bathroom and returned with a wash-cloth. Gently, he wiped between my thighs and said, "I want all your messes."

I hummed, reaching for him to lay next to me.

"You okay?" he murmured against the side of my head, planting a kiss on the side of my forehead, his hand sliding up and down my back. Through my hair. Never not touching me.

I nodded, laughing softly. "Oh yeah, I'm worn out. Completely ruined. No critiques."

"That's a first."

I wasn't used to this. Being able to touch Max whenever I wanted. I'd spent so much time, stuffing my hands in my coat pockets to resist grabbing her hand. Now she was in my bed, her head against my chest, her heart beating in tandem with mine.

— Excerpt from *Untitled* by
Rosie Maxwell and Aiden Huntington

CHAPTER TWENTY-FIVE

I woke with Aiden's arm slung around my waist. During the middle of the night, maybe between rounds two and three, Aiden found an old t-shirt for me to sleep in. It was a worn out Velvet Underground shirt that smelled exactly like him. My throat was dry, and I tried to slip out of Aiden's grasp, but he just held me tighter.

"Where are you going?" he murmured into my hair.

"I was going to raid your kitchen."

"For what?"

"I was going to start with water then see if you had Pop-Tarts."

He opened one eye. "Do I seem like the type of person to have Pop-Tarts?"

"Yes. Brown sugar."

He sighed and pulled my waist closer to his abdomen. "I'm obviously a s'mores guy." He kissed my cheek and said, "I'll get you water, stay here."

The bed dipped behind me, and I was suddenly colder in his absence. I listened to Aiden's feet padding down the hallway and stairs and slowly sat up in his bed. His room wasn't far off from what I had imagined. He had a queen-sized bed facing a window with closed white curtains. A wooden dresser sat in the corner with a few books sitting on top. The door to his closet peeked open, with sweaters and button-downs hanging on the rack. I leaned over the bed, contemplating opening the door of his nightstand. It felt like an invasion of privacy, but I was so curious. My hand reached for it tentatively before I snatched it back.

"You can open it."

I jumped at the sound of Aiden's voice. He was leaning against the door frame in nothing but boxers, holding two glasses of water. He handed me a glass of water before slipping into bed.

"I wasn't going to."

"You were and it's fine." He smiled. "I don't mind."

I scowled. "You don't know everything. I was going to feel the wood."

He nodded and said, "Sure."

I sipped my water greedily before setting it on the nightstand.

At the beginning of the semester I never would've believed I'd end up in Aiden's bed—or that I'd even want to. But he clearly wanted me the way I wanted him, which meant his hands were probably just as clammy as mine and his heart was probably racing as much as mine. There was so much I wanted to ask him and get to know about him. But all that came out of my mouth was:

"So, you kinda have a dirty mouth in bed, huh?"

Aiden choked on his own water, coughing. "Jesus Christ, Rosie."

"I was surprised!" I said defensively. "I mean you know I was thinking of you when we wrote that scene, but I thought you were just playing it up for the book. I didn't think you'd *actually* say stuff like that out loud."

Aiden looked toward the ceiling. "God, I'm going to die."

"I liked it!" I reassured. "Trust me, any romance reader eats that shit up, but I just didn't expect it from you."

"Can we talk about anything else?"

"Aww," I cooed. "Is someone shy?"

"No." He leveled me with a look. "I'd rather not have this conversation when I can see your nipples through my shirt, slowly getting me hard. If we're going to have this conversation, I'd rather have it when I can fuck you."

My cheeks turned crimson, but I grinned. "See? Dirty talker."

He rolled his eyes and handed me his glass. "Put this on the nightstand for me?"

Even in the silence, everything felt right. I had dreaded the times when Simon and I would wake up on mornings like this, curious as to what we would even say. What casually cruel thing Simon would say that I'd done wrong in bed or wasn't doing enough of for him.

"I don't want to get up," I confessed. "Your bed is so comfortable."

"We don't have to," Aiden said carefully. He looked down at his hands, his fingers playing with each other. "Look, Rosie, if last night was just a heat of the moment thing—"

"It wasn't," I said immediately. I pushed the comforter away so I could sit closer to him. I held his hands in mine. He intertwined our fingers, pulling me down to lay on his chest.

His eyes found mine, intensely focused on me. His voice was low, tentative as he said, "I'm in this, Rosie. I have trouble opening up because I've found that when I did, it scared people off. Somewhere along the way I decided it was better to keep to myself. And then when my mom died I was just so *mad* at the world, and I pushed so many people away. I let that defensive side of myself get the better of me sometimes, but I don't want to do that with you. I'm *in* this," he said earnestly.

I peered up at him placing my chin on his chest. I reached up to push his hair back from his eyes, softly. "I am too, Aiden. I know you think I have all these grand expectations for romance, but I really don't."

"I don't want to hurt you," he said honestly. "My mom really believed in Happily Ever Afters, even after everything with my dad. She got burned time and time again. I figured if someone as good as her didn't get to have one, then it just wasn't real. I don't want to burn you."

"I don't want to burn *you*," I whispered. "Maybe we haven't had our hearts broken in the same way, but you still have. I want to take care of you, too."

He cupped my cheek, kissing me softly. I pulled back and smiled, so happy that I was here with him. That my New Year hadn't started with a hangover and a headache, but with Aiden in a comfy bed.

We decided (more like I insisted) that the *only* way to spend the day was in bed. Aiden had said that was ridiculous, so I amended it to bed and couch. He ordered us some bagels for breakfast and when he went downstairs to get them, I quickly texted Jess:

Rosie: at aiden's place!! howd it go with tyler??
Jess: . . . at tyler's place
Rosie: NO WAY
Jess: literally in a daydream, debrief this weekend???
Rosie: absolutely

We talked in his bed for what felt like hours, telling funny stories from our childhood. I told him how Maria and I would catch fireflies in jars, running around in our backyard. How every Thursday night my family would play Monopoly, and I'd threaten to flip the table every time I lost. I talked a lot for the both of us at first. But once he started to open up, the words came rushing out.

I was greedy for everything Aiden revealed about himself. I'd press him for more details about his best friend from second grade or the time he learned to drive in Queens—he'd shake his head as if he was annoyed, suppressing a smile, and then tell me more.

The love I had read in romance novels was so epic and monumental. I'd spent a lifetime craving grand gestures and sweeping proclamations. I hadn't known the small moments like this would feel as good.

"You really don't mind looking over my piece for the fellowship?" I asked him, still in bed.

We sat against the headboard, him facing forward with my legs slung over his lap. He gave me a t-shirt he was never getting back because it smelled like him, and I couldn't get enough. He was rubbing up and down my leg soothingly.

"Not at all, Rosie," he said, affectionately. "I love reading your writing. Send it over now."

"Thank you," I said sincerely as I forwarded him once of my previous emails to Ida with the story attached. He reached for his phone to read through it, but I rushed to stop him. "Not now! You'll make me nervous."

He shot me a look. "We've written *together*. You don't need to be shy in front of me of all people."

I warmed at the sentiment. "Please," I said anyway. "I'll just scrutinize your every expression, and then I'll probably find it hot and then it'll lead to me wanting to go *again* with you and I really need my rest."

He laughed, shaking his head. "Fine, fine. Are you sore, baby?"

I leaned forward to kiss him quickly, thrilled that I got to just *do* that now. "Not too sore for an hour from now."

I pulled away before he could deepen the kiss because then we'd *really* be in trouble. He studied me before carefully saying, "I didn't know how important the Frost Fellowship was to you."

I scoffed. "I *need* this fellowship. I wish I'd known about it last year, too—if I'd applied and somehow won, I would be halfway through my MFA by now." I sighed. "But whatever, hopefully it works out this year."

He squeezed my calf and said, "I'm sure your piece is great."

"Have you thought about applying?" I asked, hesitantly. Aiden was more in tune with the literary world than I was. I stuck to my romance novels, always scrolling through social media on the eye for the newest releases. But Aiden knew which magazines were important, which agencies were the most reputable.

"Yeah, I've thought about it," he said quietly.

"The due date isn't until next week. You should apply." The lie tasted bad in my mouth. I wanted to be as supportive of him as he was of me. But I knew that if he submitted something, he would have a way better chance than me. As much as I adored Aiden, I couldn't let go of the part of my brain that viewed him as competition.

"We'll see" was all he said.

I was a bit relieved by this. It made sense. Aiden had more money than God, he probably didn't need the money at all. I'm sure he was submitting to other magazines, too.

After we fell into a comfortable silence, I said, "I know it shouldn't matter now, but I want to know why you hated me."

He frowned. "I didn't *hate* you."

"Puh-lease. Every workshop you had more notes for me than anyone else, and they were always harsher."

"Because you're a good writer—"

"Boo." I said, lifting my leg to push his thigh gently. "That's a cop-out. Tell me the truth."

He ruffled his hair, his hand sliding down the side of his face. "It's complicated."

"As if you and I don't know about that," I said gently. "If you don't want to talk about it, it's okay."

Aiden shook his head. "No, I do." He took a deep breath. "What I said to your parents was true. I liked you the minute I saw you. It's stupid, but I had never really been that shy in front of people. Years of my father telling me I wasn't good enough or a nuisance made me develop this thick skin where I just stopped caring. I spent *so* long as a kid trying to find the right version of myself for him. Eventually, I didn't want to live with other people's expectations of me. But for some reason, when I saw you, I was *beyond* nervous. I simultaneously wanted you to look at only me and never look my way."

He took a breath and kept going. "When my mom died, I turned harsh—cynical. The kind of person you hate," he said lightly. "I've been trying to get my shit together, but then you walked in with the widest smile and the curliest hair I'd ever seen." He smiled softly at the memory, his head tilted back against his headboard. "I freaked out. I didn't know where to place my emotions and then you said you loved romance and this vision I had of us shattered. I knew you'd want someone to sweep you off your feet, but I wasn't that type of guy. Maybe I was too much of an asshole and probably too childish, but that's why I distanced myself."

"Aiden," I said softly, tears brimming my eyes. I hated how unwanted he felt. How he had spent so long believing that no one could want him the way I do now.

"Someone made me stop believing in love. I didn't want to be that person for you. I *don't* want to be that person for you."

His fingers tightened on mine slightly as if he was scared I'd leave after all of this. Instead, I moved to straddle him, his arms settling around my waist. I buried my face into his neck, holding him close.

We stayed like this for a few minutes as I tried to convey to him, without words, how much I cared about him. How I couldn't imagine my life without him in it anymore.

"Aren't you going to ask me why I didn't like you?" I said, pulling back to meet his eyes.

"I'm going to ask you why you *hated* me."

"Again with the dramatics." I tsked, pushing his hair back from his eyes. "I didn't hate you. I hated that you hated me. You'll be happy to know I thought you were hot."

"Oh yeah?" He grinned.

"What I said to my parents was true too—I had the *biggest* crush on you after that reading. Like, I *stalked* you online. I couldn't find anything but your LinkedIn so I asked around about you and every-one warned me. They said you were a dick and I shouldn't waste my time. But I had this feeling, a pull. Even when you *were* a dick in class—" Aiden's hand curled around my hair, tugging lightly. "I'd linger afterward, just to get a few more seconds to look at you in that peacoat. I hated that you were a good writer. I was so jealous that everything you submitted was nothing short of eloquent."

He studied my face, his grip on his waist tightening. "Tell me I'm not making up the way you're looking at me right now." His voice was low and hoarse. "I can't pretend anymore. I'm so bad at it."

I grinned. "Oh, I've got you now. No way I'm letting you go until I get another look at you in that peacoat."

We were sitting on my couch, a book in each of our hands, her head in my lap. I ran my fingers through her hair, careful, as she had warned me, not to ruin her curls.

She'd been on the same page for at least five minutes. I looked down and her gaze was looking beyond the page, deep in thought.

"Hey," I said softly, tapping her temple. "What's going on in there?"

Her eyes flicked up to mine. "What do you mean?"

"I can see you worrying about something. Talk to me."

She sat up and faced me, folding her legs under her.

"I was just thinking about if we never met. If we were never put in next-door cubicles together and forced to work on this presentation together. Would we have even found each other?"

I shrugged. "No use in thinking about that now."

"Even if it meant we wouldn't be here?"

"But we are here," I reasoned. "And there's nowhere I'd rather be. I had the time of my life making you mad but loving you has been so much better."

— Excerpt from *Untitled* by
Aiden Huntington and Rosie Maxwell

CHAPTER TWENTY-SIX

I hadn't left Aiden's apartment in the few days since New Year's. We'd fallen into a comfortable rhythm and kept making up silly excuses for me to stay.

"Rosie, I read it's a full moon tonight. The train is always weird on full moons. I really think you should stay," he said one evening, right as I was slipping on my shoes.

"I think I saw it might possibly drizzle," I said the next morning. "I didn't bring an umbrella, do you mind if I stay?"

Yesterday morning, Aiden said, "I made *way* too much pasta last night. Would you mind staying for lunch and dinner and helping me finish it?"

I gladly stayed every time.

But this morning, I woke up to Aiden reading my submission piece on his phone in bed.

My head was on his chest. One of his arms was wrapped around me, taking one of my curls between his fingers, playing with it. His other was scrolling through the story on his phone.

I peeked my eyes open at him, trying to read him. After a moment, he glanced down at me, and I quickly shut my eyes.

"I know you're awake," he said, amusement tinting his voice.

"Ugh," I said, sitting up, suddenly nervous. "It's okay if it's bad."

"Shh," he admonished, still reading. "Don't draw me out of it."

I studied him as he read, trying to see any break in his expression.

"If you don't like it, you can tell me. I can take it." I paused. "But maybe be a little nicer than you were in September."

"Rosie, I can't focus with you staring at me like that." A few moments later, he clicked his phone off and faced me, smiling.

"Well?" I demanded. "What'd you think?"

"I loved it."

I groaned. "Tell me what I need to fix. I know you have something simmering in that devious brain of yours."

"I have notes, but not a lot. I think it's in really good shape. Do you want to go over them now?"

"*Please.*"

He spent the next hour going over line-by-line edits with me. Naturally, we argued over a few different key points, but it was mostly painless. The way Aiden talked about it so *seriously* and was giving me so much effort filled me with joy.

After I was happy with it, I submitted it that afternoon. I peppered him with kisses in thanks.

"It really means a lot to me," I said afterward.

He regarded me and said, "You act like it's some big nuisance that I'd do something like that for you. I *want* to, Rosie. I want to be the first one you show your writing and the one you tell all those thought in your head. I'm grateful that you let me."

I blinked away tears before they could fall. "You were worth every bit of the wait, Aiden."

Eventually, I had to leave. After I collected my things and put my shoes on for the first time in days, he pressed me against the front door, his mouth on mine.

"You sure I can't convince you to stay?" He murmured against my neck, biting softly where he'd easily discovered I was sensitive.

"You're making a really good case."

He huffed a laugh. "I can make a better one upstairs."

I groaned and pushed him away, "No, no, I need to go. I'll see you on Monday, okay?"

"Fine," he said begrudgingly. It was only Wednesday, but Monday felt so far away. He gave me a final reluctant kiss, his hand on my jaw, angling my mouth whichever way he wanted. I walked all the way home a little dazed, wishing I could turn right back around.

"I'm home," I called out to Alexa as I shoved our front door open later that morning. She was supposed to arrive home late last night. I hadn't seen her since before break ended, and I hated how lonely the apartment had felt without her. Alexa's bedroom door creaked open, and I moved to give her a hug. "How was your break?"

She hugged me back, but then stilled; she pulled back and peered at me. "Oh my God. You and Aiden fucked."

I straightened. "Um."

"Oh my God!" she yelled, grabbing my hands. "You two *fucked!* Tell me everything."

We sat on the couch, snuggled in blankets. Her eyes were wide as I relayed every detail of the weekend. Even talking about it now was surreal. It was like I was speaking about a romance novel, not my own life.

"To quote you, 'That's so romantic.'"

I laughed. "It was."

She smiled wide. "I'm so happy for you."

"Me too." I smiled to myself for the millionth time that day.

I spent the remainder of the day writing everything I'd felt this weekend into the chapters. The words came easily, remembering the way Aiden would bring me tea in bed or how he'd dutifully slip his socks on my feet when I got too cold. I'd always preferred fiction, but now I couldn't wait for the rest of my new reality.

The second semester of our class started Monday. I had taken a few days off work for the holidays, and I had to make up the shifts before class started. Aiden and I had been texting whenever we could. He even came to grab at drink at the Hideout during a slow shift, and took me back to his apartment after, fucking me nice and slow until I was nearly sobbing for relief. I was a bit nervous for today, though—we were still in this liminal beginning space, and I didn't want the workshop environment to change everything.

Aiden was waiting for me outside of the Writer's House, leaning against the front gate. Usually, he had a permanent wrinkle in his forehead, like someone had just pissed him off. Now, he had a slight smile on his face, his cheeks risen just a little.

"Hi," he said as I approached him.

"Hi," I said back. I held my arms out for a hug, but quickly pulled them back. Was that weird? I mean, we had been on dates, but were we *dating*? Even though I had slept in this man's bed, I couldn't lay my insecurities to rest.

He must've read it on my face because he tugged the scarf around my neck, pulling me closer. He kissed the top of my head and murmured, "I've missed you. Is that stupid? I saw you a few days ago, but I missed you."

I looked up at him. "No. I missed you too."

He frowned when I shuddered, wrapping the ends of the scarf around me once for good measure. He grabbed my hand, pulling me toward the building. "You're shivering, let's go in."

In class, as I read aloud, Logan and Jess exchanged a look. Even Tyler was trying to suppress a smile. Our classmates had definitely noticed the shift in our writing.

"Notes? Aiden, would you like to go first?" Ida asked.

He shook his head. "No notes from me. I loved it."

Ida raised her eyebrows, surprised. "Alright then. Tyler, let's start with you."

Later, as we walked out of class, Jess and Tyler stopped us.

"Are you two coming to Peculiar Pub tonight?" Jess asked. She looked to Aiden and said, "We usually go after class if we're not working, if you want to come."

I turned to him and smiled. "You should join us. It's super fun. We make Logan play darts, and he *always* misses the board."

Aiden shook his head. "That's okay. I've got to talk to Ida about some stuff. Go on without me."

I frowned. "Are you sure?"

His gaze flickered to Jess before whispering, "I'll see you tonight. Come over after." He pressed a kiss to the side of my forehead before heading back into the classroom with Ida.

Once he was out of sight, Logan whacked me in the arm.

"Ouch!" I rubbed my arm, pouting. "What was that for?"

"You two left the bar on New Year's Eve together, then walked into class together today," Logan hissed. "He said *come over.*"

I shrugged sheepishly. Jess and I shared a look. We'd gotten bagels over the weekend and shared every detail we could, pouring over every single moment we'd spent with our guys. After she and Tyler had kissed at the club, she confessed she had feelings for him and he did the same. They ended up back at his place, but they didn't hook up. They stayed up till the sun rose, just talking. Tyler asked her out for dinner, and they'd been on a few dates since.

Of course, I told Jess everything that happened between Aiden and me, but I hadn't had the chance to update Tyler and Logan until now.

Logan all but pushed us out of the Writer's House and down the street to the pub. We huddled into our corner booth and they all looked at me expectantly.

"Should we get drinks—"

"*No*," they all said at once.

"Spill," Logan demanded.

I tried to tamp down my smile, but I couldn't. "We hooked up. And I think we're dating? I don't know, we haven't really talked about it yet, but . . ."

"Holy shit." Logan gasped.

"I called it," Tyler said. "I knew he liked you. I can always tell. First round's on me tonight. Jess, do you mind helping me carry?"

"You need help with four beers?" Logan asked. I kicked him under the table, widening my eyes. "Oh. I mean. What a great idea," he said in a flat tone.

Once they left, I looked back at Logan. "Did he tell you?"

"Jesus Christ, did he ever," he huffed. "Tyler's been blowing up my phone. Every time Jess texts him he'll send a screenshot, super excited."

"Aw, that's adorable," I gushed.

Logan scowled. "Does no one care about Emily and me?"

"You texted us the next morning that she had a toe ring, and you couldn't support that decision," I said, flatly.

He lifted his chin. "Well, I couldn't. Anyway, I don't understand why Jess and Tyler are acting like we don't all know about them."

I shrugged. "Sometimes a new relationship is better when it's just yours, and you don't have to explain it to everyone."

"Whatever. If they start playing footsie under the table, drinks are on Tyler."

We quieted when they returned with the bottles, giggling.

"Tell us more about Aiden," Logan urged. "We want all the nasty details."

Jess smacked him on the head. "Don't be weird about it."

"Is this abuse Logan night? Did I miss the sign on the board?" Logan said drily.

"We are kind of dying to know," Tyler admitted.

They hung onto every word as I relayed the story the same way I had to Alexa. Jess grabbed my hand and squeezed it, excited for me.

"Who knew Aiden had the ability to smile? Let alone *love*," Logan joked.

"I've kind of always liked Aiden." Tyler frowned. "I never thought he was as bad as you guys said."

"He's not so bad." I shrugged, sipping on my beer. I tried to be nonchalant but I counted down the minutes until I could head to his place.

We became *that* couple. The one I always envied. Who sat on the same side of a booth at a restaurant. Who made out in stacks of books and on corners of streets and didn't care who saw.

I spent most nights at his place because I was obsessed with his brownstone. I loved just sitting by the window and reading while the sun set. Tonight, I waited at his door with a bag of Peruvian food from our new favorite restaurant, Inti. I had come straight from work and still had my tie hanging loosely around my neck. My feet were *killing* me.

When Aiden opened his front door, he was wearing a white t-shirt and my favorite gray sweatpants. I had gotten used to his casual clothes, but it had taken time. I'd been genuinely *shocked* to find out that he owned flannel shirts. He was on the phone but smiled when he saw me and beckoned me inside, taking the bag of food.

"Yes, I do understand," he clipped into the phone. He covered the speaker with his hand and mouthed, "Sorry."

I waved him off and slipped out of my shoes before settling onto the living room couch.

Katie Holt

"I'm not talking about this anymore, Dad." Aiden held the phone between his ear and shoulder, unpacking the bag onto the coffee table in front of the couch. "We talked about this months ago. I have no interest in the open position, and I won't change my mind." His tone was authoritative, and I knew it pissed his father right off. "Have a good night."

He tossed his phone on the table, running a hand down on his face. "Sorry." He sat on the couch next to me and handed me the box with camarones in it. "My dad was riding my ass again."

"Same thing?" I frowned.

"Always is. He's still hoping that one day I'll take over and run the company or I'll 'wake up to reality,' as he says. There's some management job available in the financial department, and he wants me to take it to get to know the company."

"What does your dad even do?"

"It's some stupid app that helps you trade easier on the stock market. It blew up when I was a kid, and he sees it as his son more than me. He wants to start his own Huntington legacy." He cleared his throat, deepening his voice. "Aiden, you need to think about your future. Aiden, you can't live off your mother's money forever."

"Aiden, I think you're a great writer and those pants make your ass look good," I said with a deep voice.

He laughed. "Okay, none of that." He leaned across me, planting a soft kiss on my lips. "How was your day?"

"Horrible. There was a huge baseball game on, and everyone and their mother decided to come to the restaurant. The only thing holding me over was the promise of Papa a la Huancaína and those grey sweatpants."

He ignored me like he always did when I begged him to wear the sweatpants more often. "Did you get a chance to look at the chapter I sent you?"

I scowled at him. "I'm still waiting for the *actual* chapter, because there's no way we're submitting that one."

Aiden rolled his eyes, reaching for the anticucho. "You know we're going to have to break them up sooner or later, Rosie Posie."

"Shh." I covered his mouth with my hand. "Live in the romance a little, they can break up in the last chapter."

He frowned. "I don't think—"

262

I took our food and placed it on the coffee table. Then I climbed on top of him, straddling his hips and tipping his head back to meet my eyes.

"You know what I hate about you," I whispered as I began to kiss his neck.

"I can already tell this is going to be a very confusing conversation." He gripped my hips, guiding my movement. His fingers spanned across my waist, each one of them sinking into me with just the right amount of pressure.

"I hate that you want to turn a perfectly good romance into a sad story." I ran my fingers through his soft hair. "I hate the way this part of your hair perfectly curls onto your forehead at the end of the day." I reached for the bottom of his shirt, tugging it off. "I hate when you make me feel like I can do just about anything."

He smiled, catching onto the game. He pulled my shirt off, then reached behind me to unclasp my bra. "I hate your smile. I especially hate how much it makes me want to smile."

He brushed his thumb against my nipple. It hardened beneath his finger, causing my back to arch. "I hate the white sundress you wear in the spring, too. Absolutely hate it."

"I hate that peacoat," I said, dragging my tongue from his neck up to his ear.

"You love my peacoat." He picked me up with my legs still wrapped around his waist, and we fumbled our way upstairs to his spacious bedroom. Aiden kept getting distracted, pushing me up against walls to grind into me, his tongue stroking against mine.

I clenched my eyes closed, lost in him, and begged, "Aiden, I need you now."

That was all he needed to hear before carrying me to his room, dropping me on the bed, and bending to capture my mouth with his.

"I never know how I want you," he whispered, his forehead pressed against mine. "I'm so greedy when it comes to you."

I was lost in lust, pushing his shirt up his abdomen until he took it off, urging me to do the same.

"Fuck, I love your tits," he said. He lifted me under my arms, dropping me closer to the center of the bed. "Wanna kiss 'em while I fuck you."

"Yes, please," I moaned as he took a nipple into his mouth. I arched my back, my hands flying into his hair, keeping him closer. His other hand came up to tease my other nipple, shooting straight to my core.

After a moment, I'd had enough and needed him inside me. I pushed him off me so he lay flat on the bed, and I climbed over him, just like I had on the couch. My hair was still in a clip from work, but when I bent down to kiss him, he reached up, taking off the clip and tossing it to the side. My hair fanned down, covering our faces as he bit on my lip, tugging.

I whimpered, pressing down on his cock. He took my hips in his hands, dragging me over him in delicious friction.

"I can't wait any longer," I muttered against his lips. I started to pull his briefs down, and he helped me, kicking them off. Aiden wasn't patient enough to do the same with my panties, only hooking them to the side with his finger. He carefully guided himself to my entrance.

Slowly, I sunk down on him, shuddering with relief. We both watched as I stretched to take him, my thighs quaking with the need for release.

"Goddammit, Rosie," he said behind gritted teeth. "You look so pretty right now, baby. Think you can take a bit more?"

I nodded, desperate. He pulled my hips down roughly, and I let out a ragged moan. I fell forward, one of my hands planted near his head. Once I adjusted, I began to move up and down on him, relishing in the feel. One of Aiden's hands let go of my hips, reaching up to cup my breasts, his tongue sliding over my nipples.

"So fucking pretty," he said. "Such a good girl letting me fuck you like this."

"*I'm* fucking *you*," I said a little breathless. "I think *you're* the one being good."

He smiled against my skin, "Yeah, you are fucking me, baby. You're fucking me real good." In a moment, he flipped us around so he was on top. "I'm gonna fuck *you* now, okay? Just lay there and look pretty, hmm?"

My thighs tightened around his torso, and he thrust into me roughly while his head nuzzled into my neck so sweetly, contrasting his harsh movements.

"I hate you," I said later as I reached my climax. "I really, really hate you."

"Just like that," he bit out, his hips moving faster. "I hate you too, Rosie. So much."

An hour later, we moved slower. We took our time. His lips lingered on my neck, whispering against my skin.

"I love your curls," he said. "I love when you wear your hair half up and a curl escapes in front of your face."

I grasped at his back. "I love that I can always tell what you're thinking from your eyes."

When we both got close, neither of us said what we thought. Those three words were an intimidating jump. I knew he would catch me, but I couldn't step off that ledge just yet.

His hand cupped my cheek, his green eyes as intense as ever. "Come for me, baby."

I whimpered as his hips lost their slow pace and moved faster until my back arched, my chest pressing into Aiden's. He cupped the back of my head, stroking my neck with his thumb. His careful hold of me pushed me right over that ledge.

As we lay in bed that night, Aiden's breathing started to even out. My eyes were starting to droop down.

"I didn't know it could be like this," I whispered. I could barely see the shadows cast across his face in the dark, but I could feel his cheek curve as he began to smile.

"Like what?" he murmured, his voice thick with sleep.

Gently I took the hand that rested against his chest and held it over my heart. Even hours after we'd finished, it was beating wildly.

"Like this."

SPRING

Hunter hated going on walks. He preferred going on runs or sitting in a café and talking. Something about a walk really annoyed him.

As much as he hated walks, he liked me. We walked around on our lunch break, holding burritos in our hands. I took a big bite of mine, chicken falling to the ground. Immediately, pigeons descended upon it.

"We can sit," I offered.

He shook his head. "No. It's okay. We can walk."

"You don't like to walk."

"You don't like to sit."

"That's it." I took another bite of my burrito. "I guess we have to break up, we're too indecisive."

He smiled but said nothing. He only stared at his burrito as we continued to walk around the park, almost finishing our loop.

"I was kidding about breaking up," I broke through the silence. "Unless this was a breakup walk, and I guessed it and now you're trying to find the right moment—"

"You really do worry a lot, Maxine."

"And now we're back to Maxine," I groaned. I tossed my empty burrito foil in a nearby trash can. "I blew it. You saw my Taylor Swift fan account and decided—"

He cupped my face, covering his mouth with mine. "You don't always know what I'm thinking, you know."

"Sure, I do." I smiled and pulled at his collar for another kiss. "Now you're thinking, 'Wow, she really is a nutjob. I wasn't planning on breaking up with her before, but how could I not after all of that?'"

His eyes flickered with annoyance. "I was thinking I never asked you to be my girlfriend. And then I started thinking if I even needed to ask, or if it was assumed, and then I worried that if I did need to ask, if it was too late in the game to do that now. Then, I started thinking about whether you thought of me as your boyfriend . . ." He trailed off.

"Wow," I said after a moment. "You worry almost as much as I do. That's a relief."

"You're a handful and a half, Maxine, you know that?"

"Annndd we're back to Maxine."

— Excerpt from *Untitled*
by Rosie Maxwell and Aiden Huntington

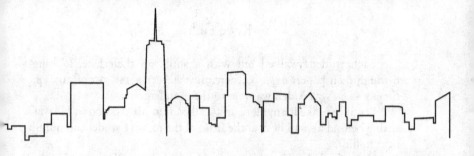

CHAPTER TWENTY-SEVEN

Grad students could teach an Intro to Creative Writing Class at the undergraduate school for some extra credits and cash. Aiden taught one in the evening and often read his students' work—muttering to himself and shaking his head—while we sat together on the couch.

We had plans after his class tonight so I thought I would surprise him outside his classroom door. He taught in the Silver Arts and Science building in the world's tiniest classroom. The classrooms in that building could hold maybe fifteen people max. I imagined Aiden as a strict, no-nonsense kind of teacher. He'd be strict on grammar and formatting, his critiques harsh as always. I feared for any romance writer in that class.

I was waiting in the lounge right outside the classroom, reading a romance novel on one of the couches, a little nervous to see his students walk out of the classroom. It'd be any minute now, and I expected to see a few tears.

When the door creaked open, I braced myself for the sobs, but heard . . . *laughter* instead. My brows furrowed in confusion. Just as I was about to check to make sure I had the right room, Aiden's voice floated out into the lounge.

"Jake, you'd better write the next chapter for next week now that you've left us on a cliffhanger." Aiden's voice had *joy* in it? He was being *kind*? "I'll see you all next week, have a nice weekend. Do something fun out in the city, don't stress so much."

Each student walked out with a smile on their face, looking through their papers *happily*. There must've been some sort of mix up; there was no way Aiden was *nice* to these undergrads.

I couldn't take it anymore and walked into his classroom. He was sitting behind a small desk at the front of the room, a student standing next to him.

"I think your dialogue is great, Henry, but I really would love to see you dig deeper." Henry was hanging onto Aiden's every word, scribbling down notes. "You know this is a safe space to experiment with your writing, so don't be afraid to get vulnerable. Write what you really feel, and if you hate it, scrap it. There's no pressure here from anyone in workshop, okay?"

"Thanks so much." Henry looked up at me, and I gave him a small smile and wave. "I think you have another student waiting for office hours."

Aiden turned to look at me, his face lighting up. He smiled kindly and said, "She's my next appointment, but if you have any questions email, okay?"

Once Henry walked past me, I closed the door and turned to Aiden.

"Ms. Maxwell, are you here for your appointment?" he said teasingly, walking over to gather me into a hug. "I missed you today."

I looked up at him, not able to keep the confusion off my face and out of my voice. "Since when are you so *nice*? Those kids were practically *glowing*."

His chest rumbled with laughter. "And?"

I pulled back. "And the man I know is *ruthless*. I expected those kids to have nightmares about workshop. Not for it to be their favorite class."

Aiden's eyes were full of amusement. His hands ran down my arms until his fingers intertwined with mine. "They're undergrads, Rosie. They're just learning how to write, and they're figuring out if they love it or not. It's where *I* got the courage to write. Their writing isn't supposed to be good or perfect, they aren't grad students. My job right now is just to get them to take another creative writing class."

I had hearts in my eyes as I beamed up at him. He took one look at me and rolled his eyes before moving back to grab his bag. "Are we going or—"

"Aiden, that may be the sweetest thing I've ever heard."

"Okay, so are we—"

"Aiden." I stepped forward, grabbed his hands, and got on my tiptoes to kiss his cheek. "I never knew you had such a soft side."

He was frowning now, all amusement gone from his eyes. But over these past few months, I'd learned enough about him to know he was just embarrassed. He waved me off and said, "Let's never talk about this again. Are we going to your place or what?"

"Fine. But I want to see your staff picture first. Are you smiling in it?"

He gave me a withering glare and walked out of the classroom with me trailing behind.

Aiden hadn't been to my apartment since Christmas. I never invited him over because he had the comfiest bed in the entire world with the softest blankets in the entire world in the nicest home in the entire world. And my place was . . . a little embarrassing.

Sure, sure, I was proud that I was paying for it all on my own blah blah blah, but I couldn't help but be a *little* self-conscious, especially when my boyfriend lived in a fucking brownstone. But when I'd mentioned to Aiden that I wished I knew how to make alfajores, he suggested that we try tonight to make up for our failed Christmas cookies. I told him I could grab the dulce de leche from my place then come over to his, but he frowned.

"Let's go to yours," he said, pressing a kiss to the side of my head. "Can I?"

I reluctantly agreed, but I knew I'd made the right decision when his eyes lit up with excitement.

New York winter had *finally* ended. My puffer coat was stored away and sadly so was Aiden's peacoat. But it made the walk home much nicer now that flowers had started to bloom and color spotted the gray streets of the city. As we approached my apartment building, Aiden's grip on my hand tightened. I looked up at him and his jaw was clenched.

"Uh-oh, angry Aiden's back. What's wrong?"

He looked between my front door and me before pinching the bridge of his nose. "Rosalinda, what will it take for you to move out of this building? Whenever you don't stay with me, I'm up for half the night worried sick."

I guffawed. "This again? You're so melodramatic. C'mon."

He sighed after a few moments, relenting, and gestured for me to lead the way.

I unlocked my apartment door, making an effort to show Aiden the multiple locks that kept me secure. I pushed in and immediately I could hear Alexa rummaging around in her room.

"Retreat," I whispered frantically. I pushed his chest toward the door. "We'll come back later."

"What? Why?" An amused smile played along his lips. I kept pushing, but I wasn't strong enough to move him.

"Alexa's home." I decided to switch tactics and tried to pull his hands rather than push his chest. He stumbled a bit, but I was too late. Alexa's bedroom door creaked open and she came out in her Hideout uniform. "Oh Lord."

"There's that country accent." Aiden grinned, pleased. He claimed my accent came out whenever I was worried or overly happy. He *loved* when it happened so much that sometimes I faked it just to see his eyes light up.

Alexa paused at the entrance to our tiny living room, her gaze shifting between me and Aiden. I had managed to keep the two of them from meeting for the past three and a half months, but I hadn't checked her schedule carefully enough today. Alexa didn't have much of a filter and I had no clue what she would say to Aiden. I loved her chaotic energy, but I wanted to hold *some* of my cards close to the chest. I wouldn't be surprised if she relayed all the details of my initial crush on him the minute they got a second alone.

"Pues, qué es esto?" She crossed her arms over her chest, a smile spread across her face.

I huffed, annoyed. "Alexa, you know Aiden. Aiden, this is Alexa."

She stepped forward, holding out her hand. When he took it, she pumped his hand enthusiastically. "I have heard a mix of wonderful and horrible things about you."

Aiden looked at me mildly. "Is that so?"

"Oh yeah. It was either the infamous peacoat or how she was going to make you regret ever writing—"

"*Okay*, Alexa, you don't want to be late for your shift, do you?" I gestured toward the door.

She nodded sweetly. "Of course. Aiden, I assume I will be seeing more of you."

"If Rosie Posie decides to keep me around." He smiled down at me.

Alexa stepped past us. She paused in the doorway and turned toward us with a mischievous grin. "I also heard you're a riot in bed. Have fun, Rosie!"

I slipped my shoe off and chucked it at the door. "Leave!"

We could hear her laughter through the door.

It took us almost an hour of pure grit and focus to make the alfajores (mostly because I kept getting distracted by Aiden rolling the dough with rolled up sleeves) but we finally finished them. We placed them on a plate and doused them in powdered sugar.

I watched eagerly as Aiden took his first bite.

"Well?" I asked expectantly. "Has your life changed forever? Has every other cookie been ruined for you?"

Aiden grimaced, obviously trying to swallow. He nodded once. "So good."

My heart sank. "You don't like them?"

"I think we missed an ingredient," he said, coughing a little. "Are you sure we made these right? They're a little," he coughed again, "dry."

I frowned, picking up the cookie and stuffing the whole thing in my mouth. Immediately I blanched. I grabbed a paper towel and spit it out. "Fuck, that's bad. My tía's never tasted like that. You put the egg yolks in, right?"

He frowned. "No, you said you were going to do that. You said, and I quote, 'It's a precise science, and you just wouldn't get it.'"

"No," I dragged out. "I said that as a joke, obviously, then I said, 'Never mind, I don't want to get my dress dirty, pretty please do it for me.'"

"You have never said pretty please a day in your life." Aiden laughed. "Especially to me. If you want me to do something, it comes with a death threat."

"I am *dainty*," I said, shocked. "I am divinely feminine."

"And you have a slight temper." He shrugged. "But don't worry, I'm into it."

I rolled my eyes. "This was not how I planned for your introduction to alfajores to go. I'll coerce my tía into sending us some. Hers are like magic." He was leaning against my kitchen counter, watching me with such fond eyes that my pulse quickened without my permission. "Now what are we going to do for a movie snack?"

"Why don't I run to the bodega and grab us something? Oreos sound good?"

"You're speaking my language."

"I'll be back soon." He kissed me quickly before slipping out of my apartment.

While Aiden was gone, I went to my room to set up for our movie night, then checked my email for the millionth time today. There was no exact timeline for when we'd find out about the fellowship, only that it would be before the spring semester ended. Aiden kept telling me not to worry about it, but I couldn't help refreshing my email any chance I got.

A few minutes later, he knocked on my front door. "Luckily the brick was there so I didn't have to buzz up."

"Shut up." I guided him to my room where I had placed pillows, blankets, and my laptop on the bed.

My room felt so small in comparison to Aiden's queen-sized bed and floor to ceiling windows. He had bookshelves and coasters; I had stacks of romance novels in the corner on the floor and used notebooks underneath my glasses.

"I didn't get to see your room at Christmas," he said, taking it all in. "I like it. It's very Rosie Posie." He leaned down and picked up one of my romances, humming as he flipped through the pages. He walked around my small room, occasionally smiling at pictures I had hung on my wall of the Peculiar Pub gang or my family.

It was surreal. Not only to be with someone like this, but for that someone to be Aiden. When people said opposites attract, I never would have thought my opposite would be someone so similar to me. Someone who understood me so well.

Once he felt like he'd sufficiently snooped, he joined me on the bed, reaching across me to snag a cookie off the nightstand. "Which rom com are we watching?"

I had been slowly introducing Aiden to romcoms, and we were working through the Nora Ephron classics. We had already watched

Sleepless in Seattle, and tonight I decided we would watch *When Harry Met Sally.*

Aiden *loved* it. He laughed throughout the whole thing and even sighed, *sighed,* at the end. He turned to me once it finished and said, "Can we watch another?"

Halfway through *You've Got Mail,* I ran my hand up his chest. "I feel bad making you watch all these movies even though you don't like romance."

"Trust me, I like this." When I pulled him on top of me, he raised his eyebrows, looking down at me. "Unless you have something else in mind?"

I shrugged. "Do *you* have something else in mind?"

"I always do with you, Rosie." Hands resting on either side of my head, he pressed his lips to mine. He coaxed my mouth open with his, and I couldn't help the whimper that escaped as he slowly dragged his hand up my thigh to my ass. He lifted me, pressing us against each other.

"Aiden," I gasped. "I want—"

"Hmm?" he murmured against my neck. "Feeling needy, baby?"

My hands raked up and down his back, scratching lightly. "I want to taste you."

His breath hitched as I slid my hand between us to grasp him firmly. He leaned back to give me just enough space to slowly unbutton his pants and slide his zipper down.

He rolled off me, and I moved down the bed until I was on my knees between his legs. I pulled his pants and briefs down and watched as his hardness lay against his stomach. For as shy as I'd been our first time, Aiden made me feel sexy and confident every single time we were together. When Aiden saw the stretch marks on my thighs or the curves of my hips, he viewed them with unrestrained desire.

Carefully, I ran my finger from the base to the tip. He sucked in a breath, his hands finding purchase in my hair, gently smoothing my hair away from my face with one of his hands. Holding his cock from the base, I slipped the tip into my mouth and swirled my tongue, sucking lightly. He grunted, still gently holding my head. I lowered my mouth, taking in more of him. I reached for his hand, telling him it was okay to guide me.

"Fuck," he spit out when I did so, his actions growing rougher as he wrapped my hair around his fist. "Just like that, baby." I looked at him through my lashes and he groaned, moving my head faster.

"You love this, don't you?" he said through gritted teeth, his eye heavy lidded with desire. "Taking me in your mouth, acting like you have control." He tugged on my hair, and I couldn't help but moan around him. "We both know you like it when I take control. We both know your panties are soaked, but you won't touch that sweet pussy until I give you permission. Isn't that right, baby?"

I nodded, desperate for him to keep talking. He was right about how much I enjoyed his words; my thighs squeezed together to relieve the ache he created.

"What a good girl," he gritted out as he began to thrust into my face. "You're doing such a good job, baby, just like that."

I swirled my tongue, knowing it would bring him closer to edge. He hissed as I did it, his grip in my hair tightening. "I'm close, baby." I moved faster, sucking him in deeper until he hit the back of my throat. He groaned as he spilled into my mouth. He leaned down, cupping my jaw before taking his thumb and pressing down on my lip.

"Show me," he whispered and I obeyed, opening my mouth with him still in it. His gaze darkened at the sight. "Swallow for me, baby."

I did, opening my mouth again to show him. He reached for me, pulling me back up on the bed. His thumb and index finger grasped my chin. "Tell me what you want," he whispered. "Do you want me on my knees, too?" I nodded, breathless. "Or do you want me to fuck you?"

I nodded to that too. "I just want *you*, Aiden." I pressed a kiss to his mouth. "All I want is you."

Three words I wished I could say but wasn't ready to yet. Three words I thought every single time I saw her. Three words that repeated in my mind over and over and over again, as I tried to gather courage to repeat them out loud.

— Excerpt from *Untitled* by
Aiden Huntington and Rosie Maxwell

CHAPTER TWENTY-EIGHT

Aiden and I were rapidly approaching the end of the semester—and our manuscript. Our characters were *this* close to confessing their love to each other, but I wanted it to be perfect. We had been writing together nonstop—and now that we could lay nearly everything we felt for each other out in the open, it felt like magic was pouring out of my fingers.

But the big love confession was our only hiccup. The right words couldn't come to us, no matter how many times we tried to write the scene. Aiden suggested moving on and coming back to that paragraph when we had the chance, but I was hell-bent on making it perfect.

I was so focused on this class and our assignment that I often *dreamt* of it. I'd see Max and Hunter in my dreams and try to make sense of it all for a scene, but rarely did anything usable come to fruition.

Until one night, my eyes flashed open. Aiden's arm was snug around my waist, my back to his chest. The words were moving around in my head, and I was desperate to get them out. We were in my apartment this time. I slapped around my nightstand until I found my phone and slipped out of Aiden's grip. Propped up on my elbow, my hair fanning over my face, I quickly typed into my notes app.

"Go back to sleep, baby," Aiden whispered, his voice thick. He tried to pull my shoulder back down to him, but I wouldn't let him.

"I think I finally have it figured out," I said.

The sheets rustled behind me and Aiden's chin landed on my shoulder as he read what I had written. "What do you think?" I asked.

"I like it."

I rolled my eyes. "Okay, what do you *really* think?"

He hesitated before reaching for my phone. "Can I?"

I nodded, and he read through the lines again, changing a few words, refocusing a few sentences.

We went back and forth like this, revising the small paragraphs on my phone, passing it between us as our backs rested against the headboard.

"She can't say that," I fussed at him. "She'd never say that."

"I'm sorry, but Maxine is the *exact* type of person to say, 'I've loved you from the very beginning.'"

"Max would use details. She'd say what made her fall in love."

"Fine, then you fix it."

He passed the phone to me, and just like we had been doing all semester, I wrote what I felt about Aiden. I wrote what I wished I had the courage to say if my heart wasn't so fragile and worried about its next break.

"I loved you before I even knew I did. I loved when someone said something funny and your eyes would find mine across the table just to watch me laugh. Or when you'd frown at something particularly sappy I'd written, even though I know now you liked it. I loved you the whole time, but I love you the most now."

I handed the phone back to Aiden with shaky hands. He read the words, slowly and carefully, before typing his own. He handed it back to me, the sound of my heartbeat creating music in the room.

"I'm not good at romance like you are. I don't have the right words to make you understand how completely wrapped around your finger I am. I didn't believe in soulmates, and for the longest time I didn't believe in love at all—until I met you. But I do love you. The shoot for the stars, shout on rooftops kind. I accepted my fate a long time ago. I don't think I could ever love anyone else but you."

After I read it, tears shone in my eyes. But neither of us said anything. We didn't need to. These words probably wouldn't ever make it into our manuscript. They were hard enough to write, let alone say, so we had to keep them tucked between the pages of a book. But we both knew it wasn't Max and Hunter talking.

We lay back in the bed, Aiden's warm arms holding me.

We were sitting at Peculiar Pub, our eyes trained on my phone, sitting in the center of the table. Logan and I were on one side, Tyler and Jess on the other side, pressed closely together. They'd been together for a while now, often lost in their own bubble.

No one said anything. Every time Logan tried to break the silence, the table shushed him.

"Are you sure it's releasing today?" Jess eventually asked.

"The email said today *at the latest*. It *has* to be today," I said. I bit my thumbnail, trying to soothe my nerves.

"God, the waiting is agonizing," Logan said. He threw his head back and groaned. "I didn't even apply, and *I'm* nervous."

I needed to leave soon to go meet Aiden for dinner at Raoul's in SoHo. I was desperate for the email to come before I left so I could either drown my sorrows in cheap beer at the pub or force Aiden to sip fancy wine with me in celebration.

"I kind of wish they didn't send the email to everyone who applied. I'd rather be embarrassed in private," I said, sipping on my water.

"You might be the only person from our program who applied. Besides, no one knows you applied," Jess reassured. "If it isn't you, only we and Aiden will know."

I picked at the skin around my thumb, staying silent.

I was the happiest I'd ever been with Aiden. Each morning felt like a new start with the whole world in front of me. I *loved* Aiden—and I wanted to tell him soon. But waiting for the fellowship decision was taking up too much of my focus. I couldn't sleep some nights from nerves, and I wanted a clear mind when I told Aiden. I wanted *him* to be my focus.

When my phone buzzed with the email, we all quickly straightened.

"I'm too nervous, I can't look," I whispered.

"Oh God, me either," Logan groaned.

Tyler gingerly plucked his phone from the table and said, "I'll read it." I watched carefully as his eyes scanned every line, waiting for him to break out into a smile. Instead, his eyes flickered to mine. He shook his head only slightly and said, "I'm sorry, Rosie."

The table was quiet. Everyone was waiting for me to react or move, and I didn't know *how* to. I was embarrassed and sad, and I didn't know how to move on from it so quickly.

"It's okay," I said eventually. "It's hard to get into for a reason. Maybe next semester."

"They're stupid," Jess supplied. "I'm sure your piece was the best one. They probably didn't pick it because it was romance."

"Probably," I conceded. "That's just how it goes. A man writes a love story and it's considered great fiction and an epic tale, but a woman does it, then it's cliché. God, y'all, sometimes it feels impossible to exist in the academic world as a romance writer."

"Rosie," Tyler said softly. "You might want to read the email . . . Aiden made it in."

He laid the phone flat on the table and we all leaned forward to skim it.

Congratulations to Aiden Huntington. A student at NYU's MFA Creative Program, his mentorship with Ida Abarough has guided him well, as his short story depicts grief in a visceral manner. We look forward to publishing him in the Sam Frost Literary Magazine and adding him to our list of fellowship recipients.

I reread the email, feeling a little dizzy. My first thought was *How many Aiden Huntingtons are there at NYU?* Because my Aiden wouldn't betray me like this, it didn't make sense.

"You didn't mention that Aiden was submitting, too. Or that Ida was mentoring him, too."

"I didn't know," I said, my words thick.

Silence fell over the table as I reread the email. It made sense that Aiden would have been accepted into the literary magazine. I didn't think he was necessarily a better writer than me, but other academics ate his shit up.

But he said he hadn't submitted, had he? And the mentorship with Ida made *no* sense.

How long had it been going on? And it wasn't like Aiden didn't *know* how much time I spent at the Writer's House with Ida. And it wasn't like Ida didn't *know* that Aiden and I were together now. How could they both keep something like this from me?

But most of all, Ida was a *romance writer*. And try as I might to keep them at bay, the words he'd said about my beloved genre ages ago lingered in my mind.

"What a jerk," Logan said.

"Logan," Jess reprimanded.

"What? It's true. He gains Rosie's trust like this, lies to her, and leaves her blindsided? He's exactly who we thought he was."

"He's not evil for submitting to the same fellowship as Rosie," Tyler said.

"No, but he should've *told* her."

"Rosie, are you okay?" Jess asked.

I didn't say anything for a moment before taking a heavy breath. "I should go. I'm meeting Aiden," I said numbly.

I couldn't stop the resentment that lingered from the beginning of the semester from infiltrating my thoughts. I was *mad* at him. How many times did I talk about the fellowship with him? How many times did he watch me anxiously refresh my email waiting for this result? He listened each time, knowing he had already submitted. And never told me. I was mad that he'd lied to me about so much and yet my heart could still skip a beat when I said his name.

"Be careful, Rosie," Jess said quietly.

The New York sun had just begun to set. Aiden had told me a million times that he was sure summers in Tennessee were nice, but nothing compared to the ones in New York. My southern heart had been reluctant to admit he was right, but he was. The sidewalks cooled down, the streets were full of people sitting on benches and at outdoor restaurants, smiling. The city came alive in the summer. After such harsh winters, it felt like every New Yorker was eager to soak up as much sun as the skyscrapers would permit.

The walk to Raoul's wasn't too far. Aiden was waiting outside for me, his hands in his pockets. A grin split his face when he saw me, and he gathered me into a hug.

"God, I missed you today," he said into my hair. When I didn't hug him back immediately, he pulled back and searched my eyes. "You okay?"

"I'm fine." I stepped away from him a little, wrapping my arms around my torso so I didn't have to touch him. He must not know yet.

His eyes tracked my motion, frowning slightly. "Okay," he said slowly. "Does Raoul's still sound good to you? If you'd rather go to La Pecora Blanca we can swing by there instead."

"Raoul's is good."

He frowned. "Is everything okay? You seem off. Usually you'd pull up the dessert menus to decide."

"I'm fine," I said a little too sharply and his frown only deepened. He peered down at me, as if he could read what was wrong on my face. "Aiden, it's nothing."

"It's not. I can tell when you're upset. Rosie, I know you."

"Maybe you don't," I snapped. "And maybe I don't know you."

His head jerked back. "Where is this coming from?"

When I was a kid, I used to get into terrible fights with my mom. I'd say mean things to her, but she'd always sit there and patiently wait for my temper to cool. The whole time I fought with her, I'd have this out of body experience where I could *see* myself acting horribly. And I'd wonder, *Why am I being such a jerk to someone I love so much?*

That's how it felt with Aiden now.

Wordlessly, I pulled out my phone and handed it to him. He shot me a confused glance, but then he scanned the screen and his expression registered understanding. He was silent as he handed the phone back to me.

"Why didn't you tell me about you applied?"

He shook his head slightly. "I don't know. I couldn't find the right time."

"I told you countless times about how much this meant to me. How *life changing* it could be . . . how I wanted to prove that romance could win a prestigious award like this."

He wouldn't meet my gaze. "Rosie, it's really not a big deal."

I reared my head back. "How could you say that? It's been *nothing* but a big deal to me."

"Are you jealous or something?"

"No, Aiden," I snapped. "I'm not fucking jealous that your tortured man piece appealed to other tortured men. It's not really innovative in the literary world. I'm mad that you fucking lied to me."

The angry words were pouring out of my mouth before I could stop them. I hated how he looked like Aiden from September, and I looked like Rosie from September. I could feel our defenses going up, and I was defenseless against it.

"I never *lied*," he insisted.

"Yes, you did," I snapped. "You *looked* me in the eye and told me you weren't applying to the litmag."

"I said I had thought about it. Which was . . . technically true. I'd thought about it and applied. But that was before everything happened between us—"

"Why should I believe anything you say?" I pushed back, growing frustrated. "You should've just *told* me."

"Right," he scoffed. "And you would've been happy for me, like you are now? You can't be mad I beat you."

My head reared back. "I'm not mad you *beat* me, Aiden. I'm mad you didn't tell me. I went to you for help and advice, and I fucking *told* you to apply, and you didn't have the courage to tell me you were already planning to. You don't even *need* this. Everyone will bow down to you the minute you finish a manuscript," I said, bitingly.

"It's not my fault you didn't get in. What, you wanted me to hand it to you? Give you the easy way out? You're already doing that by writing romance."

I stepped back like he had pushed me. The sounds of New York drowned out, and all I could hear were Aiden's words echoing in my head.

"Fuck you, Aiden. I'm not taking the *easy* way out with romance. How could you say that to me?"

"You're a good writer, Rosie. A great one. You know what sort of stories get into that litmag—you shouldn't have submitted a romantic piece."

"Ida *told* me to submit a romantic piece."

"Well that was bad fucking advice," he snapped.

I *knew* Aiden had been lying to me this whole time. I was dizzy with pain as I realized this whole time Aiden hadn't been taking me seriously. If he'd lied about the mentorship and respecting romance, what else had he been lying about?

"You meant everything you said in August?" I asked. "That romance was frivolous and not worth anyone's time?"

He shook his head. "Rosie, don't twist my words."

"I know I'm a good writer," I said emphatically. "I don't need any-one else to tell me I am. I know it the way the sky is blue and the way romances will always have an HEA. It's just a fucking fact, Aiden. Writing romance doesn't nullify my skill, and for you to imply that makes you a dickhead." I scoffed. "I really thought you had changed, that maybe you weren't like Simon and everyone else. But you're just sitting there on your high fucking horse judging me."

"So I don't like romance!" Aiden exploded. "You don't like literary fiction. Whatever. I'm not throwing some fit over it." He was getting angry now, his hands moving all over the place.

"I should've known better." I could feel the tears climbing their way up my throat. I willed them away, not wanting to cry in front of Aiden as they welled in the corner of my eyes. I was *stupid* for falling for this front he had created. Of course he'd do whatever it took to get his sad ending. "I should've known you could never really love me like I hoped."

"*I* should've known better," he corrected, his tone lashing. "I was stupid enough to believe you could actually want *me*." His jaw tight-ened. "But you don't want me. You want some guy you can mold into the words you've read in a book. Someone you could place on a damn pedestal that's destined to fall."

"So maybe I did place you on one," I snapped, wiping the stray tears with the back of my hand. "I'd rather live in a world where I see the potential for someone's best than their worst. But you know what, maybe I was wrong for that. How I felt for you included the litfic, sad endings, and all. And I never judged you for it. But this entire time you've been lying to me." For a split second, I saw the Aiden I'd thought existed peek through the shadows. But, just as quickly, his eyes hard-ened again. "Finish the book," I said, hiccupping between the words. "Kill Maxine. Give her some horrible, painful death. I'm done, Aiden."

Before he could respond, I turned on my heel, walking home so fast the soles of my feet ached. It was easy to ignore, though, with the way the pain in my heart overpowered everything.

I ignored the glass of my own shattered heart as I cut myself trying to put hers back together.

— Excerpt from *Untitled* by
Aiden Huntington and Rosie Maxwell

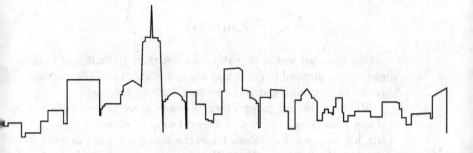

CHAPTER TWENTY-NINE

We only had one class left together. Ida wanted us to have a final good-bye session before summer began. It'd only been a few days, and the wound felt as fresh as if it had happened just minutes ago. I wasn't ready to see him.

Aiden still felt the need to update me on the book. He'd only spoken to me through email, but I never replied to them. And I never read the final chapters.

Every time his email appeared in my inbox, my heart jumped to my throat. I prayed for the grand gesture of romance novels, a love letter begging forgiveness and telling me he was wrong, that he regretted that night. That he'd been miserable every second we'd been apart, and he'd do anything to have me back.

But no. His emails were always one liners: "Chapter's done" or "Are you writing the next one or should I?" Up until his last one: "Final manuscript attached."

I hadn't seen Ida since it had all gone down either. I was just as hurt by her as Aiden. In New York, I had only really built a few foundations. Aiden and Ida were undoubtedly two of the most important ones. She knew, probably even more than Aiden, how much this fellowship meant to me, what it could do for me. And she'd never even told me Aiden was submitting, too.

Our last class would probably take less than an hour, but I was dreading it. I planned to get in and out as quickly as possible. Because three hours after class ended, I'd be on a flight to Tennessee.

When I'd told my parents I was going to move to New York, my dad had been skeptical. He told me he'd support whatever decision I made, but he cautioned, "Rosie Posie, the saying is *if* you can make it there. Not everyone can, okay? There's nothing wrong with coming home."

I had laughed when he said that because it was a ridiculous notion. I had spent nearly my entire life picturing myself as a stylish Sally Albright or a poised Charlotte York. I'd never, ever thought I'd go home.

But now I longed for the green hills of Tennessee and the peace and quiet.

Aiden was already there when I walked into our classroom. I could feel his gaze on me, but I refused to look his way.

"Is everything okay?" Jess frowned when I took Logan's seat by her, away from Aiden. I hadn't updated the Peculiar Pub gang about our breakup. I'd spent so much time reliving every word and second over in my head, and it only hurt more when I told Alexa. I didn't think I had the strength to rehash it all.

I shrugged. "I don't really know."

"Is everything okay between you and Aiden?"

I spared a glance at him but he wasn't paying attention to me.

"We broke up." I lowered my voice.

"Oh, Rosie," she said softly, grabbing my hand and squeezing it. "I'm so sorry."

I shrugged. "It was bound to happen."

Tyler walked into the room and sat across from Jess, sending her a smile. When he began to rifle through his bag, I whispered, "Things are going good between you two, huh?" Jess hesitated. "You can tell me. I'm not going to break."

She nodded. "*Really* good. He's going to come meet my family over summer break." I watched an involuntary smile spread over Jess's face.

"I'm so happy for you, Jess," I said genuinely.

"We're planning on staying in the city for the summer, and I think Logan is too. We can egg Aiden's place once you feel up for it."

I smiled softly. "I'm actually going home."

"Oh that's great! You've been so homesick—this is exactly what you need. But you'll be back in the fall, right? Because we've got that craft class together next semester, thank God." When I shook my head, she straightened. "*Rosie*. You can't go home . . . you *love* New York. You told me once you even loved the *rats* here. You can't just leave because of him."

"It's not because of him." I looked down at my hands. "It's just time. I don't think I can do it much longer."

Logan walked into the classroom and frowned when he saw me in his seat. Jess sent him a look and nodded at the chair across from Aiden. Genuine fear flitted across his face before he relented.

"I thought Logan stopped being scared of him when we started dating."

Jess scoffed. "Aiden could dress like a teddy bear, and Logan would still freak out."

Ida walked in the classroom and faltered when she saw the change in seats. Our eyes met briefly before I looked away.

It was a double heartbreak. Ida had been the catalyst for my life the past two years. Her article had pushed me to move to apply to NYU. Her kindness and advice in office hours had emboldened me. But I'd been avoiding her since the fellowship email went out.

She stood at the front of the room, clasping her hands in front of her chest. She asked us to share our experiences with our final projects, what we'd learned. I tuned it all out, my gaze firmly on the table between all of us.

"Before I dismiss you all for the final time, I just want to say how much of a joy it was to facilitate this class. It's not often I have so much talent in one place, and I feel so lucky to have gotten to know you all." I looked up at this and her eyes met mine. I quickly looked away. "If you need anything at all, please don't hesitate to reach out. Have a great summer."

The class shifted, gathering their things, and I moved as quickly as I could. The last thing I needed was a run in with Ida and Aiden. But just as I was about to rush out the door, Ida called out, "Rosie, can you hang back for a second?"

I grimaced and turned on my heel to stand at the head of the table by her.

"I just wanted to check in on you. I expected you to be practically living in my office as you worked on your final chapters."

I bit my lip. "I got busy. You know how it is."

She narrowed her eyes and nodded at the chair next to her. "Sit."

Reluctantly, I slumped into the chair, holding my hands tightly together in my lap.

"If this is about the fellowship, then I'm really sorry you weren't accepted. I think you're an amazing writer, and you have a real future in the literary world. The story you submitted was exceptional. It was honest, raw, and heartfelt and I was surprised when—"

"I'm going home," I blurted out. She opened her mouth but I cut her off. "And before you try to talk me out of it, I'm set in my decision. I . . . I trusted you. And Aiden. And neither of you told me he submitted, too. Aiden and I became so much more than competitors over these past few months . . . only for me to be the only one unaware we were still in a competition." I took a shaky breath. "Maybe Aiden and I were only meant to get together to break up like in our book. I get that Happily Ever Afters don't actually exist. I just . . . need to go home."

She softened. "Rosie, I'm sorry neither of us told you. I—"

"I'm sorry, I think it's best if I go," I said. "I can't miss my flight."

With the weight of the world on my shoulders, or at least that's what it felt like, I walked out of the Writer's House for the last time.

Logan, Tyler, Jess, and Aiden were all waiting for me. One look at Tyler and Logan, and I knew Jess had filled them in.

"We told him to leave," Logan said. He glared at Aiden from behind Tyler's shoulder. "But he won't budge."

"You don't have to talk to him," Jess insisted. "We're you're security team. We can get you out of here without even looking at him."

"I'm right here," Aiden said drily.

"Did you hear that?" Logan asked, looking around. "Sounds like a whiny bitch."

"Hey," Aiden snapped, and Logan recoiled.

I smiled slightly. "It's okay, y'all. I'll catch up with you later."

"You sure, Rosie?" Tyler asked.

I nodded. "I'll text y'all later."

All of them gave me supportive looks as Aiden and I were left on the street with each other. The silence stretched between us in unbearable lengths.

Finally, he spoke up. "Did you get a chance to read the last chapters?"

I knew better now what that look of hope meant in his eyes. It didn't mean he wanted me to enjoy it, it meant he wanted me to praise it. Couldn't say goodbye without enlarging his ego.

"Yes," I lied.

"And?" he asked carefully.

"And what, Aiden?" I sighed. "It was good if that's what you want me to say. The class is over, the book is done. It's time to move on."

A muscle in his cheek jumped. "Fine," he said, his voice laced with venom. "Good luck, Rosie." He turned on his heel and headed toward the subway.

After I said my goodbyes to the workshop group, I headed home to pick up my suitcase. I'd already shipped most of my boxes back home to Tennessee and was ready to get out of here.

Alexa was waiting for me in our living room. She was wearing all black because as she said, "I'm in mourning."

She was in as much agony as me over the breakup, maybe even more.

"Are you absolutely sure?" Alexa asked miserably. I had pulled my suitcase to our front door, all packed and ready to go. "New York City is huge. You probably won't ever see him again."

I shook my head, my heart heavy. "I tried, but it didn't work out. I need to go home."

She folded me into a hug, squeezing me tight. "If you decide to come back, you'll always have me for a roommate. Even if someone else is living with me, I'll kick her out for you."

I choked on a laugh, one or two tears slipping down my face. "You don't have to."

"But I will." She tugged on my hand. "I hope you find what you're looking for in Tennessee."

"God," I sighed. "Me too."

SUMMER

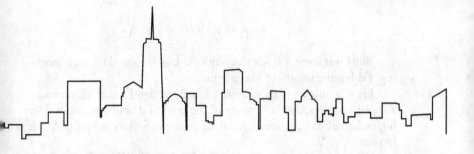

CHAPTER THIRTY

I'd been home for a month and hadn't written a single word since I got back. Some of the best lines I'd ever written had been with Aiden. I was determined to make something better, to show that I had moved on, but writing felt impossible now, as if Aiden had taken that from me, too. I loved writing, but I'd loved it so much more when it was with Aiden.

My mom checked on me every day, trying to get my spark back, but nothing worked. No matter how many rom-coms I started, I felt physically ill at my favorite scenes and had to stop.

I holed myself in my room, reading. At first, I read Aiden's mom's book that he bought for me at the Strand, *As Best I Can*. It was obviously about her divorce. Tears streamed down my face as I wondered how much was fact or fiction. Aiden had made it sound like his father was borderline emotionally abusive and negligent. But the little boy in the book, Aaron, was *desperate* for his father's attention, stopping at nothing. The story focused mostly on how the mom character tried her best, but still fell short.

I wanted to call him and tell him that I loved him. That he wasn't defined by the people who didn't. But part of me believed I'd made everything up in my head. I'd seen what I wanted to, and when Aiden didn't follow the plot I fantasized about, I let myself get hurt.

But I was *there.* I'd felt the way he'd kiss my shoulder each morning. I'd felt the weight of his gaze on me.

He was only a phone call away, but the Aiden I knew felt unreachable. I hadn't realized how many of her books I'd read when in was in high school. I pored through them, desperate to find some hint of Aiden in them.

When the first few chords of "All Too Well" by Taylor Swift played for the fiftieth time, my sister barged in my room.

"Enough," she said, whipping my comforter off me. She walked over to my speaker and unplugged it from the wall. "I love Taylor, but this song is going to make me and my baby sick."

Ever since Maria announced her pregnancy, she'd used it as an excuse for everything.

"Your baby will love Taylor Swift," I said from under my comforter. "It's never too early to prepare for heartbreak."

"Stop that," she fussed. She sat on the edge of my bed, pulling the covers away from me. "This isn't you. You're a *romantic.* You've never listened to this many break-up songs in your life. Even after Simon. Rosie, you can't keep doing this."

"Doing what?"

She gave me a flat look. "You know what I'm talking about. You can't live like this forever. Your heart was broken, and I'm sorry. Aiden wasn't who you thought he was and I'm *sorry*, Rosie Posie, I really am. But you have to start living again." She said this gently, as if it would make me feel better.

"You don't get it." I turned on my side away from her.

"Then explain." She pulled my shoulder, so I faced her again. "Talk to me. We're worried sick about you. You won't talk to any of us, you rush out of rooms at a moment's notice. You're not writing. Talk to *me* at least."

I pushed upright, sitting against my headboard. My limbs felt so heavy, my chest felt so tight. I didn't *want* to talk about it. I wanted to wallow and live in my world of misery.

I closed my eyes, taking heavy breaths. In and out, slower and slower. More in, more out.

"I just keep playing it back in my mind. All of it. I was so *certain* that we were meant for each other. And then I feel so foolish for even letting myself believe that. For letting him deceive me."

"Okay," she said slowly. "What else?"

"Aiden *should've* been my person, but he tricked me into thinking he was someone else and I fell for it. And there's no one that *really* acts the way he used to when things were good between us."

"Oh, Rosie," she said gently. She nodded her head, telling me to scoot over. I made room for her on the bed, and she pulled the covers around us, resting her hands over her belly. "You know that's not true. He's out there."

"He's in New York," I said miserably. "In the Strand. In the romance section of fiction."

"*Stop* it," she scolded. "If soulmates weren't real, how'd Mom and Dad find each other? How'd Peter and I find each other?"

I crossed my arms, hugging myself tightly. "I miss him," I said quietly. "That's the worst part of it all. I miss him so much that everything reminds me of him. I miss the scratch of his pencil when he's writing in his notebook. Or the way he'd spot me across the street and his face would light up. I miss him."

"That's okay," she said softly. "That's normal. You fell in love—"

"I never even told him!" I cried, new tears springing from my eyes. "I never even told him I loved him, and he never even told me, we just wrote in our book. I'm lovesick over a guy who probably hasn't thought twice about me since I left."

"Rosie." She sat up and pulled me with her. We sat face to face, and she pushed my hair from my face, tucking it behind my ears. "I'm saying this because *I* love you. But you need to take all of this, every tear, every piece of anger, and put it into writing. Even if it's terrible— *especially* if it's terrible. Don't let this pain be for nothing."

I opened my mouth, but she covered it with her hand.

"And before you protest, just think about it. This isn't the big sister I grew up with. How many times have you told me that love shouldn't be easy when Peter and I got in a fight?"

"Yeah, but it shouldn't *hurt*."

"Maybe," she conceded. "Love fights through dark and light. It's not always easy, Rosie. The fights, the disagreements can hurt, but at least you know you're fighting *for* something. It's not the biggest war you'll ever fight, but it can be a battle sometimes." She stood from my bed and smiled down at me. "You're gonna be fine. Write something good." She paused. "For the baby?"

"I'm spoiling them for the rest of their life. You'll rue the day you used them against me."

"Do what you do best, Rosie Posie."

When she left my room, the sun was just beginning to set in Tennessee. Soft light filled through the slats of my blinds, landing on my laptop. I groaned, taking the sign from the universe. I hobbled from my bed to my desk, lifted the top of my laptop, and began to write.

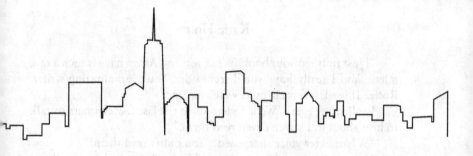

CHAPTER THIRTY-ONE

A week later, my phone rang, Ida's name flashing across it. I only had her number because I'd *begged* her to give it to me so I could send her a link to a fanfic (that she never responded to). She made me swear to only call her for emergencies.

My hand lingered over my phone, nerves spreading throughout me. And before I could think better of it, I hit the green button and answered.

"Hello?"

"Rosie? Is that you?"

I relaxed against the headboard of my bed. "Yeah. Hi, professor."

She paused, most likely unnerved that I'd called her *professor*. The first and only time I'd done that before was when we first met, and she'd immediately corrected me.

"I hope it's okay that I'm calling you," she said softly. "I haven't been able to stop thinking about how we left things and I feel horrible. I wanted to apologize again and try to convince you to come back to NYU."

"Oh, I don't know." I looked down, playing with a fraying string from my blanket. My throat was thick with the threat of tears. It hadn't been an easy decision to leave. I missed New York every day, but I couldn't go back and walk streets that would only remind me of him.

"I just finished your book. What you and Aiden have is such a rare talent, and I really hope you'll reconsider. You're an amazing writer, Rosie. Those last few chapters were amazing."

I rolled my eyes. "Well, Aiden wrote the last few chapters so talk to him about it. I haven't even read them."

"What?" Her voice sharpened. "You didn't read them?"

"I know that could get me in trouble, but I dropped out. So if you have to take it out on someone's grade, make it Aiden's."

"No, Rosie, I think you really need to read them," she said, her voice strained.

"No."

"*Rosie,*" she said urgently. "I don't want to tell you what's in them, but—"

"Then don't," I cut her off. "I *chose* not to read them. I have no interest in reading them, and I don't ever plan to. I appreciate you calling and apologizing but it's no use." I sighed, tears forming again in the back of my throat. "Thank you for everything, but I need to go."

I hung up without another word and sunk into my bed, tears streaming down my face. Part of me was curious about how Aiden had tied it all up. But I wasn't really in the mood to read how Hunter got promoted to CEO and Max was hit by a bus. I turned over in my bed, soaking my pillow with tears.

Later that night, my mom called for me from downstairs.

"Rosie. ¡Tienes un visitante!"

I rolled my eyes. My old high school principal had been bugging me to start subbing at the high school.

"¿Quién?" I called back.

"Ven abajo y mira."

"If it's Mr. Terra tell him I'm not teaching bratty fourteen-year-olds."

"It's not Mr. Terra."

I paused, frowning. But soon curiosity had me padding down the stairs, the wood creaking beneath me.

"Mom, if this was a trick just to get me to talk to Mr. Terra, then I'm moving out. And I mean it this time. I'll get a job at Dollywood and never look—"

"Hi."

Aiden Huntington was standing in the doorway of my front door, his head skimming the top of the doorframe. He was holding a bouquet of roses wrapped in white paper. He was wearing a suit of all things—and he was *here*.

His suit jacket was crumpled, like he had been wearing it for hours. It looked like he hadn't slept or combed his hair in days. Whenever his hair was like that—sticking up in every direction, the perfect combination of bedhead and gorgeous—it meant he had been running his hands through it, probably grasping at the ends.

"What're you doing here?" I asked harshly. I was still on the bottom step. I shifted my weight, ashamed of myself for feeling self-conscious in running shorts and a ratty t-shirt from high school. I shouldn't care what I looked like in front of him anymore, but part of me wanted to appear as if the breakup hadn't destroyed me.

He wasn't affected by my tone—his face was open and hopeful, his eyes soft and pleading. "I hoped we could talk," he said gently.

"So, talk." I crossed my arms over my chest. I wanted to keep as much distance between me and Aiden as possible. I couldn't even stand to look at him, my chest hurt so bad.

"Could we talk outside?" He was eyeing the kitchen behind me. My parents and Maria and Peter were having dinner together, their boisterous laughs flooding through the house.

"Fine."

I walked past him out onto my front porch, my breath catching as my shoulder brushed his chest. He followed slowly behind me and took a seat on the porch steps next to me. There wasn't enough distance between us, and I had to resist the urge to scoot to the opposite end of the steps. His long legs were folded, his knees pressing against his chest as we sat.

"These are for you. I got them from the shop downtown." He pushed the bouquet of roses toward me, and I took them tentatively. I laid them down next to me, resisting the urge to sniff them.

"How'd you know where I lived?"

"I begged Alexa."

"Traitor," I muttered.

"I came here to explain."

I scoffed. "Of course."

"Rosie—"

"No, no, go ahead. Clear your conscience. I'll sit here and listen, then you can head on home."

I was provoking him. I wanted some sort of reaction because I'd truly rather fight with him at this point. It was so much better to be at war with him than to sit here and hope that maybe he had changed his mind.

"I plan on apologizing, too, but—"

"But only after you feel better about yourself."

"Would you let me talk?" he snapped.

"Why should I?" I snapped back. "You've had a month to talk. I don't know why it's taking you so long to just spit it out."

"It's a two-way street, you know. You could've talked to me if you wanted to." He was getting angry now.

"The difference is I don't have anything to say to you." I stood from the steps onto the pavement, suddenly needing to be away from him again. Any piece of myself I had begun to put together these past few weeks was falling away fast, and I couldn't protect myself from him if he was sitting right next to me.

"I'm not doing this, Aiden. I'm not indulging you so you can go back to New York and feel good about yourself while I'm here in Tennessee, trying to figure it all out. I don't care anymore."

"That's not true." He stood, too. I had to look up at him to meet his eye and that just pissed me off further. I moved past him to the top step, so we were the same height. He rolled his eyes but stayed put.

"You don't have to lie anymore, Aiden. It's over. You don't have to pretend you want to be with me."

He looked like he'd been punched. "Rosie, what are you talking about? I've wanted to be with you this whole time! I never lied about that."

"Oh please!" I said, throwing my hands up. "You hated me that first semester. You berated me constantly in class—"

"I didn't know how else to get you to notice me. I *told* you this, Rosie. I thought I was protecting myself—and you."

"What a fucking cop-out," I spat.

"It's not." He pushed. "I liked you the moment I saw you, Rosie. I wasn't lying at all."

I'd done this before. I'd convinced myself that a relationship was something it wasn't for nearly a decade. I let Simon walk all over me, because I thought it was better to love than to be loved. But I wanted more, I *deserved* more.

"All you *did* was lie. You lied when you said you liked me. You lied about the fellowship. You lied—"

"I *didn't*, Rosie." He stepped toward me and reached for my hands. I snatched them away, but that didn't stop him. "Rosie, I'm an idiot. I don't do romance. I don't know *how*—but I'm trying right now to be one of your heroes."

"Well, you're doing a shit job."

"I'm doing the best I can, Rosie," he said his voice low and pleading. "I'm new at this."

"I've read plenty of romantic heroes, Aiden. I've seen all different types of grand gestures, and I can say with certainty those heroes didn't go in yelling."

"You're the one who started yelling," he muttered.

"Whatever!" I threw my hands up. "You broke my heart, Aiden. Sorry if I'm not so keen on accepting your red roses." I tried to keep the tears in. His eyes locked with mine, studying me. The only sounds, besides the birds chirping and cicadas singing around us, were the sounds of my beating heart and his ragged breath.

"I came here because you didn't read the last chapters." He grew serious at this, his voice low and intent. He held out the chapters between us, but I ignored the papers.

"Yes, I did," I lied.

"No, you didn't. Ida told me."

I rolled my eyes. "Of course she did."

He pulled his phone out, scrolling through it before holding up the screen to me. I squinted, reading an email from Ida:

I thought you should know Rosie hasn't read the last chapters. I hope you both can forgive me for mentoring you one last time.

"She emailed me this morning. I went down to her office, and she explained everything. I didn't know you hadn't read the last chapters. I didn't know you went back to Tennessee."

"None of this even matters." I turned around and started toward my door, but he was at my tail.

"I went to your apartment every day. I hit your buzzer a million times until Alexa would send me away, and that stupid fucking brick wasn't there when I needed it the most. I went to Think Coffee every morning. I ate nearly every meal at the Hideout, hoping to see you there. I didn't just lie down and die, Rosie, I just *didn't know*."

"Stop!" I said, tears finally brimming over. "Don't tell me this! I don't want to know any of this. How do I know you're not lying again?"

"Rosie, if I knew you weren't in New York, I would've gotten the first flight out here. I *did* that. The minute Ida told me everything, I went straight to LaGuardia." He paused. "I didn't write our breakup."

"Sure," I scoffed. We'd spent so much time writing ourselves into our book, but I'd never really known how similar we truly were to Max and Hunter. Competing for the same fellowship like they would for clients. We had written our fate, and I wasn't naïve enough to think Aiden could let it end on a happy note.

"I didn't," he said emphatically. "I asked you after class if you had read it, and you said you did. I thought you were rejecting me, but that's no excuse. I shouldn't have let you walk away that second time."

I squeezed my eyes shut, trying to make his words feel like nothing to me. I felt myself believing him, but I couldn't do this again. I wouldn't let myself fall in love with the faux version of himself he was presenting.

"Rosie, I'm begging you to read them."

"Don't you see it doesn't matter?" I snapped. "I don't *want* to, Aiden. I don't want to forgive you. I don't want to get hurt again. I won't do it."

"So, I've got no chance?" He asked, raising a brow.

I swallowed. "None."

"I find that hard to believe," he said gently.

"Why? Because you know me so well?"

"Yeah, I do. You're the most stubborn person I know, and if you didn't want to hear me out, you wouldn't be standing here in your front porch light, looking at me like that."

"Like what? Like I want to gouge your eyes out?"

He smiled genuinely for the first time since we'd come out here. "There's my Rosie."

I turned away because I knew if I kept looking at his smile, I'd fold. And I wanted to. I wanted to throw my arms around him and leave it all in the past. But I couldn't take another heartbreak.

"I'm not yours anymore."

"Fine. If you're not mine, then know that I'm yours. The minute I saw you, you had me hooked, and I never wanted you to let go. The entire time we were together all I could think was you were better than any dream, any piece of fiction I could ever write." He reached into his back pocket and pulled out a stack of papers. "Just read them. Whenever you want to. If not today, tomorrow. If not tomorrow, then next week. If not next week, then know I'll be waiting for you in New York to come home to me."

I glanced at the papers between us, convincing myself I didn't care. That I wouldn't ever want to know the words he'd written to get me back. But the romantic in me couldn't resist. Hesitantly, I took them from his grasp and relief flooded his entire demeanor.

"I'll wait for you, Rosie, I swear it. I'm in it for the long haul. I want all your tomorrows. Every single one you're willing to give me," he said pleadingly. Almost like a promise.

I took a shaky breath, holding on tightly to the papers. I narrowed my eyes at him. "You can't wait here while I read them. I want to be alone."

"Of course," he said immediately. "I'll wait at the coffee shop you told me about. The one where the kid you were tutoring spilled coffee on you? The one where your best friend had six coffees your sophomore—"

"Honeybee. Yes. I know the place, Aiden."

"Just trying to prove I listened to you." The corners of his mouth lifted. He reached for me this time, his hands grabbing my arms, and this time I let him. "I'll be there. I'll be there all night."

I nodded once and watched as he made his way to the rental car. The blue sky was already turning pink and orange.

"What if I don't read until the middle of the night?" I called after him.

He glanced at me over his shoulder. "Then I'll sleep in the back of my rental car."

I smiled ruefully then turned away from me so he couldn't see me. "Okay," I said, voice thick. "Okay."

I watched as he pulled out of my driveway, down the street, and into the sunset.

Part of me wanted to wait to read the chapters. To make him suffer like I was and to call him on his bluff. But I couldn't resist.

I unfolded the pages and turned to the first page.

I lived a life waiting for the other shoe to drop. When life became too good, there were consequences. When my mom got successful, she got sick. When I finally felt settled into college, she died.

I walked on eggshells around Max, petrified that I would be the one to cause us to break. That something would inevitably mess up everything between us.

We had submitted our final presentation. The project drew us closer, but I was waiting for it to drive it us apart. Max was hoping this presentation would serve her well in her application for a promotion. She didn't know that I was vying for that promotion, too. I wanted the promotion for different reasons than Maxine. I wanted a tangible way to prove to myself that if my mother were still here, she'd be proud of me. That she, and even my father, could see that I was living up to her legacy while making my own.

But after discovering Maxine's motives for the promotion, the way it would change everything for her, I tried to back out. I spoke with our supervisor, but if I backed out now I jeopardized my reputation, and I couldn't go through with that. I walked with that regret with every time Max spoke about the promotion, every time she hoped for it. We were supposed to find out soon, and I was dreading it.

We were meeting for dinner and the promotion was the last thing on my mind. I always felt a buzz of anticipation when I knew I'd be near her soon.

I spotted her walking toward me from across the street. Her eyes were hard, her mouth turned down in a frown. Something must be wrong because my Max smiled.

When she approached me, I couldn't stop myself from wrapping her into a hug. My parents had never been affectionate growing up, even my mom. She'd lay a hand on my forehead if I was sick or hug me when I hurt, but that was about it. With Max, I found myself in a constant state of wanting my hands on her. In the middle of the night, if we drifted apart, I'd reach for her until we were pressed close together. It was impulsive, instinctual.

"I missed you today," I said, kissing the top of her hair. She was stiff in my arms. I pulled back, search in her distant eyes. "Everything okay?"

"Fine" was all she said.

"Okay. Dinner here still sound good?"

She could barely meet my eyes. I had always been good at reading Max. From across conference tables, I could see her eyes light up when she thought something was particularly funny. In our tiny office, I could hear in her voice when a client made her mad, but she refused to be impolite. But I couldn't read her now.

"This is good."

Whenever we would get in a fight, I could sense it in my chest. Like the universe would unbalance and my body was preparing for me to quickly construct walls. I could feel the animosity between us and slowly, my defenses built.

I frowned, refusing to let it go. "Are you sure you're okay?"

"I'm fine," she said sharply. I peered down at her, trying to read her face. Trying to detect any sign of anger or hurt, but it was impassive. "Hunter, it's nothing."

"I know when you're upset, Max. I know you."

"Maybe you don't," she snapped. "And maybe I don't know you."

"What're you talking about?" I asked, even though I knew. I didn't have to check my phone to confirm that everything I was dreading was right here, right now.

"Why didn't you tell me you applied for the promotion?"

Before my parents got divorced, my father spent most of his time at home yelling at us. He'd sling words at my mom and me like they were weapons. He yelled until his voice was raw and our tears were all shed. The older I got, the more I realized how much he'd fed off that fear in our eyes. I'd learned to keep my face still, unreadable, until I knew how to respond. It was my fight or flight response when I feared losing. And I was desperately scared of losing Max.

It was the way she said it that hurt the most. I'd not only broken her trust, but I'd hurt her. I knew I should just apologize, but all I knew how to do was defend until I was blue in the face. I was still learning how to love, slowly taking notes from Max as she did it so fiercely, so carefully. I was new at all of this and fucking it up.

"I don't know. It didn't seem relevant," I said slowly.

"I told you countless times how much I wanted that position. How it could change everything for me. I must've brought it up every single day, and you didn't think to even tell me?"

Her hurt morphed into anger in front of my eyes, her voice sharp like I had never heard before. Like she hadn't had the time to consider the true impact of them before they fell from her mouth. My first thought was that maybe she'd spent too much time with me.

"Why are you making such a big deal of this?" I narrowed my eyes.

"Because it is a big deal," she insisted.

"You can't be upset that I beat you, Max." My anger was boiling over and while trying to salvage what we had, I knew I was close to destroying it.

"I'm not upset you beat me, Hunter," she said. I could see the anger and frustration in her eyes and voice. "You should know me better than that. If I had known you were applying, I would've cheered you on. Instead you kept a secret like this from me for months. I thought I could trust you."

"I never lied, Max." I was clawing at scraps. I didn't want to fight. I wanted to sit with her in the corner of a crowded restaurant and watch her eyes spark up every time she spoke. I wanted to have my hand wrapped around her knee under the table and to roll my eyes when she stole the food off my plate. I didn't want to stand at the edge of a block and lose all I had. "You're just mad that I'm going to beat you."

She jerked back, as if I had hit her. "I'm not worried about that. I don't care. I thought we had gone to a place where we could be honest with each other, but you're hiding from me."

"It's not my fault you feel so inferior, Maxine. What, you want me to hand it to you? Give you the easy way out? You're already doing that by living in your own daydreams."

The words rose in my throat before I could shove them down. Acid burned the back of my throat at the hurt written across her face as the other shoe finally dropped. The way she was looking at me was destined to haunt for me a lifetime.

She didn't say anything, just turned around on her heel and walked away.

A foolish man would've let her walk away. He would've been too scornful and proud to ever try again. He would've let weeks pass by without begging for forgiveness or hearing a word from her.

I hadn't thought love was ever in the cards for me. I watched the people I loved, and the people who were supposed to love me, walk away without a second thought. I settled into a life without love, never looking back, because if I were to fall, I knew it'd be slow and rare. I gave up the worst parts of myself to my words on paper so no one thought I was hiding. So everyone knew precisely what they were getting into with me. And maybe my characters didn't get their Happily Ever Afters, but they'd survive. They'd walk out limping, but walk out, nevertheless. I couldn't help but imagine how it could've been had maybe I tried a little harder. I didn't know how to love, but for Maxine, I wanted to learn.

"Maxine, wait." I jogged down the block after her, pushing past the people. "Max, I'm sorry."

"It was all a lie." Tears were pooling in her eyes.

"None of it was."

"It all was." She hiccupped between her words. "I really hate you some-times, Hunter, I really do."

"Well, I hate you, too," I said, softly. "I hate the way you laugh at every joke in a TV show, even if it isn't funny, because I know you just get caught up in the moment. And I hate how you get caught up in the moment, too, because it feels like you go somewhere without me, and I wish I was your shadow so I could never be apart from you."

She shook her head. "Hunter, it's not that easy. I—"

"But I love you too," I said softly. "I haven't told you enough just how much I love you. I love the way you look at me and make me feel like you're shining a spotlight on just me. I love the way you smile at me first thing in the morning, even though you're not a morning person. And I love the way you always have to win every fight we have—and you can win, Maxine. You can win this one. Because I miss you more than I've ever dreamed of missing another person. And I'm sorry. I know I'm not easy to love, either. I'm too angry and jaded, but I want to be someone you can see yourself loving. The kind of guy that you instinctually look for. You can win every fight we ever have for the rest of time, just don't give up on me."

I tentatively grabbed her hands. She gripped them back tightly, her eyes shining with tears.

"You're lucky you're wearing your peacoat."

I choked on a laugh, pulling her into my arms. Moments like these, when we were bundled up in each other and I had no clue where she started and I ended, made me believe in Happily Ever Afters.

Not in My Book

Rosie, I'm sorry. I love you. You once told me that when you fell in love, you didn't want to have to second-guess what you felt. I've never second-guessed what I feel for you. I know you prefer what's in your books, and I pretend I don't want to be like them, but I do. I want to be the person you picture when you're reading and dreaming because you're who I picture every single time. I love you. In light and dark, in romance and litfic. In this lifetime and the next.

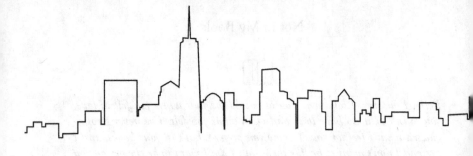

CHAPTER THIRTY-TWO

True to his word, Aiden was waiting for me at Honeybee Coffee. I'd read the final pages in five minutes, speeding through to read every word Aiden had written to me. Then I read it a second time, carefully analyzing each line because Aiden didn't waste words. Then I read it until the sun set and there was no light left in my bedroom except for the streetlight in front of my house barely brightening the room.

Honeybee was closed now, Aiden's car the only one in the parking lot. The hatchback of the car was open, and he was lying inside it on his back, his legs swinging back and forth, skimming the gravel.

When my car pulled into the lot, Aiden sat up and stepped out from his trunk. His suit jacket was off, his white dress shirt rolled up to his elbows.

"Hi," I said.

"Hi," Aiden said cautiously.

My heart swelled at just the sight of him, the frantic hammer in my chest screaming at me that he loved me. That the imperfectly perfect man standing just a few feet away loved me, and he was here and wanted me like I wanted him.

"Before you say anything," he said, "I want you to hear it from me because you deserve to *hear* it. You deserve more than a second-hand I love you. And I do—I love you. I love you so much. And I'm so sorry.

If I could, I'd go back in time and change the way I handled everything so you knew how much I cherish what we had."

"Aiden—"

"I'm sorry I was an asshole about the fellowship and that I've been an asshole about romance. I should've told you that I applied. I went to Ida first thing in January and tried to rescind my application because I knew by then how important this was to you, but she said the applications had already gone through, and I was too late. I wished every day I wouldn't get it and then, when I did, I tried to pretend like it didn't matter. But it did and it does and I'm sorry. You deserve everything I can't give you, but I swear every single day, I'll try."

I didn't say anything, I just pulled the two sheets of papers from behind my back and stepped toward him, handing him his copy.

He frowned. "What's this?"

"You wrote your last chapter, and I wrote mine."

He looked down at me, a little dazed it seemed, and carefully took the paper, slowly unfolding it. I watched his green eyes skim the first few lines until they snapped up to meet mine.

"Rosie—"

"I've got mine, too," I said. I held up my stack of papers and cleared my throat. "*Hi.*"

When he continued to stare at me, I nodded at his paper, prodding him to continue.

"*Hi,*" he read.

"*I've spent my whole life defending what I love. Prepared to jump to the defense of romance with nothing else in sight. But it wasn't fair for me to not celebrate your success. Love should be come hell or high water, and I'm here for all of it with you. I'm sorry. I should've listened to you instead of just running away when it all got too hard. But the truth is I'm scared. Because you're right that I've set every expectation too high, but it's because I'm scared of showing who I am and for it to not be enough. I've always wanted to be someone somebody can love. Not just like or admire, but* love. *I've yearned to find someone who looks for me in crowded streets and smiles in relief. Or wishes for me every chance they get. Someone who genuinely knows me and wants to figure out how to know more. But I feel like I never figured out how to give love, too.*"

Aiden looked down at his paper and said, "Do I really have to start a sentence only for you to interrupt me?"

"Yes."

A hint of a smile appeared. He cleared his throat. "*Rosalinda, I don't—*"

"But I love *you*," I interrupted him. The pages were empty after this line because I didn't need to remind myself why I loved him. He looked up at me, waiting. "I love the way your hands find mine when we walk in a crowd, like you're protecting me. I love the way your feet hang off the edge of my bed and how you've never complained once about it. I love that fucking peacoat." He shook his head, rolling his eyes. But he was smiling. "I love you. It's the easiest thing I've ever done. I've never had to second guess it. I shouldn't have walked away from you."

I reached forward and grabbed his hands. He interlaced our fingers.

"I'm scared too," he confessed. His hands traveled up my arms until his hands cupped both sides of my face. "But I look for you in every crowded street, and when I see you, I smile in pure awe and relief. I wished upon every star and birthday candle for the idea of you, but when I met you last January, I wished for *you*, Rosie Maxwell. The girl who loves romance. The girl who can't go three hours without chocolate. The girl who gets so annoyed with me, I can see it in the way her nose scrunches up. I wished for you until I didn't know how to not long for you anymore." His eyebrows creased as tears pooled in my eyes, his thumb caressing my cheek to swipe one away. "We're both learning. And we're both going to make so many mistakes, and we're probably going to fuck this up a million more times."

I laughed through the tears, my eyes shining up to meet his.

"But know that every single time I fuck up, I'll come home to you. We'll work together to make it better because we won't abandon each other. We'll make mistakes, we'll learn lessons, and we'll be tested. But we'll come out so much stronger on the other side."

I nodded, pressing my forehead against his chest. His hand cupped the back of my head, holding me to him.

"I'll come home to you too." I hadn't meant to cry, but tears began to fall anyway. "There's no one I'd rather fight with. I love you, Aiden Huntington."

"I love you, Rosie Maxwell. I love you more than any person has loved another."

"Wrong again," I whispered before his lips captured mine, moving slowly against mine.

It had only been a few weeks without him, but I felt for the first time in as many weeks like I could breathe. I clutched the collar of his shirt in my hand, and he wrapped his hands around both sides of my waist.

And it was just like a romance novel.

EPILOGUE

"No."

I wanted to strangle him. I genuinely wanted to wrap my hands around his neck and shake until he complied.

"Why not?"

"Because I don't want to."

"That's a bullshit excuse," I snapped.

"Rosalinda. I'm not wearing my peacoat at our wedding."

"But you'd look so handsome," I cooed, running a hand up his chest. We stood in front of Juanita's truck, our last meal before we headed off to Tennessee tomorrow morning. "For me?" I batted my eyelashes at him, but he shook his head.

"Not going to work this time." He kissed my forehead. "Your mother would have my head if I did that."

"So what? You're not marrying her."

He snorted. "As if I'm going to risk disappointing your mother. I do that, then we can say goodbye to the alfajores she's been sending us."

I groaned. The wedding was only a week away, and Aiden had refused to grant my one bridal wish of him wearing his peacoat.

Aiden proposed a year after we got back together. I came home from work one day, and he had shipped roses from the shop in downtown Rogersville and scattered them all over his brownstone. He was waiting for me in candlelight on one knee, Taylor Swift playing softly in the background.

"Did you send the latest revision to Jeanine?" he murmured, rubbing my arm. We had spent the year revising our novel before querying and striking luck with our agent.

"I thought you were supposed to do that."

"No, *you* were."

I straightened, frowning. "I sent it last time."

"No, you were supposed to send it last time and forgot. So I sent it and we agreed you were next."

I squinted at him, knowing he was right, but not wanting to admit it. "What happened to me winning every fight?"

He looked down at me fondly. "We'll never publish a book that way, baby."

Jeanine was pretty flexible with deadlines anyway. After reading our book, she knew how easily we bickered and how much time that took up.

"Fine. I'll send it—*if* you wear the peacoat."

Aiden looked toward the sky. "Lord, help me."

I laughed, nudging him with my shoulder. "I'm kidding, I'm kidding. I'll send it later."

"Here you go." Juanita held the tin foil wraps out for us. "Mateo and I are finishing our food prep, and we'll see you both in Tennessee later this week."

With the stress of wedding planning, I told him I wished Juanita and Mateo could just cater for us. He offered them a ridiculous amount of money and to pay for their flights and accommodations down there. I think he did it more because I'm still desperate for them to get together.

"Thanks, Juanita." I smiled up at her. "Maybe while we're all down there, you two could talk a little more."

She blushed. "I'll see you later, okay?"

My phone buzzed with incessant texts. I glanced at our group chat now titled *raiden weekend*

Logan: which of ur cousins are hot rosie

Jess: don't ask her that! the bride doesn't care about ur weekend hookups

Logan: i'm doing this for HER. SHE'S the one that likes romance
Tyler: Logan, stop.
Rosie: leave my cousins alone
Rosie: you'll get along well with carla
Logan: LOVE YOU ROSIE see you in tennessee!!!

We walked from the park toward Aiden's brownstone, eating our burritos. Aiden was excited to see Cori, Maria's daughter. He thought it was adorable how everyone called him Tío Aiden already. At first he'd thought it was weird since he wasn't Hispanic, but I assured him, "I call my uncle on my dad's side Tío Sean. No one cares, trust me."

In Aiden's living room, which was soon to become *our* living room, boxes of my stuff were piling up. We kept saying we'd unpack it later, but neither of us really wanted to.

Aiden cast me a sidelong glance. "You know, we could knock this out in a few hours. Then we'd come home from the wedding to *our* place."

I nodded. "You get the box cutter, I'll handle the music."

So for the next few hours, deep into the night, Aiden and I unpacked all my boxes, melding my stuff with his. We'd get distracted every so often, laughing at photos we found or chasing each other around the house or when Aiden sat me on the kitchen counter, his face cradled in my hands.

Aiden was still skeptical about Happily Ever Afters. We'd gotten in plenty of arguments about Max and Hunter's future. Eventually, he agreed they were meant to be. But honestly? I didn't care what happened to Max and Hunter. Because I *knew* what my future with Aiden held.

People say there's a thin line between love and hate, and you know what? They're right.

— Excerpt from WHAT LIES BETWEEN by Rosie Maxwell and Aiden Huntington

ACKNOWLEDGMENTS

I can't believe I'm writing my acknowledgements for my own book! I'm a dedicated acknowledgements reader so shout out to the romance readers who search for a bit of extra love in these paragraphs ♥. This book was a labor of love, tears, chocolate, and barbeque chips, and I'm so grateful for everyone who's supported me through this!

I am everything I am because of my parents. Mom and Dad, I love you both so much more than a book dedication and acknowledgments section could ever contain. From the very start, you've supported everything I've hoped to be. Writing a book never felt like a pipe dream because of your support. My whole life has been nothing but an absolute joy. I miss you both and Holt 5 dinners every day. I wouldn't be writing this without all the trips to the Cedar Bluff Library, homemade puppet theater, and the penny-a-page contests. I am so sorry for all the smut (but not sorry enough to delete it). Mom, I am sorry for how many curse words there are in this, but since you all seem to think this is an autobiography it seems fitting . . .

Leah Marie Holt, my best friend! My twin flame! Thank you for being my number one defender and for bracing our family in a café in Paris for what kind of books I read and write (*"she* puts it in *him"* haunts my worst nightmares). There is no one I'd rather live with, giggle with, and stand awkwardly in the corners of open bar events with. Thank you for letting me talk out nonsensical plots, being my brand ambassador, and always singing along to every random Taylor song that gets stuck in my head. Gleep glorp. William, you slay, too.

Drewcifer! (Sorry for immortalizing you as Drewcifer in my book but I had to.) I've spent my whole life looking up to you, trying to read books as fast as you did. I wouldn't have my taste in music or my sense of humor without all those *Arrested Development* and *The Office* marathons where the jokes we told were *way* funnier (do you think we have an ego problem when it comes to comedy?) Thank you for always validating my love for The Smiths and trying your very best to understand my love for romance novels. Joyce is fun, too! I love you bunches and I *wish* you'd just move to NYC already!

Thank you, Beth, for all the sleepovers and buying me countless books as a kid. Thank you, Reba, for the sleepovers with extra-strong margaritas and buying me pink hair dye at Walmart. Thank you, Boom Boom, for our late night talks and helping to teach me how to drive (it's why I'm the best in the fam). I have loved our sleepovers and beach trips my whole life. Uncle Andy, I miss you all the time and I always think of you. Tia Janecita, I love all of our Waffle House visits, and I can't wait for the next one. Tia Anita, I miss you all the time, thank you for always buying me books whenever I visited and making me chocolate chip cookies.

Granddaddy, I admire you so much. I love coming to visit you and picking your mind on traveling. I love hearing all your stories, jokes, and general wisdom. I've cherished every phone call and visit we've had. Grandma, I wish I had had more time to get to know you. Every time I learn something new, I hoard the fact as if I could've discovered it all by myself. Lito, me siento profundamente honrada de conocerte y valoro enormemente todo el tiempo que compartimos. Admiro sinceramente tu forma de vivir y la ambición que te caracteriza. Lita, usted siempre ha sido una modelo a seguir en cómo actuar. Su constante amabilidad y empatía es hermosa. Me encanta su risa con facilidad y espero poder ser como tú cuando sea mayor.

I only know Momo through stories and what stories they are! I hope I make her and all her loved ones proud by writing and publishing a novel. She wrote in her autobiography, "Building castles in the air is one thing I have always done best." Although I never got to know her, I've grown to admire her and eagerly read every word she's written I can find.

Not in My Book

Thank you to the entire team at Alcove Press who made my *literal dreams come true!* Jess, thank you so much for seeing something in my feral, peacoat-loving heroine and helping me shape this book into something I'm so so proud of. Dulce Botello, Mikaela Bender, Cassidy Graham, Stephanie Manova, Megan Matti, Rebecca Nelson, Thaisheemarie Fantauzzi Pérez, Doug White, and Matt Martz and everyone who even thought the words *Not in My Book*, thank you all for your hard work!

My wonderful agent, Steffi Rossitto! Oh my God, I have the *world* to thank you for! None of this would've been possible without your help, smart edits, and patience as I wrestled with this book. Thank you for explaining math (royalties) to me and answering every little question I've ever had. I'm so excited to continue working together!

Mazey Eddings for being my other mother, mentor, bff, and guide to historical romances and soup dumplings. Clare Gilmore for all your support and making me miss Tennessee every single day and writing such soft heroines. Tessa Bailey for giving me the confidence to write steamy scenes without worrying about what other people think about it. Also for the dugout scene in *Fix Her Up*. Krista and Becca Ritchie, just because you invented Connor Cobalt. Christina Lauren for being such a kind pillar of the community. And to every romance writer who has inspired me ever since I was way too young to be reading them.

McKenna, don't even get me *started*. From high school until we literally die, I'll love you so much for all the times you let me rant about boys, books, and life to you (which in high school was *far* too much). Nothing compares to our wine nights and your brussel sprouts with aioli. *Cori Purcell*! My jelly! We were girls together. We were just fourteen when you insisted that my first book was good (it was not). Ten years later and I still feel like you're my biggest cheerleader. I love you so much. And Mrs. Purcell, I love you too! When is our NYC girls trip?! Addie, Mara, Casey, Kyra, Ashlyn, thank you all too!! Rachel Bazzoon, my identical twin. Thank you for all the Texas Roadhouse rolls, Shirley Temples, and laughs. Ugh, Bella, I miss you *so* much. Thank you for always supporting me and getting the big bottle of wine even when I say I want the little one. Maria, thank you for watching smutty movies with me and understanding me on a molecular level. Gabriela, Gabby, Ashley, Lilly, Natalie, and Hailey, y'all made NYU bearable because sometimes crying in Washington Square Park is cute and sometimes it's traumatic. Carson, Yasmine, Bailey, Lianna, Rachel, Steph, Sophie, Julia, and Anna, thank you all for your support and friendship!! And all my Strand friends! Alex, Jenny, Collie, Rickea, Jordan, Marissa, Walker, Boice, Grecia, Niccolo, Joel, and Maria, you made shelving history and Americana bearable.

DFH for you, always.

The Talented Bastard Co-op!! You all were the first people to make me feel like I had an actual shot at publishing a book. I was so happy during those weeks and pushed myself so hard. I loved our Zoom writing sessions, and I cannot wait for a reunion. Rachel Carter, you changed my life that summer, and I wouldn't be writing this without you.

Miss Mynatt, Miss Williams, Mrs. Lentz, Mrs. Phillips, Miss Murphy, Mrs. McCarter, Mrs. Hopkins, thank you all for always encouraging me to read and write and being the kind of teacher someone thinks about ten years later. Professor Row, you were the only professor at NYU that was nice to me about romance! One day Darla and Lucas will see the light of day! Professor Weintraub (sorry, I know you hate "professor") although it was screenwriting, I always appreciated how much you helped me with my romcom! Lanie and Clark will probably stay buried.

Taylor Swift because I often thought "if she can perform for three hours with a broken heart, I can finish this edit." I listened to Speak Now, 1989, and Midnights *religiously* while writing!

Finally, thank you reader! I cannot even imagine someone walking into a store, picking up my book, and reading it down to the very last word. And to *enjoy* it? It's almost too much to ask! It means so much more than I'll ever be able to express.

MWAH! ♥

Katie